"I marvel at the wisdom tucked away inside these pages, at the generosity and artistic grace on display here. This is a fine, fine book."
—STEVE YARBROUGH, author of
Prisoners of War and *The Oxygen Man*

"A sprawling Southern epic that covers a number of years and generations and crosses racial lines." —*New Orleans Gambit Weekly*

"Bev Marshall has not so much written a novel as she has drawn back the curtain on a South-facing window, a view of Mississippi fifty years ago, of forty and thirty years ago. . . . They are not so much characters as people we have known; their stories not so much witnessed as shared. The shifting points of view—female and male, black and white—never shift away from honesty and authenticity."
—SONNY BREWER, author of
The Poet of Tolstoy Park

"A brilliantly crafted page-turner, *Right as Rain* spins a cinematic tale of familial love, everlasting friendship, and secret desire that will entrench you in the lives of its characters so completely you will never want it to end." —SUZANNE KINGSBURY, author of *The Summer Fletcher Greel Loved Me* and *The Gospel According to Gracey*

"In the tradition of . . . *Gone with the Wind* and . . . *To Kill a Mockingbird* . . . Pitch-perfect." —*Roanoke Times*

"Marshall has managed the mixing of history and fiction and magic and memory. She keeps the reader glued to the pages with love, friendship and secret desires that will summon you into the lives of the characters. You don't want the story to end!"

—*Magnolia Gazette*

"Catches you from the first page . . . Marshall knows how to capture the life and language of the rural South."

—McComb *Enterprise Journal*

Right as Rain

Also by Bev Marshall

WALKING THROUGH SHADOWS

 BALLANTINE BOOKS | NEW YORK

Right as Rain

BEV MARSHALL

A NOVEL

Right as Rain is a work of fiction. Names, places, and incidents either are the products of the author's imagination or are used fictitiously.

2005 Ballantine Books Trade Paperback Edition

Copyright © 2004 by Bev Marshall
Reader's Guide copyright © 2005 by Bev Marshall and Random House, Inc.
Excerpt from Unanswered Prayers *copyright © 2005 by Bev Marshall*

Published in the United States by Ballantine Books, an imprint of The Random House Publishing Group, a division of Random House, Inc., New York.

Ballantine and colophon are trademarks of Random House, Inc. Ballantine Reader's Circle and colophon are trademarks of Random House, Inc.

This book contains an excerpt from the forthcoming hardcover edition of Unanswered Prayers. *This excerpt has been set for this edition only and may not reflect the final content of the forthcoming novel.*

Originally published in hardcover in the United States by Ballantine Books, an imprint of The Random House Publishing Group, a division of Random House, Inc., in 2004.

Library of Congress Cataloging-in-Publication Data
Marshall, Bev, 1945–
Right as rain / Bev Marshall.—1st ed.
p. cm.
ISBN 0-345-46842-2
1. African-American women—Fiction.
2. Landlord and tenant—Fiction. 3. Southern States—Fiction. 4. Tenant farmers—Fiction.
5. Race relations—Fiction. 6. Women farmers—Fiction. 7. Landowners—Fiction.
I. Title.
PS3613.A77R54 2004
813'.6—dc22   2003063775

Printed in the United States of America

Ballantine Books website address: www.ballantinebooks.com/BRC

9 8 7 6 5 4
Book design by Barbara M. Bachman

To Lisa Bankoff, who believed;
Butch, my whole in one;
and Dad, who is always right as rain

In memory of my father-in-law,
Francis Chester Marshall,
who knew a lot more about cars than Mr. Larry

Acknowledgments

On my list of people to thank, the name of my editor, Maureen O'Neal, appears on the first line. My respect for her editing skills and knowledge is boundless. From the beginning of our relationship and continuing through publication, she has cheerfully been a source of help and inspiration that far exceeded my expectations. The professionalism and talent of the Ballantine family is truly phenomenal, and I offer my heartfelt thanks to each of them, especially Nancy Miller, Johanna Bowman, Kim Hovey, and Cindy Murray, who is possibly the smartest and sweetest publicist in the business. I dedicated this book to Lisa Bankoff, my agent and friend, who believes all things are possible and whose faith in me and this novel confirmed my suspicion that she is one of the most remarkable women I will ever know. Patrick Price and Tina Dubois are angels in disguise, and I thank them both, past and present.

Thank you to the St. Tammany Writers Group, who read the first drafts of this novel and encouraged me to write on and on and on: Andrée Cosby, Jan Chabreck, Tana Bradley, Maat Andrews, Mark Monk, Dan Butcher, Melanie Plesh, Wade Heaton, Phillip Routh, and Kate Hauck. I also appreciate the continuing support of my fellow writers: Katie Wainwright, Karen Maceira, and Tracy Amond. The early encouragement I received from Douglas Glover and Paul Cirone, who read the first manuscript of this saga, meant more to me than I can find words for.

I am grateful for the support of the independent bookstore owners and managers, who are some of the nicest and most special people in the business. I am especially thankful for Sonny Brewer at Over the Transom, whose talent and generosity are boundless and whose friendship is truly a blessing.

In the past two years I have been fortunate in meeting many talented authors (too many to name) who overwhelmed me by generously sharing their knowledge and supporting me with grace. Your friendships are a privilege I will forever cherish.

I thank Allen Orillion for sharing his knowledge as a firefighter and Corvette lover. In researching the civil rights movement, I am indebted to Townsend Davis for his splendid account of that era in his book *Weary Feet, Rested Souls*.

Finally, through all of the drafts, highs and lows, the support and love of my family and friends was essential. Jim Forrest, Shirley and Irvin Tate, Joey and Mandy Marshall, Zora Marshall, buddies Tana, Andrée, Jan, and my lifetime editor Emily Heckman, I love and appreciate all of you. My dad, Ernest Forrest, never runs out of stories to tell, and for that and many other reasons, I'm blessed to be his daughter. My other blessings are Angela and Chess Acosta, and I thank you both for loving me on my worst days. I am most thankful to live each day with Butch Marshall, whose love makes my life right as rain.

JOHNNIE WILKS WAS LAID OUT IN HIS LIVING ROOM IN A PINE box balanced on two ladder-backed chairs. He weighed only 132 pounds, and the borrowed black suit his wife had dressed him in was tucked and folded beneath his back. The starched white shirt covered the bullet hole in his chest just fine.

Feke Parsons, the man who had murdered Johnnie, stood looking into his coffin. He wiped the sweat from his forehead with a thin white handkerchief stained brown from the tobacco juice that dribbled down his chin daily like a small muddy stream flowing from the corners of his mouth. Feke was thinking about Dolly, his best working mule, whom he had shot with the same rifle he had used on Johnnie. He'd have to buy another animal if he was going to finish the plowing.

At supper on the day of the "accident" Feke had looked across the oilcloth-covered table and said to his wife, "Niggers. They're all good for nothing."

His wife had kept her head down, her eyes on her candied yams like they were the answer to a mystery she had been trying to solve. His twenty-year-old son, James, had half believed the story Feke told the sheriff. The first part of Feke's explanation of the death was accurate. Johnnie had sprinted up to the Parsons' house, gasping for air, his eyes bulging out with fear. "Dolly," he said, his voice a high screech, "Dolly done fell with the plow, look like her leg be broke." Feke made two trips to the ditch, a ribbon of red clay dividing the green rows of pole beans and tall cornstalks. He had followed Johnnie's half skip, half run to where the mule, braying horrid, squealing sounds, lay on her side with one hind leg crunched beneath her. On his second trip out to the field, Feke carried the rifle he had bought for thirty-five dollars in Summit, Mississippi. He shot the mule in the head between her twitching ears, watched her jerk until she lay still, and then he turned the gun on Johnnie and fired into his chest. Johnnie's body, lifting from the ground, slammed back into the ditch and landed crosswise on top of the mule. As the scent of gunpowder and blood wafted around him, Feke stood with his gun cradled against his chest. He spit tobacco juice onto the red clay ground, shouldered his rifle, and, looking down on the two corpses, addressed them. "Dumb animals," he said.

By the time the sheriff, Ed Duncan, and Johnnie's forty-five-year-old wife gathered in the front yard where Johnnie lay in a deceptively peaceful repose, Feke had polished his story so that it was entirely plausible to the sheriff, who borrowed Feke's hunting dogs every quail season. Walking away from the wailing wife on her knees beside her husband's body, Ed leaned into Feke's shoulder and whispered, "Johnnie was a dumb nigger. It figures he'd jump in your line of fire, cause you to have to waste a bullet." Feke said nothing to this, but he lifted his hand to his mouth to cover his smile.

Turning away from Johnnie's bleached pine box, Feke hurried out of the Wilks' house. He had paid his respects and now he was eager to begin his search for another nigger and a smarter mule.

He found both at an auction some forty miles away on the Martin Place. After purchasing David Martin's best mule, Feke hired Uncle Kurt, a strong, dark-skinned man who was unaware of the fate of his predecessor.

In the fall, six months after Johnnie had been laid to rest in the colored cemetery, Feke's son, James, married Euylis Bearden, the daughter of Jarvis Bearden, a schoolteacher whose family had migrated to Lexie County in the mid-1800s. Euylis' daddy loaned them five hundred dollars for a down payment on the old Reeves' homestead, and the newlyweds settled happily into the modest white farmhouse. Their new home sat on the rise of a hill half a mile off Enterprise Road and four miles west of Zebulon. James' deed included 185 acres, a pond, a barn, a pine grove, and two tenant houses across the field to the left of the main house.

Euylis hated to visit James' parents. She was afraid of her father-in-law, suspecting that, if she were to open the mirrored doors of the big black wardrobe in his bedroom, she would find a white sheet and hood that was worn on nights when the moon turned bloodred. She made James promise that he would treat his Negroes better than his father. She was a Christian, she told him, and she couldn't abide violence against her fellow man, even if he was colored. James assured her that he would be kinder than his father had been; and in return, he asked for her promise to learn to cook—but Euylis couldn't keep her vow. Her biscuits came out of the oven black on the bottom, gooey in the middle; the crust of her fried chicken fell off before James could lift it to his mouth, and her sun tea had a bitter sharpness to it that made him snap his teeth together after each sip.

When Euylis stopped her menstrual flow for two months in a row, she learned to crochet. After she mastered the chain and purl, she bought cream-colored plastic needles and soft yellow yarn. When the baby, named Browder after Euylis' grandfather, had mastered walking bowlegged down the wide center hall, Euylis was tying pink ribbons on her daughter, Ruthie's, booties. Her cooking skills deteriorated even more as the demands of the children occupied her time. She would put a hen on to stew and hours later run back into the kitchen when the smell of charring bird wafted into the living room where she sat on the floor playing pat-a-cake with the children. James, who was rapidly losing weight and dreaming of chocolate pies and big thick pancakes covered in maple syrup, threw down his fork of mushy butter beans one night and said, "We've been here five years, and we've nearly got the note paid off on the place; I made good money on the cotton, the corn, and the two bulls I sold at the Summit auction. We can afford more help if we rent out one of the tenant houses. Let's hire a first-rate cook and another hand."

Euylis nodded, but her hands trembled with joy as she swallowed a hard ball of dough. She was hungry, too. "I heard Uncle Kurt's daughter, Tee Wee, is an excellent cook. She lives in Magnolia I think."

At twenty-three Tee Wee was six feet tall, big-boned, and round-stomached. From her birth, weighing twelve pounds, eleven ounces, she had outstripped all eight of her siblings in both weight and height. Tee Wee's great-grandmother, a slave named Sadie by her owners but called Yulanda in her native land, was said to have been a tall, regal woman with large strong hands that could crush corncobs into dust. She lived on Windsor Plantation near Port Gibson, and it was fitting that the largest antebellum mansion ever built in Mississippi was her home. Sadie was renowned for her culinary surprises, like the sweet potato pie with cinnamon that she served to the guests at the long mahogany table in the

Windsor dining room, and the recipes for the pie and many other delica-
cies were her legacy to her great-granddaughter, Tee Wee.

When James Parsons knocked on the screen door of her ramshackle
two-room house, Tee Wee answered the door with a scowl on her face.
Her husband, Curtis, had lost his job at the Thompson Dairy, her four
children were fighting over the last piece of corn bread, and earlier that
day her employer, Ida Quinn, had falsely accused her of stealing a set of
embroidered pillowcases from her linen closet. James, intimidated by her
girth and countenance, backed perilously close to the edge of the sagging porch and stammered out his offer. Work for both her and Curtis, a
tenant house, land for planting their own crops. Tee Wee listened to his
words with an immobile face, and then suddenly her set mouth spread
into a wide and scary jack-o'-lantern grin. "When you want us?"

After James left, Tee Wee turned to her husband and burst out laughing. "Praise the Lord," she said. "He done sent us a savior." Then, grabbing the upper arms of her children, she lifted each of them from the
floor and pushed them toward the back room. "Get packed," she told
them. "We movin to the Parsons Place."

Part One

1950

EE WEE STOOD ON HER FRONT PORCH, ARMS FOLDED OVER her huge breasts, black, bare feet wide apart. She weighed more than two hundred pounds, and in her Sunday navy blue dress with red stripes, over which she wore a small white apron, she resembled a large mailbox. On her head she wore a straw boater with black streamers. As she reached to straighten the hat, adjusting the streamers so that they curled around her neck, she thought how unfair it was that the Parsons had chosen Luther to be the one to go get this Summit woman who called herself Icey. And on a Sunday, too! Tee Wee's day had begun at five when she had stumbled to the kitchen to make pies for dinner at Mount Zion. Then at meeting four sinners had been called to Jesus, which meant an extra hour of testifying and singing, and when she had finally gotten home after three o'clock, she barely had time to make her famous chicken pie and put her Sunday clothes back on before Luther was due back.

When Tee Wee saw an orange ball of dust swirling up the hill, she crossed her arms and took a deep breath. Now she could see the black car slowly moving toward her. The 1940 Ford was ten years old and didn't run half the time, but its chrome bumpers were still shiny, and it was the only car owned by a colored on Enterprise Road.

Now another woman was sitting in the passenger's seat of that Ford. "Here she comes," Tee Wee said. "Here comes misery up my drive." Last week Mrs. Parsons had broken the news that Tee Wee's daughter Ernestine wasn't going to get the housekeeping job after that no-good Pansy had quit. No, she was giving the job, the tenant house next door, and half of Tee Wee's vegetable garden to this Icey. And all because Icey's man had run off and she was kin to Idella, who cleaned up the white Methodist church. "So she got young'ns to feed. We all got them," she mumbled to herself. And the worst insult of all was Luther having to drive up to Summit to fetch her and her children. Didn't the woman have no friends to help her? Like as not, she thought. Woman can't hold her man can't hold no friends.

Luther pulled into the small circle of shade offered by the only oak in their yard. Tee Wee began counting heads in the car. Luther's. Hers. Three young'ns. Tee Wee smiled. Four of her six were in the house behind her. The back doors of the car opened and the passengers began falling out of the Ford. None of them had on shoes. She kept smiling. Then she saw a pair of black patent leather pumps dangling from beneath the door of the passenger's side. Her smile vanished. She wished she hadn't taken off her shoes, but they were two sizes too small, and her feet had been killing her after wearing them to meeting this morning. When Icey finally got out of the Ford, Tee Wee saw that she was nearly as large as herself and also in her early thirties. The woman's skin was walnut-colored, and she was wearing a white lace dress with a blue aster blossom stuck in one of the holes over her left breast. Her head was, Tee Wee saw with relief, hatless. Luther, who normally limped from an injury caused by a mule falling on his left leg, swung around the car like he'd never seen a jackass, much less had one fall on him.

Tee Wee didn't move. Let them come up to her. "Bout time. Supper's on and gettin scorched."

Luther laughed like she'd said something funny. "This here's our new neighbor, Tee. Name of Icey."

Icey nodded, dipping her head to show a big silver barrette holding up her black curls. "Tee Wee," she said. "Look like we gonna be neighbors a spell."

Tee Wee turned her back and opened the screen door. "Look like that," she said, pulling the door open and stepping over all the children who had been leaning against it. "Ernestine, Crow, you girls come for these young'ns," she called to her daughters. Let this Icey know she had help in her house; let her know she didn't raise no trash. And she grinned, hurrying back to the kitchen. Let her smell my chicken pie and greens cookin and see them four pies on my windowsill when she look out hers.

—

ICEY DIDN'T NOTICE the pies because she was too busy inspecting her wonderful new home. After Luther followed Tee Wee into their house, Icey had led her children inside the adjacent, identical one, where they would now be living. Four rooms—more than she'd ever had before—a roof that looked like it wouldn't leak, and most wondrous of all, electricity! Every bare bulb hanging from the ceiling in each room came magically alive with a small orange glow when she flipped the little lever on the wall.

Looking to her left, she saw the small kitchen, which had a wood-burning stove, a washstand, and even some shelves to put dishes on. The other door from the front room led to a back bedroom, and from there she could see into another small bedroom. No windows, but there was one in the kitchen and one in the front room, and only two panes were broken. "Thank You, Lord Jesus," Icey said, lifting her head to the wooden ceiling. Preacher Smith had said the Lord would provide and He had.

The house was furnished with only a few sticks of furniture: a couch with broken springs and stuffing protruding out both cushions, a small wooden table in the kitchen, two straight ladder-backed chairs, and one mattress on the floor. Icey kicked off the shoes she'd stuffed paper in to make them fit and threw herself down on the couch. She sagged to the floor. "Okay, young'ns," she called to the children who were wandering through the house like scattered ants. "Bring all them boxes in; we home."

WHEN TEE WEE turned out the lights at nine, she noticed Icey's house was aglow with pumpkin light. Hidden in the darkness of her own window, she stood looking through Icey's kitchen into the front room. Two naked children were sprawled out on the floor on sheets and blankets, and what Tee Wee declared to herself were "nothin but rags." Craning her head sideways, she could see Icey sitting on the couch, still wearing the lace dress and shriveled blue aster; she held something in her hand that looked like a book. Raising the window, Tee Wee stuck her head out into the cool night air. It *was* a book, and the woman's head was down like she was reading it. Tee Wee felt enormously jealous. Her secret dream was to learn to read and write. Her Ernestine could read, Crow,

Rufus, and Paul, too, but Tee Wee herself could barely make out her name. "I said this woman was trouble, and here it is sittin right there next door to me." She slammed the window down and made her way in the darkness to her bed, where Luther lay sleeping with his mouth wide open. Crawling in beside her man, Tee Wee curled her big body around his bony form. Readin ain't everythin, she told herself. Let her sleep with that book; I got a man.

Icey and Tee Wee came out of their houses the next morning at the same moment and stood planted on their porches staring over at each other like gladiators about to enter an arena. This Monday morning was an overcast, gray fall day, and the obscured sun gave off little warmth. Tee Wee pulled her sweater arms down over her square hands. She knew it would be hot in just a few hours, but for now the wool felt comforting to her. Icey, she saw out of the corner of her eye, had no sweater, but she looked perfectly warm in her sleeveless print housedress. Tee Wee yawned and stretched, stalling for time to decide how to handle this situation she'd have every morning now that Trouble had moved in. Well, she decided finally, weren't no help for it. They'd be going to the same place at the same time every day. "Mornin, Icey," she called across the few feet between them.

Icey nodded. "Look like a beautiful day."

Tee Wee took another look up at the gray sky. "Might rain, though," she said.

"Might at that," Icey said, sauntering down the three wooden steps to wait for Tee Wee. "I hopes not. Children will get wet walkin to school." She wanted Tee Wee to know that all of her children went to school.

Tee Wee was smiling as she came down her three steps. "Yes, mine's got a umbrella, though." With three broken ribs, she wasn't going to mention.

"Oh," Icey said. "Well, maybe it won't rain anyway."

"Maybe not," Tee Wee said, walking on toward the Parsons', "but I believes I just felt a drop on my head."

Icey caught up with her. "I didn't feel nothin. You sure a bird ain't found you?"

Tee Wee walked faster. These morning walks to work were gonna be nothing but misery from now on. "I knows the difference between droppins and water," she said.

Icey smiled. She thought to herself that these walks with Tee Wee might turn out to be the best part of her day.

AT THE PARSONS' HOUSE the two women gave each other wide berth. Tee Wee hardly ever left the kitchen, and although Icey's cleaning chores included that area, Tee Wee made it clear that she trusted no one to clean her domain. Icey, who was allowed to take her noonday meal at her employer's, never complimented Tee Wee on her fried chicken, blueberry cobbler, tea cakes, or even her chicken pie, which all the Parsons declared to be the best in Mississippi, and so the two continued as they had the first morning, sparring with words. They wore dresses normally reserved for Sunday meeting; they waved starred schoolwork their children brought home in each other's faces; they mentioned nearly every possession they had acquired of any worth at all. When Icey set her iron wash pot on her front porch, Tee Wee produced her own with red plastic flowers peeking out of it. On Wednesday Tee Wee set a china milk pitcher on her kitchen windowsill, and by Thursday Icey had placed a china sugar bowl on hers. And every evening when Tee Wee pushed a protesting Luther out onto her front porch, Icey would respond by going inside and opening her Bible, which she read aloud in a voice that sounded like the preacher's when he was ordering devils out of the hearts of his congregation.

Icey's and Tee Wee's children were, however, fast friends by the weekend. They shared the few homemade toys they possessed between them: corn husk and clothespin dolls, slingshots, balls made of twine, pine straw and chinaberry jewelry, and whittled wooden swords and guns. At Sunday meeting the children sat together while Icey and Tee Wee chose separate pews. Icey wore her white lace again, and Tee Wee had sewn a bit of red ribbon on the sleeves of her navy blue Sunday dress. If Icey noticed the addition, she showed no sign. Thus, Icey's first week in her tenant house ended as it had begun: Icey went to bed with her Bible, Tee Wee with her man. And both warriors, already battle-weary, dreamed of victories in skirmishes yet to come.

Icey's second week as Tee Wee's neighbor brought only more stalemates, and on Thursday Icey grudgingly complimented Tee Wee on her lemon meringue pie. At first Tee Wee thought Icey was only baiting her again and watched her face carefully before answering. When she saw genuine pleasure in Icey's eyes after forking another bite into her mouth, Tee Wee straightened her back, lifted her head, and said, "It's in how long you beat the whites makes meringue right. I beats four minutes longer than most."

"Well, it sure taste good."

They were sitting on the back steps of the Parsons' house resting between the noontime and evening meals. Icey continued to look at Tee Wee without the ice in her eyes Tee Wee thought she was named for. "Well," Tee Wee said, scraping her plate with her fork, trying to think of something nice to say back. "You done a good job on that old mirror in the hall. Seem like the woman Parsons had before you just smeared it up every time she touched it."

"I use newspaper and vinegar. That do the job right on mirrors. Windows, too."

"Parsons is pretty picky bout their help." Then, in the habit she'd fallen into, she couldn't resist adding, "I guess you ain't used to workin for such fine folk."

Icey stood up and held out her saucer and fork to Tee Wee. "I don't reckon the Parsons is any more picky than them Manchesters I work for in Summit. They used to entertain the governor of this here whole state, and he came to visit one day and said, 'Icey, you does keep things nice round here.' That what he said."

Tee Wee stood up, ignoring the saucer and fork Icey was holding out. She couldn't think of anybody who'd visited the Parsons worth mentioning. Silently, she turned and entered her kitchen. A governor, she thought to herself. Imagine that.

Icey, following her in, set her dish on the table. "Well, that pie was good, Tee. I best get back to dustin the furniture. See you later."

"Yeah, I'll see you whether I wants to or not," Tee Wee mumbled, slinging the saucer into the sink with such force it shattered into tiny pieces.

THE NEXT DAY on their walk to work Tee Wee brought up the subject she'd been burning to know about ever since she'd met Icey. "What happened to your man?"

Icey looked down at the brown grass, which wore a slight dusting of early white frost. "Run off. Same's the two before him."

Tee Wee glanced over and, seeing Icey's chin drooping over her chest, felt a stirring of sympathy in her own. "Well, before Luther, I had three men. First one, by the name of Frank, I married when I weren't but fourteen, had Ernestine, who's eighteen now, then next two years I had my boys, Rufus and Paul. They moved to town. Work at the Co-op. Back then we lived on the Dyson Place and Frank was plumb crazy. The things that man done." Tee Wee shook her head. "Anyways, I run him off and then along comes David Jefferson, who is Crow's daddy. We moved to Magnolia and then he got in trouble with the law and left. Crow ain't got over him leavin yet. Next one was Curtis, a good man. Then we come to this house. Birthed my twins, Lester and Masie. Curtis was older than me, wore hisself out I reckon. Died in bed one night. Bad heart."

"How'd you feel? Bout that last one I mean?"

"Sad. And mad, too."

"Was he good-lookin?"

Tee Wee laughed. "I reckon. All the gals at meetin wanted him to get called to Jesus just so they could look at him on Sundays."

"My last was right good lookin, too. He was tall and big, and had hands wide as a plate. Good hands, but he weren't no good. Ran with anythin, stole, lied, played dice, and got so lickered up on weekends, he'd get in a fight and end up in jail." Icey slowed her pace, turned toward Tee Wee. "Still I miss him anyhow. Miss havin somebody to laugh with."

"I knows, girl. Waited a year before Luther come along. He's a good man. Ain't been with me that long, but so far as I can tell, this here one is gonna stay." Tee Wee looked back at her house anxiously. She shouldn't have said that. Say it and it won't be so. Everybody knew that.

Icey looked back, too. "I got to get a man to stay. I can't do enough work to pay rent on the place by myself. My sixteen-year-old Eli is plannin on movin out so's he can work in town, but when he does he ain't gonna make enough to help me. Jonas ain't but twelve and got to get schooled, and Glory, well, she just cost money."

Tee Wee patted Icey's shoulder. "I'll keep my ears open. One'll come. Men. They always do."

Icey smiled. "Yep, they's like rain. Just when you thinks your beans is gonna dry up, along comes a thunderstorm and drowns em."

Tee Wee slapped her thighs. "Girl, you right about that. We gets drowned all right."

Both women entered the Parsons' back door, laughing together for the first time, and when Mrs. Parsons said she wanted beans for dinner, their earsplitting laughter rang out over the entire house.

Chapter 2

RUTHIE STOOD IN THE CENTER HALL, HER EAR TO THE door of her parents' bedroom. They were discussing whether or not to keep Icey on their place. Her father's voice sounded bored with the topic.

"Do what you want, Euylis. If she keeps breaking things, not doing what you ask, fire her. Tee Wee's girl Ernestine isn't going anywhere. She's too ugly to find a man."

"But, James, three children, no man," her mother said. "Where's she going to go?"

"Well, then keep her."

Ruthie tiptoed down the hall. She didn't want to be caught eavesdropping again. Her mother had told her over and over that it was impolite to listen to other people's conversations, but no one ever told her anything nearly as interesting as what she overheard.

On the front porch she stretched out on the swing. She was hot and bored and mad at Browder for running off with Crow. Ruthie had hoped to listen in on Troy Greer's and Dimple Butler's conversation, but the phone had rung only once all afternoon even though there were eight people on their party line. Ruthie wished she could drive. She'd go into Zebulon and get ice cream at the Dairy Freeze, then go to the Saturday double feature, stop at Woolworth's later and buy her doll Josie something nice like a new plastic feeding set or a bonnet. But no one wanted to go to town today. "Too close to Christmas," her mother had said. "Everybody and his brother will be shopping over in Zebulon."

When the telephone rang, Ruthie jumped out of the swing. Two short, one long. It was Dimple's number. She raced to the phone and counted to ten before lifting the receiver. "What was I doing? Nothing much," she heard Dimple say.

"I think somebody picked up," Troy said.

Dimple laughed. "Of course, somebody always wants the line when I'm on it."

Ruthie held her hand over the mouthpiece, afraid her breathing would be heard. Troy's voice was soft. "So, you got a date for the hayride Saturday?"

Ruthie imagined Dimple smiling, twirling her hair, as she said, "Sort of."

"What's that mean?"

"John Welbourne asked me, but I haven't said yes or no. Are *you* asking me?"

"Uh-huh."

"Wellll, there's poor John Welbourne to think about."

Troy's voice sounded deeper when he said, "Think about me, not him."

The line clicked. "It's Rose Coker. I need to make a call. You still on the line?"

Dimple gave out a long sigh into the phone. "Getting off. Okay, Troy, pick me up at seven."

Ruthie replaced the receiver, squeezed her hands together over her heart, and skipped down the hall. She'd said yes. Ruthie thought Troy was the best-looking boy in the Enterprise community and Dimple, who was a senior at Zebulon High, was glamorous enough to be a movie star. John Welbourne wasn't nearly handsome enough to date Dimple. Although Ruthie was only ten, she knew there was something special about Dimple that men were drawn to. She didn't understand what it was, but she was very sure she wanted to have it, too.

Leaving the house, Ruthie set out to find Browder and Crow. Maybe if she asked very nicely, they would play a game of chase with her. She began her search in the barn. Next she looked in the car house, the feedlot, and the pine grove. At the pond, as she stood looking across the waving cattails, it occurred to her that Browder and Crow might be at Tee Wee's house. Crow often had to baby-sit for her mother, and sometimes Browder would help her chase the children around the Weathersbys' yard.

As she walked toward the tenant houses, she spotted Tee Wee and Icey sitting on the steps in front of Icey's house. From the serious expressions both of them wore, Ruthie guessed that they were discussing something important. Softly sliding her feet across the grass, she crept around to the side of the house where she could eavesdrop unseen.

"This one'll be my last. I gettin too old to go droppin anymore," she heard Tee Wee say.

"How you gonna be sure of that, girl?" Icey asked.

"Ole Auntie Seline live over in Osyka gives you stuff to drink to stop it. She's part Indian. She know all about plants and herbs and animal insides that fixes the miseries of humans."

"Sound like Devil doins to me," Icey said in a scared voice. "I don't hold with nothin to do with Satan."

Ruthie craned her head around the side of the house. Icey was snapping late string beans into the big white enamel dishpan balanced on her lap. "It ain't voodoo. Just doctorin," Tee Wee said.

"So when is your young'n due?"

"July. Hope it ain't gonna be hot."

Icey nodded. "Had my boys, Eli and Jonas, in August. I bout died in the heat."

"I had worse," Tee Wee said. "Three in July, one in August, and two in September. August ain't nothin to September."

Icey, pulling the string from her bean and snapping it vigorously into small bits, said in a louder voice. "Huh, nine years ago, I had one born in February that froze solid comin out. My girl, Glory, it were, and I had to hold her over boilin water for a spell to thaw her out. You don't know what that's like."

Ruthie stood up. More birthing stories. She'd overheard enough about ripping and shredding wombs to fill four five-year diaries. If women weren't talking about bearing children, they were telling about the amounts of liquids they excreted monthly onto the cloths they wore between their legs. She'd overheard her mother and her aunt Ola whispering about red female juice and raging blood falls pooling around their feet, and Ruthie had decided she wouldn't grow up to have any of that. She'd wished on a first star and a four-leaf clover that she'd be spared that part of being a woman, and she believed that something would happen to change her present destiny.

"I know you there," Tee Wee said. "Come round here, Miz Ruthie. What you wantin?"

Ruthie shuffled around the corner of the house. "Hey, Tee. Hey,

Icey." She tried not to stare at Tee Wee's stomach, and after a quick glance at her midsection, she climbed up the steps to the porch. "Have y'all seen Browder? Or Crow?"

"I ain't seen em," Tee Wee said. "Crow was suppose to watch the twins, but they inside sleepin, and she run off somewheres."

"Well, I've already looked for them at the henhouse, the car house, the barn. They've just disappeared."

Icey set her pan of beans on the porch boards. "You can play with my girl Glory sometime. She the same age as you. Right now she got chores in the house, though."

Ruthie scratched her leg with the toe of her sandal. "Well, I guess I'll keep looking then." She turned and started toward the pasture. "See y'all later."

"Bye," Tee Wee called. "Hope you finds them."

When Ruthie was out of earshot, Tee Wee turned to Icey. "That child is so lonely; she pretends her baby doll's a livin baby."

Icey grinned. "Well, come July she can play with your livin baby. She can change diapers with real doody instead of pretend poop."

Tee Wee laughed. "I reckon she would want her doll back then."

After Icey went home, Tee Wee set her beans on the kitchen table and returned to the porch. She thought about Crow and Browder off somewhere together. Crow was an expert on vanishing. If she didn't want to be found, all the looking in the world wouldn't help. She worried more about Crow than any of her children, and she didn't like her spending so much time with a twelve-year-old white boy. Especially Browder. Tee Wee had had to tie him to a fence to keep him from running off when he was toddling around the farm. Ruthie had been the easy child in the Parsons' house, content to play with her doll on the kitchen floor while Tee Wee did her cooking. She felt sorry for her because, although she was only a year and a half younger than Crow and her brother, they never included her in their games. Tee Wee had heard Crow call her some terrible names, all having to do with her freckled white skin.

With every one of her babies she had felt sleepy the first few months, and now she closed her heavy eyes. In minutes she began snoring softly in rhythm with the yard dogs who sighed in their sleep beneath the oak tree.

"Miz Weathersby?" Tee Wee's head jerked up, and she saw a young man she vaguely recognized, but couldn't put a name to, walking across the yard. "Miz Weathersby, you know me. Sam Jackson."

Tee Wee straightened her dress and stood up. "Hush," she yelled to the dogs, who had begun to growl and bark at the boy, who had surprised them, too. She did know Sam. Ernestine had introduced him to her at church. He was brother to that Willie Jackson who Ernestine was so crazy about. "Ain't he a dreamboat, Mama?" her oldest daughter had said, and Tee Wee had looked at the long turkey feather sticking out of the "dreamboat's" hat, the polka-dotted bow tie at his skinny neck, and she had shaken her head at her daughter's taste in men. She walked down the steps toward Sam. "Your brother ain't here if'n you lookin for him. I reckon he and Ernestine off somewhere."

Sam ducked his head. "No. He ain't hereabouts. I come to tell you where he at."

Tee Wee frowned. She didn't need to know where any of the no-count Jacksons were on this Sunday afternoon. Just then a cloud moved across the face of the sun and cast the boy into a shadow. It was a bad sign. "Oh Lord," Tee Wee said. "What you got to tell me?" But she knew. Ernestine. My baby. What you done now?

"They gone. Willie, he got a job in Alabama. They catched a ride with my cousin Toot. He live over that way." He stuck his hand into the pocket of his overalls and withdrew a scrap of paper. "Ernestine said to give you this."

Tee Wee stared at the white sheet. She wasn't gonna let on she couldn't read what was written on that paper. "You read it to me. I too upset to take that from you."

Sam unfolded the note, cleared his throat. "It say, 'Dear Mama, I hope you get somebody to read this to you besides Crow. She gonna be mad cause I took her money outta that hole in the floor by her cot. But me and Willie needed it bad. Tell her I'll try to pay her back. We getting married soon as we get to Alabama. I'll write to you where I am when we find somewhere to live. Don't be mad. Love, your daughter, Ernestine.'

"That's all." He held the note out to her. When Sam looked up into Tee Wee's face, contorted with fury, he dropped the sheet of paper, turned, and ran straight through the pack of barking dogs toward Enterprise Road.

WHEN ICEY LOOKED out through the front door screen and saw a colored boy flying down the driveway, she wondered who he was. And what did he want over to Tee Wee's? Pushing the door open a crack, she poked her head out and saw Tee Wee standing in her yard lifting a piece of paper from the ground. Icey stepped out on the porch. "Everythin all right over there?"

Tee Wee shook her head, but didn't answer. "I better go see what this is about," Icey said to Glory, who stood behind her with her hair wild around her face. "I'll braid your hair when I gets back. And Jonas"—she shook her finger in his face—"you finishes your homework. Tell Eli to help you if he ain't forgot what he learnt already."

When Tee Wee handed her the note without a word, she looked into her face and saw why the boy had run. Her eyes were narrowed into slits, her mouth pooched out like she had swallowed something bitter, and her skin had taken on an ashy hue. Icey forced her eyes to the paper and quickly read the block-printed words. "Ernestine," she said. "She your oldest, ain't she?"

Tee Wee nodded. Icey recalled the girl as she had seen her this morning in church. She was tall and skinny; bones stuck out from her body like pins on a cushion. Ernestine's faded dress hung down straight from her waist, not a curve to give shape to it. She was plain-out ugly, and before she could stop herself Icey said, "How'd she get a man with her looks?"

Tee Wee backed up to the steps and fell heavily onto the bottom one. "I reckon there's other things besides looks. Ernestine is right smart." Then, with tears welling up, she said, "But not smart enough to see that Willie Jackson is a no-good nigger who's gonna ruin her life." She lifted her apron to her face and wept into the brown-stained white cloth.

Icey put her arm around her and patted her broad back. "There now. Ain't as bad as all that. There's a silver linin to black clouds, darkness before the dawnin, rainbow after stormin, uh, good things a-comin when there's, uh, somethin not so good."

Tee Wee lifted her head. "Ain't nothin good gonna come of this. My baby gone off to a faraway place. And maybe she be kilt on the way, her money stole. It ain't safe over there in Alabama. Them folks is mean to coloreds."

Now Icey could ask the question she was most curious about. "How much money did Crow have in that hidey-hole?"

"I don't know. Didn't know she had no money."

"Oh, Tee. My heart is hurtin so for your trouble. I sure is sorry." Icey truly was filled with sympathy for her friend. She dreaded the day when one of her young'ns would fly out of the coop. Eli, who had just turned sixteen, was already looking for a place to roost in town. But he wasn't going far, and she couldn't imagine how it would be to have one fly so far away. "She'll come back. You wait and see. Ernestine get homesick over there and come a-runnin home to her mama."

Tee Wee wiped her eyes with the back of her hand. "I hope you right, Icey. I hopes you sayin the truth." She shook her head. "The Good Lord have to look out for her till then."

Icey nodded. "That's right. Jesus be walkin on that road with her." She frowned. "I reckon He can stand to go to Alabama if He has to."

Chapter 3

RUTHIE CONTINUED HER SEARCH FOR BROWDER AND CROW behind the tenant houses, but she saw only rusty-red chickens, two yellow mutts, and one lone speckled guinea looking for its mate. After checking the Weathersbys' car house and the outhouses, Ruthie finally gave up hope of finding them. It seemed that Browder and Crow had evaporated like wisps of steam.

Ruthie could vanish, too. Her favorite hideaway was the closet between her parents' bedroom and the bathroom. It served as storage space for seldom-used luggage, and Ruthie would often slip into the dark space between the black trunk and the brown leather suitcases to sit and listen to the private conversations between her mother and father. It was there where she had learned about Mamaw Parsons' cancer, Uncle Gene's drinking problem, and her mother's jealousy of Irma Nelson, which her father had declared totally preposterous since Irma was "at least thirty pounds overweight and stupid to boot." Ruthie understood her mother's envy, though. Irma laughed and moved her body much like Dimple Butler.

Starting back across the pasture toward home, Ruthie began humming Johnny Ray's new song, "Walking My Baby Back Home." She swung her hips to the music in her head, thrusting her pelvis forward as she took long strides across the hard ground. Her cousin Catherine loved the song, too, and she wished she were over at Catherine's right now. Let Browder and Crow hide all they wanted from her; her cousin was more fun than they'd ever be. Josie liked her, too. Catherine never minded if Josie cried or needed changing while they were playing, but Browder would say Josie was just a doll and she could wait till they finished a game of Parcheesi before being changed. "A doll don't feel, stupid," he'd said last night when Ruthie had asked to leave the dinner table to check on her. Her father had frowned at Browder and said she could be excused but to come right back and finish her turnips.

Turnips. Turnips were all they ate late in the year. Ruthie hated them. Even when Tee Wee put lots of fatback in them, they still tasted bitter to her. Looking ahead into the bright sunlight, Ruthie shaded her eyes. She could just make out two figures crawling out from beneath the house. Browder's blond head emerged first; then Crow's darker one appeared behind his left shoulder. What were they doing under there?

AS CROW WATCHED Ruthie flying over the brown pasture toward them, she turned to Browder. "You reckon Ruthie will tell?"

Browder shook his head. "She didn't see anything. I saw her first."

Tossing her long braids over her shoulder, Crow said, "Don't matter anyhow. We wasn't doing nothin wrong." But she knew her mother would think crawling under the house with a white boy, lying beside him, touching body parts was as bad as lying, skipping school, or running off when you had chores to do—which she routinely did. Luther never punished her, but Tee Wee would tear a limb from the quince tree and beat her bare bottom and legs until welts rose up on her black skin. No matter how severe these beatings, Crow would never cry. Years ago she had learned that, if she twisted her tongue into a coil inside her mouth, concentrating on keeping it tightly wound, she wouldn't feel the switch biting into her flesh. Tee Wee, thinking her beating was having no effect, would sigh, drop the switch, and usually say, "Girl, you worries me. What gonna become of a stubborn child like you?"

Ruthie probably never gets a spanking, Crow thought, as she watched her galloping on her thin freckled legs toward them. She hated hearing her mother call her Miz Ruthie. It was Miz Ruthie this and Miz Ruthie that. Crow would rather die than call her Miz Ruthie. "Hey, runt," she said to her now.

"What were y'all doing under the house?" Ruthie wanted to know. She crossed her arms over her chest the way Mrs. Parsons did when she was displeased with someone.

"None of your business," Browder said in a loud defiant voice, which belied the dark pink flush rising up from his neck to his cheeks.

Ruthie's eyes, the dark blue of a Morton Salt box, scanned her brother's face; she turned to Crow. "I looked everywhere. Why were you hiding under there?" she asked, pointing to the dark space beneath the white clapboards.

Crow knew how to handle Ruthie better than Browder did. "Where's your doll, Josie? Hadn't you better be lookin for her? I ain't seen her all day. Maybe she be kidnapped like that young'n over at Tylertown they found dead in the woods last week."

Ruthie's voice wavered. "Did you all take Josie? Did you hide her?"

"Well, you better go see." Before Crow's words were spoken, Ruthie began running toward the house, calling Josie's name.

Browder dropped to the ground, laughing. "What a stupid mule I got for a sister."

Crow looked down at him. She stopped smiling. "Yeah, well, she loves that doll like it was a real person. You don't love nothin that much."

Crow had never had a real doll like Josie, but she'd loved a tabby cat once. She'd named it Caddie after Caddie Woodlawn, the heroine in a library book she'd stolen from a white girl's book satchel propped beside the door of the Ben Franklin store. The cat had followed her everywhere, rubbing against her legs, purring contented little sounds. She remembered how she felt the day she had found her on the road in front of the house torn to pieces by some animal. She had stood a long time staring down at the cat's little broken body, the bits of yellow fluff scattered around her. She hadn't twisted her tongue and her tears had fallen and mingled with Caddie's blood. Gathering up the bits of fur and the small body, she'd cradled the dead kitten against her chest and carried it to the pond, where she dug a grave beside the cattails. That day, walking home, Crow began to understand the awful risk people took when they chose to love something, and she had decided that she didn't want to love anything anymore.

Reaching out, she yanked Browder's arm. "Get up. You promised to give me a nickel if I'd go under the house with you. I kept my end of the deal; where's the money?"

Browder passed his hand over his blond crew cut. "Did I say that I had a nickel? Hmmm. I don't remember having any money left over after I went to the show with Tommy King last night." His pale eyes were fixed on Crow's face, which remained expressionless. She'd wait him out. He knew better than to cross her.

"Is that a fact? Well, you better go butter up that sister of yours and get it out of her cause I ain't leavin without my pay, and when your mama asks me why I ain't left, I guess I'll have to tell her what her son did with me this afternoon."

Browder hesitated. Crow knew he was considering calling her bluff. They both knew she'd be in worse trouble than he, but he was more afraid of Crow's wrath. Slowly rising, he slid his hand into the right pocket of his navy shorts. As he pulled out a small cloth coin purse, Crow stuck out her hand, palm up. Browder tried to smile. "Well, maybe I've got a five-cent piece or two left after all. Lemme see." He opened the purse, withdrew a nickel, and flipped it into the center of her palm. "How about that? Five cents. Just what I said I'd pay."

Crow's fingers curled around the hard coin. "You know you better not ever try to cheat me. You'll be sorrier than anybody on this place ever been if you crosses me."

Browder's cocky smile vanished. He believed her.

Crow's real name was Sharmaine, but she had been called Crow before she'd learned to walk. Black as her namesake, sleek and shiny, she'd lain in her bed, cawing her own peculiar sounds. Scooting across rooms, she would swoop her head down, and, with her always open mouth, she'd snatch up any objects in her path. She had eaten crayons, chewed a shoe into three pieces, and swallowed Tee Wee's thimble as if it were a bean. When she was tired, she'd sit still as a statue, with only her dark eyes sweeping back and forth like windshield wiper blades until suddenly her eyelids would close and sleep would overtake her.

Crow's father was a Natchez man who had moved south of Zebulon to Magnolia. David Jefferson had laughed at this child his wife had borne him, and he'd begun calling her Crow. "She more like a bird than anything," he said to Tee Wee.

After she began walking, Crow stopped eating strange objects, but her behavior worsened. She threw tantrums whenever she was barred from doing something she desired. Pulling her hair, she'd shriek, spin, stomp her long slender feet on the ground, and then pummel anyone who came near to stop her. Tee Wee would stand a few feet away, shaking her head at her strange child, crying out, "Lord, what You done give me this time?"

Only her father could calm her when she flew into one of her fits. "Coo coo, my baby bird," he'd croon to her in a singsong voice. "Coo coo come come," he would say, holding out his arms. And Crow would fall into his arms, weeping into his overalls, shivering with sobs that tore out of her small chest. David would lift her up, take her hands, and, turning around, swing her up and down. Legs splaying out behind her, flying in her father's strong arms, head thrown back, she watched the sky spin above her. Her tears dried in the wind, and she laughed as both she and David fell dizzily to the ground.

When Crow was four years old, her father left without saying goodbye. One August night he crept out of Tee Wee's bed, met his friend Lucius Taylor, and, after the two men got drunk on corn liquor, went to Greel's Store for more. They kicked open the flimsy front door and were helping themselves to some good Jim Beam when Ned Forrest drove by in his white Dodge and saw the open door. Ned could grab only one, and that one was Lucius, who was slower, drunker, and weighed a lot less than David, whom Ned couldn't have held on to. David ran only three blocks before deciding Lucius would tell his name and the sheriff would come looking for another nigger to throw in his jail. He had been incarcerated once in Natchez and, on the day he'd been released, had vowed never to spend another night in a white man's custody. And so Crow's daddy flew on his strong legs toward Jackson, where he knew safer places to roost than the shack he shared with his family. Tee Wee never heard from him again.

Crow had not wanted to move from the small house near Magnolia she'd always lived in. She worried her father wouldn't be able to find her when he came home, and nothing Tee Wee said convinced her that David Jefferson wouldn't be back to lift her off the ground into the open sky where she knew she belonged.

But David hadn't returned, and now, as Crow, nickel secured inside one of her braids, walked home, she knew it was Luther who'd be waiting for her with a frown on his face and a list of chores for her to do before supper. When she reached Icey's yard, she looked up and saw Tee Wee, arms crossed, feet spread wide, standing on the porch like a gargoyle guarding the entrance to hell. Crow approached her slowly, but she lifted her chin, set her mouth into a tight frown. Whatever had caused her mama's fire, she would meet with icy waters.

Tee Wee unfolded her arm, pointed to the far side of the house. "Your sister's run off," she said. "Gone with that no-count nigger, Willie Jackson, to Alabama. Took the money you hid in the floor by your cot." Tee Wee fell silent, but big droplets of tears splashed out of her eyes. "Gal gonna get herself in a mess of sorrow."

"With my money," Crow said. Reaching up to her braid, she felt the nickel there. One damn nickel left. That was all she had now. "Hope she do get into trouble. Hope she dies," Crow yelled. "No-good bitch."

Before she'd spat out her last sentence, Tee Wee gripped her arm. "You hush up that talk." She tightened her grip. "You hear?"

Crow twisted her tongue, felt no pain. She didn't care what her mother did to her. She'd get Ernestine someday. She'd make her give her money back. She thought about the twelve dollars she'd been saving for her own flight from this dirty, rat-infested house she despised. Twelve dollars she'd counted on to find her daddy who most likely lived somewhere in a house as good as the Parsons'. Maybe better.

She loosened her tongue. "I'm sorry, Mama. I shouldn't said that bout Ernestine. Maybe she'll get homesick over there in Alabama and come back."

Tee Wee let go of her. "I hope you right, child. Maybe she come back home. You think she know how to find us again?"

She found my money, didn't she? Crow started to say, but she smiled at Tee Wee's dark puffy face. "She'll figure it out. She smart, Ernestine is."

Tee Wee pulled Crow to her and squeezed her tightly against her large breasts. "You right. Ernestine be back. We just pray for the Lord to take care of her until she back where she belong."

Crow breathed in the scent of her mother. She smelled like rancid bacon grease and something else. Something was different. Maybe it wasn't the smell. Maybe it was the way she felt. She lifted her head backward, pushing her body into Tee Wee's stomach, and then she knew. Between the soft folds of fat, she felt a new hardness, another beating heart separating Crow from her mother. Another damn baby to take care of, Crow thought. Another squallin young'n to feed. And wasn't Luther gonna strut around like the big black rooster now. Crow jerked away from Tee Wee. She ran up the steps, onto the porch, into the house. She'd find another hiding place for her nickel. She'd start over, saving in some secret place to find a way to get away from here, from these people, from the Parsons, Browder, and Ruthie, and that stupid Icey and her idiot children. She wasn't gonna rot here like the potatoes stinking in the ground beside her house.

Chapter 4

ROWDER GAVE HIS DIME TO THE SKINNY WOMAN BEHIND the glass window and hurried inside the Palace Theater. Only a few minutes remained before the show started, and he had been waiting to see this new Roy Rogers movie for weeks. After purchasing a red-and-white striped box of popcorn, he stood at the theater door, searching for his friends, Bobby Hall, Derek Moon, and Sammy Westheimer. He found them slouched in their usual seats—two down, center section.

"Hey, you late, Brow," Sammy said, as Browder fell down onto the seat beside him.

"Yeah, yeah. Mama had to drop Ruthie off at my cousin's and yak yak."

The theater darkened and a blast of music quieted the noisy crowd. When the words MOVIETONE NEWS appeared on the screen, Browder slumped down in his seat and began eating his popcorn. By the time the feature film began, he had emptied the box and torn it into strips, which he rolled into a tight coil. On the count of three, all four boys lofted their cardboard streamers over the heads of the people sitting in front of them, and then ducked as giggles and shrieks from girls rang out in the theater.

When Roy Rogers appeared on the screen, Browder sat higher in his seat. He watched as Roy strode across the front yard of his ranch house with fingers on the brim of his white cowboy hat. After Dale strolled over and greeted Roy with a big smile, Browder frowned. Dale was a dog; he couldn't figure what Roy saw in her. Browder was a heinie man, and Dale's butt looked like nearly deflated balloons. For the next hour and a half Browder traveled the dusty roads with Roy on Trigger, shooting, worrying, singing, and accepting the praise from the grateful people he and Roy had saved. He was limp with exhaustion when the show was over.

When the theater lights came on, Browder rose from his seat and looked up at the coloreds filing out of the balcony section. He knew Crow wouldn't be among them, but he looked for her anyway. Mostly, town Negroes went to the show on Saturdays, but sometimes he would recognize a face from the Enterprise community. In a way he was glad Crow never came because he often improvised the plots of the movies, which he paid Crow to playact with him. Next week he planned to go see a Tarzan show, and he shivered just thinking about Tarzan's naked chest, that small rag he wore to tease Jane, whose role he would assign to Crow. Of course, he couldn't wear Tarzan's outfit, but the thought of standing in front of Crow so scantily attired excited him.

After the show the boys went over to Gillis' Drug Store for cherry Cokes. Over his glass, Browder watched Missy Jordan come in with a pack of her stupid friends. She sashayed over to the stool where he sat. "You threw that popcorn box streamer right at me," she said, shaking her blond ponytail to punctuate her words. Browder glanced over at her three girlfriends, who stood, giggling, with their hands flying all around them like a bunch of sparrows flapping around a camellia bush.

"I didn't throw nothing at *you*. Your head was in my way is all." Browder turned back to his Coke and sipped from the paper straw. "Go away," he mumbled into his drink. His buddies were ignoring him now, but they'd have plenty to say later. Bobby had given Missy a half heart last year, and he had worn the matching half for only three weeks before she'd given hers back. She isn't getting any heart from me, Browder thought, as he slurped the last bit of Coke from the bottom of his glass. He was saving his money for something better—somebody who didn't have brown freckles all over her face and had a much better heinie.

At home Browder placed his ticket stub in the Buster Brown shoe box with his other keepsakes, which included his grandfather's old pocket watch, a speckled guinea feather, a chinaberry necklace Ruthie had made for his eleventh birthday, and a small lock of Crow's hair, which had cost him a nickel. He fingered the coarse hair, lifted it to his nose, and sniffed. The hair had lost its odor, but he knew the musky scent of Crow from memory.

"Browder." His father's voice carried through the closed door. "Get out here this minute."

Browder dropped the lock of hair back into the box, slammed the lid down, and stowed the box behind his shoe tree rack. "Yes sir. Coming," he called.

His father was standing outside his door. "Did I or did I not tell you to wash your mother's car when you got back from the show? If memory serves me, you were wolfing down one of Tee Wee's big biscuits when you nodded your head that you heard me."

Browder looked up at his father's six-foot frame. He wasn't ever going to be that tall; he was only three inches over five feet, and he couldn't imagine stretching that many inches in the few growing years he had left. In fact, he looked nothing like his father, who had curly brown hair and green eyes. Browder's blond hair was straight and stuck out if he slept on it wrong. But he was glad he wasn't thin and bony like his father's side of the family. He was more like Grandpa Bearden, short, but stocky with strong arms and big thighs. He looked down at the polished floor. "Yes sir. I was going to. You didn't say it had to be done the very minute I got back."

"Oh, I see," Mr. Parsons said in a tone that Browder knew meant he certainly did not see at all. "Get your butt out there and get busy."

Browder waited until he heard the back door slam. Why couldn't Luther wash the car? Why couldn't the Parsons have enough money like Derek's family to hire more help? Derek never had to do any chores, and it seemed to Browder he was constantly being summoned by somebody to do something. Even Tee Wee would bark orders at him about picking up his room, carrying his plate to the sink, stupid things she could do herself. Well, at least washing the car meant he'd get to drive a little. Maybe Crow would be around somewhere and see him behind the wheel when he pulled it beneath the shade of the oak tree.

Browder didn't see Crow, but Ruthie and her sidekick Josie were perched on a low limb of the oak tree when he drove the Chevrolet up to it. "Hey," Ruthie screamed like she was a mile away. "Catherine's dog had puppies, and we got to play with them. Mama said I can go back over there tomorrow."

Browder rolled up the driver's side window. He could still see Ruthie's mouth moving. "Shit," he said. "Now I got to listen to her yapping." He got out of the car. "So, big deal."

Ruthie jumped down from the tree, dropping Josie in the dirt. She scooped her up and brushed dust from her dress. "Oops, you're okay. You're not hurt, Josie."

Browder snatched the doll from Ruthie's hands and flung her as far as he could across the yard. "She's hurt now. Better go for the doc."

Ruthie screamed and ran to her doll's rescue. "I hate you, Browder." Lifting Josie from the grass, she cradled her in her arms. "I'm gonna tell Mama on you. I'm gonna tell her you and Crow were playing under the house, too."

Browder dropped the hose. "Wait a minute, Ruthie. Wait." He walked to where she stood, one foot on top of the other, her hands on her hips. "You don't wanna tell Mama nothing."

"I do, too."

"No, you don't. Think about it. You tell Mama about Crow and me under the house and she's gonna be mad as hell at Crow, too."

Ruthie chewed on her bottom lip. "Yeah, y'all will *both* be in trouble."

Browder nodded. "That's right, and then when Crow finds out you are the one who told on her, who's she gonna be mad at?"

"Me?"

"Uh-huh. You want Crow mad at you?"

Ruthie shook her head.

"Well, you tattle and that's what's gonna happen." Browder started back toward the car. He was still a little worried Ruthie would tell, but he was counting on the scales to tip toward her wanting to please Crow rather than take revenge on him. He picked up the hose and began spraying the car. Besides, he told himself, Ruthie doesn't really hate me; she thinks hating others is a big ole sin she'll go to hell for.

Browder slapped his soapy cloth on the car hood. "God heard you yelling at me, and I wouldn't want Him and Crow mad at me." He stole a glance over his shoulder. Ruthie was sitting on the ground now, her knees up to her chest, squeezing Josie against her with her thighs. He wiped down the side of the car in fast circles.

Ruthie lowered her legs. "Okay, Browder. I'm not gonna tell."

Picking up the hose, Browder turned the nozzle toward Ruthie, and then, deciding not to push his luck, he directed the stream at the back window where he imagined his father's stern face looking out at him.

Lying in bed that night Browder crossed his arms behind his head and stared at his feet. He wiggled his toes, splaying them as wide as he could. He could pick up objects with his toes, pinch Ruthie with them, grip the top metal bar of the swing set good enough to nearly be a tight-rope walker. Once he'd thought about being a high-wire performer in a circus when Barnum and Bailey had come to town. Then he had imagined going out to Nevada and being a cowboy. Later when he had gotten a .22 for his birthday, he had thought maybe he'd be a soldier or a tough PI like Sam Spade. But what he really wanted to be was a movie director or a producer or even an actor.

Browder swung his legs off the bed and sat up. He wasn't going to do any of those things. He was going to finish school and then go to college. He wished he could go out for football, become a star quarterback, but he knew that he couldn't catch or run fast enough to make the team. Looking around his room, Browder's eyes fell on the violin case leaning against his dresser. He could become a musician. Everyone said he had a beautiful voice, a gift for music. His mother had insisted he play the violin instead of the drums he wanted to play. "Anybody can play drums," she had said. "You aren't going to waste all that talent beating sticks against a bucket like Tee Wee's boys." Browder leaned over and beat his palms on the top of his night table. "Bam. Bam. Bop bop bop bop." He drummed faster and faster. He imagined that he was Gene Krupa, his long, dark hair falling forward onto his face. He conjured a scantily clad Crow dancing with wild abandonment around his room. With her head back, arms slithering against her body like snakes, she came toward him with her pelvis thrust forward, bumping her hips against his thigh. Yeah, a drummer in a big band would be all right. He and Crow could go up to New York City. They'd live in Harlem where all the really good musicians hung out. Or they could go to California; he'd get in the movie business, become a big star.

He locked his door, switched off the light, and, just as he was getting into bed, heard the phone ring. He counted. Dimple Butler's ring. Now there was a piece of fine woman flesh. Dimple reminded him of the chestnut quarter horse Ruthie had begged her father to buy when they'd taken the Jersey cows to auction last month. The horse had pranced out into the arena, his shiny hooves kicking hay, shaking his mane and tail as if to say, *I'm beautiful and none of you mere mortals can ride me.* The horse was uppity and so was Dimple. Crow, on the other hand, he likened to the black Arabian Derek's father had bought. She weighed about a thousand pounds and stood sixteen hands high. Her dark eyes were moist and sensual. The mare had turned in the ring, seeming to stare straight through each man whose eyes followed her high steps. Her owner, Sid

Nunnery, had dropped her lead, and unrestrained she had galloped around the ring, throwing straw and dirt on Sid and Mr. Waller when he tried to help catch her. Browder lay on his back, then threw his pillow in the air and caught it with the raised soles of his feet. Just like Crow, can't catch her unless she wants to be caught. He juggled the pillow with his feet. He would catch her tomorrow; someday he would mount her like a horse and ride on her sleek back. Faster and faster he bounced the pillow until he felt the heat of his passion rising in his underwear. He turned over, shoved the pillow between his legs, and in the darkness he thrust his hips into the soft fabric, whispering Crow's name again and again.

Chapter 5

O N SATURDAY WHEN MRS. PARSONS CAME BY TO COLLECT TEE Wee's rent money, she reached into her purse and drew out a blue envelope. "This is addressed to you. I see the postmark is from Alabama, so it must be from Ernestine," she said.

After Mrs. Parsons left, Tee Wee plopped down on her porch rocker, and, lifting the envelope, she stared at the small circle in the upper right-hand corner. She knew that this was the post office mark for where mail came from, and she guessed the red-ringed letters said ALABAMA. Moving her fingers over the blue ink, she recognized her name and knew that the lines beneath it were the Parsons' address, but after she tore the flap away and pulled out the two sheets of lined paper, she gaped in confusion at the words written there. A letter from Ernestine meant her firstborn was safe. She hadn't been kilt on the way there at least. But was this bad news or good news in here?

Tee Wee shooed a fly away from her face and looked over toward Icey's house. Icey could read; she could go over there, ask her what Ernestine had written. Placing her hands on the arms of the rocker, Tee Wee lifted herself up with a groan. She was fast gaining some weight with this baby. She stood with the envelope in her hand staring at Icey's silent house. She hadn't seen her all morning; most likely she was lying down in there just being lazy, doing nothing. As she started across the yard, she remembered the look on Icey's face when she read that Bible of hers, big flat nose flaring out in an uppity way. She thought of that snooty preacher tone of Icey's voice. No, she didn't want her reading no mail belonging to any of the Weathersbys.

She'd get Crow to read it. But Crow had taken the twins fishing and they wouldn't be back until time to eat dinner. Okay, well, she would just have to wait to find out Ernestine's news. She could wait. She went back to her rocker and looked at the pages again. It sure was a lot of little letters all strung out together on the second line, and some of the words was underlined. Probably them was more important than the little bitty ones beside them. What if Ernestine had bad news to tell them? What if she was sick? Dying? She'd just have to let Icey read this, tell her this bad news. This time she was halfway across the yard before she stopped and turned back. Icey would make such a show of reading this, and for weeks she'd be saying, *Remembers when I read that letter of yours?* No, she would wait for Crow, or maybe one of the boys would get off from work down at the Co-op feed store where they was working and come by and read their sister's letter to her. She climbed the steps back to the porch and sat down again. No, they wasn't gonna come by. They would stay in town drinkin and dancin all night.

As Tee Wee fanned herself with the letter, she saw that the back of the pages was written on, too. It must be a lot of things that Ernestine had to tell, and her oldest daughter hadn't been no talker when she lived here. This letter must have important news in it to use up so many words. Tee Wee pushed her toes against the boards beneath her feet and began rocking furiously. "Oh Lord," she said out loud. "What happen to my poor child over there in the faraway place of Alabama?" Tee Wee stopped her chair. She couldn't stand it. She was gonna have to know what was in this letter even if it meant Icey was gonna strut around like a new laying hen in the chicken coop.

Before Tee Wee could raise her fist to knock, Icey flung open the screen door. "Hey, Tee. Come on in. I got a mess of greens cookin. Reckon you ain't got none over by your house."

Ignoring this insult, Tee Wee walked into the dark living room, where she stood waiting for an invitation to sit. But Icey turned toward the kitchen. "I best check on these here greens. See if they's got enough fatback in em." Tee Wee started to follow her but then stopped. She wasn't going in no kitchen uninvited.

After banging pot lids, Icey returned to the living room where Tee Wee was still standing, holding the letter behind her back. "Sit down, girl. Sit on the couch," Icey said, waving her arm toward the sagging cushions.

Slowly Tee Wee lowered her big body down until her butt hit the floor beneath the worn-out springs. She groaned, knowing she'd have one devil of a time gettin up from here.

Icey sat in the straight-backed chair across from her. She leaned forward, eyeing the blue envelope and paper Tee Wee had dropped in her lap. Icey would no more ask her about the letter than she would ask Mrs. Parsons her age even though they'd had an argument over it. Icey said she was at least forty-five, and Tee Wee had said she wasn't near that old, and she knew that for a fact, but Icey wouldn't believe her.

Jonas came into the room. "Mama, can we go to Mister Moore's store? Get some candy?"

Icey's face transformed into a mask of ferocity, and, speaking through clenched teeth, she growled, "Mama has company. You don't come in the room when Mama has a guest, and you don't ask no questions in front of one." Jonas backed out of the room so quickly Tee Wee thought she'd imagined him standing there hopping on bare feet.

Staring at Tee Wee's lap, Icey's voice softened into the sweetest of tones. "I reckon you didn't get up from your nap and come all the way over here for nothin."

Tee Wee drew herself up as high as she could from her awkward seat. Her legs were spread out in front of her, so that she was nearly lying down. "Nap? I ain't had no nap in I can'ts think how long. No, I was cookin, too. Not just greens, but field peas and corn bread and cobbler, too."

Icey leaned over and straightened the crocheted doily on the arm of the couch. Tee Wee noticed the other arm didn't have one. "New doily I got the other day. I starched it good, but it still seem a little limp."

It looked like the doily that was under the telephone at the Parsons'. Tee Wee wondered if Mrs. Parsons gave it to Icey; she didn't think Icey was dumb enough to steal it, but did she really know this woman all that well? She cleared her throat. Wasn't gonna get into no conversation with herself about no doilies. She had a reason for being here, and much as she hated to ask Icey to read her letter, she knew that that paper lyin on her thighs was gonna start burnin a hole in her dress if she didn't find out what was written on them pages. She held up the envelope. "I reckon you wonderin what this be?"

Icey feigned surprise by arching her back and thrusting out her chest. "Oh. I didn't see that."

Tee Wee picked up the two sheets of blue paper. "You seen these I'm sure. This is a letter come all the way from Alabama. It addressed to me, gone through the mail to the Parsons, and Miz Parsons personally done delivered it to me." Icey didn't get no mail from far off.

Icey, Tee Wee saw with great satisfaction, was impressed. "Alabama? Imagine that. I once knew a man lived over that way. Junior, somethin like that, was his name."

"I be thinkin you knows lots of mens from plenty of places, but ain't none of em write you no letter."

Icey shook her head. "No, not that many peoples reads like I does."

Tee Wee smiled. Now they were gettin to it. "No, lots and lots of folk don't read." Tee Wee pushed herself forward a bit on the couch. "And I ain't much of a reader myself. Seem like I used to read good, but these days I ain't makin much outta them letters. Reckon I may be needin eye spectacles."

Icey's face lit up like a lightbulb in a well. Tee Wee frowned. This was gonna be worse than she'd thought. "So you sayin you got that letter, but you can't read it?"

"Icey, you knows that now. I just told you." Tee Wee took a deep breath. "Will you read this here letter to me?"

Icey smiled like a baby with a full tummy. "Well, course I will, Tee. Be glad to help you out. Hand it here."

Tee Wee thrust the pages at her and Icey made a big show of flattening them out, examining them, turning them just right before she spoke again. "I see there's lots of readin to be done here. Your girl must have lots to tell. I know you are some worried to know what all be in here." After a long minute of silence during which Tee Wee thought she might scream if Icey didn't get on with it, Icey said, "Well, I begin." She sat up straighter, held the sheets in front of her face. " 'Dear Mama. And everybody. I hope y'all ain't mad at me for leaving like I done.' " Icey lowered the paper. "I reckon she means runnin off without tellin you."

Tee Wee ground her teeth together. "Uh-huh. Go on."

Icey lifted the letter again. " 'I reckon I was afraid you wouldn't let me go.' " Icey stopped reading aloud, but her eyes were ricocheting across the page. "Oh my," she said.

"Icey, I didn't come here for you to read my mail to yourself. You gonna read it to me or not?"

"Sorry. I just read so much faster to myself; I couldn't help it. I'll start over. 'Dear Mama. And everybody.' "

With several more pauses, personal observations, and exclamations, it took Icey fifteen more minutes to read the three-and-a-half-page letter, but by the end of that time Tee Wee was smiling and thanking Jesus for all her good luck. She and Icey had learned that Ernestine had landed a job at a fine white person's laundry and dry-cleaning business. Ernestine was doing alterations for extra money. "Just simple ole stuff like hemming," she had written. "People can't do it pay lots of money for me to do it for them." She and Willie were living in a fine boardinghouse owned by a black lady everybody called Auntie Gert. Every morning she stood outside the house and a bus would come along and pick her and other coloreds up and drop them off downtown. The most surprising news that Icey had had to read twice was that Ernestine was enrolled in a Negro college called Tuskegee. Her employer was loaning her money to pay for this, and she was determined to make good grades, pay him back.

"Praise the Lord; He sure is good to me," Tee Wee said with a broad smile on her face. And, she added silently, thank You for givin me the bonus of Icey being the one to read the news.

Icey stood up. "Well, that was all good news. I just hopes the next letter won't be bad. You can never be sure anythin gonna last in this world."

Tee Wee was struggling to stand. After grunting, grabbing the couch arm, and pushing forward, she finally managed to stand upright. "Phew, I reckon that Ernestine know how to get along in the world. I gots to go." She turned and walked to the door where she paused and turned back to Icey. "I thanks you for readin this. I'll send you some corn bread over for payment."

Icey waved her hand. "No. No. Don't need no payment." She walked to where Tee Wee stood, put her hand on her arm. "I truly glad your girl doin good. Ain't nothin worse'n worryin bout your young'ns."

Without warning, Tee Wee felt her eyes filling with tears. She was so relieved to know Ernestine was okay, so happy now. "You right. Ain't nothin worse. And, Icey, I'm glad none of yours ain't gone off yet. Everybody safe here on the Parsons Place."

Icey nodded her head vigorously. "Amen to that. Amen, Amen."

Chapter 6

*I*CEY WAS LONELY. IN HER NARROW BED AT NIGHT, SHE SPOONED her body around her feather pillow, pressing her face into the soft folds of her cotton sheets. She had not slept alone since the day she turned fifteen and moved into the fine yellow clapboard where Abel Wilkerson made room for her in his wide mahogany bed. Abel was the richest of her three husbands, the kindest, and the ugliest. His protruding eyes were his worst feature; they had a habit of wandering off in different directions when he was talking to someone. Although small-boned, stringy, and jerky in his movements, reminding Icey of a small clothespin doll dancing on a string, Abel Wilkerson had been gentle and tender in his lovemaking to his bride who was twenty years younger and a head taller than he.

Some nights Icey traveled back to Abel's house where she sat in the cozy kitchen at the square table covered with a shiny red oilcloth. Matching red-and-white-checked curtains flapped gaily over the open window above the spotless white sink, and the scent of lilacs drifted into her dreams mingling with the aroma of Abel's strong black coffee bubbling on the big enamel stove. Across the table sat Abel dressed in his black Sunday suit, white shirt buttoned tightly into the folds of the sagging skin of his goose neck. When he spoke the glimmer of his beautiful gold tooth winked out like one shining star appearing in the night. Such happiness! She was thin then and pretty, dressed in her favorite green-and-black-striped shirtwaist Abel had given her for her sixteenth birthday. In the full-skirted dress, Icey stood and twirled across the room, singing, laughing, falling across her husband's lap. His arms wrapped around her flat stomach, infusing his love into muscle, tissue, and bone.

And she would awaken in the small iron bed Mrs. Parsons had loaned her to feel the terrible coldness of her empty arms. She would delay rising, remembering the losses she had suffered. Abel was dead, George gone off to God knows where, Pete living with that trash, Sarah Long. Her last man, Webber (whom she hadn't actually married), had left more than a month ago now. On that Sunday morning she'd awakened, stretched out her hand to feel the cool pillow he had abandoned in the dark hours of the night. He'd left her with no money, bills to pay at Carter's store and the Lazi-Dazi bar, and he'd taken the garden rake, the grass sling, his tools, and the watch from the dark blue velvet box she'd opened with such joy last Christmas.

She missed all of her bed partners, but she missed Abel the most. Why'd he have to go and die on her? Two years. That was all she had with him. Of course, Icey admitted to herself, he wasn't perfect, but she hadn't known that until after his other wife came knocking on her door waving a paper in her hand that said she was Abel's lawful, wedded, and entitled-to-everything-in-the-house wife. The big angry woman had sauntered through the house, noting her every possession. She stood in the bedroom, a saccharine smile on her face, watching Icey fold the wedding-ring-patterned quilt she'd brought to the house on the first day after her so-called holy union to Abel. Bigomony, or some fancy word, was what the woman said describing Icey's marriage. She said he had run off from the house in Memphis where he had lived with her and her mother and five sisters. He'd left his job as undertaker at Hart's Funeral Home without a word to her or anyone, and after two and a half years she'd caught the train to Zebulon and walked into Perkins' Funeral Parlor to learn she was one week too late to kill him because he was already dead—drowned in the Tangipahoa River after his Nash had skidded on the gravel and fishtailed off the flimsy bridge.

Icey groaned, swung her feet onto the cold floor of her dark room, and entered her present life. Times now might not be so good, she reminded herself, but they was better than they had been. As she made her way to her tiny kitchen, she lifted her hand to her face remembering the mornings she'd awaken with a swollen jaw or puffy eye or a bruise as big as an apple on her arm or leg from the long, hazy nights she spent with Webber. He wasn't nothing to miss. That the truth, she said to herself, slamming her frying pan onto the eye of the stove. She took three brown eggs from the basket beside the sink and cracked them over the pan. With her long fork, she poked the yolks one by one. "Take that and that and that," she said aloud to Webber. Then, lifting her head to the low wooden ceiling, she said, "Send me a better man this time. Please?"

"Mama?" Glory stood in the doorway. "Who you talkin to?"

"Nobody, baby. The Lord. I guess."

Glory peered around the room as if expecting to see Jesus and His lamb from her Sunday school paper sitting on the linoleum. She was George's child, and like him she believed in miracles. To Icey's knowledge neither of them had witnessed one, nor did they actually, to her mind, have any hope of a miracle occurring to either of them. When she was married to him, George had squandered most of his railroad paycheck on get-rich-quick schemes that resulted in Icey having to spend her evenings ironing white people's shirts and tablecloths after she had scrubbed their floors all day. And here was little Glory, wearing his jutting chin, ten years old now, still watching the bean stalks in the garden, thinking one of them would grow up to some castle in the sky where she'd find the goose that laid one of them gold eggs.

Whipping the ordinary chicken eggs in her skillet, Icey shook her head at her daughter. "Wake up Jonas. Get dressed. School ain't waitin for you to start."

"I ain't feelin good, Mama. That's what I come to say. I got a bellyache."

"Too many pieces of apple pie off Tee Wee's dish, I'll say."

Glory shook her head. "I ain't ate but one slice, and my gut, it hurts bad."

Icey turned to her child. Her eyes were unnaturally bright, and when she pulled her toward her and laid her cheek against her forehead, she felt as hot as the frying pan. "Lord have mercy, girl. You got the fever. Go lay down on my bed. I'll be in directly soon as I finishes these eggs."

After Icey sent Jonas over to Tee Wee's to ask her if she had any powders for fever, Tee Wee returned with a pinkish concoction she declared was better than aspirin tablets, but when Glory swallowed it, she immediately began vomiting. "Wipe her with a cold rag," Tee Wee suggested, and Icey ran to kitchen for her dishrag, soaked it in cold water and slapped it on Glory's head. Glory was moaning with pain now; clutching her stomach, she rolled into a ball. "It hurts, Mama, hurts so bad."

Tee Wee looked across the child to Icey, who stood against the wall on the far side of the bed. "It serious, I'm thinkin. Ain't no whiner, this child. She hurtin all right."

Icey began wiping up the pink mess of vomit with the rag she'd swept over Glory's face. "What you think it be?" she asked.

Tee Wee shook her head. "Don't know, girl, but I think we better get Luther to get the car out and take her to the doctor's."

Icey's eyes grew round with fright. None of her children had ever been taken to a hospital. Like nearly all the coloreds in Mississippi, Icey had always relied on home remedies, which didn't cost much money. How would she ever pay some fancy doctor's bill? She looked down at Glory, who was thrashing against the corn shuck mattress, barely conscious now. Icey nodded her head. "Let's go," she said.

They sat in the colored waiting room in the basement of the Zebulon Infirmary Hospital on Lincoln Street. Icey held Glory on her lap, the child's head thrashing back and forth against her bosom. The hard metal chair bit into her back. The room was hot and stuffy and dimly lit by a single light, placed not in the center, but toward the back of the small square room. A boy, who looked to be around Glory's age, sat in the row of chairs in front of Icey and Tee Wee and Luther. He coughed, a deep rattling reverberation, and, pushing his head into his mother's shoulder, he whimpered. The woman's arm stretched out around her son, patting him on his thin shoulder. "Shush. Be a big boy. Ain't gonna be long now," she said. Then after a moment, she tilted her head back toward Icey and Glory. "We been here three hours already. Doctor don't come until the whites is taken care of first."

Icey nodded. She'd expected this. She felt for her brown cloth purse on the floor beside her. Two five-dollar bills was all she had, and she wondered if they'd be enough for treatment. She'd heard stories of folks getting turned away if they couldn't show no money.

A starched white nurse wearing a peaked white cap appeared in the doorway. She was carrying a brown clipboard with white papers flapping on the top of it. Glancing down at the paper, she called out. "Jessie Newman?" The woman in front of Icey stood up. "That's us," she said, jerking her son to his feet.

Tee Wee leapt up from her chair. "Miss?"

Half the distance to the door, the nurse stopped and turned. "Yes?"

"Our little girl, Glory here, she real sick. She got the fever bad. This one's an emergency patient."

The nurse's hand rose to the gold pin on her cap. Her eyes roamed over Tee Wee in her ragged, faded blue housedress clutching the back of the chair where the boy had sat. Tee Wee's head was bowed, but her eyes lifted to the nurse's chest where a little rectangular pin bore the letters, P. SIMPSON. The nurse lowered her hand. "Well," she said, looking toward Glory who was writhing in delirium against Icey's tense body.

"Please," Tee Wee whispered. Reaching up, Luther clutched his wife's arm and gently pulled her down to the chair between him and Icey. The nurse stood for a moment longer, her pale gray eyes appraising them, and then she nodded. "Yes, she looks like an emergency. I'll be right back." Pivoting on her white rubber-soled shoes, she hurried after the mother and son down the long cream-colored hall.

Glory was an emergency. Within the hour she was lying on the operating table, her face covered with a rubber mask leaking ether into her nose and mouth. Her appendix had nearly ruptured, Dr. Uleland said to Icey. "Close call, could have lost her." He had come into the colored waiting room so silently and swiftly, Icey had jumped up from her metal chair, nearly crying out when he spoke in his cheerful, booming voice. He was one of the whitest white people Icey had ever seen. From the green surgical clothing that covered his hair and body, his white face and hands stuck out like fluffy cotton bolls on a dark green plant. Icey grabbed one of his hands, brought it to her lips, and kissed the soft flesh of his palm. Her tears dripped onto the fine orange-red hairs on his wrists.

"Thank you. Thank you."

Reaching across Icey, Tee Wee jerked the young doctor's hand away. "You saved our baby's life," she yelled at him. Pumping his hand, she continued on. "I knowed Glory was an emergency. I'm the one who told that nurse. I knowed she was knockin on death's door."

Dr. Uleland smiled, tried to pull his hand away, but Tee Wee paid no attention. "That child, Glory, is like one of my own young'ns. Just last night she was over to the house eatin pie." She stopping whipping the doctor's hand up and down and squeezed it between her two, oblivious to the grimace that appeared on Uleland's face. "That's what I'm gonna do. I'm gonna bake you a pie and bring it down here. You ain't never ate no pie like my lemon pie. No sir, you ain't."

Icey, watching Tee Wee and listening to these last words, wiped her tears and stepped forward. "Glory is *my* daughter. *I'm* the mother," she said, giving Tee Wee a nudge with her hip. "I got money to pay. Doctors want money, not pie." She looked up into the widened eyes of Glory's savior. "How much?"

Dr. Uleland, who had finally managed to drag his hand out of Tee Wee's grip, inched backward across the room. He waved his hand at Icey as she swung her purse up from the floor. "No, No. I don't take the money. A bill. You'll get a bill when your daughter goes home." He'd nearly reached the door, and he talked more quickly now. "Recovery. You can see her in recovery. Upstairs. Down the hall. Left turn. Then, we'll keep her a few . . ." His last words were lost as his green suit vanished around the wall.

Icey, Tee Wee, and Luther stood in front of their chairs aligned like soldiers at attention. After a moment or so, Luther relaxed and shook his head. "You women. You two. I ain't never in my life seen nothin to beat it."

Both Icey and Tee Wee turned toward him, and Luther jumped backward, falling onto his chair. Over his head Icey and Tee's eyes met. "She okay!" Icey screamed. "Glory gonna be fine." Tee Wee grabbed Icey around her waist, and, laughing together, they jumped up and down on the wooden floor, knocking the chairs against each other. "Praise the Lord," Icey said. "Glory saved."

"Amen. Thank You Sweet Jesus," Tee Wee yelled.

Dropping his head, Luther spoke to the floor. "I got work to do. Hogs and cattle and wood choppin, and I'm sittin here with two crazy gals dancin in a hospital like some floozies down at Burglundtown Bar."

As he twirled his straw hat in his hands between his knees, Icey stared at the yellow brim circling between his long brown fingers. He spun it faster and faster until it looked to Icey like there was a streak of rich golden butter flowing right out of his hands.

Chapter 7

FTER GLORY WAS RELEASED FROM THE HOSPITAL, RUTHIE became her most frequent visitor. She was fascinated by the large, ugly wound on Glory's right side, and Glory happily lifted her gown to allow Ruthie to examine the line of black blood-clotted stitches that rose from her smooth brown stomach. Glory's prized treasure sat in a quart jar on the floor beside her mother's bed, where she had been sleeping since coming home from the Zebulon Infirmary Hospital. Glory's appendix, a gray-purplish mass, which Ruthie declared looked a lot like chicken in-nards, floated inside the jar in a clear solution. For the first time in her life, Ruthie contemplated her own organs. At night she'd lie in her bed, her hand over her heart feeling it beat against her palm. Thump, thump, thump, her chest would rise and fall like a slow bouncing ball, and she would move her hand to press against her stomach, trying to feel the yards of ropy intestines beneath her pale skin. She thought that maybe she'd like to be a nurse. A nurse in the operating room who routinely looked at the mysteries inside other people's bodies.

When school let out on Friday, Ruthie raced across the pasture to the tenant house for her usual visit; today she carried a letter her mother had instructed her to deliver to Icey, and, bounding up the steps, she jerked open the screen door and called out Icey's name.

Her voice boomed out from the kitchen. "Hey, Miz Ruthie, come on in. Glory back in the bedroom."

Ruthie walked into the hot kitchen and held out the letter. "You got mail."

"I got a letter?" she asked, reaching out to take the envelope from

Ruthie's extended hand. Icey pulled out a chair and sat down beside the small wooden table. She read her typed name through the cellophane window and then lifted her eyes to the return address. "Zebulon Infirmary," she said out loud in a voice filled with dread. Slowly she worked open the flap and pulled out a thin sheet of pink paper. After staring at it for nearly a minute, she dropped it on the table as if it were covered with mites. "Oh Lord," she cried. "Seventy-five dollars! I ain't got the money for this."

Ruthie laid her hand on Icey's slumped shoulder. "Maybe we could loan you some, Icey. Daddy sold a calf at the auction last Saturday."

"I already borrowed some for a coat for Glory and a pair of shoes for Jonas." Icey lifted the bill and stared at it as if willing the figures written there to disappear. "Six days in the hospital. Who'd of thought it cost this much?" Folding the bill into its original creases, she stuffed it back in the envelope, positioning it with her thumb so that her name once again appeared in the cellophane window. "Well, I gonna pray on it. The Lord will think of a way. He found me this place and this job. He gonna provide."

"I'll ask Him, too. Tonight when I say my prayers, I'll say, 'Please help Icey to find some money,'" Ruthie said.

"You do that. Icey need all the help she can get." Then, pushing her toward the door, she said, "Now you go see Glory. She been waitin on you."

When Ruthie woke up Saturday morning and remembered she'd forgotten her prayers last night, she hastily scrambled to her knees beside her bed and folded her hands into a tent. She knelt silently for a while wondering how to begin since the usual *Now I lay me down to sleep* wasn't appropriate, and the *dying before I wake* part didn't fit, either. She closed her eyes. "Jesus, help Icey to find some money for her bills and help Dimple Butler to get Troy for a boyfriend. Forgive me of any sins I forgot I did. Bless Josie, Mama and Daddy and Tee Wee and Icey, Glory, and . . . Browder, I guess. Thank You. Amen."

She hoped the Lord was listening to her prayers and all those Icey had offered up each day as she flicked a feather duster around the Parsons' house. "Religion is the only comfort we humans have in this world," Tee Wee had told Ruthie when she'd asked how come Icey kept talking to Jesus all day like He was accompanying her every step. Ruthie believed in Jesus, but she didn't think He followed her around the house like Icey did. One afternoon she had seen Icey in the living room on her knees dusting the legs of the piano, talking to Jesus like He was sitting on the bench practicing the scales. Jesus was in the living room, but He was immobile, standing in the gold-painted wooden frame that hung over the sofa. The picture was called *Portrait of Jesus as a Young Man*, and Jesus looked to be about Uncle Homer's age, twenty-eight or so. He had long brown wavy hair, and the gown He wore was a soft-looking vanilla-ice-cream-colored material. Sometimes He looked serious, other times sort of sad, and once in a while, when Ruthie was lying on the couch looking up at Him, He stared back at her with a stern unforgiving look in His blue eyes. This usually happened when Ruthie had borrowed Catherine's *True Confessions* magazine and was reading the parts about aching breasts and throbbing feelings. She would be stretched out, reading along, and then she'd feel His eyes on her. Quickly stuffing the magazine down between the cushions, Ruthie would then walk over to the piano and play "What a Friend We Have in Jesus," which seemed to appease Him and make His face kind again.

Jesus was white, of course, but Icey, Ruthie guessed, knew that Jesus loved the red man and the yellow and the black man, too. In Sunday school she had learned that Jesus loved all the different-colored children of the world just the same, and she was glad about that because she wanted to believe that, if Glory had died, she'd go to heaven just like white people did. She believed Glory would most probably go to heaven; she wasn't old enough to have committed very many sins. Ruthie had only just begun sinning in the last year or so, and that was why she had amended her nighttime prayer to include a last rejoinder to God to ask His forgiveness for anything she was doing that might be a sin, but she didn't know it was yet.

Besides solving Icey's problems, Ruthie hoped God was also working on the romance between Dimple and Troy Greer although she believed Dimple's chances of success were far better than Icey's.

On the following Sunday, when the congregation of Pisgah Methodist Church gathered on the lawn for the annual dinner, Ruthie decided that Dimple didn't really need the Lord's help. Everyone had worried delaying the celebration dinner until December would mean moving it to the church basement, but the day was mild and the trestle tables were set up outside beneath the oaks and pines that stood on the side of the parking lot. After the service and handshaking, Ruthie didn't join the children who began a game of Devil in the ditch. She wasn't all that fast, and she knew she'd be the Devil for the rest of the game.

When she spotted Dimple Butler talking to Troy Greer, Ruthie ran across the church grounds toward them. They stood beside the long planked tables covered with white cloths on which rested mounds of fried chicken, okra, field peas, butter beans, corn on the cob, chicken and dumplings, stewed tomatoes, and assorted pies and cakes and cobblers. Dimple was wearing a white piqué dress trimmed with blue ribbon, and in her red hair she'd pinned an artificial gardenia. She stood with one hand on her right hip, the other resting on Troy's left bicep.

As she neared them, Ruthie slowed and crept up to stand across the table within earshot of their conversation. Reaching over, she picked the crust from a chicken leg, and as she popped the brown crunchy batter into her mouth she heard Dimple's warm laugh. "Well, Mister Troy Greer, I don't know what to say to such an invitation."

Looking over at them, Ruthie saw Troy's acorn-colored long-lashed eyes swoop over Dimple's plunging neckline, then lift to her face. "All I'm asking for is your company on a short ride in the Caddy." He pointed toward the back of the churchyard, where Ruthie saw his long white Cadillac convertible with red cloth seats, a big red steering wheel, and a fancy rearview mirror that had a flip button to adjust it for day and night vision. From it, on a piece of gold braid, hung a dark blue velvet bag, which Ruthie guessed had once covered a bottle of store-bought whiskey.

Ruthie sidestepped closer to Dimple and Troy and stuck her finger in some kind of red icing on the bottom of a cake plate. "So what do you say, honey? I'm promising to be a good boy," Troy said in a husky voice.

Dimple twirled one of her red curls. She smiled. Her breasts rose and fell like she was going to cough, but her voice was clear and soft. "I just don't know what my mama would say about me going off with someone with your reputation. I might get into trouble. Would it be worth it?"

Troy laughed. "Since when did Dimple Butler start worrying about getting into trouble? You been in trouble since the day you was born." He winked at her. "Just like me, baby. We're cut of the same cloth."

Ruthie nodded agreement. Troy certainly did have a bad reputation. His mama had died when he was an infant, and folks said his daddy just grieved so, he couldn't pay any attention to Troy and left him to run wild. The Greers were rich in cattle and Shetland ponies and cotton, too. So Troy got whatever he wanted as long as he left his daddy to sit in the front parlor drinking whiskey and listening to old records on his phonograph. Tee Wee had told Ruthie that Bernadine Wilson, who had worked at the Greers for years, said Mr. Troy weren't no good. She said he started drinking and carousing and gambling when he wasn't growed much more than a tadpole.

As for Dimple being of the same cloth, Ruthie couldn't say for sure. She was the only seventeen-year-old Ruthie knew who could cuss as good as a man. Now she watched Dimple squeeze Troy's bicep before her fingers ran down his forearm. Leaning over, she whispered something in his ear, and Ruthie saw Troy's eyes go all watery like a calf's at feeding time. As Troy and Dimple walked away from the table, Ruthie raised her arm in a wave, but they didn't notice her. She lifted a chicken leg and bit into it, her eyes following them to the Cadillac. Dimple slid in on the driver's side and moved over to leave just enough space for Troy to get behind the steering wheel.

Her prayers were answered. Ruthie sighed as she watched the car drive away in a cloud of dust. "Someday I'm gonna be driving off with a dreamboat like that in a car like that," Ruthie told the pyramid of corn on the cob beside her. Then, wiping the chicken grease on her dress, Ruthie headed toward the ditch where the Devil waited to catch her.

Chapter 8

*O*N SUNDAY AFTERNOON TEE WEE SAT ALONE ON HER FRONT porch listening to Luther's and the children's snores and whistles coming from inside the house. She hadn't been able to fall asleep, and she had crept out of bed and come out here to sit and think. She couldn't stop worrying about Ernestine lost somewhere over there in Alabama. None of her children had left home before, and she felt the loss of one of them like a missing tooth, constantly feeling for it with her tongue and finding only a gaping sore hole.

She'd mentioned how she was feeling to Icey, but Icey couldn't think about anything but Glory's brush with death. She was convinced her illness was a message from God. "What message?" Tee Wee had asked her. "I don't know, but trouble don't come with no reason. First I loses my man, then I nearly lose my girl. God tryin to tell me somethin."

In church meeting this morning Icey had leapt up from her bench and staggered out into the aisle where she fell on her knees begging Preacher Dixon to pray the Devil out of her home and save her children from his evil. Tee Wee had then been moved to leave her own seat, leap in front of Icey, and beg the preacher to pray for Ernestine who was living in the Devil's kingdom over in Alabama. Both Icey and Tee Wee had had to be fanned and given water to revive them enough to go home and eat Sunday dinner.

Tee Wee closed her eyes. Maybe she could catnap a little out here in the crisp fall air. She folded her arms over her stomach. Soon she would feel life stirring inside her again. This one would be her last. She wanted this baby, though. Wanted Luther's son. It would be a boy; she knew because the button on the string Icey had held over her womb swung left and right and that meant boy. They would name him John Paul after Luther's daddy and hers. Call him J. P. maybe.

"You sleep?" Opening her eyes, Tee Wee saw Icey standing on her porch with her neck craned toward Tee Wee's rocker.

"No. Come on over. Sit a spell. I just wool gatherin."

Slowly Icey walked down her three wooden steps and made her way across the yard to Tee Wee's porch. She walked like an old woman, stooped and careful of where she put each brown foot. Holding on to the porch post, she eased down onto the top step. "I reckon I ain't over my faintin spell I suffered at church this mornin."

"You over it," Tee Wee said. "You just tired is all. Like me. I ain't got no energy at all. Course I'm pregnant and you ain't."

Icey smoothed down her blue apron over her yellow print dress. "I wish I was. I felt good with all of mine. You get *more* energy with the extra soul you carryin."

Tee Wee rocked back, a frown on her face. Why'd she have to come over and bother her when she was feeling so happy? She changed the subject. "How's Glory feelin?"

Icey's sorrowful face vanished. She smiled. "Right as rain, that child. She healed up quicker than anybody ever did. Doctor Uleland said so hisself."

"Miz Ruthie told me you got his bill last week."

Icey lowered her head. "Yes ma'am. That bill sittin on my kitchen table right now. I ain't got the money to pay it. Don't see no way to ever have it. I can't even send in some every week. There just ain't none left after I pays the rent and the bill at Mister Moore's store. Eli's spending his railroad paycheck on that gal he moved in with in town."

Tee Wee stopping rocking, leaned forward in her chair. "You needs somebody to help you pay the rent. A man who can make more wages than you makes."

Icey nodded. "But where is I gonna find me somebody? The good men I know already taken."

Tee Wee resumed her rocking, a smile on her face. She had an idea, but she wasn't ready to share it with Icey yet. "Well, somethin might come along, girl. It looks like rain to me. Remember what we said about men and rain comin round sure as Christmas and snow at the North Pole."

After Icey returned home, Tee Wee went inside, too. She plopped down on the corn shuck mattress Luther was lying on. "Wake up, lazy man. You done slept past feedin time. Cows has come up and is bellowin down at the lot."

Luther stirred only enough to open his eyes and lift his hand to wave her away.

She shook him, poked her big thumb into the center of his stomach. "Wake up, Luther. I got somethin to ask you."

Luther lifted his hand to his eyes. She poked him again. He sighed. "Okay, what?"

Tee Wee grabbed his shoulders and hauled him up from his pillow. "You wake enough to listen?"

Luther yawned. "I'm up, ain't I? What you studyin on now, Tee?"

Tee Wee grinned. "It Icey I'm thinkin of. Icey needin money, which mean a man."

"Uh-huh. What we gonna do about that?" Luther swung his legs down, placed his feet on the floor. A cow bellowed loudly. "Hear that? I needin to get down to the Parsons' before they send that Browder for me. Ain't nothin worse than that white boy barkin orders like he is lord of the world."

Tee Wee pulled him back when he tried to stand. "Wait a minute. I'm gonna tell you what we gonna do."

"Later. Gotta go feed now," he said. Tee Wee waited. Luther understood he wasn't going anywhere until she was done with whatever she had to say.

As she helped him pull his arms through his overall straps, she said, "Okay, but listen to this first. You know your cousin, the one from Memphis? Deke. That's him. Deke. Didn't you say he was come back here to live?"

"Yeah, but he ain't got no money to give Icey. Ain't got no work yet, and he ain't brought no money with him from Memphis. Reckon that woman he was livin with got what all he had. I told you bout meetin up with him."

"Tell it again," Tee Wee said, smiling widely.

"I went to town to the Co-op store to get some horse and mule feed and some chicken scratch for the Parsons, and after I left with the trunk and backseat filled with fifty-pound sacks, I stopped in at Caskell's to treat myself to a little Jax beer."

Tee Wee started to say something about the beer, which he'd omitted to tell her before, but thought better of it. "Go on."

"Well, sittin at one of them yellow enamel tables I sees cousin Deke, who I ain't seen in sixteen or so years. I wouldn't of known him, but Caskell called my name when I walked in, and Deke looked up and yelled, 'Luther, that you? It's me, Deke. I was just askin folk where you lived so's I could come visit you.'

" 'What you doin back, boy?' I says. When Deke stood up, I could see he weren't no boy no longer. He was only fifteen when he run off to Memphis to be a riverboat captain."

"A captain? You never said nothin bout no riverboat."

Luther held up his hand. "Wait and hear this out. So, I sat down in the metal foldin chair beside Deke, and I said, 'You ain't on the river no more?' Deke, he shakes his head and says, 'Nooo. I got tired of the water. It the same every day going the same direction, rollin water, slappin gainst the boat, the bank. Make you dizzy you watch it too long. Course I was too busy to see much. Worked down in the engine room. I'm a mechanic now.' That what he said to me."

Tee Wee inched her hips forward on the bed. "Mechanic, huh?"

"Then I says, 'Mechanic, huh?' Deke, he took a sip of his beer. 'That's right. I can fix near bout anythin. And that's why I was gonna look you up. See if you know anybody needin a mechanic.' That is all he said." He looked over at Tee Wee, sitting on the bed like a cat waiting for a bird to fly by. "That's the end of it. I said I didn't know nobody, but I'd keep my ear to the ground."

Tee Wee smiled. Luther was taking his time getting to it.

Finally, he said the words. "You thinkin Deke be right for Icey?"

Tee Wee clapped her hands together the way she did when the children got stars on their schoolwork. "I was thinkin he could get a job at the Parsons' and move in over there to Icey's. Help pay the rent."

Luther shook his head. "I don't know. Parsons ain't got no need of him. I do all they need done."

"You said he was a mechanic. You don't know nothin bout machinery. He could fix that broke tractor they got sittin in the barn. And there's other stuff, too. The machines they pays to get fixed, the combine, the bush hog. He'd save em money in the long run."

"Yeah, mebbe you gots a point here. I wouldn't have to go into town to get somethin fixed. And no matter the price, Mister Parsons is always sayin he is robbed out of his hard-earned money. The Ford is making a knockin noise; maybe Deke could figure that out and save us money, too." Luther found his boots and began to pull them on. "I'll think on it some. Deke, he might have other opportunities. Might not want to come out here in the country. He weren't no country boy even when he live with his mama."

Tee Wee reached down to help him pull the boot over his heel. "But, Luther, you could talk him into it. You good at talk. You know you is." Then she leaned over and brushed her lips against his cheek. "You was good talkin me into you, wasn't you?"

Luther laughed. "Okay, when I go to town next, I'll ask him. And I'll talk to Mister Parsons tomorrow. That good enough for you and Miz Icey Ice?"

"Good enough, but don't say nothin to Icey yet. Let her keep on prayin for a while. She so sure God gonna help her out. Let her see it's *me* she got to count on."

After daily reminders of his promise, Luther arranged a meeting between Deke and Mr. Parsons on the following Friday. That morning Tee Wee ran back and forth to the kitchen window, watching for Luther, waiting for him to report the outcome to her.

She finally spotted him outside the Parsons' back door where she was sitting on the steps peeling the potatoes she would fry later. He was lumbering across the yard, dragging a tree limb out to the burn pile. Tee Wee yelled to him. "Did he get hired?"

Luther didn't stop, but trudged on with the limb as if he hadn't heard her loud voice. Halfway across the yard, he turned his head to her and called over his shoulder. "Deke hired, but I see troubles a-comin from it. He tried to shake Mister Parsons' hand . . . a *white* man."

"Well, he ain't from round here, don't know no better. You worries bout nothin. Is he still here?"

"He here. Down to the barn," Luther said before he disappeared behind the pump house.

Tee Wee dumped the potatoes into a pan of water so they wouldn't turn brown, and, wiping her hands on her apron, she went out and headed for the barn. On the way she practiced the words she planned to say to Deke. " 'If'n you be needin a place to stay . . .' " She shook her head. "No. I'll say, 'I *might* knows a place you could stay.' He has to take Icey. Just has to. I got a good plan here and he got to go along with it."

When she reached the barn, Tee Wee stood for a moment in the open door breathing in the smell of axle grease and hay and damp earth before walking inside. She stepped around the boxes of old spark plugs and rusted plow points and hoes and rakes that were strewn helter-skelter on the dark earthen floor. She called out into the dimly lit barn. "Yoo hoo!" When she saw Deke's rounded back hunched over the front of the tractor parked at the back of the barn, she cleared her throat, then said, "I be Luther's wife, Tee Wee. Come to say hello."

Deke straightened and turned to her. "Howdo." He wiped his hands on a green rag lying on the tractor seat and then thrust his right one toward her.

Unaccustomed to such gallantry, Tee Wee shuffled her feet. Deke took a step forward, lifted her hand, and shook it vigorously. "Pleased to meet you," he said.

Tee Wee snatched her hand back and ran it down her apron front. "Well, well, I . . . uh . . . I pleased, too," she said in the smallest voice she'd ever heard herself use. This man wasn't nothing like the other colored men she knew. She wondered if all the men on riverboats was like him.

Deke leaned back against the side of the tractor, his elbows spread wide across the smooth red enamel. His tan work shirt tightened against his broad chest. Tee Wee guessed the curly red letters over the pocket were those of his name.

"Luther told me you're going to have his baby," he said with a knowing smile.

Tee Wee dug her fingers into her wiry hair. Men didn't talk bout women's things, neither. This one was a caution. "That right," she said. "It be a boy."

Deke nodded. "Well, I'm glad Luther got hisself such a fine woman like you."

Having no idea what to say to this, Tee Wee saw that at least this last sentence was an opening for saying what she'd come for. "Uh, you ain't got no woman, I reckon?"

Deke laughed. "Not yet. Not here anyway."

Tee Wee licked her lips. "Well, you needin a place to stay, and I knows a woman needin a man to help out with the rent." She lowered her eyes, not ready to see if he was gonna laugh at her. "She a good church woman," she added before peeking up at him.

"Church woman, you say?" Deke straightened up, took a cigarette and a single Red Ball match out of the named pocket. He struck the match on the bottom of his shoe, held it to the cigarette he'd placed in the center of his mouth. Blue smoke curled up around his brown face.

Icey wasn't gonna like no smoker, Tee Wee thought. But then, when did she get the chance to be picky? I gonna do what I come to do even if'n I has to tell a little ole white lie. Tee Wee smiled. "Well, she go to Sunday meetin like we all does. I ain't sayin more'n that."

Deke sucked in on the cigarette, blew the smoke up toward the rafters. "Where she live? I'll go over there tonight."

Tee Wee smiled. She had him; he weren't no different than the rest of them when it come to womenfolk. "Real close to right where you is now. Real, real close."

Chapter 9

THE RAPPING ON THE SCREEN DOOR STARTLED ICEY. HARDLY anyone ever knocked; most folks just opened the door and called her name. She waited, listening for a voice, but she heard only louder and more persistent banging. Leaping from her bed, Icey threw her plaid robe on over her thin blue nightgown and hurried to the front room.

In the pale yellow moonlight she could just make out the form of a very large man standing on her porch. "Oh, Sweet Lord," Icey said out loud. "Now You sent me more trouble." She looked around for a weapon, and taking up Jonas's toy wooden sword, she crept to the window. She lifted the window a crack. "Who there? I got a sword and I ain't scared to use it," she said, holding up the blunt-ended blade to the window. Nobody could tell it weren't real in the shadows, could they?

"Miz Icey Hamilton?"

"That right. What you want?"

"My name's Deke. I'm Luther's cousin from Memphis."

Icey stood framed in the window a moment longer, thinking. Tee Wee had said something about Luther's having a cousin in Memphis. "Okay, just a minute." She closed the window, laid the sword on the couch, and went to the door. Opening it, she stepped out into the cool night air. She folded her arms over her chest. "Luther and Tee Wee live next door." She nodded her head toward their dark house.

The man's teeth flashed in the night. "I know. It's you I come to see." He held out his hand for her to shake. She stuffed her own hands farther into her armpits. His arm dropped, but he moved closer to her. "You needing a man to help you around this place?"

Icey backed up to lean against the door. "Maybe I do and maybe I don't."

"Tee Wee over there"—he jerked his head left now—"said your last man run off and you needing someone to help with the bills and planting." She knew he was guessing about her man because Tee Wee wouldn't say that. Icey's eyes began to take him in, appraising and weighing and judging. She noticed his thick forearm muscles bulging beneath the rolled-up sleeves of his dark blue shirt, his wide chest, the thighs that strained against the cotton cloth of his black pants. "I ain't no rich white woman can pay help," she said. She knew she needed a big strong man like this one because she was over 180 pounds, prime woman she knew.

"I got money be coming in over to the Parsons'. Not just no field hand. Mechanic. I can fix tractors, equipment, anything." He was tall and when he lifted his head, saying this, he reminded Icey of that black horse, Shiloh, the Parsons bought at the last auction. A thoroughbred they had said.

Icey pushed away from the door toward him. Her nose was level with his shoulder. "So, you really just needin a place to stay?" she said.

Now Deke smiled. His tongue crept out to the corner of his mouth. He chuckled softly into the stillness of the night. "I left a good bed in Memphis, Tennessee, and I reckon I can find another one here if it ain't gonna be yours."

Icey swayed on her feet, allowing her robe to fall open. She was glad she'd decided to wear her one good gown tonight. It was an omen, picking that gown outta the cardboard box beneath her bed where she kept her few personal belongings.

Deke noticed the gown. She saw his eyes roving from her neck to her breastbone on down to her toes. She walked around him to the porch post beside the steps. "I reckon you could find somebody, but you won't find nobody like me." She shrugged the robe off her shoulders, exposing the thin pale blue straps that held up her short gown.

Deke whirled around and in two steps was beside her. Lifting his hands to her shoulders, his fingers worked their way under the two nylon strips. "You gonna show me what you like, so's I'll know?"

Icey smiled. "How much you say you gettin paid down at the Parsons'?"

Deke's tongue went back to the corner of his mouth. "I didn't, but money ain't everything, is it, Icey?"

Icey felt his breath on her face and she wondered how much longer she could hold out. She closed her eyes. Please God, don't go gettin mad at me. I'll get him to marry me. In church, too. She opened her eyes. Remember what's important here, she reminded herself. She pressed her back into the post. "Money ain't everythin maybe, but it be big in your mind when you ain't got any." She could feel his large fingers rubbing against her collarbone. She knew she was losing now. If he was lyin and nothin more than a low-down polecat, she was gonna love gettin clawed.

Deke leaned forward, put his lips to her ear. "I got enough of everything to take care of a woman like you." Icey nodded; he did. "Let's go inside and talk some more." Deke opened the door and walked into his new home. Before she followed him, Icey looked up. "Thank You, Jesus. Thank You, thank You," she whispered to the silver moon.

Icey skipped church the following Sunday. She sent Glory and Jonas off with the Weathersbys, saying her head was "bout to split open like a watermelon." Tee Wee knew she was lying, but she shooed Icey's children out to Luther's already filled car. Icey stood on the porch, holding a rag to her head watching the car bottom out at the end of the drive, then turn left down Enterprise Road toward Mount Zion.

Deke was waiting for her in the back room. He hadn't bothered to make up a story about missing church. He wasn't saved, he'd told her. He wasn't going to wade in no cold river and get half drowned while a horde of colored people stood on the bank screaming out songs about cherry-os going up to heaven. Icey hadn't liked hearing that, but she figured there'd be plenty of time to save Deke's soul. She was, she admitted, a lot more interested in his body right now. She wondered if all Memphis men was good lovers. First Abel and now Deke had both proved to be a lot smarter bout women than all the Mississippi men she'd known.

When she'd confided her thoughts about this to Tee Wee in the Parsons' kitchen on Friday, she'd gotten no response, except a "Humph" and a quickly turned back. Of course, Luther hadn't never been to Memphis, so she guessed Tee Wee couldn't know what she was talking about. Icey had been sitting at the table polishing the big silver tea set the Parsons never drank any tea out of. Taking up the creamer, she rubbed its little belly sides with her cloth-covered thumb. "All I'm sayin is I happy with him."

Tee Wee didn't turn around, but continued on dipping chicken pieces into her famous flour, cornmeal, egg, and milk batter. Finally, she said, "You wouldn't got him ceptin for me beggin for you."

Icey put the creamer down on the newspaper she'd spread on the table. "You sent him over. That's true. But I'm the one had to sell him on me. He picked me."

Tee Wee whirled around, her dark eyes were flashing. "I picked him to help you with them big bills of your'n. You do better to worry about your young'ns stead of a pole to straddle." She lifted a chicken breast and threw it into the big iron skillet, spraying grease across the stove and onto the floor. "And that one in your stomach ain't got no daddy till you marries him."

Icey slammed her hands down on the table and jumped up. "*What?*"

"You heard me."

"What make you think I got one growin when he ain't been here but for five days?" She sat back down, took up the large coffee urn and began rubbing it. "You don't know nothin."

Tee Wee moved the chicken pieces in the skillet around with her fork. "I knows. I can tell. I sees it in your face. You growed a new hair on your cheek. That be a sign for sure."

Icey dropped the pot on the floor, denting the handle as it banged into the baseboard. She lifted her hand to her face. It was true; she'd seen that hair sprouting out to the right of her nose in the Parsons' hall mirror. "Oh, Lord. It be true. I gonna have another one."

Tee Wee turned from the stove, stabbed the air with her fork as she said, "That right. And you ain't married. Now you the sinner you always talkin bout." She lowered the fork. "That what good come of readin that Bible you always wavin around."

Icey put her head down and cried onto the newspaper until Tee Wee's hand patted her back and she heard her say, "I'll get Luther to talk to him. He'll marry you, even if he is from Memphis and ain't saved."

Now slipping into bed beside Deke, Icey wondered if Luther had talked to him. She'd planned this time alone with him so that she could tell him about the baby he had fathered. She snuggled against him, put her nose into his neck, and breathed in the wonderful aroma of him. He smelled like chicory coffee mixed with Big Red tobacco and Unger's toilet water. She was in love with everything around, in, and about him. She sighed with happiness.

"What got you purring, cat?" Deke whispered above her head.

"Like you doesn't know."

"You lucky, woman. Seven days I been here, and I ain't tired of you yet."

Icey punched him in the stomach. "You better not be. And not be ever."

Deke pulled her on top of him. "Well, we'll just have to wait a spell and see what come about from this here. Meantime . . ." His hands traveled down her back. Icey decided her news could wait just a little longer.

THE YOUNG'NS WAS gonna be home soon and still Icey hadn't said nothin to him about jumping the broom. And he had to get saved first. But this one wasn't no easy horse to break. He was skittish, hadn't never been married he'd told her. He liked his freedom. That was why he'd run off so young to the river. "You know that song, Icey, the river he jest keep rollin on? Well, I'm like that river, rollin and rollin on and on. Don't want to come up gainst no dam."

They were sitting at the kitchen table drinking the dark, syrupy coffee Icey had brewed early this morning. Deke smiled at her over the rim of his cup. He looked happy.

Icey stirred a little cow's milk into her cup. She licked the spoon. "You think you could be happy here a while?"

Deke sat his cup down. "Seem like it," he said in a quiet voice.

"You think you'd be happy with a young'n of your own?"

He frowned. "Don't know. Far as I know I ain't never caught no egg with my pole. Maybe it ain't the right shape." He laughed, looking down into his lap. "What you think, gal?"

Icey didn't smile. "I think you caught somethin already and just don't know it yet." She looked over at Deke now, watching his face carefully for his reaction.

He shook his head. "What you talking bout?" His brows knitted together. He didn't understand what she was saying.

Icey leaned closer, touched her fingers to his cheeks. "You gonna be a daddy."

Deke shoved his chair back. He didn't look happy now. His eyes went blank and cold. "If you pregnant, it ain't mine."

Icey could feel her heart beating hard against her gown. She hadn't expected this. A knot of fear began to form inside her. She should of kept her mouth shut. Luther hadn't said nothin to him yet. It was too soon. "Deke, I ain't had no man ceptin you for a long time. I ain't sure, of course, but I feels like last Sunday we made us a baby."

The muscles in Deke's face relaxed a bit. He rubbed his bare chest with the palms of his hands. "Oh. Then we'll see. Wait and see. Might not be. You women go jumping off the bank before you know if there's water in the pond." He dropped his hands and smiled at her. "What you got to eat? Ain't you gonna feed your man, woman? I near starving to death."

Icey stood up. "I got corn bread and greens. That suit you, mister?" She walked behind his chair toward the cupboard. As she passed, she said silently to the back of his head, "You the daddy, all right. Like it or not. You him."

Chapter 10

S URROUNDED BY LAUGHING SHOPPERS HOLDING UP SUITS, shirts, ties, and belts, Browder stood against the wall in the men's section of Alford's department store feeling like a cornered rabbit. Christmas music wafted down the narrow aisles of the store lavishly decorated with the customary red and green of the season. Browder, dressed in jeans and a patterned yellow-and-green shirt, felt the eyes of the clerks upon him. He imagined they thought he was a country boy with no sense of fashion. He stared at the racks of gray and navy and black suits hanging from wooden hooks thinking he would look like Alan Ladd or Jimmy Stewart in one of those.

"Can I help you?" Browder turned and saw an elderly man wearing a tape measure around his neck.

Nodding his head toward the women's end of the store, he said, "No, I'm waiting on my mother." He had refused to go through the lingerie area with his mother and Ruthie, who was acting like she was a princess in a palace. Moving away from the clerk, Browder wandered over to where a mannequin wearing a Santa hat and dark blue suit stood with its hands on its hips on a cloth-covered stand. Sitting beside the dummy, he sighed, knowing his mother and Ruthie would take their time. Ruthie was known for not making up her mind any faster than a turtle could crawl a mile.

Turning toward the Fifth Street entrance, Browder spotted Troy Greer sauntering past the display of leather wallets. As he approached the mannequin's stand, he pointed to Browder's chest. "What's up? You modeling that shirt you're wearing?"

Browder's face turned as red as the Santa hat above him. Why did he have to be in here? Why did he have to wear this stupid shirt his mother bought for him? "I'm just waiting on the womenfolk."

Troy laughed. "Whoo-whee. This time of year they all act like nuts about to crack." He leaned closer, and the woody scent of his cologne sailed toward Browder. Lifting the toe of his boot to the mannequin's stand and resting his forearm on his thigh, Troy leaned down and asked, "So what's Santa gonna bring you? You been a good boy?"

"Oh, I've been good and I want lots of money."

"When you get a girlfriend, you'll need it, kid. Dimple Butler is expecting a big ole present from yours truly this year." Troy straightened up. "Matter of fact, that's what I'm here for. What do you think a filly like Dimple is wanting this Santa to bring her?"

Browder blushed as he thought of Dimple's long red hair, her curved hips in jeans that stretched and wound around her like a rubber hose. He hoped Troy couldn't read his mind. "Well, something expensive, I'll bet."

Troy slapped Browder's shoulder. "You better believe it. I'm thinking something over in the ladies' undies section. I'm thinking of getting her something I can enjoy, too"—he winked—"if you know what I mean. I'd better get over there. See you, Browder."

As Gene Autry's version of "Jingle Bells" began blaring out of the store's speaker system, Browder watched Troy, bouncing on his toes to the rhythm of the music, saunter over to a salesgirl who gazed up at him with a coy smile. When Troy stretched out his hands as if he were measuring the size of Dimple's hips, the girl laughed and shook her head as he moved his hands wider. How does he do it? Browder wondered. Troy sure had a way with the women. Keeping Dimple Butler interested was proof of that.

As Browder watched Troy point to a red see-through nightgown, he thought of Crow. He wished he could buy her a present, but he knew better. Glancing back at Troy, he watched as he held the sheer nightgown against the blushing salesgirl. Crow would look like something in that. Her breasts were already bigger than his mama's. That lace would barely cover her dark nipples and the . . . Browder shivered and looked away to a fat lady who was selecting a tie from the round table in front of him. His mother had bought a new tie and shirt for his father to wear to the Christmas program at Pisgah.

Browder bumped the heels of his loafers against the mannequin's stand. He wished his father wasn't coming to hear him sing. He would make fun of him most likely. He made a joke of just about everything Browder did. As the chorus to "Silent Night" began, Browder lifted his head and saw his mother and Ruthie threading their way through the shoppers toward him. A rectangular silver box was tucked beneath Ruthie's arm, and the frown on his mother's face told him that the dress had cost a pretty penny. Standing on his toes, Browder waved them over. At last, he could get away from the crowded stores and back to Parsons Place, where he belonged.

When his mother parked the car beside the house, his father walked over to the Chevrolet. Before Browder opened his door, his father's face appeared at the window. "I thought you were going to help me worm the new calves," he said. "Didn't know you were going to town with the girls."

Browder slammed the car door. "Mama asked me to go. Wanted someone to carry packages and stuff."

His father slapped his work gloves against his thigh. "Well, I got them all finished up now. Luther helped me. I reckon he knew more what to do than you anyhow." And without a word to his wife or Ruthie, he turned and walked toward the barn. As Browder stood watching his heavy work boots stomping down the grass, he thought of the steel-toed boots as weapons his father used to beat the cows, horses, and pigs to his will. When one of the animals died from a disease or an accident, his father would usually curse and kick the carcass with the toe of his boot. Just last week, his father, standing over the sow who had lain down and died on top of her piglets, had booted her belly and said, "You old fool."

When his father disappeared into the barn, Browder lifted the packages from the backseat of the car. "Merry Christmas, Daddy," he said.

In his room Browder stared at his reflection in the mirror over his dresser. He stroked the soft down over his upper lip. No trace of a beard yet, but there were definitely more hairs growing there. He hoped he'd see Crow later today. He wanted to tell her about the solo he would sing during the program, how Mrs. Laird, the choir director, had praised his voice, said he had real talent. But he knew Crow wouldn't be impressed. She sang solos in the Negro choir every Sunday, and she had bragged that someday she was going to make records and be a big star like Bessie Smith. Turning away from the mirror, he fell back onto his bed. The only way to impress Crow was to show her a pocketful of money. He'd get some for Christmas, but would it be enough? She'd charged him a dime for a quick glimpse of her left breast. He'd never have enough to get all he wanted from Crow. He wondered where she was right now, what was she doing? Closing his eyes he summoned her to him. He slipped the straps of her sundress down her smooth dark arm.

THE FLESH-AND-BLOOD Crow was in Tee Wee and Luther's bedroom. Everyone had gone off visiting or shopping, and she was alone in the house. She walked to the old chest Tee Wee had brought from Magnolia to her new home and flung open the doors. Reaching behind the piles of scraps of material her mother had saved, she felt for the loose strip of wood that lifted forward when she pressed on it. Stretching her arm into the small hole, her fingers felt the tobacco can. Quickly, she pulled it out and pried off the lid. She dumped out the contents and began counting the bills and coins strewn across the floor. Eighty-six dollars and thirty-four cents. Crow grinned. Old stupid Ernestine hadn't known about this money her mother and Luther had been stuffing in here all this time. But when I leave, there won't be no money I don't find, Crow thought. She replaced the money and the can and then went into the kitchen and sat at the small table. She grinned up at the lopsided picture that hung over the table. The picture, speckled with bacon grease and yellow flecks of corn and egg yolk and framed in blond wood, was a fall scene of a farm. There was a white house, a red barn, and three Holstein cows, one chestnut horse, and a huge maple tree with gold and red leaves. Tee Wee's dream house, Crow guessed. "I'm the one who gonna live there," she said. She looked back at the painted cows. "No, not there. I'm gonna live in a big city where there ain't no whiff of cow shit. Mama can have that house if she want it."

Chapter 11

EE WEE PATTED MRS. PARSONS' BACK. "SHE'LL BE FINE THAT one. Miz Ruthie strong as a mule. Them little holes she got in her head ain't nothin. She most likely fainted and fell on some trifle left on the floor of y'all's church."

Mrs. Parsons picked up the dish towel from the kitchen table where Tee Wee had just finished rolling out biscuit dough. "You're probably right. Swooning runs on my side of the family. My mama and all of her sisters were sensitive people, and Ruthie takes after them."

Taking the dish towel from Mrs. Parsons, Tee Wee wiped the back of her blouse where she'd left a white handprint. "That's true. I remembers you tellin me your mama have to lie down in the afternoons with a rag on her head just to keep from faintin."

Mrs. Parsons sighed. "Well, I'm glad Ruthie's okay. I was so scared when I realized she was missing. And to be locked in the church all alone! No wonder she fainted. If she were a year or so older, I'd say this fainting spell might have been caused by her time coming, but she's still a little young for that."

"Hump. Granny Red come to Crow two years back. She were Ruthie's age. Now she wearin the cloth every month same as us."

Mrs. Parsons pushed the rolling pin around on the floured cloth. "Really? Well, maybe Negroes start earlier. I never heard of a ten-year-old white girl getting it that early."

Tee Wee took the rolling pin from Mrs. Parsons. "Well, coloreds do grow up a lot faster than whites, but I spect it's cause they has to work while they's still young. Me, I was workin the fields when I weren't but about five." She dropped the rolling pin in the pan of dishwater beside the sink. "You goin to your ladies' circle meetin today or not?"

Mrs. Parsons looked down at the white-gold watch on her wrist. "Oh no, I'm late. Check on Ruthie for me."

"Yes'm. I do that," Tee Wee said, as Mrs. Parsons hurried out of the kitchen in search of her keys and purse.

After she'd taken the golden brown biscuits from the oven and pronounced them "perfect as always," Tee Wee looked in on Ruthie, who was sitting on her bed with paper dolls spread out across the sheets. Josie reclined beside her, a blond-haired paper doll wedged between her vinyl fingers. Ruthie looked up. "Hey, Tee Wee. Me and Josie are playing hospital. She's the nurse and I'm the patient."

"You feelin okay? Wantin somethin?"

Ruthie shook her head. "No, it's stupid to make me stay in bed. I just got scared and fainted is all. And Mama gave me an aspirin for my headache. It's gone." She touched her fingertips to the bandages across her forehead. "I'm fine now. Mama is making such a fuss about it."

"Well, you most likely fine all right, but your mama needin to worry about somethin, and you gonna be it for a while."

"Mama ought to be worrying about Browder. He's the one most upset after he embarrassed himself so bad at the program last night."

"I didn't hear nothin much about it. What happened? I reckon there was a big crowd."

"Uh-huh. When we got to Pisgah, nearly every pew in the church was filled with folks. Tom Harvey had to set up extra folding chairs in the back, and, oh, Tee Wee, everyone looked so nice in their Christmas dresses. There were poinsettias on the altar, red candles, and the room smelled like holly and mistletoe. Christmassy, you know?"

"Yeah, Mount Zion smell right good, too, if you don't notice Sister Evelyn's cheap scent she bound to take a bath in."

Ruthie sat up straighter. "I was wearing my new red-and-green-plaid taffeta dress Mama and me got at Alford's, but I wished I had a dress like Catherine's. Hers was black, and her hair was twisted in a doughnut on top of her head, and underneath the bun she had pinned a cream-colored silk rose. I felt like a baby next to her."

"What'd your mama wear?"

"Oh, that ugly brown suit she wears every year. But the dress that everyone was talking about was Dimple Butler's."

"Pretty, huh?"

Ruthie grinned. "Yes, I wish you could have seen her, Tee Wee. When she walked in with Troy, everyone craned their heads around to watch her walk down the aisle. The dress was green, the color of pine needles, and it was an off-the-shoulder cut." She poked Tee Wee's arm. "Very low cut, too. You could see the tops of her breasts, and when she walked in those high-heeled shoes, they jiggled nearly right out of her bra." Ruthie covered her face with her hands and laughed. "You should have seen everyone whispering with their heads falling sideways like dominoes as she passed by to the front where Harry Wells had saved a seat for her."

"But what happened to Mister Troy then?"

"Oh, he went right up to the front with her, wearing a big grin, kind of bouncing behind her on his pointy-toed boots. Somehow they all managed to squeeze in together on the front pew. When Miss Wilda played 'Hark the Herald Angels,' the choir began to come out from the door behind the pulpit. Missy Jordan was first, and she near bout fell down on the loose carpet the volunteers had pieced together, but hadn't finished tacking down. Browder was next to her, and he caught her by the elbow. The choir sang one song. Then Browder stepped out of the line for his solo. That's when everything happened that was so funny."

"I heard Browder practicin that song, 'O Holy Night.' I reckon that's what he sang." Tee Wee sat down and Ruthie scooted farther over across the bed.

"Yeah, and at first, it was going good. I saw a couple of the ladies daubing their eyes with hankies when he got to the chorus, but near the middle of the song, Dimple leaned over to get something off the floor, and Browder saw her breasts nearly falling out of her dress, and he just went dumb. I mean his mouth was open, but wasn't any sound coming out."

Tee Wee laughed. "Struck dumb, huh?"

"Uh-huh. And it got worse! Miss Wilda played louder and people were whispering and snickering, but Browder didn't even know it. It was like he was gone off to some fantasyland where he and Dimple's breasts were all alone."

"Poor Browder. That must have been some awful for him," Tee Wee said, but she couldn't keep the smile from her face. "So what happened after that?"

"Missy Jordan saved him. She started singing right in his ear and Browder kind of woke up and his face turned as red as the poinsettias, but he managed to sing the last verse, and he was real good. Everyone said so at the reception afterward in the fellowship hall. But everyone was grinning a lot when they complimented him."

"And that's when you told your mama you was goin home with Miz Catherine to spend the night?"

Ruthie frowned. "Yes, but Catherine thought Mama said I couldn't go and they left me. And Mama and Daddy and Browder had already left, and then . . ." She closed her eyes. "I don't want to talk about that part."

Tee Wee hugged her. "You don't have to. I know it ain't no good memory gettin locked in like that and faintin and all." She stood up. "I got to get back to my kitchen." Then, remembering her conversation with Mrs. Parsons, Tee Wee said, "Miz Ruthie, you ain't seen no bleedin comin out twixt your legs, has you?"

Ruthie stared at her. "What?"

"You know, the monthly. You is old enough now for it to happen."

Ruthie looked away from Tee Wee. "I am not." She turned her head toward Josie. "Besides, it isn't going to happen to me. Not ever."

Tee Wee patted her leg. "Oh, yes'm, it is. You can't stop nature from doin its job. You is gonna have to bear the load God give you when He decided you was a girl baby in your mama's stomach."

"You'll see. I'm right. Not you." Ruthie threw her head back on the pillow. "You don't know anything. You're a nigger."

Tee Wee's face showed no emotion, but she wanted to snatch this child up and beat her good with a broom.

Ruthie ducked her head. "I'm sorry."

She sighed. Ruthie didn't mean what she was saying. She just scared is all, Tee Wee said to herself. "I know, baby." She walked to the door, then said in a quiet voice, "My body is black and yours is white, but the blood what come out tween our legs is the same color. We is equals in that."

When she returned to the kitchen Tee Wee found Icey sitting at the table drawing faces on the floured cloth with her finger. "How the patient doin in there?"

"She fine. Ain't nothin wrong with that child, but Miz Parsons want her kept quiet. You know how white folk are. They got to make them mountains out of their molehills."

Icey nodded. "I looked in on her when I gots here this mornin, and she look fresh as a daisy. Just a little ole bandage on her head. Ain't nothin like what I went through with Glory."

"No, but Glory doin good now. All your children is. What Deke say about that one of his?"

Icey wiped her fingers on the front of her dress. "Well, he ain't said much." She opened her mouth wide, stuck out her tongue, and wiggled it from side to side. "Truth is he ain't much of a talker. More of a doer."

Tee Wee grinned. "I hears that. He kin to Luther. They both got good butts."

Icey giggled. "Girl, I can't hardly get my work done cause I'se so tired in the mornin from them nights he stay with me."

Tee Wee stood and began gathering up the floured cloth, folding the edges to the center. Luther hadn't been keeping her up at all. He was tending a sick mule half the night on Friday, played cards in town on Saturday, and got too drunk to do anything with his pole on Sunday. She carried the cloth to the sink. "I know what you mean. Luther just pesterin me like I was a bitch in heat. Can't go round me without catchin my scent. Course we man and wife and that make the bed better than if we was just alley cattin."

Icey pushed her chair back from the table. "We ain't gonna be cattin much longer." She walked to the sink to look into Tee Wee's face. "Right after Christmas we plannin to get hitched for life."

Tee Wee smiled. "I am some glad for that. Reckon I'll be makin weddin cake then."

"I reckon you will, and, Tee Wee, I wants you to stand up with me. Deke got a brother to stand up for him, but I ain't seen none of my family in a long time, and sometimes it seem like you is kin."

Tee Wee slapped the sink with her rag. "I be honored to, Icey. Yes, I will."

Ruthie was reading a book when Tee Wee brought her lunch to her on the Snow White wooden snack tray. "Ain't much here. Just some biscuits and syrup, bologna, boiled egg, and peach cobbler."

Ruthie dog-eared a page of her book and laid it beside her.

Tee Wee set the tray down on the bed. "What that book you readin bout?"

"It's about a horse, named Black Beauty, and he gets sold to different people, and some of them are so mean to him. It happened a long time ago in England." Ruthie pried open her biscuit and poured syrup onto both sides. "I can't wait to find out what's going to happen to him next."

"And the horse lived in England?"

"Uh-huh. I wish I could go there. I'm learning a lot about the country from reading this story."

Tee Wee picked up the book and leafed through the pages. "I'd like to read bout other places in this country, like Alabama or Chicago or the city of New Orleans. I reckon there's books bout them."

Ruthie chewed and swallowed. "Mmmm. In the geography section at the library there's lots of travel books. You could get a card and check them out." She frowned. "I don't think coloreds are allowed in the library. I haven't ever seen any Negroes in there."

Tee Wee laid the book beside Ruthie's tray and pointed to the bologna. "Eat that. Well, don't make no difference to me. I can't read no how. Have to get Icey or Crow to read me the letters Ernestine writes."

"How come you didn't learn to read?"

"Well, weren't no schools for coloreds where I grew up, and even if'n there had been, I had to work. Didn't have no time for such."

"Do you know your ABCs?"

Tee Wee nodded. "Yeah, I can make out letters some, a few words, just don't know enough to make sense outta nothin."

Ruthie pushed the tray aside, sat up on her knees. "I could teach you. I can read good. We could play school for real."

Tee Wee slapped her thighs with both hands. "Me learnin to read old as I is? Let me think on this." She walked over to the window and looked out on the front lawn. While her eyes wandered from the tops of the trees to the eggshell color of the sky, her thoughts reached back to a day when she had heard the story of Jacob Reddix, the president of Jackson College, a college for black teachers. He was from over at Vancleave, and he had learned to read and write by the time he was seven. Tee Wee was thrilled by this story of a man rising to such a high position with no better chance in the white man's world than her. And besides him, there was Jessie Thomas, who was born in Pike County. He had gone to a one-room schoolhouse, had lost his mama to Jesus when he was little, and still he had gone to Washington, DC, and become a big shot in the Red Cross.

"Well, what do you think?"

Tee Wee didn't turn around. "Just a minute. I am considerin more on this." Them famous men's success had given hope to colored people, had shown them they could better theirselves. And wouldn't her life be way better if she could read, and hadn't her own children proven you didn't have to be all that smart to learn? Ernestine was goin to college and most of her young'ns could read now even though their schools didn't have books enough for all of them. They didn't have books, nor a big yellow school bus to ride on, or as many teachers as the white children. Their school year was a lot shorter, too. Still, her children learned. They could read. Well, cept for Lester and Masie who was just gettin started in school. Turning from the window, Tee Wee walked back to the bed and stared down at the wasted food on Ruthie's tray. When she brought the leftovers back to the kitchen, Icey would eat the rest of that biscuit. A huge smile broke out on Tee Wee's face. Icey! Wouldn't she be surprised when she found out Tee Wee could read as good as her!

Ruthie reached up and took Tee Wee's big hand in her small one. "So do you want to try to learn to read?"

Tee Wee squeezed her fingers. "*No.* Ain't no tryin to it. I mean to *do* it, but this got to be a secret. A secret between just you and me. I don't want Icey knowin nothin bout this."

"Okay. I won't tell a soul. Let's start right now."

Tee Wee pulled her hand away. "Right now, I has work to do, but tomorrow we gonna start and we ain't stoppin till I learns to read every word on Ernestine's letter paper."

"Every word. I promise," Ruthie said wearing a big smile on her pale face.

Chapter 12

AFTER TEE WEE LEFT HER ROOM, RUTHIE LIFTED *BLACK Beauty* and opened it to the page she had dog-eared, but her eyes wouldn't focus on the words anymore. She closed the book and tossed it across the bed. Although she didn't want to think about what had happened to her, images of the night before kept recurring in her mind. It was as if God were sending her messages, and He was going to keep on calling her until she answered. But she didn't know how to respond. With a sigh, she lay back on her pillow. If only she hadn't thought of spending the night with Catherine, she wouldn't have gotten locked in the church and none of the terrifying events of the night before would have ever happened.

Closing her eyes, she saw herself in the fellowship hall filled with people talking and eating and smiling as they wished each other a Merry Christmas. She was standing beside the refreshment table holding a gingerbread cookie in one hand and a glass cup filled with pink punch in the other. Her new red purse lay on the white tablecloth beside a bowl of mixed nuts. As she ate her cookie, she thought of the ride home, of sitting in the backseat of her mother's Chevrolet beside Browder. What would she say to him? He would be in a terrible mood after humiliating himself. But she wouldn't have to talk to him if she went home with Catherine, would she? Her mother would most likely allow her to go since school was closed for the holidays, and by the time she came home the next day, maybe Browder would be over the worst of it.

Pleased with her plan, she set the punch cup down beside her purse and went to the ladies' room, where she found Catherine standing in front of the mirror smearing bright pink lipstick on her puckered lips.

"Hi," Ruthie said. "I wish Mama would let me wear lip color." She knew the longing she felt could be heard in her voice.

Catherine dropped the gold lipstick tube into her purse. "Your mama thinks you're still a baby. Treats you like one, too."

"I know. She does. Hey, I was wondering if I could go home with you tonight."

"Sure. Mama won't mind. I'll go find her and tell her you're coming. If your mama says you can, meet me at the car."

Ruthie pulled the door open. "If I don't show, you'll know she said no." Her mother gave her permission to go to Catherine's, and as she stood on the porch steps watching the Chevrolet's taillights disappear down Carterdale Road, Ruthie realized that she had left her purse on the refreshment table. When she ran back to the fellowship hall, she saw that everyone had left now, and the table was bare except for a few cookie crumbs scattered on the white cloth. After a quick search around the room for the missing bag, Ruthie guessed that someone must have taken it to the church office. Hurrying back through the sanctuary, she tried the office door, but it was locked. As she retraced her steps down the hall, she heard car doors slamming, people calling good-bye, and tires crunching on the gravel outside. She would have to hurry to catch Catherine. Racing down the center aisle of the church, Ruthie pushed on the door that led back into the fellowship hall, but now it was locked, too. Spinning around, she ran to the front door, her last hope of an exit, but the cold brass knob was unyielding, offering no escape. Ruthie raced to the stained-glass windows and peered out into the darkness. Catherine's family car was no longer parked by the hedge where Ruthie had seen it earlier. In fact, not a single car was left in the parking lot. "Everybody's gone," she whispered.

Ruthie checked all the doors again. She pounded on each one and yelled as loudly as she could, "Hey somebody. Hey. I'm in here." Someone would come and get her out. But who? Her mother thought she was with Catherine; Catherine must have thought her mother said she couldn't go with her. Looking around the dark church, the silent pews became long open coffins, the lectern rising above them, a grave marker. Ruthie's eyes lifted to the huge wooden cross behind the pulpit, and her heart hammered against the bodice of her dress. How could a place so familiar suddenly become so frightening? She would not panic. This was her house of worship; she came here every week. She hadn't yet joined the church although she was saved through baptism, she knew. Her mother had told her when she was twelve she'd be old enough to understand the significance of becoming a member, but Ruthie felt she was old enough now. Slowly she rose and walked down the aisle toward the altar. She knelt on the step where the preacher stood when he called souls to Jesus. Rising, she turned and held out her arms. "Sinners, come down. Sinners, save yourselves tonight." She imagined the congregation singing "Just as I Am" in soft voices as she waited for the lost souls to fall on their knees at her feet.

After a few minutes, Ruthie stepped down and sat on the first pew in old Mr. Stokes' customary seat. She needed divine help; she would pray herself out of here. She bowed her head. "Dear Jesus, it's me, Ruthie Parsons. I need You to send somebody over to rescue me."

A shiver passed over her body. What if Jesus were really here? She switched her plea to God. "Dear God. Please send someone here to this church tonight." She heard a scratching sound; her head flew up. What was that? She told herself it was just a mouse or a bird against the window or maybe she was only imagining she'd heard something. But what if God Himself was in this church with her right now? Her throat tightened; she could barely get out the faintest of whispers. "I know You love little children; I am just a child really. I don't wear lipstick like Catherine." But Ruthie reminded herself that God knows everything; He knows all secrets. She thought of Jesus in the portrait over the couch, His piercing eyes. What if He was watching when she'd put her hand down there between her legs? "Please God, forgive me. I won't do that anymore. I promise."

Then in the still church she thought she heard a voice, *His* voice. "You break your promises, Ruthie."

Terrified, she whispered, "What?" She looked up at the cross and now she saw that Jesus' body had appeared. Nearly naked, He was bleeding, crying, lifting His arms out to her. "No," she cried out. "Go away. Stop." Squeezing her eyes shut, she willed Him to go away, but when she lifted her head, Jesus was still staring down on her with a sad expression on His face. I am imagining all this, she said to herself. It is just like when I hear Josie's little doll's voice. It's all pretend, not real. But deep inside her heart she knew the shadowy figure in front of her was definitely Jesus. She fell to her knees, folded her hands into a tent, and with her neck stretched back as far as it would go, she forced herself to look up into Jesus' face. He was frowning now. When His lips began to move, His body swam in and out of her vision. She put her hands on the floor to keep her balance. His lips moved again. He wanted her to do something to prove she was truly sorry for her sins. He knew what was in her heart. He knew about her lies, about spying on her parents in their bedroom. He wanted her to prove to Him that she wasn't a sinner lost to the Devil.

She would repent, beg for His forgiveness. When Ruthie, keeping her eyes on Jesus, hurried toward Him, the toe of her shoe caught the loose carpet and, losing her balance, she pitched forward. As her head hit the floor, the sharp tacks sticking up from the new carpet pierced two small, but deep, holes in her forehead. Dizzy and nauseous, she grasped the altar railing for support. Blood seeped from the punctures in her forehead, and when Ruthie saw the dark wet spots forming on her dress, she sank back to the floor. She lay with her knees tucked to her chest, rocking herself, crying out into the empty church.

Ruthie didn't know for sure if she had fainted or fallen asleep, nor did she know for how long, but it was late, in the middle of the night, when she woke and heard a voice calling her name. "Ruthie! Are you in here?"

"*Mama!* Mama, I'm here. I'm bleeding," she screamed. And then she felt her father's arms lifting her; his clean white handkerchief soft on her forehead. As he carried her down the aisle, Ruthie looked back at the cross. Jesus was gone.

RUTHIE TOUCHED THE BANDAGE on her forehead. She wasn't in pain; she would get dressed and ask Tee Wee if she would help her make Christmas cookies. She was glad her mother had gone to circle meeting. She didn't want to be questioned anymore. This morning when she'd opened her eyes, her mother, standing over her bed, had asked the first of many questions. "Ruthie, how are you feeling, baby?"

And Ruthie had answered with questions of her own. "How did you find me? I was so scared."

Her mother had pulled her up into her arms and cradled her against her chest. "I know. You must have been terrified. My poor Ruthie, locked in the church, thinking no one would come for you." She squeezed her tighter. "It was a miracle! Something woke me up and told me that you needed me. I just knew something was wrong. I got out of bed and called Ola just to make sure you were okay, and when Ola told me you hadn't gone home with them, I nearly fainted. I woke Daddy up, and he called the sheriff and told him you were missing."

The sheriff! No one ever called him except for big emergencies like when Tom Willoughby shot his brother over his date with Millie Barnes, who was engaged to Tom. "Then what happened?" Ruthie asked.

"Well, the sheriff said to meet him at the church where we'd last seen you, so we got Browder up and raced down to the parking lot. And the sheriff drove up almost immediately." She smiled. "Both his and Daddy's pajama legs were sticking out of their pants. Anyway, the church was dark and quiet, and we didn't have a key to get in, so Browder ran over to the parsonage and woke Brother Thompson, who seemed to take forever to get dressed and bring the key." She wrinkled her nose and smiled again. "I guess he thinks he's too dignified to wear pajamas under his pants."

Ruthie's head was starting to throb. "Go on; you went in and found me?"

"Yes, when I called your name, and you said 'Mama,' it was music to my ears. I was sure you'd been kidnapped. And you were injured. What happened to you?"

Ruthie looked up at the ceiling. This was the question she had dreaded answering. "I was . . ." She hesitated. What should she tell her mother? Was this a secret between her and God? Would her mother understand if she tried to explain what had happened? She remembered a conversation she had overheard when her mother had been the hostess for the Methodist Women's Circle meeting. They had been talking about the "Romans," whose church was on the corner of Delaware and State Street in Zebulon. Aunt Ola had said that they did strange mysterious things in the gray stone building. Mrs. Lot said they talked to Mary and Joseph and other people in the Bible, and Katie Greene's mother said she knew for a fact that they drank spirits during communion and believed that it turned into blood. Blood! She remembered seeing the picture Betsy McCosker held up to her in Miss Walker's fourth-grade classroom. A man's upturned palms were bleeding, and Betsy said he was Saint somebody. A saint was what these people were called who saw Jesus and talked to Him and bled from the places on their bodies where He did on the cross. Was she a saint now? Ruthie dragged her eyes back down to her mother, who was looking at her with even deeper creases between her eyes. No, she would think she had turned Roman if she said the truth. She sighed. "I don't know. I was bleeding. I must have hit my forehead on something."

Her mother looked relieved as if she had known Ruthie was about to say words she didn't want to hear. She smiled. "Well, you're a smart little girl, but sometimes you don't use your brain."

"I know. But, Mama, my brain is hurting bad. Can I have an aspirin?"

The aspirin had helped her head, but there was no medicine to take for the doubts that she would live with from now on. Ruthie dropped to her knees beside her bed and closed her eyes. "Dear God, I hope I did what You wanted me to do. I know I told another lie, but I think Your sending Jesus is supposed to be a secret. And I don't have to confess my sins to my mother, just You. Right?" She waited a moment, half expecting God to answer; then she went on. "So, after all that happened, I'm forgiven for my sins now is what I'm thinking. I'm pure and washed white as snow like the song says, and I'm not going to do anything bad ever again. Am I a saint now? Amen."

Chapter 13

ROWDER WAS ANGRY. HE HAD LEFT THE HOUSE AN HOUR
ago and now sat hurling pinecones at the trunks of the tall trees. When
he and Ruthie were younger they had come here to the grove and made
houses with rooms of straw walls. Browder knew that Ruthie still took a
rake out here occasionally and continued her fantasy world, but now he
felt he was too old to be playing such fool games with her. He rose from
the damp ground and, kicking through the pine straw, walked farther
into the woods where only a small amount of sunlight filtered through
the canopy of tree branches. He would go to the creek, maybe wade in
the clear water. Even though Christmas was days away, it was warm
enough to swim. He wished he lived somewhere where it snowed, like
the scenes in the movies with snowballs and sleighs and candlelit Christmas trees reflecting on snow-covered lawns.

When he reached the creek, he sat on the bank and stared at the
swirling water. His anger returned. His mother had been constantly nagging him to leave his room where he'd taken refuge since the Christmas
program at Pisgah. His face grew warm thinking about that awful day.
Night after night, lying on his bed he had practiced singing "O Holy
Night," anticipating the applause that he deserved. Everyone knew it was
a difficult piece to do properly, and he had reached the high notes perfectly. But his father had said that he could sing tenor because he didn't
have a man's voice yet. Browder reached for a rock and threw it in the
water. Not a man, not a man. He'd never be a man in his father's eyes.
Just because he liked movies and singing and didn't want to spend all day
working his tail off, his father thought he was a sissy. Browder pulled off

his shoes and socks and plunged his feet into the water, which was colder than he'd thought. He rolled up his pant legs and planted his feet in the soft bottom sand of the icy stream. He waded out into the middle of the creek. He knew more about being a man than his father thought.

Last year when he'd seen the movie *Johnny Belinda*, he hadn't really understood some of the scenes, but he had been excited sitting in the dark theater watching Jane Wyman's face when the big brute of a man lunged toward her. He had known then that women were scared of men who were more powerful than they. His father was always saying that women were the weaker sex, and now Browder thought he understood what he meant.

Browder waded back to the bank and dug his toes in the muddy bank. He thought of Crow; she wasn't afraid of him, but someday . . . Someday he'd show her; he'd show his father, and the embarrassment of the Christmas program would be forgotten. His anger left him, and, with a ray of optimism lighting his way, Browder picked up his socks and shoes and headed home.

Before he reached the front yard, he knew something was amiss. The dogs were barking, his father's truck was gone, and Tee Wee's and Icey's children were running in the yard, sliding left and right like bowling balls thrown out on the green lawn. He walked faster. When he reached the side yard, he called out. "Hey, what's going on?" No one heard him, but as Glory ran by, he reached out and snatched her arms. "Hey, what's all the fuss about?"

Glory wriggled in his grip like a little worm caught on a hook. "Let me go. I gotta go."

"Hold on. You're not going anywhere until you tell me what everybody is so worked up about."

"Panther!"

"Panther? Where?"

Glory rose up on her toes; she waved her arms at her sides. "A black panther come up to the door, scared Mama so bad, she bout turned white. He done ate up a calf of your daddy's and he tryin to get us little children." She stretched her arms out as far as she could reach. "He be a big big hungry panther."

Browder looked across the yard and saw Masie and Lester climbing on the hood of his mother's Chevrolet. "Where are the adults? My daddy?"

Glory was edging away from him, her eyes darting around the yard as if she were seeking her own hiding place. "Got guns and went trackin him. Over to the pond."

"Why don't y'all get in the house where you'll be safe?"

Glory looked back at him and began to run. "We wants to see him get kilt. Can't see nothin inside," she called over her shoulder.

Browder wasn't sure what to do first. He started for the barn, then, realizing he needed a gun, he ran into the house and got his .22 from his closet. Loading it quickly, he shouldered the gun and headed toward the pond. He was Glenn Ford now or Audie Murphy, or maybe John Wayne. People were counting on him to save them; he knew he was their best hope. As he approached the pond, he saw large paw prints in the red dirt. The panther had taken off in the direction of the Kepper Place. Browder began to run.

When he reached the Keppers', he walked toward the large group of men assembled in the front yard. His father's voice rose up from the others. "Well, since we lost the track, the best thing to do is spread out and walk in a line toward Moore's store. First one to spot him, call out." The six other men standing in a circle around his father began talking all at once. As Browder approached the group, his father looked over at him. "Get on home, Browder. We got plenty of help. You're not a good shot anyway."

Browder's jaw muscles locked up. His father wasn't going to cheat him out of this. "Daddy, I can hit him. Let me go." Browder felt the other men's eyes on him. His father said nothing. Finally, Mr. Whittington spoke. "Let the boy come. He ain't gonna be the one to find him no way."

Browder waited. His father shifted his sixteen-gauge into the crook of his arm. "Okay, time's wasting. Let's go."

Following the men, Browder walked across the pasture toward Mr. Whittington, who waved him on. Browder hoped his pride in being here didn't show on his face. Keeping his head down, he walked on past Mr. Whittington far out to the right of the line of men.

He entered the Keppers' cornfield, where he marched between the rows of dried brown stalks. He saluted them. These stalks were his soldiers lined up for inspection on either side of him. "All right, men," Browder said to them. "We're in the show. The German line is behind that hill. We're going to take it. A lot of you won't make it, but you're brave men, and we're fighting for the best damn country in the world." He crouched down, tucked his rifle under his arm and duckwalked forward. "Follow me," he called out in the empty field.

Five minutes later Browder came out of the field and climbed the barbed-wire fence that kept the Keppers' cows out of the cornfield. At first he saw no cows, but, veering farther right, he heard the bellowing of several Jerseys. They were so far away, he could barely make them out beneath a grove of pines. Browder slowed his pace, trying to decide which direction to take. His boot hit something soft, and, looking down, he jumped back when he saw the dead calf lying in the tall grass. Its side was torn open and entrails trailed out from the gutted section the panther had eaten. Browder stood over the calf, shivering. This must be a huge animal to eat two calves in one day, he thought. His finger felt for the trigger of his rifle. He had never seen a panther up close, but he knew one could leap five or six feet in half a second. He swung his head left and right. The panther could be lying in the grass ready to leap those few feet toward him. Browder turned and looked across the pasture. He'd strayed too far from the men to see any of them. He could enter the woods, but he imagined the animal up in a tree, ready to pounce down on him as he walked beneath it. Sweat formed on his forehead and beneath his arms. The cows continued to bellow, but he could hear his panting breath over their cries. He lifted his gun, and then lowered it. He needed to clear his mind, think what to do. Scent! Was he downwind of the panther? He stuck his finger in the air and could feel no breeze. He turned to his left, then his right. Which way to go?

Suddenly he heard a shout and an explosion. "Here," a man's voice called out. "Over here." Browder ran toward the woods. "He's hit, but he ain't down."

Browder, running with his gun tucked beneath his armpit, had nearly reached the woods when he saw the panther in the dark shadows of the pine trees. Its scream pierced the air and Browder dropped his gun and stood shaking uncontrollably. A shot rang out; someone yelled, *"Got him."*

As his father walked toward him, Browder tried to quell the whimpering sounds that came from his quivering lips. He looked up into his father's red face, the tightly drawn mouth, the accusing eyes. Browder shifted his eyes to the ground where his fallen rifle lay. He wished he could stop crying, but it seemed his body wasn't his and he had no control of it. And then with horror he realized he had wet himself.

Mr. Whittington and three other men came running over and stopped just short of the panther's body. "Man, I'll bet he weighs more'n a hundred pounds," Mr. Kepper said. Mr. Whittington stepped across the panther and picked up Browder's gun. He handed it to his father.

"It's my . . ." Browder stopped speaking as his father shouldered the gun beside his own. He knew that the rifle would not be given back. With his head on his chest, Browder turned away from the men and slowly walked back across the field. He hoped that his father would call to him. But he knew he would not.

He walked past the Keppers' and then past his own house. Veering off the road, he entered the cemetery where his ancestors were lying beneath high grass and crumbling tombstones. He wandered through the leaning markers until he stood before the grave of his great-uncle Will, who had died of pneumonia when he was fourteen. Browder's grandmother said he reminded her of poor Will, and she would part his blond strands down the middle of his head into the style her brother wore in his portrait. Will's headstone was a square column of gray, weathered marble. On the top of the stone a one-winged angel poised ready for flight to heaven. Right now Browder wished he could exchange places with his look-alike. It would have been better if the panther had gotten him. Anything would be better than the humiliation he was feeling now.

Browder sank down on the grave and rested his back against the marker. He hated his father. He hated his mother, who would avoid looking at him when his father told her how stupid her son was. Most of all, he hated himself. He looked across the cemetery at the silent tombs, then walked over to the O'Neal plot. "I was so scared I peed my pants," he said to Toby and Virgil and Maryanne. He crossed the rutted drive to the far side of the cemetery. To the dead Wells, Hiram, Rose, Eugene, Maude, and Taylor, he whispered, "I couldn't even run. I stood there like one of your damn tombstones."

From grave to grave Browder stumbled up and down crumbling steps, over tiled borders, across the mounded earth of newly dug homes for the dead. He told the cemetery dwellers all of his humiliations; he told them about his feelings for his father, his mother, and his secret longing for Crow.

By the time Browder left the cemetery and walked down the road to the Parsons' drive, he had mapped out his plan. He would need money, and he would have it. Christmas was only two days away, and he always got cash from his uncles and aunts. He would need courage, too, and he resolved to carry out his plan at any cost. As he walked up the drive to his house, he looked to his left at the tenant houses sitting side by side like twin boxes on a hilltop. Crow was the tenant; he was the master. She would learn to respect him, and maybe someday he would win her love. He lifted his arms into the air like a boxer entering a ring. Shaking his fists at the sky, he chanted, "Browder! Browder! Yes, yes, yes."

Chapter 14

CLUTCHING A FIFTY-CENT PIECE IN HER FIST, CROW RAN HOME racing against the fading light. Browder wouldn't tell her how much money he had gotten for Christmas, but she figured he'd gotten quite a lot. He had asked her to meet him at the pond to playact some picture show about a woman who couldn't hear or talk, and after he offered to pay her fifty cents, she'd agreed to it.

When she met him an hour ago, she had ignored his complaint that she was late and said, "I see you wore your new jacket for me."

Browder had pulled his sleeves down over his hands. "I wore it because it's cold."

Crow laughed. "No, it ain't. I feel just right in this cotton dress," she said, lifting the edge of her short, blue floral print skirt, exposing just a bit of her dark thigh. The dress had belonged to Mrs. Parsons' niece and it had a big red stain on the bodice. Crow had refused to wear it when Tee Wee had first brought it home with some other castoffs from the Parsons' relatives. But when Crow had been given a red scarf for Christmas, she'd decided to wear the dress, since the ends of the scarf covered most of the stain.

Browder's eyes were on the folds of her skirt covering the flash of thigh she'd allowed him to see. "Well," he said, "you wanna play the movie or not?"

"I'm here, ain't I?"

Browder looked relieved. "Okay, then. Let's go over by the cattails."

Crow followed him, smiling at his tan back. "What'd you say I was suppose to be?"

"A dummy. You can't talk or hear. You make signs with your hands, but you don't say anything."

They had reached the tall cattails and Browder pointed behind them. "That space back there is your house, and I'm gonna just walk in because you can't hear me knocking."

Crow nodded. "Okay, what am I supposed to be doin when you comes in?"

"It doesn't matter. We start acting the movie when I come in. Go on back there in your house."

Waiting behind the clump of cattails, Crow had looked up and seen a wild turkey flying overhead, and she watched it falling into the trees behind her. Luther had shot one for their Christmas dinner, but even though Tee Wee had seasoned it well, it had tasted gamey. She knew that the Parsons had eaten the store-bought turkey that her mother had cooked before she trudged home exhausted to begin their very late Christmas dinner. That night Tee Wee had told Crow that, after buying a few toys for Santa's bag, there wasn't any money left to buy the older children gifts. Crow shrugged her shoulders. She didn't care. She would be adding fifty cents to her savings today, and she wasn't spending it on some dumb present for herself. She was saving for the big exodus to the Promised Land up in the North.

Browder called to her. "You ready?"

"Yeah," she said, and, pushing back the cattails, she lay down, nestled between the waving stalks, thinking that this picture show would be easy to playact. She didn't have to remember any lines at all.

NOW CROW SLOWED as she neared her house, and, tucking the coin into her braid, she took a deep breath and stopped beside the oak tree. Closing her eyes, she saw Browder's face as she had earlier when she looked up at him framed against the gray winter sky. His features had contorted and grown out of focus as he leaned down to kiss her lips. He had murmured crazy nonsense in her ear, words about how beautiful she was, how someday they would run away together. She had lain beneath his hard body without words of her own, but had she spoken, she would have told him that she wasn't taking no white boy with her when she left Parsons Place someday. Browder wouldn't have heard her anyway; he was nervous, the breath rushing out of his open mouth as he stroked her skin. He asked her to let him kiss her in places she hadn't ever thought about.

The raucous voices inside the house roused her from her reverie, and, patting her braid, she moved away from the tree to cross the yard. Before she mounted the steps, Crow looked up and saw the first night star winking overhead, and she smiled, thinking that it resembled a shiny fifty-cent piece in the darkening sky.

RUTHIE WRAPPED HER ARMS around the small pine tree where she knelt on the mahogany-colored needles it had shed. She wished Browder would hurry up and go home; it was getting dark, and her mother would be looking for her soon. She had been watching Browder and Crow over in the cattails for nearly half an hour and her knees were sore and scratched. Crow must have been getting paid a pretty big sum for play-acting whatever picture show Browder had seen. I'm smarter than Browder, she thought, too smart to give my money to Crow for letting me feel her titties anyway. She smiled. She was so glad God had decided to make her a girl. And now that she was a secret saint, she felt protected from sinning. She frowned. Was just watching a sin? Glancing up at the sky, Ruthie saw that night was falling fast now. Browder better hurry up or she'd have to leave before him and run the risk of his catching her spying on him. Crow probably knew she had watched them. Whenever Ruthie was around Crow, she always got a funny feeling in the pit of her stomach that Crow knew things about her that she wanted to hide. It was like Crow was God and could see right into her brain and read the thoughts that ran across it. And yet, she admitted to herself, she sort of wanted her to know the things she'd never ever want her mother to know. Ruthie felt that Crow, and Tee Wee, too, would think her sins weren't so bad, wouldn't judge her like God and the folks at Pisgah would. When she'd gone to Mount Zion with the Weathersbys a couple of times, she had loved the singing and hollering and dancing they did. Church at Mount Zion was actually fun. The colored congregation seemed a lot happier about worshiping the Lord than the Methodists.

A cricket's loud chirping startled her out of her reverie, and Ruthie stood up. She watched Browder bend forward, pick up his jacket, and stuff it beneath his arm. "Go on. Go home," Ruthie whispered. If her mother missed her and realized she was out after dark, she'd get a spanking for sure.

Finally Browder shoved his hands into his pockets and walked away from the pond, following Crow's path toward home. Ruthie crept out of the woods and ran to the cover of the cattails. She discovered the flattened grass where Crow had lain, and on impulse, she flung herself down on the spot. There was still a bit of warmth rising from the ground, and Ruthie inhaled Crow's scent, which still lingered in the grass. She closed her eyes; she was Dimple lying here waiting for Troy to press his lips on hers. In *True Confessions* she'd read about this young girl, Dorothy, who met her boyfriend in a deserted parking lot, and she hadn't meant to go all the way, but he'd begged and begged and she couldn't help the "tide of passions that washed over her body." Ruthie wiggled in the grass. She (Dimple now) felt this passion washing her body. "Troy. Troy," she said with a little moan.

"*Ruthie!*" It was her mother. "Ruthie, where are you?"

Ruthie crawled through the cattails, and, bending them back, she could see her mother, looking left and right as she walked across the field toward her. "Shit fire and save the matches, I'm dead," Ruthie said aloud. She stood up, waved. "Here I am, Mama. Coming."

As she ran to her mother, Ruthie thought up the lie she was going to tell. There was this poor injured cat howling outside her window. She'd followed it across the pasture, trying to catch it to get medical attention for it, but she'd lost it in the woods, and then . . .

Later that night Ruthie did hear wailing outside her window. She'd been dreaming about riding her bicycle down a steep hill, and although she pushed the pedals back trying to brake, she careened on at a faster and faster pace. There was a yellow school bus at the bottom of the hill, and she saw that she was going to smash into its side. She thought it was she who was screaming when she woke, but then she realized the shrieks she heard were coming from the yard.

Ruthie threw off her pink coverlet and ran to the window. In the moonlight she saw Crow, in a light-colored short gown, flying across the yard, waving her arms. Ruthie shivered; something terrible must have happened.

Within seconds the Parsons were all on the porch listening to Crow's frantic stuttering as she ran up the steps toward them. "Sick. Th-th-they all dyin up there. P-P-Poison. They done all been poisoned."

"I'll call the doctor," her mother said, running into the house. Mr. Parsons stood for a moment, looked down at his striped pajamas, and then said, "Shoes. Be right there."

As Crow wheeled about and jumped down the steps, Ruthie looked over at Browder. "Wait. I'm coming," he yelled.

"Me, too," Ruthie said, jumping off the porch. Crow had already reached the side yard and plunged through the hedge toward home.

"How did they get poisoned?" Browder yelled at Crow's back.

"Corn bread," she said without breaking her stride.

Browder slowed, looked at Ruthie as she struggled on her bare feet across the prickly grass. "Did she say corn bread?"

"Uh-huh," Ruthie gasped. "Think they're dead already?" She hoped not. She hadn't ever seen dead people except in coffins, all fixed up by Mr. Jenkins.

"Might be," Browder said. And he took Ruthie's hand in his cold left hand. "Come on. Don't be scared." The tremor in his voice told her that he was as frightened as she.

Before they reached Tee Wee's porch, they could hear the retching and moaning inside. "Oh, Sweet Lord Jesus," Icey's voice rang out. "Save these here poor wretches."

Browder opened the screen door and Ruthie followed so closely, her head rammed into his back. Looking around her brother's shoulder, her mouth fell open. On the floor the Weathersbys lay writhing like snakes, clutching their stomachs. Lester was on his hands and knees, Tee Wee was curled into a fetal position, and Masie had rolled her body into a perfect circle resembling a little burned doughnut. Rufus and Paul, whom Ruthie guessed had been invited to dinner, were shaking the furniture as they rolled back and forth across the floor.

Icey ran to Masie and lifted her up, wiping her face with a cloth. "This littlest one gonna die for sure."

"Shut up," Tee Wee screamed. "She ain't gonna die; none of us is."

Ruthie looked at Browder, who hadn't moved an inch into the room. "What should we do?" she asked him.

Browder looked over at Crow. "What's wrong with them?"

"Told you. They ate poison. Rat poison."

"Why'd they do that?" Ruthie asked.

Crow shot her a look of disgust. "They didn't do it on purpose, stupid. Didn't know what they was eatin."

Ruthie was relieved to see her parents opening the screen door.

"Doc Uleland will be here in a minute. Said to make them vomit," her mother said, walking into the house. In her green chenille robe, her hair wrapped in toilet paper, she fingered the little silver clasp that held the paper together over the center of her forehead.

"Some of them's already puked," Icey said, thrusting Masie toward Mrs. Parsons. "This one ain't."

Mrs. Parsons took the child and absently patted her dark apple cheek. Looking down at Masie, she wrinkled her nose as if the horrible stench in the room had just now reached her nostrils. "Yes, well. We'll have to, uh, have to see who needs to, still."

Icey was hoisting Tee Wee up into a sitting position. "Deke, he got Luther outside in the back, urping in the yard. Tee ain't done nothin cept scream like a panther."

Ruthie sidled along the wall toward Crow. "How come you aren't sick?" she asked her.

"Didn't eat no corn bread," Crow said. She had refused dinner so that she could deposit her fifty-cent piece in the hole in the floor she'd whittled out for her new hiding place in the back bedroom. After counting her money, she had replaced the rag rug over the hole, and then sat on the bed pretending to read the *Weekly Reader* she'd been given at school. Tee Wee had called her, but she hadn't come until fifteen minutes or so had passed. She was going to tell her mother she wasn't doing no dishes cause she didn't eat, but when she walked into the kitchen, she saw her entire family doubled over with stomach cramps.

It hadn't taken long for Tee Wee to figure out what had poisoned them. The greens and yams they had eaten the day before; only the corn bread had just been baked. When she told Luther she'd taken a sack of cornmeal from the Parsons' barn, Luther's eyes had gone wild as a startled horse's. "That was bait! Parsons tryin to get rid of rats in the barn, and I mixed two boxes of rat poison in that meal for em to eat."

"Oh, Lord have mercy," Tee Wee had screamed. "I done poisoned my family." She clutched her stomach. "My unborn baby, J. P., he's most likely dead already."

Luther had staggered toward the door. "I'll get Icey and Deke." Turning back, he yelled at Crow. "You run to the Parsons'. Get a doctor."

And Crow had rushed out behind him. Sailing across the pasture on her bare feet, her teeth chattered and weak moaning sounds rose up from her throat. She was the only one. The only one who would live. Why? Why was she the one chosen? Her heart hammered wildly as she ran on leaping over dead limbs and anthills. Why me? She chanted over and over. Why me? Why me?

Now she looked at Ruthie in her flannel nightgown with pink kittens printed on the white background. A darker pink ribbon laced through the ruffle at Ruthie's throat. She looked so clean, so perfect. Even her disheveled hair, fluffed out around her little round face, was shiny and smelled of lemon. "Reckon ain't no worry of you eatin no rat food. You ain't got to steal nothin out of nobody's barn to eat, has you?"

Ruthie heard the hatred in Crow's tone, but she put her hand on Crow's arm. Her whole family was about to die. She had a right to be mad. "Maybe they'll be okay. Doctor will be here soon."

Crow nodded. She hoped so. She didn't even want that money now. No, she didn't want to be alone in this house. If they all died, she'd have to leave; Parsons wouldn't rent to just her. Where would she go? Now, Crow admitted to herself, she wasn't going to find her daddy. He wasn't going to rescue her. Ernestine over in Alabama would be all the family she had left. "Mama." Crow pushed past Ruthie and went to her. "Mama, you gonna be all right. You be fine."

Tee Wee, half lying in Icey's arms, opened her eyes. "Don't be scared, baby. Your mama ain't gonna die. Ain't gonna leave you." She lifted her arm, patted Crow's cheek. "We all be better. We tougher than them rats, we is."

Icey laughed. "Yeah, and you a whole lot bigger than em, too."

When Doc Uleland came, Icey told him her joke, but he didn't laugh. He said it was the truth; the Weathersbys would survive. They were stronger than rats, and a lot more determined to live.

When Crow heard this and realized the crowded Weathersby house would return to its normal state of daily turmoil, she slipped outside and walked across the field. Looking up at the crescent yellow moon, she lifted her arms high above her head. She still wanted to fly, wanted to fly toward that gold up there. She'd get there one day; one day she'd leave, but not now. More moons would fill and empty their light in the sky, and beneath one of those future full silver ones, she'd finally fly into that light.

Chapter 15

ICEY WOKE AT FIVE ON HER WEDDING DAY. SHE HAD TOLD Deke to spend the night with the Weathersbys because she wasn't starting this marriage off with no bad luck. No siree, this man was gonna be the forever one, she said to herself, as she slid out into the cold room from beneath the warm covers. Today, on December 30, 1950, she would become Mrs. Deke Taylor, and the child growing inside her wouldn't be no bastard now. If it was a boy, she had decided to name him Memphis after the place where all the good men in her life had lived.

Icey went into the next room and clapped her hands over Glory's ears. "Get Jonas up and going; we got a weddin on this here day to go to."

Icey went into the kitchen to put the kettle on the stove. She would wash herself in the hottest water she could stand. And her children was going to get the scrubbing of their lives. Tee Wee wasn't gonna say hers wasn't spick-and-span today.

After the last pan of bathwater was thrown out into the yard, Icey went into her bedroom and hooked the latch on her door. She needed alone time to get dressed. She laid her white taffeta dress out on the bed; beside it, she placed her new white shoes she'd paid out of layaway at Sears & Roebuck. She would be beautiful today. All brides were, was what everyone said. Propping the mirror up against the foot of the bed, Icey turned sideways, looking at the curve of her growing stomach. "Can't tell yet," she said. She had missed only one monthly, but her bosom was considerably bigger already. She hoped the dress wasn't gonna be too tight across her front. Icey turned back facing the mirror; she put her hands on her wide hips and grinned. She hadn't been this happy in a long, long time. Deke was a good man, a good wage earner, a good lover, and he was gonna be a good daddy, too. She'd make sure of that. She raised her eyes to the single lightbulb dangling over her head. "Thank You, Jesus. Thank You for sending this man to your faithful servant, Icey. I knowed all along You would help me out. Amen."

WHILE ICEY WAS standing before her mirror, Tee Wee was glaring into her own. She was to serve as matron of honor for Icey, and she hated the pearl-gray dress she was going to wear. The dress had once belonged to Miss Wilda, who was about her size. She didn't have anything else near as nice as this dress to wear, but the color made her skin look ashy and wasn't all that becoming. She sighed. Well, there wasn't no help for it; she was wearing it and that was that. Tee Wee threw the dress over her head and wiggled it down over her hips. It just fit. Her stomach stuck out considerably now, and the dress cupped beneath the mound of her baby son. Tee Wee slapped her hips with her broad hands. Two of us carryin in a weddin, she thought. I reckon that be a first at Mount Zion. She turned her head to the door. "Luther, Crow, where you all at?" she yelled. "We ain't gonna be late, is we?"

"No, Mama. It's two hours yet," Crow called. "Everybody ready ceptin you. Glory is here and her and Masie got their flower girl outfits on and looks cute. Come see."

"Be there in a minute," Tee Wee said. She yanked the brocade cloth farther down over her stomach and patted her new hairdo. Crow had insisted she should weave it for the day, but Tee Wee didn't think it mattered since she was wearing a big picture hat anyway.

When she went into the living room, her eyes widened when she saw Deke, standing in the doorway. "Land's sake, Deke, you looks like you a moving-picture star."

Deke bowed. "Got me a new suit for the occasion," he said, straightening the lapel of his pin-striped black jacket. "You looks right nice, too, Tee. Folks will think you is the bride."

Tee Wee lifted her chin higher. She chuckled and said, "Well, I does try to look my best for my friends on this here big day." She looked around at the scrubbed children, the bowed and ruffled girls, the boys with their slicked-down hair and royal blue bow ties she'd cut from an old dress. Then she frowned. "Where's Luther?"

Deke looked away. "I believe he gone to the store."

"Oh, no. I told him not to buy no hooch. That where he went, ain't it? We don't need no drinkin at the weddin."

Deke kept his eyes on the children. "Well, Tee Wee, some folks think you got to toast the bride, and I reckon Luther one of them."

Tee Wee snorted. "Humph, ain't just a toast that man be after." She straightened the bow in Masie's hair. "Well, we just have to keep an eye on that man today. He better be back in time to drive us to the church."

Deke nodded. "He will. He will. Don't you worry none," he said as he smoothed his hair around his ears. "He knows he got to make two trips."

LUTHER MADE THE TWO TRIPS and nipped on the Old Crow bottle both ways both times. By the time he was sitting on the second pew in Mount Zion Church, he was feeling much better than he had in weeks. Deke had taken only one sip from the bottle hidden in a paper bag beneath the driver's seat in the Ford. He was worried about saying his lines.

Mount Zion Church had never held as many flowers or people as it did on this day. Icey, standing just inside the front door in the back of the church, looked over the scene with satisfaction. She and Tee Wee had worked all day Friday placing red and white poinsettias on the altar, greenery on the end of every pew, and they had spread white butcher paper across the scarred wooden floor where the bride and groom would stand. The choir box was draped with silver Christmas garland, and bright red holly berries stood gaily out of their waxy leaves on Preacher Dixon's lectern.

Icey straightened the bit of net across her forehead. It dipped a little over her right eye and, each time someone on that side spoke to her, she cocked her head sideways to see them better. No matter how many times she moved the circle of net around, it continued to droop unevenly, and Icey suspected Tee Wee had cut the short veil lopsided on purpose.

But now Tee Wee was smiling at her with such sisterly warmth that Icey felt rebuked for that thought. She just had a case of wedding day jitters. That was all. "You looks good, Tee," she said to make up for her suspicious thoughts.

"Thank you, Icey. You makes a beautiful bride. Just waits till you see

Deke. He's got on a new suit," she added, knowing she was spoiling his surprise.

Icey wasn't listening, though. "Is that 'Oh Happy Day' Sister Ida is playin now? I think that's the last song before the Wedding March starts."

"Yeah, here comes Deke and his brother, Jimmy. Where're those girls?" Tee Wee and Icey began looking around frantically for the two flower girls, who weren't where they were supposed to be. "Glory, Masie, where you got to?"

Icey turned and opened the door. "They outside I bet, gettin theirselves all dirty." She leaned out calling, *"Glorree! Masieee!"*

Everyone sitting on a pew in Mount Zion turned their heads to see the bride yanking the girls in through the front door as they came running up the steps to the church. Glory's hair bow was missing and Masie had stepped in a puddle, covering one of her new black patent shoes with red mud. Tee Wee quickly cleaned Masie's shoe with the good handkerchief she had hidden in the sleeve of her dress to use to wipe her eyes during the vows. Sister Ida, oblivious to the commotion, continued to pound chords on the old black upright in front of the choir stall.

"Go on, Tee," Icey commanded, pushing her toward the aisle.

Tee Wee stumbled forward, then turned back, swept up her holly wreath bouquet from the program table, and began again marching slowly to the front of the church. Smiling and nodding to each side, she majestically swayed forward toward Deke and Jimmy and Brother Dixon, who stood looking up at the ceiling as if he were praying already.

Glory and Masie, holding a single basket between them, followed Tee Wee, and, nearly halfway to their destination, both remembered to throw out the paper rose petals and began scooping handfuls up and tossing them over the heads of those sitting on the ends of the pews they passed by.

When Sister Ida saw that everyone was in place, she hit the first chord of the march three times for Icey's signal and pounded the keys as hard as she dared to cue the congregation to stand. Slowly, Icey began her last walk as a single woman. She nodded to the Parsons on the left, the Redmonds on the right, the Walkers, the Tates, and the Hendersons. Then, looking forward, she caught her breath when she saw Deke standing in front of Brother Dixon. He was the handsomest man in the whole church, and he was about to become all hers. By the time she reached his side, her veil had fallen completely over her right eye, which was filled with tears of happiness.

—

EVERY MEMBER OF Mount Zion agreed that Icey and Deke's reception, held in the back room of the church, was the best one they'd ever attended. Tee Wee preened like a peacock with every slice of cake she served. She received so many compliments on her three-layer creation of white-frosted lemon cake, she'd convinced herself she was most likely the best cook in the whole state of Mississippi. Miss Ruthie had eaten three pieces, and when she'd come back for the third piece, she'd told her that she thought Miss Wilda's dress was "simply divine" on Tee Wee. Without thinking, Tee Wee licked the cake knife and then smiled across the room at all her friends and family. This day was better than her own wedding day, she thought. Luther hadn't even worn a suit when they went to the courthouse. Tee Wee's eyes began roaming the room. He wasn't nowhere. "That man," she muttered to herself, as Preacher Dixon approached her cake table. "He drinkin outside; I'll bet money." She slapped a piece of cake on a saucer and thrust it toward the preacher. "Ain't you been here twice already?" she asked.

Preacher Dixon smiled. "Well, yes I has, Tee Wee, but I can't resist just one more slice of your cake."

"Well, it ain't gonna last all day if you keeps eatin." Tee Wee slapped the knife down on the table and walked away. "Luther Weathersby," she called. "Anyone seen Luther?"

Crow tapped her on the back. "He outside with Deke and Deke's brother, Jimmy, and Tom, and his son. I just seen them when I went to the outhouse."

Tee Wee frowned. "Is they drunk?"

Crow nodded. "As skunks." Quickly she turned and walked away. She hadn't told her mother that Browder was out there, too. Let her hear it from the Parsons when they found out their precious son was getting drunk off Luther's bottle.

As if reading her thoughts, Mrs. Parsons stopped her. "Crow, have you seen Browder? Mister Parsons wants to take everyone's picture with his new Brownie camera, and we can't find Ruthie or Browder."

Crow shook her head. "Ruthie was here just a minute ago, eatin cake on a foldin chair."

"I know. I saw her then, but now she's gone and I haven't seen Browder since the service was over." She waved her white-gloved hand toward the cake table. "Now I don't see Tee Wee, either. Who will cut the cake?"

she asked, as she wandered toward the line of people waiting in front of the shrinking cake.

RUTHIE WAS SITTING on a tree stump behind the Parsons' car watching Browder and the group of colored men take turns sipping from the pint bottle of liquor Deke's brother had drawn out of the back pocket of his Sunday pants. Luther's empty bottle of Old Crow had been discarded on a pile of leaves behind them. The men were talking about "hot weddin nights" and "limp poles" and "Mammies' milk" and some other topics she didn't totally understand. In the center of them, Browder stood grinning stupidly. He was pretending he understood every word they said, but Ruthie knew he didn't. She smoothed her red-and-green-checked skirt over her knees. This had been a wonderful day, one she'd never forget. She sighed. Icey and Deke were in love. She could tell by the way they looked into each other's eyes during the saying of the vows. Ruthie had craned her neck to see the couple around Miss Wilda's big black hat. When Icey had said, "I do," she'd felt a little tear falling on her lap. She'd been thinking about her own wedding day and imagining a tall man slipping a ring on her finger, squeezing her hand, and brushing her lips with a gentle kiss after the pronouncement.

She looked up at Deke, who was leaning against the pine tree now. He had kissed Icey hard. And everyone had laughed when Icey had pulled away and frowned at him. His grin reminded Ruthie of Troy Greer, and she knew Dimple wouldn't lean back from him the way Icey had. Now the muscles in Deke's face had dropped; his eyes were vacant, and his mouth hung open. He was dead drunk, Ruthie decided. They all were. Luther had stretched out on the leaves beside his bottle, Jimmy was dancing around in a circle, holding the pint over his head, and Browder was giggling at him like a girl.

Ruthie heard the crunch of footsteps on gravel, and, looking up, she saw Tee Wee marching toward Luther. Before he opened his eyes, she began yelling. "Man, you is nothin but a cow pile. Get up off that ground."

Luther scrambled up, brushing leaves from his suit coat. "Tee, I was just restin here. Big day, you know." He moved sideways toward Deke. "All that drivin, excitin day." He pried Deke from the bark of the tree and slung his arm across his shoulders. "I takin care of Deke here."

Tee Wee lifted the empty bottle from the ground. "I see your medicine right here." She flung the bottle at the tree. Both men ducked even though the bottle landed in a bush two feet to their right.

Ruthie covered her mouth with her hands. She couldn't wait to see what Tee Wee was going to say when she recognized Browder in the group of openmouthed men behind her. But Browder was smarter than she thought. He began inching backward toward their black Chevrolet. Ruthie waited. When the car touched his back, he crouched down and duckwalked around the bumper toward the stump where Ruthie sat.

"Hey, Browder," Ruthie whispered.

He wheeled around. "Ruthie! What you doing here?"

"I'm not drinking nobody's liquor like you were."

Browder squatted down beside her. He wiped his mouth with the back of his hand. "Ruthie, you're not going to tell Mama on me, are you?"

Ruthie pinched her nose with her fingers. "I won't have to. She's gonna smell it on you when you open your mouth," she said.

Browder sat back on the ground. Ruthie knew he was remembering his mother had told them drinking spirits was a sin, and she could smell it on anybody's breath from a mile away. He looked over at her with frightened eyes. "What am I gonna do?"

Ruthie crossed her legs, swung her patent shoe up and down. "You should've thought about Mama before you starting acting a fool with Luther and them."

Browder dropped his head. "I know."

Now Ruthie felt a little bit sorry for him. She would like to know what that brown liquid tasted like herself, and if she'd been born a boy, she'd probably have tried it, too. She uncrossed her legs and stood up. "I got a peppermint candy cane in a bag in the car. Think that would take the smell away?"

Browder was already opening the car door. "It's got to."

MR. PARSONS, looking through the glass box on top of his camera, could see everyone except Browder, who stood on the edge of the back row of the group. "Move in, son," he said. When Browder inched over toward Crow, he nodded with satisfaction. He had them all now. In the center a beaming Icey stood in the circle of Deke's arm. Beside her Tee Wee stood squeezing Luther's upper arm. Both of them were scowling. In front of the group Masie and Glory knelt holding their basket between them. Lester and four or five cousins leaned in on Luther's right, and six more children flanked Icey's left side. Behind them, he could now see Crow's and Browder's heads. "Where's Ruthie? I don't see her."

"Here," Ruthie called, lifting her arm over Icey's head. "I'm right behind the bride and groom." She pushed her head forward so that the center of her chin was exactly midpoint between their shoulders.

As Mr. Parsons pressed the button, Tee Wee tilted her picture hat in front of Icey's face, Masie stuck her finger in Glory's ear, Luther slumped to his knees, Crow bumped Browder out of view with her hip, and Ruthie screamed, *"Cheeese everybody!"*

Part Two

1958

ALTHOUGH IT WAS ONLY SEVEN O'CLOCK, THE EARLY-MORNING sun was already burning its way through the wispy clouds floating over rural Mississippi. Below the sky on the rough wooden steps of Tee Wee's small house, Memphis and his best friend, J. P., sat discussing the possibilities offered by the long day that stretched before them. Thoughts of the cool pond, the shady pine grove, or the abandoned car house were usually among the first considerations of both boys, who met here before J. P.'s house nearly every morning. Today J. P. was puffed up from his status as the honored at his seventh birthday party last Sunday, and Memphis, who wouldn't turn seven until August, was feeling some jealousy still. "We could go fishing," he suggested with the thought that he might catch a bigger fish and thus regain some of his rank with J. P.

"No, ain't no fish biting this time of day." J. P. was twirling a whistle attached to a ten-inch black cord. On his birthday the whistle, a gift from his mother Tee Wee, had been wrapped in white tissue paper and tied with a red string.

Memphis eyed it now with longing. "Can I blow it?" he asked.

"Nope. Mama said don't blow it in the house."

"We ain't in the house. We on the porch."

J. P. drew the black cord over his head. "Too close to the house. Let's go over to the Parsons' and see what's going on." As he rose from the steps, his bulldog Bob ambled across the porch to his master. J. P. stroked his white head and then slapped his side. "No, Bob, you gotta stay here. Last time I took you to the Parsons' you got in trouble when you chased the chickens off'n their roosts."

Stuffing the remains of the biscuit in his mouth, Memphis hurried after J. P., who was streaking across the yard. "Wait up. I'm coming," he yelled.

When they reached the fence that enclosed the Parsons' Jersey cows in their pasture, Memphis ran ahead. He loved the big swinging gate the Parsons had erected last April when the old wood-and-wire gate had rotted beyond repair. This new gate was shiny gray metal, constructed of eight horizontal poles spaced six inches apart and held together with two slanting crossbars. When the latch attached to the fence was unhooked, the poles could be swung back into the yard, leaving enough space in the entrance to the pasture for the Parsons' green pickup truck to drive through. The first time Memphis had seen the gate, he had thought of the pearly gates, sparkling with heavenly radiance. In fact, the metal poles reflected the noonday sun's light so brightly, he had thought the gate could really be the entrance to heaven, and it was only after blinking his wide eyes several times that he was convinced the cows standing placidly behind the gate weren't supernatural heavenly beings.

The cows were nowhere in sight today. They had taken refuge from the sun farther back in the pasture where a few scrub oaks offered some shade. Memphis hopped on the fence, and, curling the arch of his foot around the pipe, he called to J. P. "Unlatch it. Let's take turns swinging."

J. P. grabbed Memphis' arm and pulled him down. "No, we going to the house. If we sit on the back steps, we may get us something good to eat."

Memphis jerked away and began to run. "Beat you there," he yelled. But J. P. was already shooting past him before he'd finished his sentence.

AFTER SHE HUNG the last shirt on the clothesline, Icey lifted the empty basket and walked toward the washhouse. Crossing the yard, she spotted the boys sitting on the Parsons' back steps, muffins in both pairs of hands. "Memphis! What you doin over here? You suppose to be snappin beans with your sister."

Memphis' toes curled under, his physical reaction to telling a lie. "Didn't say nothing. Didn't even see her." He *had* seen Glory, and she'd screamed his name in her worst screechy voice, but Memphis had taken off without answering her.

Icey saw the curled toes. "Well, you gonna get it later. I got more work to do, but when I get through, you gonna get it, you hear?"

Memphis nodded. He expected to get it, but he figured a day with J. P. was worth it. Later when his mother's switch hit the back of his legs, he'd just think back to the fun they'd had and he'd hardly feel it. Icey didn't spank that hard. Memphis was small for his age, skinny with an elongated face and head that made him appear sad even when he was smiling. Nearly always covered with scabs and bruises from frequent falls and born with a pronounced bowed left leg, Memphis often escaped Icey's peach tree limb by wobbling off balance on her first blow.

After Icey disappeared into the house, J. P. turned to Memphis with a malicious grin. He enjoyed Memphis' humiliations because they served as consolations for his own misfortunes. Tee Wee wielded her switch more often than Icey and with much greater force. J. P. fingered his whistle. "Reckon you can't go fairy calling with me now."

"Fairy calling? What you mean?"

J. P. lifted the whistle from his chest. "Well, you didn't know, but this here whistle is a magic whistle. When I blows it a certain way, black fairies come out of the woods and dance. Then I rub the whistle and, uh—" He hesitated, trying to remember which tale was which—"and a genie comes out and grants my any wish."

Memphis didn't think there was any such thing as fairies and genies, but then he hadn't ever seen a magic whistle, and here was one dangling on a cord right before his eyes.

J. P. stood up. "You coming or not?"

Memphis scrambled to his feet. "Yeah, I'm coming. I ain't afraid of genies," he said, immediately wishing he hadn't mentioned his fear to J. P.

ICEY HAD JUST tucked the last fold under the pillows on Browder's bed when she looked out the window and saw the boys speeding toward the woods. Walking across the room to the dresser, she lifted her head to the mirror and smiled. She touched the tip of her forefinger to her left incisor. She was the only colored woman on Enterprise Road with a gold tooth. She had begged Deke for the money to buy it, but he had kept on refusing her until in desperation she had agreed to do that one sinful act in the night in exchange for the tooth. She'd had pain, too. Lots of burning pain which didn't go away for several days, but when she'd seen the envy on Tee Wee's big broad face, she'd known the tooth was worth the price. She slapped the mirror with her dust cloth. She was a lucky woman. Four fine children, one grandson, and a good man who worked and didn't drink too much except on Saturday nights. She lined up Browder's hair-brush, comb, and cologne bottle on the dresser. Deke didn't wear no cologne, but she loved the scent of him just fine. She'd whiffed the same tangy odor on Memphis when she had hugged him to her breast last night before he jumped into bed. Icey dipped her mop into the bucket and, with her broad hands, wrung it nearly dry. Slapping it on the oak floor, she thought how alike Memphis and his daddy were. They had the same habit of touching the tip of their tongues to the sides of their mouths when they was feeling good about theirselves.

Backing out of the bedroom, Icey propped the mop against the wall. Memphis was her favorite young'n because, unlike the others, with him there weren't no bad associations made with bad men. She hoped none of her children were going to take after their fathers. She worried even though Jonas had married, had a good job driving the delivery truck for Wells Furniture Store, and was a good daddy to his little baby. Eli, now, had some bad bad habits; he'd lost his job and moved to Biloxi, and she knew for sure he was runnin hooch from Louisiana to them white night-clubs. She wished Glory would find a man and get on with life, but Glory took after her, was a little too heavy around the middle, and some men just didn't appreciate a full-sized woman. Icey dropped to her knees and began wiping the big white baseboards. The Lord didn't offer no guaran-tees in this life, but if He was merciful, He'd forgive her for those other no-good men and allow her children to find happiness in this world.

"*Icey.*" She lifted her eyes to Tee Wee, who stood over her wiping her hands on her apron. "You seen J. P.? Parsons want blackberry cobbler. I needs him to go pickin."

Icey struggled to her feet. "I seen him and Memphis headin out to the woods a while back."

Tee Wee slapped her hands against her big stomach. "That boy. He must've knowed I was gonna put him to work. Smart. Just too smart that boy."

Icey frowned. "He ain't that smart. He just lazy." They faced each other in the narrow hall, their wide bodies filling the space between the walls. Icey believed that Tee Wee was jealous of her baby Memphis be-cause he was by far the most handsome of any of their children. Even the one bowed leg only made Memphis more interesting. Special, she'd told herself, turned by God's hand into a soul destined, by his curved bone, to glory someday. She smiled now, displaying her gold tooth. Luther wouldn't ever have enough cash to get Tee Wee one.

Tee Wee stabbed her index finger in Icey's face. "You just can't admit J. P.'s smarter than Memphis, can you?"

Icey dropped back to the floor to resume her work. "J. P. is older than Memphis, but when Memphis turns seven, he won't be playin in the woods when his mama want him for a job. He'll be right here sayin, 'What you need, Mama? I'll do it.' "

"You can think that, but the proof's in the puddin," Tee Wee called over her shoulder as she walked back to the kitchen.

"Yeah, it sure is," Icey said, slapping her mop down the hall toward the heavily draped, gloomy living room. Mrs. Parsons wouldn't allow the drapes to remain open, but Icey threw them aside when she dusted because she was secretly frightened of the dark corners of the big rectangular room. She knew for sure that the Devil hid in darkness, waiting for a chance to grab you and make you do things you wouldn't do in the light. Mrs. Parsons said light was bad. It fades the furniture, makes the house hotter, and isn't flattering to a lady's complexion. If this was my house, Icey thought, I'd buy white curtains and keep em open to let in all the light God wants to send me. The Devil and his evil messengers couldn't find no spot in her house to hide. She squirted the marble-topped coffee table with furniture polish even though she'd been told not to. Mrs. Parsons didn't know everything just because she was white. Polish made the marble glisten and it hadn't turned yellow like she said it would. As she wiped the table, Icey thought about the birthday party she was going to have when Memphis turned seven. She'd make the party Tee Wee threw for J. P. look like a piddling attempt when she brought out the store-bought cake she was saving for. Let J. P. blow that lousy whistle all he wants, she thought. I'm gonna buy Memphis a real horn to blow. Icey suspected Memphis had musical talent because he hummed in his sleep. She'd heard some beautiful combinations of notes when he took his nap on the cot on the porch. Icey began taking the figurines off the whatnot shelves and laying them on the floor. Yes, a horn or maybe even a drum would show Tee Wee that a whistle was a trifling gift.

MEMPHIS WAS FAR from agreeing with his mother. He was sitting on a bed of pine needles watching J. P.'s round, dark cheeks puff in and out as he blew air into the silver opening on the end of the whistle. Short staccato blasts reverberated through the tops of the pines, and in the intervals between the toots, Memphis imagined that he could hear the tiny footsteps of black fairies on the woodland floor behind him. "Let me have a turn," he begged.

J. P. was tired of blowing on the toy, but he said, "Nooo. You too young. Fairies don't come for folks under seven; they think they ain't old enough to know secrets."

"But I'm almost seven," Memphis said. "Just let me try it once."

"Okay," J. P. said in his most adult voice. "But just remember to keep the calls short and quick. Long blows can call up mean monsters instead of good fairies."

Memphis sat with the tip of his tongue in the corner of his mouth as he watched J. P. lift the cord over his head and roll it into a ball before handing it to him. He wiped his sweating hands down the front of his overalls before accepting the toy, and after he hung it around his neck, feeling the weight of it against his chest, he lifted it to his mouth. Scrunching his eyes shut, he blew with all his might. Startled robins, blue jays, and sparrows flushed from tree branches and, beating their wings frantically, flew away from the offending noise. When Memphis heard their flurry, he opened his eyes expecting to see monsters, witches, and maybe the Devil himself. He saw only J. P. holding his palms over his big ears. He tried again, puffing his checks and expelling his breath into the hole in the magic whistle, but now no sound came from his efforts. He looked over at J. P., who shook his head in disgust. "You got spit in it. Give it back. You too little and stupid to do nothing right."

Reluctantly Memphis lifted the cord over his head. "I didn't mean to, J. P. You think any fairies heard my first blow?"

J. P. tapped the whistle against his thigh. "No, too long. Most likely there's a monster waiting behind a tree to grab you fore you get home."

When Memphis digested this fact, his eyes grew rounder, and, imagining a great hairy monster, his heart pounded faster in his chest. He didn't want to cry in front of J. P., but his lips quivered, and then with horror he felt tears sliding down his thin dark cheeks.

AT THAT MOMENT, Icey was crying, too. She had just broken Mrs. Parsons' antique vase she'd been told never to touch. She had only lifted it a little ways off the marble-topped sideboard where it sat on a white lace doily. She had wanted to look at the beautiful pictures painted around the base of the vase. There were dancing ladies in pastel dresses, lilies and gladioli at their feet, and over their heads, silver and gold birds were flying up toward the slender, curved handles of the vase. One handle had just broken off for no reason Icey could guess and the vase had crashed to the table, shattering into what looked like a hundred or more pieces. Her tears fell on the head of one lady who looked up at her with a gentle smile. Icey cried silently, her big square shoulders shaking, her rag-tied head dropping to her chest. She would be fired. Mrs. Parsons was not a forgiving woman even if she was president of the Methodist Women's Circle group. When Icey had cracked her vanity mirror, she had told her that if she broke one more thing, she was gonna get Tee Wee's Crow to be her housekeeper.

Crow. She wasn't no good, couldn't trust her to do nothin right. Icey couldn't bear to be replaced by her. If that happened, Deke wouldn't be able to pay the rent by hisself, and then they'd have to move. Icey looked around the room like she'd never seen it before, like she hadn't polished that big silver teapot a hundred times. She turned away from the broken shards scattered on the table and walked over to stand beside the long mahogany table. She pulled out a chair and sank down onto the peach-colored brocaded seat. Resting her elbows on the table, she cupped her chin in her hands. Her mind wandered around and away from her predicament, and she suddenly realized she'd never thought much about the whites who sat here eating Tee Wee's roast chicken, corn casseroles, and lemon meringue pies. Icey lifted her eyes to the painting hanging on the wall above her. Inside the wide gold frame men dressed in red coats, black derby hats, and shiny boots rode on white, black, and reddish brown horses following a pack of hunting dogs. The grass over which the horses' hooves ran was brilliantly green. The trees were full-leafed, tall and straight. In the background a miniature white farmhouse sat on a hill not unlike the house in which she sat now and from which, she now reminded herself, she was about to be banished. She turned to the china cabinet filled with crystal goblets, china plates, a silver candle snuffer, a rose-colored glass compote. There was a lot of expensive stuff in this room. She wondered if Mrs. Parsons had done something sinful in order to get Mr. Parsons to give her money for all this. Did white ladies have to barter with their husbands, too? No, white people didn't have to suffer like colored to get what they wanted. They didn't clean no toilets, squat under tables to dust spindled legs, and they wouldn't be crying over breaking a vase that cost more money than a gold tooth.

Tee Wee's voice from the kitchen drifted under the closed door between the dining room and the kitchen. She was singing about chariots
and going home to Jesus. Icey hated that song. She didn't want to go to
no heaven; she wanted to stay right here with her man and her children
and watch Memphis grow up to be something better than any of them.
Icey slapped her hands on the table and stood up. "I ain't goin," she said
aloud. "Crow ain't gettin my job, and Tee Wee ain't watchin me slink out
of here like no stray dog she kicks out the yard."

She knew she'd have to do something quickly now, and as her thoughts
focused on her problem, panic set in. Her breath quickened as she spun
around in a circle looking at all the beautiful objects in the room. Expensive stuff, she thought again. Parsons is lucky they ain't been robbed.
Why just last week two hoboes had broke into Mrs. Taylor's house and
ate a pie, takin her frying pan and two dollars in change she'd left in the
soap dish by the sink. Those two hoboes could come back here and steal
from the Parsons. Icey walked over to the window. Suddenly she knew
what she was going to do. Raising the window, she took a deep breath,
reared back on her heels, and thrust her massive body forward. Her
balled fist shot through the screen, ripping its center. Pulling the torn
ends wide, she fashioned a hole large enough for a body to pass through.

Wheeling around, Icey grabbed her broom and swept the vase shards
into a brown paper sack she used for extra cleaning rags. She snatched the
candlesticks from the table and tossed them in the bag along with a compote, the creamer and sugar, two figurines, and a little crystal bell en-
graved with the date of the Parsons' tenth wedding anniversary.

Clutching the heavy bag to her chest, Icey tiptoed out the front door
and hurried around to the side of the house. Squinting up at the sun, she
calculated that it was nearly noon. They'd all be back soon. She had to
get rid of the bag quickly. The hydrangea bushes in full bloom would be
a good hiding place for now. After dark, she could retrieve the bag and
bury it far away in the back of the pasture.

MEMPHIS AND J. P. had just left the woods and were running across the
lawn when they heard Icey's scream. Memphis' first thought was that he
had called up the monster that J. P. had told him about. It might be his
fault that a creature was in the house.

Icey's screams were frightening J. P., too. "Robbers. We been robbed,"
she yelled. Then the boys heard Tee Wee shouting, "Oh Lord oh Lord."

When Ruthie's head appeared through the hole in the screen on the side of the house, J. P. and Memphis ran toward her. No one they knew had ever been robbed, and both J. P. and Memphis felt a delicious thrill of horror run up their backs. Stumbling over clumps of dry, brown grass, they exchanged wide grins, which they were trying to suppress when Ruthie yelled to them. "J. P., Memphis, y'all go get Daddy. He's down at the cow lot."

BY THE TIME the sheriff arrived, both Mrs. Parsons and Browder had returned from their trip into town. Mrs. Parsons told the sheriff that she had heard a noise in the night, but had assumed it was just some stray dog, and Browder volunteered that he had come home around two A.M. but hadn't seen anything unusual. Mr. Parsons said that he had slept soundly, heard nothing at all, and hurried back to his sick calf, which he said was more valuable than all that fancy stuff that cluttered up the dining room. Sheriff Patterson believed that hoboes had robbed them and that they had most likely hopped the four A.M. train and was maybe in Jackson or Natchez by now. Icey cataloged the missing items for the sheriff. "Because I dusts it every week, I knows what's missin," she said, looking down at the patterned carpet. She patted Mrs. Parsons' arm. "I know you cares about that vase more'n anythin. You sure did love that vase."

Tee Wee, jealous of Icey's role as a central player in the scene, hustled off to the kitchen mumbling about her pork chops getting cold and not having no blackberries to make no cobbler with. Mrs. Parsons told Icey she could take the rest of the day off, but Icey shook her head and said she wasn't one to not finish a job and she was gonna tackle Ruthie's room right after dinner.

When the sheriff returned just after the late lunch with two mat-haired dogs, Memphis and J. P. trailed along behind them. Black noses pressed to the ground, the dogs zigzagged from beneath the window across the lawn to the woods. They were following a scent, but the sheriff said they weren't all that reliable and had once dragged him ten miles on the trail of a raccoon they mistook for a runaway wife. The dogs found the exact spot where Memphis and J. P. had been sitting blowing the magic whistle. Circling the area, they hiked their legs on a tree and then doubled back toward the house.

Running full out alongside J. P.'s trotting gait, Memphis, his voice wavering with the motion of his pounding feet, said, "You reckon it's fairy scent them dogs has got?"

J. P. kept his stride. "Naw. It's hobo smell. I believe I smell it myself." When they returned to the yard, he said, "We ought to look for clues."

Looking down, Memphis saw a doodlebug hole and thought about sticking a piece of pine straw in to haul one out, but then remembered he was looking for something called clues. "What's clues look like?" he asked J. P.

J. P. was peering into the washtub Icey had set beside the steps. "A piece of shirt, a billfolder, a gun. Things like that."

"Oh." Memphis hoped he'd find something before J. P., and he peered under the steps hoping he wouldn't find no snake instead of clues.

ICEY, WIPING THE SINK in the bathroom, was thinking about clues, too. Had she left any in her haste to hide her bag? Her hands shook so, she could hardly hold on to the rag she swished around in the sink. What had she done? She was evil. Evil and crazy, too. "Oh Lord," she prayed, "please don't let them find me out. I ain't never *ever* gonna do somethin this bad again. I'll have this gold tooth taken out. I'll give it to Tee Wee if You let me bury that stuff tonight and don't let nobody find it. I won't say nothin mean to Tee Wee again. I'll tell her J. P. is smarter than all my young'ns, and I won't use no more polish on the marble table. I swear I'll change if You'll just let me go this one time."

Icey moved over to the bathtub, knelt beside it. She folded her hands. "Please, Jesus, if not for my sinful self, forgive me for the sake of my boy Memphis. He's special. You marked him for special. Don't do nothin to his only mama he got in this world." As she sprinkled Ajax in the tub and began to wipe it with her rag, a deep nauseating sickness overwhelmed her and she knew it was no use. She would be caught. She would go to jail, and she saw her children lined up behind bars looking through them to where she lay on a narrow cot in a dark cell. Rivulets of her tears made little pathways through the white Ajax powder, and she dropped her head on the cool white porcelain tub. In her experience God hadn't been merciful even though she was a churchgoing woman and lived a mostly Christian life. She'd never owned but two store-bought dresses, never had a matched set of dishes. Then she'd gone and done that act in the night and squandered Deke's money on a gold tooth instead of using it to purchase something for her children. She was a sinner and there wasn't nothing going to save her. Wearily, she rose from the tub, walked out of the bathroom, and went out to sit on the back steps to await her jailers.

Chapter 17

EMPHIS FOUND THE BAG, BUT J. P. INSISTED HE'D SEEN IT first. Both boys reached for it simultaneously, and when they had peered inside and seen the glinting silver, they shouted for the sheriff to come quick. J. P. belatedly thought to blow his whistle just as the sheriff, the dogs, Mrs. Parsons, Ruthie, Browder, and Tee Wee assembled beside the hydrangea bushes. They were all talking at once, but the shrill whistle drowned out their voices so that everyone began shouting louder and louder until Tee Wee snatched the whistle from J. P., breaking the cord and causing a red welt to rise on the back of his neck.

After the sheriff had finally quieted the group, he took the bag from Memphis, and kneeling on the ground, began laying out the objects on the grass. "Okay, Missus Parsons, can you identify these items?" He held up the crystal bell for her inspection. "Is this your dinner bell?"

Mrs. Parsons reached out and grabbed the tinkling bell from the sheriff. "Of course, it's mine. The question is what's it doing here? Why didn't the robbers take it?"

The sheriff reached back into the bag and drew out a shard of the vase. "Looks like this here got broken when the other stuff was piled on top of it."

"Oh, no! That was my great-grandmother's vase. I didn't even allow Icey to dust it. Icey!" She looked around the group clustered beside her. "Where's Icey?"

Ruthie looked at Tee Wee, who looked at Browder, who shrugged. "She's not here, Mama."

"Here I is," Icey called, coming around the corner of the house. "What's all the commotion about?"

"Mama," Memphis said, running toward her. "The robbers left the stuff and broke Miz Parsons' granny's vase."

"What? Robbers broke it?" Icey couldn't take in this turn of events. She had been practicing her confession, and now she looked wonderingly from her son's upturned face to the sheriff, to the dogs who were whining and sniffing J. P.'s feet.

The sheriff lifted his arms above his head as if appealing to God to solve the mystery. "Folks, gather round. Come over here. I'm gonna tell how this crime was committed." When the group had shuffled into a semicircle around the sheriff, he cleared his throat, dropped his arms, and began to deliver his theory. "Last night. Sometime before two A.M., hoboes come up out of them woods." He pointed toward the right. "They entered the house by ripping the screen in the dining room window, climbed in, and began helping themselves to Mrs. Parsons' good stuff." Everyone nodded, except Icey, who stood on the edge of the circle with her mouth hanging open, her eyes fixed on the "stolen" objects scattered on the ground. The sheriff continued his scenario of the night's events, saying that Browder had come home and surprised the robbers, who had hastily run out of the house and hidden in the hydrangea bushes.

"But why didn't they take the bag with them?" Mrs. Parsons interrupted.

The sheriff frowned. He was coming to that, he said. Stooping down, he scratched behind the ears of the dogs, who lay stretched across his feet.

"They was gonna come back and get it tonight," Icey blurted out and then clapped her hand over her mouth. What was she saying? Shut up, shut up, she told her mouth.

The sheriff wheeled toward Icey. "I'm telling this. You hush till I finish." Icey nodded vigorously. She was hushed. "Then they decided to come back tonight and get the stuff cause they waited in them bushes till daylight, and they figured someone might see them with the bag and get suspicious."

Still holding the bell, Mrs. Parsons shook it gently and said over the tinkling sound, "Why would they wait till daylight? Why didn't they just leave after Browder went to bed? This doesn't make any sense to me."

The sheriff stuck his thumbs in his belt. "Criminal mind. Doesn't make sense to you because you haven't got a criminal mind. They think different. I've dealt with them; you don't have the experience I do. I'll set up a stakeout on these bushes tonight and catch them when they come back." Taking the bell from Mrs. Parsons, he gathered up the loot and put it back into the sack. "I'll have to take all this in for evidence."

Mrs. Parsons fingered the bow at the neck of her cotton blouse. She didn't look convinced. "Well, still, I just don't see, don't understand why. I mean it just doesn't add up, and how come the bell didn't break, too? It's all so, so . . ." She broke off, not knowing how to finish her sentence.

"Surprisin," Icey said.

After the sheriff drove away, the group dispersed except for Icey, Memphis, and J. P. "Can we come over and watch the sheriff catch the robbers tonight?" Memphis asked.

"No, you ain't comin over here. You ain't goin nowhere but to bed." Suddenly Icey's knees buckled and she sank to the ground with blessed relief. "It all over now. All over," she whispered. "Thank You, Jesus."

"It ain't over till they catches them," J. P. said.

"Ain't gonna catch nobody now," Icey said, holding her palms to her breasts.

"Is, too." Memphis nodded at his friend's words. But then, looking at his mother's drawn face, he remembered that it was usually she who was right about things, and not J. P. There hadn't been one sign of any fairies or monsters.

J. P.'s certainty wavered. "But the sheriff said he is gonna come back, lay in them bushes, and when the robbers come, he'll pull out his gun and blow their heads off."

Icey stood up. "Only head's gonna come off is yours if you don't go pick them blackberries your mama wants for cobbler. Memphis, you get home and snap the rest of them beans."

"Yes'm," they yelled, as they sprinted across the yard in opposite directions.

AROUND EIGHT O'CLOCK darkness fell on the Parsons' hydrangea bushes, and at midnight the quarter moon offered only a sliver of light to guide Memphis and J. P. over the pasture to the Parsons' fence. Unlatching the gate, they crept through and made their way along the blackberry bushes lining the fence. After a few yards they stopped and squatted down behind a bush to wait for the robbers. Memphis was already sorry he had come, but he'd promised to meet J. P. behind his house after everyone was asleep and he was more frightened of J. P.'s disapproval than his mother's. Maybe she wouldn't miss him. She had looked tired and was unusually quiet when she had tucked him in bed.

Memphis squinted out into the darkness. He was shivering from a deeper fear than he had ever known. He thought of Icey's admonitions about the Devil and his workers who lurked outside his house in the inky blackness. And he still wasn't absolutely positive he hadn't called up some monster with the whistle that J. P. now carried in the pocket of his overalls. Memphis glanced back over his shoulder. The cottonwoods looked like giant black monsters, rising in a line behind him and creeping forward across the grassy stubble to grab him for Satan's army. He said the only prayers he could recall. "Now I lay me down to sleep. Thank you for this food."

"Shush up. They'll hear you," J. P. whispered.

"Let's go home. Ain't nothing happened."

J. P. drew out his whistle. "It will, and when we sees them robbers, I'll blow this and I'll be the one who catches them. Probably get a medal or prize for it."

"And me, too?"

"Yeah. You, too, if you stay, but if you leave me here by myself, you'll just be known for the coward you is acting like."

Memphis peeked back at the trees. They hadn't moved much. Maybe the robbers would come soon. He wanted a medal, but he wished he knew where the sheriff was.

ICEY WAS ALSO WONDERING where the sheriff was hiding. She hadn't been able to sleep and had crept out of bed to the porch. Looking over toward the Parsons' house, she saw no sign of the sheriff. No sign of life anywhere about the place. She ran her tongue across the smooth edges of her gold tooth. She remembered her promise to Jesus, but she knew she couldn't part with it. What did He care about an old tooth anyway? It wasn't nothing to Him. She looked around her porch. There was her rocker, her wash pot, her straw broom. She wouldn't have to leave these things. Memphis and her other children wasn't going to get throwed out of their home. Safe. They were all safe. She closed her eyes and saw Mrs.

Parsons' pasty face, saw her holding that little bell. Served her right. That vase wasn't nothing but a piece of china, and her so haughty acting about it. Didn't Jesus say, "Lay not your treasures up on earth"?

"Icey? Icey?" Tee Wee scampered up the steps to where she stood.

"What you doin over here this time of night?" Icey asked, staring at Tee Wee's long cotton nightgown. Where'd she get that? she wondered.

"Is J. P. over to here? He ain't in his bed." Tee Wee drew up her night-gown and formed a little knot in her fist with it. "I'm worried them boys is down there where them robbers is. Go see if Memphis is gone, too."

When Icey returned from inside the house and confirmed Memphis' disappearance, Tee Wee clutched her chest. "Wake up Deke. I'll go get Luther." She wrung her nightgown around her wide hips and started back down the steps.

"Wait," Icey called. "Ain't no need. They down at the Parsons' is all. They be back directly."

Tee Wee stopped and turned. "What kind of mama is you? Robbers out there with maybe guns, knives, big boards to kill them children with. Don't you care what happens to your young'n?"

Icey stiffened with anger. "I am so a good mama. I ain't worried cause there ain't no robbers." She clamped her hands over her mouth as she had earlier in the day. Big mouth of hers always opening when it ought to be shut. She stared at Tee Wee, praying she hadn't heard her, praying that somehow she'd be saved again.

Tee Wee took a step toward Icey, then stopped and dropped her gown. She pulled on her nose, her lips. "I smells truth here. And I'm re-memberin somethin I heard." She poked her finger into Icey's chest. "You the one said them robbers would be back tonight, and you said that because you is the robber. You was gonna go back and get them things tonight, sell em and buy somethin for yourself. What? Another gold tooth?"

Icey sank down onto the rocking chair. "No. You got it wrong, Tee. I ain't never stole nothin in my life. I ain't no thief."

Tee Wee pushed her chair back and leaned over her. Her breath was hot on Icey's face; her eyes looked like two big white eggs bulging out of her dark face. "I known you a lot of years. You lyin. You done it."

Icey pressed her head into the back of the chair. "Okay, you right, I done it, but I didn't steal nothin. I mean I didn't rob nobody. I broke the vase is all. I was just tryin to study on some way to hide the vase, and I thought about them robbers, and I was gonna bury the stuff. That's all. I ain't no thief." She fell forward out of the chair and knelt at Tee Wee's bare feet. "Please don't tell nobody, Tee. Please." Icey reached up, grasped her hand. "I am your sister, not them Parsons."

Tee Wee's eyes narrowed. Her mind was quickly assessing the possibilities the situation offered. Icey's sobs turned to wails. "Shush up. I can't think with you makin noise. Besides you gonna wake up your house." Icey stuffed her fist in her mouth; her shoulders heaved, but she made no more sounds. "That better. I got to study some on this here crime. I needs more time. I let you know tomorrow."

Icey rose to her feet. "Tomorrow? Can't you tell me now?" She knew she wouldn't sleep. She felt Tee Wee was being unreasonably cruel, but she also knew it was what she would do in her place, and she realized further pleading was futile.

"Tomorrow," Tee Wee said, turning to go back to her house. "And while I'm thinkin, you go down there and get them boys home."

MEMPHIS WAS THINKING of going home alone. His terror of the dark, of the robbers, of gigantic hairy monsters, and the trees themselves had been steadily mounting, and if he continued to squat beside J. P. in the bushes much longer, he felt his heart would surely beat right out of his chest. Great wrenching sobs burst out of him, and as he gulped the hot night air, his sobs deepened into moans.

J. P. grabbed Memphis' arm and gave him a shake. "Shush up. Robbers will hear you. I reckon I'm gonna have to take you home," he said with relief. He, too, was frightened of the dark and welcomed this opportunity to return to his safe bed without losing face. "Follow me, but stay down," he said, rising to a half crouch.

Memphis followed him along the fence line, keeping a close distance, never taking his eyes from J. P.'s hunched back. They had nearly reached the gate when Memphis stepped on a sharp stick J. P. had avoided. *"Ow ow ow!"* he screamed, straightening up and hopping furiously on his injured foot.

SHERIFF PATTERSON, who had fallen asleep in the Parsons' green pickup truck where he'd been lying in wait for the robbers, heard the boy's screams. Befuddled by the noise, which had interrupted his dream of chasing a roe with a rack of twelve antlers, he peered into the darkness. Detecting movement by the fence, he watched two figures dart out of the bushes toward the gate. Frantically, he turned the ignition key and shifted the truck into gear. He would catch them thieves now. Two on foot and him with a vehicle.

Icey heard the screams, too. On her heavy legs she ran surprisingly fast across the rutted ground, and, as she ran, she saw the sheriff driving forward toward the two boys. J. P. had crossed the gate opening, but Memphis, limping along behind, grabbed the unlatched gate for support, causing it to swing open. Icey screamed her son's name. The sheriff, fully awake now, saw that it was Memphis who was hanging on to the gate. He stomped on the brakes as the truck shot through the opening into the pasture.

Icey saw the brake lights and sighed. She was nearly there now, and she thought of how she was going to say, *You're gonna get it, Memphis.* Then as if in a slow-motion dream, she watched Memphis' hands slip from the gate, watched him fall sideways through the air toward the skidding truck. She heard nothing; not even her breath sounded in her ears. All was silence and her legs seemed not a part of her as they moved her around the truck to the front left bumper where her son's bowed leg jutted out from beneath it.

Icey watched as the sheriff pulled Memphis out from beneath the truck. He laid his hand against his neck, shook his head. He waved her backward. "No, girl. No. He's gone. Don't look." And she stood not looking. Not seeing or hearing anything. She had fallen into the black void of Satan's evil world where God had thrust her away from His salvation. Sheriff Patterson told J. P. to run for Tee Wee and the boy's father, then he vomited into the bushes before he rushed to the Parsons' back porch. She stood enveloped in the evil cloud from which only her gold tooth shone into the darkness.

Hadn't she told Memphis not to walk into the darkness where the Devil reigned? Slowly, she walked over to the gate. Standing before it, she saw the unearthly light on the poles glinting into the darkness, and she lifted her head to the slivered moon. She hadn't kept her bargain with God, and He had allowed Satan his dark deed. "You took him through Your gate, didn't You?" she whispered. "Why didn't You take me? Why?" Reaching out, she grasped the top pole of the gate in her hands. She gripped the hard metal in her strong hands, twisting and pushing, grunting inhuman guttural cries.

Then, dropping her hands to her side, she fell silent. She knew why God was punishing her.

When Icey felt Tee Wee's hand on her back, she turned to her without tears. Wordlessly, she pushed her head into Tee Wee's soft breasts, and, cradled there, she waited for Deke. With dry eyes, she watched her husband running toward them, watched him lift his son into his arms and lay him on the seat of the truck. And as the sheriff drove away, she gazed after the taillights waving across the pasture, growing smaller until they were merely red specks blinking in the night. When she felt Tee Wee's hand in hers, she walked with her away from the gate toward their houses standing side by side, silent and dark, waiting for the light.

Chapter 18

J. P. AND BOB WERE HEADED DOWN ENTERPRISE ROAD ON THEIR way to Johnny Moore's store when they saw Luther's Ford coming toward them. Stopping the car alongside them, he called from the window. "Where you goin to, J. P.?"

J. P. moved closer and leaned into the car. "Mama sent me to the store for sugar. She's making cake for Memphis' laying out."

Luther patted his son's cheek and said, "Well, get on home soon as you can. I'm helpin with Deke's chores and you got to slop the hogs before dark."

He stepped back. "Okay, Daddy. Me and Bob be back quick." He stood in the road until the Ford was out of sight, and then reached down and scratched behind Bob's ear. Straightening up, he waved the dog on toward Mr. Moore's store. Bob hadn't left his side all day. The bulldog seemed to know he was needed more than ever, and he had left his usual shady spot beneath the oak tree to accompany J. P. on all his errands and chores this hot, sunny day. J. P. did need Bob's company today. He'd awakened forgetting about the events of the night before, and, throwing on his overalls, he had run to the kitchen to grab a biscuit before meeting Memphis on his porch. But when he'd seen his mother's broad back standing at the stove, he remembered. Memphis wouldn't be meeting him today; he was lying in a box in the front room of his mama's house. Without a word, J. P. had backed out of the kitchen and returned to his room. There, lying on his cot, arms crossed behind his head, he had relived all the events of the night before.

J. P. turned on his side in his narrow bed. "If only he hadn't climbed up on that gate," he whispered. "If only, if only . . ." He covered his eyes with his forearm. His misery was too deep for tears, and he wondered at the emotion he felt bottled up just under his ribs. Physically, he felt sort of like he had when he had contracted the mumps. He felt swollen and stiff and achy, and when Tee Wee sent him outside to gather the hen eggs, he felt as if his legs were swinging on metal hinges that needing oiling.

Bob had come along with him to the henhouse and with his protruding round eyes watched J. P.'s every movement. Even now, the dog looked sideways at him as he waddled along in the heat. His wrinkled white skin quivered in waves as he walked; his long pink tongue hung down in the dust that billowed up beneath J. P.'s feet. He had lived with J. P. for six years now, and he seemed to understand that his master derived some comfort in the feel of him brushing occasionally against his leg.

J. P. usually meandered off the road into the ditch that ran beside the packed red clay on which he walked, collecting grasshoppers and slugs, bottle caps, and shiny round pebbles. But today J. P. strode with purpose, keeping his eyes focused on his destination. The mid-afternoon sun beating down on his head added to the weight of his sorrow, and he lifted his forearm to his brow to wipe the beads of sweat that formed around his cropped hair. He kept to the center of the road, unaware of passing the Thompson Place, the Keppers', the Tate pastureland. He heard a mockingbird's cry, a cricket in the tall grass that lined the ditch, a Jersey cow's bellow to her calf as he continued on his mile walk to the little store that sat in a wedge of pie-shaped land where Enterprise Road and Carterdale Road forked.

The store, a white wooden building, sat in the middle of the vee between the roads. It was narrow at the entrance, with a center door that opened into a long rectangular room. Mr. Moore's daddy had added on the store before Carterdale Road was widened for cars, and when Johnny Moore had included a single gas pump to his business, he had placed it in the vee, precariously close to both roads. Traffic was usually light, but when cars passed the store, dust clouded the pump and billowed through the screen door into the interior of the dark store, coating the merchandise with a fine layer of red powder. Whenever a customer handed over a purchase (whether it be a can of soup, a bag of tobacco, or a stick of peppermint), Johnny would lift the merchandise to his mouth and blow off the dust before ringing up the amount on his big gold metal register.

Today Johnny Moore was sitting outside his store in one of the three cane rockers lined up close behind the gas pump. Mr. Whittington and Mr. Kepper occupied the other two rockers, their heads wreathed in clouds of smoke from the cigars stuck in the sides of their mouths. J. P. and Bob slowed their steps as they approached the men. Ducking his head, J. P. whispered to Bob. "You lays down quiet. White men don't like for dogs and coloreds to disturb their talking." The dog ambled obediently over to the shade offered from a pine on the side of the store and lay down, closing his eyes, but lifting his ears to follow his master's steps. J. P. slowly and quietly walked toward the front door. He needed sugar and Tee Wee had told him he could buy a peppermint with the change from the wrinkled dollar he had stuffed in the pocket of his overalls.

Ten feet from the men, J. P. stopped and waited until he was noticed. Mr. Moore looked over at him first. "You needing something today, boy?" he asked.

"Yes sir."

When Mr. Whittington motioned him forward, J. P. saw the brown dribble spots on his shirt from the cigar he was chewing. Ducking his head, he looked over at Mr. Kepper's big brown boots. "You Luther and Tee Wee's boy? You the one who was with Deke and Icey's boy that got hisself killed?" J. P. nodded. He could sense the quickening interest of all three of these white men, and he felt his heart thumping with fear. He hadn't done anything, had he? Heaving his shoulders, he breathed in the white scent. These men smelled differently from the white men in town. Their aroma was more familiar because they were farmers who carried the pungent odors of manure and molasses-based feed, and the acrid pesticide that never completely left the skin.

Mr. Moore rocked back in his chair. "Sit down, boy, tell us about what happened. What'd you see? How bad was he mashed up?"

Looking around, J. P. didn't see another chair, so he sat a few feet back on the ground in front of the dust-coated red pump. He didn't know exactly what was expected of him; his face immobile, he waited. Mr. Kepper leaned forward. "Sheriff Patterson I heard run right over the middle of him, squished him flat. That what you saw?"

Still J. P. couldn't find his tongue. He looked across the yard at Bob lying in the dirt, ears lifted. Bob's presence was a comfort, but he couldn't make himself put on the smile like he usually tried to wear when talking to white people.

Mr. Moore was growing impatient. "What you got to say? Cat got your tongue?"

Now J. P. succeeded in managing a small smile for the men . "No sir. Memphis, he laying out at his house. Ain't squashed none I could see. Got on a white burying suit Missus Parsons brought his mama this morning."

"Doc was out, patched him up, I bet," Mr. Kepper said.

"Yes sir. Doctor was to the house last night. We knowed he were dead, but Missus Parsons, she sent for him anyhows." J. P., rounding his back, hunching his shoulders, drew back into himself. He had never spoken for so long to so many white men, and he needed to find his identity inside himself again.

"Was you there when they pulled him out beneath the truck? I heard the truck was so gunked up with blood and guts they had to wash it out before it would run."

"No sir. I don't know, sir. I weren't there long. Sheriff sent me to the house to get Memphis' daddy and my mama."

Mr. Whittington spat out more tobacco juice, which landed only a foot away from where J. P. sat. "What about his mama? Why didn't you get her?"

"Oh, she was already there," J. P. said, understanding now that all the attention of these three men was directed on him and that he was expected to give a performance. Sitting up straighter, his voice took on a louder, more lively tone. "Yes siree, I was right in front of Memphis when he jumped on the gate, and I turned back and seen Memphis' mama running up just when Memphis fell off the gate, and the truck were skidding, and there was a thump. Then she screamed such a scream it was to make your blood go cold in your body and I was feeling I gonna freeze to death just hearing that awful screaming." Checking the men's faces, J. P. knew he was giving them what they wanted. " 'God, Lord Jesus,' she said. Sheriff Patterson, he jumped out of the truck and he seen his shoes covering with the blood of Memphis and he puked in the bushes, and I says, 'Somebody got to help this woman and this here white man.' And I starts to run for help, but I seen Memphis' leg sticking out from underneath the truck and I smells the blood and I knowed God done took my best friend, and . . ." These last words brought J. P. back to himself, and now he remembered his loss. He fell silent and glanced over at the men. They were staring at him with an intensity he'd never seen in white men's eyes. He thought perhaps this was the way they looked at their own children, and he began to experience an emotion he'd never had before. Although he couldn't quite identify it, J. P. knew that the close listening these men had given him wasn't something even his daddy would know about. And then he did something he had never done. He violated his mother's taboo. He lifted his eyes and stared right back into the faces of these men. When his eyes met Mr. Moore's, he saw the tightening muscles at the corners, the lift of the brow. Instantly he realized he'd been too bold. The spell he'd bound was broken. Quickly J. P. tucked his chin in and lowered his eyes.

He heard Mr. Moore rising from his chair, opening the screen door. "You wanting something to buy? Come on in and get it and be off."

J. P. scrambled up and followed him into the dark room. He couldn't make out anything for a minute or so, but when his eyes adjusted, he roamed them over the shelves of tinned goods, dry goods, barrels of nails and pickles, jars of licorice and peppermint. He lowered his head and mumbled, "I needs sugar for my mama, and I got money to pay." He drew out his rumpled dollar bill and laid it on the counter.

Mr. Moore lifted a brown one-pound paper bag, blew on it, and snatched the dollar from the counter. Opening the cash register, he drew out some change and slapped it on the varnished wood. J. P. scooped up the coins and dropped them into his overall pocket. Then, taking the bag, he silently backed out the door.

Bob was waiting for him, keeping one eye on the men in the rockers. That he was nervous showed only in his continual tail twitching. J. P. slapped him on the head to turn toward home. Trying not to run, he walked as fast as he could away from the store, and he kept the pace until he knew he was out of sight of the white men who'd somehow won something from him he didn't understand.

As they walked on more slowly, J. P. began to talk to Bob in a low voice. "I feels like I done something wrong back there. We ain't gonna say nothing to Mama. She told me to just say yes to whites; don't go telling nothing to em. But I done told about Memphis, and now I feels like Memphis would be mad at me for it."

Bob banged against J. P.'s leg. Hearing the tremor in his master's voice, he quickened his pace toward home. They were passing the Kepper Place now, which meant they were nearly halfway there, and J. P. stopping talking, remembering now that he'd forgotten to buy a peppermint for himself, and feeling glad that he at least hadn't rewarded himself for his disloyalty. He didn't notice the blue tick hound sitting in the Keppers' yard.

Bob lifted his head, sniffing the dog's proximity. As J. P. and Bob continued on, the blue tick rose up and, standing on his long sturdy legs, watched them move toward him. Out of the corner of his eye, J. P. saw a shiny object lying on the other side of the ditch that served as a boundary to the Keppers' property. He thought of the medal he'd promised Memphis they would win when they caught the robbers. But there hadn't been any robbers. Jumping the ditch, he squatted down to pick up the bottle cap. It would be a medal for Memphis; he would lay it on his chest beside the whistle he would send with Memphis to heaven. He heard the hound's growls and Bob's bark at the same time. Dropping his sugar and bottle cap, he turned to run back to the road, but he slipped on the loose gravel and fell back into the ditch.

Nothing had seemed normal all day and now Bob let all his anxieties work their way out in this natural savage urge he felt toward this threatening enemy who was bearing down on his master. He bounded across the ditch and met the dog with his wide jaws open. Although the blue tick was faster than Bob, he was no match for the strength of a bulldog. Pushing his way underneath the hound's belly, Bob's strong teeth tore into soft flesh.

J. P. scrambled out of the ditch. Frantically, he forced himself to move toward the melee. He tried to grab Bob's back legs but he wasn't strong enough to budge them. When he tried to pull the blue tick away from Bob, the enraged dog tried to sink his teeth into J. P.'s arm. "Stop. Stop, Bob," he yelled over and over as he continued to try to separate the dogs with his trembling hands. But Bob was oblivious to his commands. In only a few minutes the fight was suddenly over. The blue tick fell on his side. His throat was torn open.

The dogs and J. P.'s shouts had brought Mrs. Kepper out of her house, and when she saw what had happened on the road, she, too, began screaming as she ran toward them. Grabbing Bob behind his neck, J. P. dragged him backward away from the dead hound. Mrs. Kepper swooped by them and knelt on the ground beside her dog. Lifting her head, she looked over at Bob. His folded face and squared white paws were covered with blood; his parted mouth revealed cherry-stained teeth. Panting heavily, Bob sat docilely beside J. P.'s feet, and when J. P. didn't reach his hand down to stroke him as he usually did, the dog looked up at him, seeming to wonder why he hadn't been praised for saving his master.

Mrs. Kepper lifted a shaking arm toward Bob. When the dog lifted his head to her, J. P. held him tighter by the heavy folds of skin around his neck. "Stay, boy. Don't move," he said, wanting to run away as fast as he could himself. But running wouldn't change anything, and he stood holding the dog, waiting.

She walked a few steps closer. Her yellow and white hair, knotted on top of her head, fell around her pale face, splotched with blemishes, the ugliest white face J. P. had ever seen. Squinting her colorless eyes at him, her mouth twisted into a squiggly line. "Boy, this here was a prime huntin dog. Blue tick. You know that?"

J. P. shook his head. He hadn't had time to notice what kind of dog Bob had fought.

Mrs. Kepper swung her finger at Bob. "You got a killer dog there."

J. P. opened his mouth. He wanted to say, *He ain't no killer, that dog just came at him too suddenlike.* But he knew better. A dog who had killed another dog would do it again. As young as he was, he knew that.

Mrs. Kepper drew herself up against the setting sun behind her back. "Here come Mister Kepper. He'll deal with this."

J. P. wheeled around, surprised to see Mr. Kepper getting out of his truck. He hadn't seen or heard the truck pass behind him. He watched as the big man walked toward his wife. J. P. felt some relief; this was one of the men who had wanted to hear his tale about Memphis, but then he saw the outraged look on Mr. Kepper's face when he looked down at the dead hound, and he knew that he was only the owner of a killer dog now.

Mrs. Kepper grabbed her husband's arm. When she had blurted out her version of the massacre, she turned around to J. P. and said, "There's the dog that done it. I saw it with my own eyes. Blood all over him, as you can see."

Mr. Kepper walked over to where Bob and J. P. waited, and with his boot, he kicked the dog hard on his right flank. Bob yelped, looked up to J. P. for help. "I said that was a mean dog when I seen him back at Johnny Moore's." He turned to J. P. "You know how much money your dog just chewed up with his ugly face?"

"He scared him," he whispered.

"What's that?" Mr. Kepper yelled.

J. P. shook his head and kept silent. There wasn't any use pleading Bob's case, especially to a white man.

"Wait here," Mr. Kepper said, walking off toward his house. Mrs. Kepper opened her mouth, then closed it and followed her husband across the yard.

J. P. thought about running, but there wasn't any use in that. The

Keppers would find him, and they'd find Bob, too. Still, he looked long-ingly down the road toward home. The sun seemed to be running down the sky now, escaping with its light beyond the fields. It shot out beams of reddish orange light over the tops of the scrub oaks in front of the Keppers' house, and behind the trees the house took on an unnatural golden glow. In the dimming light, J. P. squatted down beside Bob. He stroked his head, scratched behind his drooping ears. "You done wrong, Bob," he whispered. "I know you didn't know no better, but you gonna have to pay for it now." Bob nudged his head into J. P.'s leg, hiding his face, as if he knew what the tone of the voice meant. "You was always a good . . ." J. P.'s voice broke off. He stood up. He heard Memphis' small voice rising across the space between them. "Now I lay me down to sleep. Thank you for this food." Then J. P. heard the crunch of gravel be-neath Mr. Kepper's boots.

"Step out of the way, boy," Mr. Kepper said, raising the tip of the big double-barrel shotgun.

J. P. jumped across the ditch, and stood on the road. Bob rose up from the ground and turned to follow him. "Stay," J. P. commanded. And Bob stopped, looking confused, as if he were unsure of what he was sup-posed to do next. J. P. looked away from him, stared at Mr. Kepper's stub-bled chin, then at the hairy knuckles that held the gun. He watched the puffy index finger crook around the trigger. The knuckle whitened a split second before the explosion.

Without looking at Bob or Mr. Kepper, J. P. moved forward, picked up his bag, and began the half-mile walk home. He thought about his mama. She was gonna be waiting for the sugar she needed for Memphis' funeral cake. And as he walked on in the twilight down the newly widened road, J. P. felt he was coming home from a very long journey from a distant land. He began to quicken his pace, walking faster and faster. When he finally saw the silhouette of his house outlined in the pink sky, his bare feet were skimming over the ground so fast, it seemed to J. P. he may have lifted off the ground and flown through the open doorway into his mama's arms.

Chapter 19

RUTHIE KNELT ON THE FLOOR BESIDE HER BEDROOM WINdow. Resting her elbows on the sill, she gazed up into the nighttime sky where God had placed the stars in perfect patterns. The moon, hanging above the water oak in the front yard, cast its pale silver light on the walk leading up to the porch where Memphis had sat on her lap playing cat's in the cradle with a piece of string. She bowed her head. "Please help me to understand why You took Memphis." Lifting her eyes to the moon, she imagined God's hands shaping its circumference, forming its craters with His fingerprints. After creating the universe, it was His breath that had given life to man. Why had He taken away the life of an innocent child? Did He have a plan, a purpose that humans could never understand?

She had believed God had a plan for her when she was in Miss Sherman's fifth-grade class. She thought that what had happened to her on the night when she was locked in Pisgah Church meant that she was special. When she was ten, Ruthie had imagined that in the reindeer herd, she stood out like the red-nosed Rudolph, and God had chosen her over all the others to drive His sleigh. But as time passed Ruthie began to have doubts. Why would God choose her, and if He had, what did He expect from her? She had searched the Bible for clues. God talked to a lot of people in the Old Testament, and there were many words of guidance from Jesus when He was on earth in the New Testament, but none of it seemed relevant.

Ruthie was twelve when she had finally tried to talk about her doubts.

She and her mother were sitting on the rockers on the back porch. "Remember that night when y'all thought I was kidnapped?" she asked.

Her mother looked up from the baby bootie she was crocheting for Dana Mills' upcoming baby. "Hmmmm?"

"You know, when I got locked in the church."

Her mother smiled. "Oh, of course. You were so scared, and so was I really." She lifted her plastic needle. "What about it?"

"Did y'all ever figure out how I got those holes in my head?"

"Holes? Well, you did have some little punctures. They weren't all that deep. Probably bumped your noggin on something or other. Why?"

Ruthie shrugged. "No reason. I've just always wondered about it." She had decided then that there was no use talking to anyone else. If her own mother hadn't cared how she got those holes, who else would?

A Catholic priest might. She remembered the picture of a bloodied Jesus that Betsy McCosker had passed around the fourth-grade class. The Romans didn't sugarcoat suffering like the Methodists. And a priest would be a safe confidant. She had heard that they weren't allowed to tell what they learned from the sinners who spoke to them in a wooden booth, which Ruthie envisioned as a kind of penalty box you had to go in when you were out of bounds in a game of kick ball. She would never confide in Brother Thompson, who had been known to tell secrets if you had him over to Sunday dinner. But Catholics were different; they knew how to keep their mouths shut.

Father McCormick was older than Preacher Thompson. When he opened the door to his office and beckoned her inside, his round stomach and white beard reminded her of pictures of Santa Claus. Ruthie had imagined he would be wearing a floor-length black outfit, but he was dressed in a fairly ordinary-looking dark suit with a round white collar. Following him into his office, Ruthie was disappointed to see that it, too, was quite ordinary. Apparently, she was not going to go to the penalty box and was supposed to tell him her secret sitting in the one small chair in front of his blond wooden desk. But the familiar surroundings didn't take away her anxiety. She had entered Roman territory. When she forced her eyes to meet the priest's, he smiled, and Ruthie took courage, found her voice, and plunged into her story.

After she had recounted everything she could remember about her experience in Pisgah Church, Father McCormick sat staring up at the tall bookcases that lined the side of his office. "You are not of our faith, so it may be hard for you to understand some of what I have to tell you. No one can truly know the will of God; priests are called by Him to help our parishioners receive the sacraments, absolution, be closer to Him." Ruthie hadn't known what a parishioner was or the meaning of *absolution*, but she nodded as if these were everyday words. "God can certainly appear to those in need, speak to us through dreams, and there are cases—" He paused. "—cases of actual miracles occurring in modern times. But most likely your fear caused you to imagine Jesus and His words."

Ruthie swallowed. He wasn't going to be much help. "But what about the blood from the holes on my head? Isn't that a sign that a person is a saint?"

Now the priest's smile reappeared. "Stigmata." He reached for a gray clothbound book behind him. The binding was frayed; the yellowed pages crackled as he flipped through them. When he had found the page he sought, his index finger traced down a column of names, dates, and figures. He lifted his eyes to Ruthie's face. "There are records of more than three hundred stigmatics, people who bleed from the wounds similar to those of Christ on the cross. Wounds from the palms and feet are most common, but there have been instances of forehead punctures like those on Jesus arising from the crown of thorns." He tapped the page before him. "Saint Francis of Assisi is probably the best-known saint who was given the stigmata, but there have been many cases of females who received it, like Saint Marie de Moerl, who bled only on Thursday evenings and Fridays. Blessed Margaret Mary Alacoque is one who bled from the crown of thorns like you described." Father McCormick closed the book, replaced it on the shelf, and then walked to Ruthie's chair. He put his hand on her shoulder. "Ruthie, all these saints lived unusual lives, spectacular ones in their devotion to God. The likelihood of your having stigmata is extremely remote. You mother is probably right. You hit your head on something." He squeezed her shoulder tighter. "You haven't had any more of these visions or incidents of bleeding since that one time, have you?"

"No. So, it would happen more than once if it were true?"

"Probably, but I think the important thing to remember here is that you felt close to God, that you desire to receive His love and forgiveness. That's what matters."

Ruthie had left the church disappointed, reluctant to give up the idea that she was chosen by God to become a saint. But within a month she had sinned by lying, masturbating, and coveting Sarah Young's C-cup bra. And during every Sunday service and Wednesday-night prayer meeting, she would stare up at the cross, waiting for a sign from Jesus that she was forgiven, that she was special to Him. But He hadn't appeared, had not spoken to her even once.

Six years had passed since then. She had gone on with her life, saying the Lord's Prayer, singing about salvation, and joining Pisgah Church as she was expected to. But none of life's routine had erased her longing for comprehension. She rose from her knees and wiped her tears with her forearm. God wasn't talking and that was that. He took Memphis, and He wasn't going to say why. She was ordinary, not a saint, not chosen, and not privy to God's plan—if He had one.

Tomorrow she would go back to summer school. She had graduated from Zebulon High the week before and had taken a typing course just to be with her boyfriend Dennis, who had failed Mr. Donaldson's chemistry class. Tomorrow she would place her fingers on the black keys, watch the letters strike the white paper curled around the black cylinder, and she would hammer out the words given to her, the nonsensical words that now seemed appropriate in a world without order. She would finish her timed test scoring seventy-plus words per minute, she would meet Dennis, and his eyes on her breasts would be the only truth she could be sure of.

It was late; she should go to bed, but she was restless and she doubted she would sleep. Ruthie lifted her left hand, weighted with Dennis' gold class ring wrapped with a wad of white adhesive tape that kept it from slipping off her finger. It signified to all the other girls who wanted him that he belonged to her. She remembered all the nights the summer before her senior year when she had lain in bed, listening to Johnny Mathis records, dreaming of Dennis, fantasizing his lips soft against hers. When school began in the fall, Myra Addison was wearing his ring, and Ruthie had prayed nightly for them to break up. Her prayers were answered three days before the homecoming game when Dennis called her and told her that he and Myra were quits. He figured she had a date to homecoming already, but he thought she was cute and fun and was there any chance?

She twisted Dennis' ring around on her finger, remembering how badly she had felt about breaking the date with George, her good friend since eighth grade, but that night had been worth the guilt. Dennis had arrived at her door with a pink carnation wrist corsage that perfectly matched her low-waisted, ballerina-length dress. In his dark blue suit and white shirt, Ruthie thought that he looked like Rock Hudson. He was shorter, but he had the same wavy dark hair, straight white teeth, tanned skin. In the gymnasium, gliding beneath the purple and gold balloons, Ruthie felt the envy of nearly every girl who danced beside them, their arms wrapped around their plain boyfriends with reddened necks squirming inside tight collars. Dennis wore his suit like a tuxedo, and Ruthie especially liked the way he flipped back his jacket before moving toward her when they danced. He was sure of himself, not at all like the nervous, pimpled George, whose palms sweated when they danced. Dennis' palms were cool and dry, and when he wiggled his third finger against her hand in the code for wanting her, Ruthie had looked up into his eyes, saying yes with hers.

Lying back on her pillow, Ruthie closed her eyes. She had said no to him later when she sat beside him in his dark green Ford that night. They had parked in the woods by the Rennick Place, and as soon as Dennis had turned off the engine, he reached beneath the seat and brought out a pint of Jim Beam. "Let's toast to homecoming, to winning against Tylertown." He took a swallow and handed her the bottle.

She remembered her cousin Catherine saying that guys tried to get girls drunk so they could take advantage of them. "I don't like whiskey," she said, "but you go ahead if you like it. I'm not a prude, a Goody Two-shoes, or anything."

And she had decided that first night that it was the Jim Beam that made him try to put his hands on her breasts after she had kissed him only once. She had pushed his hand away, but his touch had stirred a desire within her that had frightened her nearly as much as his anger when she asked him to take her home. Beside her bed that night, she had knelt and asked God for His help. "Please take away these feelings, but please let him call me."

God had granted only part of her request. Dennis had called her, apologizing for his temper, but her passion for Dennis had grown more intense. Now Ruthie leaned over and picked up the gold Seth Thomas clock Dennis had given her for Christmas. "To mark the time until we get married," he had said, but they weren't going to get married for a very long time. Lying back on her bed, she set the clock on her stomach, pressing it against her navel. She watched the second hand circumnavigate the Roman numerals: V, VI, VII. Time. How she hated the idea of time. Either it went too fast or too slowly. Why couldn't she have a minute that would last an hour when she stood at the door saying good night to Dennis? Why couldn't the years speed by until she would be old enough to marry? Sex wasn't a sin if you were married. But if you weren't married! God was sure to punish her if she went all the way. He was capable of vengeance; this Ruthie was sure of. She didn't know why or who God was punishing when He took Memphis from them, but she remembered reading the scripture that said, "The wages of sin is death." Ruthie set the clock back on her nightstand and knelt beside her bed. "Lead me not into temptation, deliver me from evil. You have the power and the glory, Lord. You've just proven that to everyone on Parsons Place."

Rising, she slid beneath her covers and closed her eyes. Tomorrow she would be with Dennis again, and when he kissed her and told her he loved her, whispered how much he wanted her, it would be he, not God, who possessed the power and the glory forever amen.

Chapter 20

CROW RAN ACROSS THE PASTURE, SIDESTEPPING COW PILES, dodging the long-horned Angus bull, scowling at the numerous Jerseys who followed her movements with their dark eyes. When she reached the pine grove, she stood panting beneath the tall pine where J. P. and Memphis had sat only a few weeks earlier. Sinking down onto the pine needles, she drew her legs up to her chest, and, resting her head on her knees, she cried for the first time for Memphis, for Icey, for herself.

She had stood dry-eyed at the tiny grave, watching Icey's display of grief without emotion. Tee Wee slapped her hard during the wake when Crow said that now Icey and Deke would have one less mouth to feed. After the funeral, when Ruthie tried to encircle her in her arms, she pulled away. "What do you care about Memphis? Now there's just one less nigger in this big ole white world to worry about." Ruthie had reacted just as Crow would have predicted. She had patted her arm. "I understand," she said although, of course, she didn't understand, could never understand one damn thing about being black.

Crow wiped her damp face with the hem of her sundress. She was glad it hadn't been J. P. who had fallen from the fence. J. P. was special. He was smart, way smarter than stupid Ernestine, who had come home for the funeral from over there in Alabama. Even though Ernestine had a college degree to be a teacher, she had married that loser Willie, had two squalling babies, one on each hip, and now her husband had run off to New Orleans. Ernestine had tried to impress everyone with her news about the bus strikes and fighting for civil rights and the great orator and preacher Dr. King who was gonna change the world. "We got desegregation way back in nineteen fifty-four, and our children are still going to separate schools. You got to stand up for yourselves. Vote for somebody who will see that the law is carried out," Ernestine had said to them on the day after Memphis' funeral. Masie and Lester had ignored her. Lester had dropped out of school after failing sixth grade twice, and Masie wasn't making A's in eighth. But J. P. had listened to Ernestine. Later that night Crow had found him sitting on the floor playing with the Tinkertoy set Mrs. Parsons had given him. He was building a bus for coloreds, he told Crow. "A bus can't no white folks ride on," he said in a grown-up voice.

Crow walked out of the grove toward the pond. She felt her throat closing and tears forming again. Poor J. P. He had lost both Bob and his best friend within twenty-four hours. She had seen him slip the little whistle Memphis wanted so badly into his coffin. He had told Tee Wee that Memphis could blow it in heaven now. Crow stopped and looked up into the gray sky. Heaven. Behind that gray was just more black clouds. There wasn't no streets paved with gold up there. The only gold any of them was gonna see was what they earned with the sweat of their backs. When she reached the pond, she sat on its bank and tossed a few pebbles into the water. As she stared at the whirling water, she thought how most folks lived their lives like small pieces of rocks, going in little circles round and round until they became nothing and evaporated into the air. She stretched her hands out from her side, and when her fingers closed over a large rock she snatched it up and threw it into the muddy water. A great jet of water rose up before the stone sank to the bottom of the pond. That's me, she thought. That rock. I ain't going down with a little ripple; I'm gonna make a big splash before I sink.

She looked toward the house. She was supposed to be ironing, cleaning, doing all of her own chores and Icey's, too, because she hadn't left her bed since Deke and Tee Wee had carried her home from the burial. Crow knew Tee Wee expected her to give Icey the money she earned for doing her work. Maybe I will and maybe I won't, she thought. She was so close to having enough to escape. She would have left already if Tee Wee hadn't moved the tobacco can from the old chest in her room. But soon she would have enough to leave. She would move up north to sing in fancy nightclubs; she would make records and so much money she'd never have to clean toilets in a white person's house ever again. Someday she would leave this stinking place.

Crow stood and brushed the dirt from the dress Tee Wee had made from coarse flour sack material. She'd go down to the Parsons' now and iron their fancy clothes made of the soft fabrics she would buy for herself one day. She had counted $332 dollars in the pile hidden in the hole beneath the rag rug, but she figured she needed an even $500 to start her trip. "Five hundred," she said with each step she took across the pasture. And I'll get it from Browder and them black men I visit. By September I'll have all of it. She walked on, a smile on her face, her face dry and cool in the early-morning breeze. By the time she reached the Parsons' back porch, she had left her tears in the pond, her grief in the pine needles; she would keep nothing in her heart now. It was drained, hollow, and light; it felt just right.

Crow saw that the heavy round ball of sheet-enshrouded clothing wasn't on the kitchen table, and she knew that Browder had carried it to the sewing room where he was waiting for her. She slipped into the Parsons' bathroom. Closing the door, she leaned against it for a moment before walking to the sink. After splashing cold water on her face, she scrutinized her image in the mirror. At nineteen she believed she had finally grown into her intended beauty. She was tall and straight-backed, with a fine round butt she carried high in the air. Her ebony skin wasn't ashy like Luther's and Tee Wee's, but shiny and oiled looking. Her almond-shaped eyes were fringed with long straight lashes, and she knew her full brown lips were perfect in the setting of her oval face.

When Crow sashayed down the hall and entered the small sewing room, she pretended she didn't see Browder sitting on the floor just inside the door. Bending over to plug in the iron, she felt his eyes on her, and, quickly turning around, she widened her eyes as though greatly surprised. "Browder! You up early for a college boy, ain't you?"

"Mama woke everybody up early with her coughing. I carried your ironing in."

Crow looked over at the big pile. Why couldn't these people wear something a few times before they threw it in the laundry bin? She moved behind the ironing board, lifted the iron, and spat on its shiny metal base. As she watched the spittle sizzle, she said, "Ain't you gonna hunt for a job this summer?"

Browder looked across the room. She followed his eyes to his mother's dress mannequin wearing a bodice with no skirt. It stood like a sentry near the door beside the Singer treadle sewing machine. Beneath the machine, patterns, bits of cloth, colored threads, and shiny pins were strewn about in chaotic disarray. A one-legged pair of pants was draped over the chair. "I guess I will," he said at last. "So much going on since I came home from Ole Miss, I haven't had much of a chance to look for work."

Crow reached inside the mound of clothes and drew out one of Mr. Parsons' white shirts. "What you studyin to be? If you could be anythin, what would you be?"

Browder lifted his eyes to her. She rose up like an apparition in the cloud of steam from the heavy iron she was wielding. She lowered her eyes to her work, knowing that Browder was admiring the curve of the muscle of her arm, her lashes against her ebony face, her pink tongue when she parted her lips. "I'm majoring in business, but I hate it. What I'd really like to do is learn how to make movies. That'd be the life, you know?"

Crow flipped his father's shirt off the board and hung it on a wire hanger. She reached into her pocket, drew out a Lucky Strike, and lit it. Cigarette dangling from the corner of her mouth, she took up a lace doily and began to move the heavy silver-and-black iron over it. Breathing deeply, her breasts rising, she inhaled the mingled scents of boiled starch, perspiration, and tobacco. "I know what I'm gonna be."

"What?"

"A singer." She hummed a few bars before she sang. "Well, since my baby left me, I got a tale to tell." She stopped and laughed. "I ain't Elvis, but I can sing."

"Go on," Browder urged. "More."

After she sang the chorus of "Heartbreak Hotel," he clapped his approval, and she took a little bow over her board. Now, she said to herself. Now is the time to get what I want out of old stupid Browder. Snuffing the cigarette out in the small ashtray on the windowsill, she turned and snatched a pair of Ruthie's shorts from the laundry pile. Shaking them in the air between them, she drew her brows together and frowned.

"What's the matter, Crow?"

She shrugged. "Usual, just the usual."

Browder rose and walked over to her. "Maybe I can help."

Crow fitted one leg of the checked shorts on the board. "Doubt it. You ain't got a job, so you ain't got no money, has you?"

He placed his hands on the board, making it jump a little on the linoleum floor. He laughed. "So it's money again, huh? Always cash with you, Crow. What do you do with all your money anyway?"

"None of your business," Crow said, holding the iron up over his left hand.

He jerked both hands from the board. "Okay, okay. So, you don't want to tell me, but you're hoping I can help you out, aren't you?"

Crow set the iron back on its metal plate. "Yeah, I'm thinkin I could earn a few extra dollars." She met his eyes. "I ain't too particular about what I got to do to get it." Browder's skin turned a bright pink; he was breathing shallow and fast. Crow kept her eyes steady, her mouth tight. She lifted her hand and rubbed her palm against her right breast. Still staring into Browder's eyes, she cupped both breasts and leaned forward.

Slowly, almost involuntarily, Browder stretched his hand across the board. Crow took it and laid it on her breast. As his thumb moved against the thin fabric over her nipple, Crow kept her dark eyes on Browder's face. "Well?" she whispered.

"Anything? You'd do anything to get money?" His voice was hoarse.

Crow pushed his hand away, picked up the iron again. "I already said that, but it don't matter. You ain't got no money." She slapped the iron down on the bright material.

"I got some." He was nearly shouting. Then lowering his voice, he said, "How much?"

She didn't look at him. "Twenty-five dollars."

Browder turned away and walked toward the mannequin.

Crow began singing again, "Well, since my baby left me . . ."

Browder punched the half-dressed mannequin in its stomach and watched it fall backward into the wall. Crow sang on, "I got a new tale to tell."

"Shut up. Wait a minute." Browder lifted the dummy back to its upright position. He straightened the bodice. "I'm thinking," he said in a little-boy voice that told Crow she'd get twenty at least.

"How long would you stay with me? For that kind of money, I'd expect time."

Crow smiled. Carefully, she smoothed the ironed creases of the pair of shorts. "After everybody's asleep, I got all night to myself."

Browder ran his hands over the mannequin's breasts. "When?"

"When you show me twenty-five dollars."

Browder walked back to her; his eyes were on her breasts. "I'll get it. And I'll get it quicker than you think."

Crow stood behind the ironing board until he left the room. Then she walked around it, and holding her arms out wide, she spun around

the room. "Twenty-five," she whispered. "I should of asked for more."
She threw her head back and watched the light globe spinning above her.
Opening her mouth wide, she laughed, and, lifting on her toes, she
twirled faster and faster until she fell dizzily against Mrs. Parsons' sewing
machine. "I'll give him his money's worth," she said to the mannequin.
"That Browder, he always gets a good deal."

Chapter 21

HE NIGHT AIR WAS HEAVY WITH THE SCENT OF GARDENIAS, magnolias, and the tea roses that lined the side of the Parsons' house. The humidity and stillness of the evening held the perfumes close, and Icey's hands, wet with perspiration in the stifling heat, slipped on the wagon handle she pulled along behind her. She turned and looked back toward the paint-chipped slats. "Hold on, now, Memphis, we got tree roots up ahead. Don't want you bouncin out, gettin yourself hurt." She struggled with the wagon, hauling it forward over the rutted ground toward the back pasture. Icey had lost weight, and her blue nightgown hung in dips and folds over her shrunken bosom. The cotton cloth dragged the ground, and occasionally she stumbled when her bare feet stepped on the uneven hem. Still she persisted, panting short feeble breaths. "Almost there now. We gonna see Jesus and His lambs pretty soon." She leaned over and adjusted the blankets she had piled in the wagon. "Suffer the little children to come unto to me. That what He say." Resuming her path, she sang, "Jesus loves me. This I know for the Bible tell me so."

When she reached the barbed-wire fence, Icey didn't retreat, but lunged forward, pushing her chest into the wire. Although the barbs caught in her gown, she continued thrusting her body forward until tiny dots of blood stained the thin material. Impervious to her pain, she threw herself harder against the strong wire, yelling until she grew hoarse. "Satan, get away. We goin forward. You can't stop us with your pitchfork. Getawaygetawaygetaway." When streams of blood began running in small rivulets down her stomach and legs, she grunted and dropped the wagon tongue in the grass. "Gotta get through," she said, and, lifting her hands to the top strand of wire and digging her heels in the ground, she pushed against the fence with all her weight. The barbs dug deeper into her coiled hands. Lifting her head to the nighttime sky, she searched the constellations for a solution to her problem. She saw the shape of a goat overhead; there was the answer. She would be a goat and butt the Devil out of her way. Stepping back, she lowered her head and charged the fence. When she hit the fence, Icey saw the Devil lifting his pitchfork. The top strand dug into her forehead, the second gouged her throat. She staggered backward and fell to the ground. "Memphis," she whispered. "Jesus?"

TEE WEE DIDN'T HEAR Deke's knock on the screen door. J. P. was wrestling with Lester on the living room floor; Masie was screaming at Crow, who was singing about blue suede shoes, and the yard dogs were barking at a cat. When she finally heard his call, she hurried from the back bedroom where she'd been altering a dress for Masie. "Deke, come on in. Luther's down at the Dunaways helping with a droppin cow." She yanked J. P. up by his arm. "You children get in the back. Crow. Masie. Y'all hush up."

Deke's eyes swept over the room. "I'm looking for Icey. She ain't in the house."

Tee Wee's hand flew to her forehead. "Oh, Lord. She ain't over here. Ain't been out since the funeral, has she?"

"No, and neither me nor Glory seen her go out. She was in bed last we saw, didn't eat no supper again."

Tee Wee frowned. "I got a feelin. I spect she done gone down to that gate. She was mumblin yesterday about Jesus bein down there." She turned. "I'll get my shoes."

Following Deke across the field, Tee Wee struggled to keep up with his long, fast strides. Her voice bumped in uneven waves. "I been some worried about Icey. Reckon you is, too."

Deke didn't answer, but quickened his pace.

"Her mind done come unraveled like yarn. Her thinkin just strung out, not makin no sense." Tee Wee stumbled and grabbed Deke's arm. Looking down to her feet, her eyes fell on Icey's Bible. "Yes, she come this way. Here her book," she said, stooping over to pick it up. She wiped the cover and then handed it to Deke.

"She ain't let this book loose since I brought her home from the funeral. Something bad wrong."

In the moonlight Tee Wee could see the fear in his eyes. Her own breath sounded like thunder in her ears.

When she spotted the wagon, Tee Wee for a moment thought that Memphis must be down here, too, hauling kittens in his wagon like he so often did. Deke called Icey's name, but there was no answer.

They found her on the ground nearby. Tee Wee screamed when she realized the dark puddles on Icey's gown were blood. "She done killed herself," she cried.

Deke knelt down beside his wife. "No, she talking. She's alive."

Tee Wee leaned over them. Icey, was mumbling something about Satan. "Oh, thank You Sweet Jesus. She awright. She hurt bad, though."

"Yeah. Get the Parsons to call the doctor."

Tee Wee heard his words, but she was already several feet away, running toward the Parsons' back porch.

ICEY OPENED HER EYES and looked around the room. She wasn't lying in her own bed. Her gaze swept past her feet, covered in a yellowed patched sheet, to the metal bedstead across the room. An old woman with white hair propped up on pillows stared back at her. "Who you?" Icey tried to say, but her voice was only a whisper and her throat burned with the effort. She raised her bandaged hand to her neck, felt more thick bandages there. She was hurt! Her fingers walked up the side of her neck to her face, where she felt bandages across her forehead, too. Her head throbbed with her movement.

The old woman was staring straight into Icey's face. She's a witch, Icey said to herself. A witch sent to cast a spell on me. Some of Tee Wee's doins most likely. But where was she? Carefully turning her head, she looked to her left. A dirty green wall, a wall she had seen before. She recognized the paint chips along the top. They looked like white ears of corn growing high on a stalk. Icey rotated her head in the other direction. There she saw the row of empty iron beds just like the one the old woman was resting on. Now Icey remembered. She was in the hospital, in the very room where Glory had stayed after her appendix operation. Had she had an operation, too? She didn't care if she had. She closed her eyes and drifted back into a warm darkness.

When she opened her eyes again, she saw Tee Wee's big round face hovering over her. She smiled. "You awake. I said you'd wake up pretty soon."

Icey frowned. She was talking too loud, making her head hurt again.

"Yes siree, I telled that skinny nurse that I'd just come on in and see if you wasn't gonna wake up while your ole Tee Wee was here to visit with you."

Icey lifted her hand and tried to wave Tee Wee's big mouth away from her ear. The pounding in her head was getting worse with her every word. "I knowed you'd be fine. Deke, he thought you was dead, but I said, 'No. That Icey is gonna live.' Praise the Lord." She clapped her hands together on her last word, and now Icey found the strength to scream. "Shut up, Tee."

Tee Wee backed up to the wall. Her eyes narrowed and she drew her black vinyl purse up to her chest. "Well, well. I see your ole self is back."

Icey sighed. She wanted water to cool her burning throat. She pointed to the tray beside her bed. Tee Wee leapt forward. "Water? You wantin somethin to drink?" When Icey nodded assent, Tee Wee poured the water and gently lifted her head for her to sip from the curved glass straw. She managed a few swallows, then pushed the glass away.

"Thank you," she whispered. "What happened to me?"

Tee Wee leaned over the bed. "All's we know is you was down to the Parsons' with the wagon and you was bleedin like a stuck pig when me and Deke founds you."

Icey thought for a minute. She closed her eyes again. Some images floated to her. Memphis' old blanket, a slice of yellow moon, a pitchfork, Jesus' face in the picture of Him with the lambs on the church wall. She was trying to get to Jesus and those lambs, but why had she taken the wagon? "I don't know, Tee. Don't know what I was doin."

Tee Wee patted her hand. "Don't matter none, Icey. You run into that fence. Blood and bits of your nightdress was on it. I reckon you didn't see it in the dark."

The dark. She was running in the dark. She saw the fence. The metal gate. The sheriff's truck. Raising her hands to her ears, she tried to block the noise of the engine, but she heard its roar. She saw it all now. Memphis spinning through the air. Memphis under the truck. He was dead. Her son had been killed, laid out and buried in the cold ground. She moaned aloud. "My boy. My boy." Tee Wee stroked her arm, patted her leg. "Memphis," she cried, holding on to Tee Wee. "My baby is gone, ain't he?"

She rocked in Tee Wee's arms, rocked on while the nurse gave her an injection, rocked until she fell into a soft warmth that wrapped around her body like a blanket and she snuggled into it. Tee Wee kept vigil while Icey slept; she stood against the wall, arms folded across her bosom. She watched the gentle rise and fall of Icey's chest; she wiped her tears with the clean handkerchief she had brought. When the old woman across the room began to laugh an idiot cackle, she tiptoed across the room to the foot of her bed. Slipping her hand beneath the sheet, she grabbed the woman's big toe and twisted it hard. Her laughter ceased immediately. Tee Wee smiled and released her. She wagged her finger in the woman's face. "You opens your mouth again, I'll twists that ole dried-up nigger toe of yours plumb off."

WHEN ICEY WOKE AGAIN, the overhead light was on. She looked across at the old woman and saw that she was curled into a small ball with the sheet completely covering her head. I reckon she got tired of starin at me, Icey said to herself. She ain't no witch. She's just a poor sick ole lady. I knows the truth now. Tears rose in her eyes. She'd never see Memphis again. Not on earth. Not until she went home to Jesus, too.

Icey cried for a long time and then wiped her eyes with her sheet. When a nurse brought in a plate of food, the aroma of greens and fresh corn wafted up from the tray. No, she wasn't gonna die yet. She was feeling hungry now. She was craving something sweet and warm to fill up the hole in her shrunken stomach. She raised herself up in the bed and, leaning forward, lifted her fork and began to eat.

Chapter 22

THE AUGUST SUN WAS WHITE HOT; IT HADN'T RAINED IN MORE than twenty days, and a haze lay over the land. The dry, brown grass along the road swayed in the scorching wind; the hard-packed ground was like cement beneath Crow's bare feet. She stopped walking, and, lifting the hem of her skirt, she wiped the sweat from her face. Dropping her cloth valise on the loose pebbles beside the melting tar of the blacktop road, she considered opening it and taking out her shoes, but she thought of how hard she had scrubbed them with the stolen white shoe polish in Mrs. Parsons' bathroom. She must look clean; that was the important thing. Feet would wash. She lifted her valise, and as she walked on, she began humming the gospel song that she had sung at meeting last Sunday. Although she wasn't sure she believed in God, she loved His music. Now she opened her mouth wide and, throwing her head back, sang the chorus to "Troublesome Waters." "Gently I feel the touch of His hand. Guiding my boat to that better land." She was guided now to Flower, Mississippi, where she believed with all her heart she was destined to find her father.

Destiny. That's what it was, she thought. We go wherever our fate leads us, and this fateful journey had begun when Icey was in the hospital, and Crow had taken over her chores. She had used newspaper to clean the mirrors and windows like Tee Wee had ordered her, and before she crumpled the paper into balls for cleaning, she scanned the headlines. There hadn't been all that much that interested her at first, but gradually she realized that some of the articles were about people who were on television or in the movies, and their lives fascinated her. Then only two days ago, she was led, yes led, she believed, to find the article about a colored man who had been awarded Citizen of the Week by the Flower Chamber of Commerce. The caption read, "Jefferson and Mayor Underwood in front of Jefferson's Eatery." Crow had nearly skipped the story beneath the picture of the handsome Negro dressed in a suit shaking hands with the mayor, but something about the tall man drew her attention. She read that this man's full name was David Jefferson, the same name as her father's. He was the right age, mid-forties, and, squinting closely at the photograph, she saw that he was dark and, his coal-black eyes were almond-shaped like hers. It was him! "Daddy," she'd said. "It's you. I know it."

That night she had taken the paper to her house and hidden it beneath the floorboards with her money. She would go to Flower and find him. Tee Wee would tell her to forget it. She would say, *Baby, if he wanted you to find him, he'd of come down here and got you.*

But we've moved, Crow would argue, and Tee Wee would say that they wasn't that hard to find; he hadn't tried.

Crow heard the whine of a car engine coming up behind her. She turned and waved, hoping for a ride, but the white driver took no notice of her. Her father could have tried to find her, Crow thought. But even if he didn't, he'd be happy to see her, wouldn't he? She remembered him tossing her in the air, coo cooing to her, laughing and smiling as he held her close. A man like that—he would want her to find him. Crow walked on; she hadn't brought any food and her stomach rumbled. She had money. When she reached a town, she would buy a hamburger. She patted her chest, felt the crackle of dollar bills and the newspaper article. She knew what it said by heart.

David Jefferson, a resident of Flower for nearly one year and the owner of Jefferson's Eatery, has single-handedly cleaned up the block between Restin and Tyler Streets. When Jefferson opened his diner for Negroes, the block was littered with bottles, broken bricks, trash, and was rat-infested. The street was an eyesore to the citizens of Flower. But in less than a year, Jefferson has changed all that. On Friday at the courthouse Mayor Underwood named Jefferson Citizen of the Week for his efforts in beautifying his block. Friends, drive down Eighth Avenue and see what Jefferson has accomplished on the block between Restin and Tyler. You will see no trash, no rats, no broken concrete. What you will see are impatiens, bachelor's buttons, and azalea bushes in front of Jefferson's diner, which has been painted bright blue. Jefferson has even purchased a wooden bench for customers to sit outside to admire the beauty while they wait for their delicious ribs, chicken, and wide variety of home-style dinners. Hats off to David Jefferson and a big thanks for making Flower the best little town to live in all of Mississippi.

When she heard the sputtering engine of an approaching vehicle, she flagged down the dust-coated truck. Crow opened the passenger door and smiled at the driver, a man the color of pecan shells, with a grizzled gray beard. "Mighty hot for a little gal like you to be out walkin in the country," he said. "Jump in, gal."

Crow slid in. "You goin anywhere near Flower?"

The man shifted gears and eased back onto the road. "Goin right through it. Better not blink, though, else you'll miss it." Crow wasn't about to miss it. She felt light-headed, weightless. She leaned forward toward the cracked windshield, impatient anticipation pushing the relic truck toward her destination. "Faster, faster," she whispered, urging the truck to keep up with the tempo beat of her dancing heart.

In less than two hours Crow was standing across the street looking up at the bright, yellow sign over the blue wooden door. "Jefferson's Eatery," she read. It was just past lunchtime, and the street was deserted except for two small boys, who looked to be about six and four. They wore faded overalls with no shirts; their bare feet chased a shorthaired white mutt. "Here, Dusty," they called. "Here, boy. C'mere." Crow looked down at her shoes. The dark scuff marks were barely visible beneath the heavy coat of shoe polish. She had washed her feet in a cow trough just outside of town and changed into her best dress behind some blackberry bushes. The navy blue shirtwaist was a hand-me-down of Mrs. Parsons', but the linen collar and cuffs were still clean and as white as Crow's teeth, which she'd rubbed hard with baking soda on her finger back at home. She sucked her stomach in over the wide cloth-covered belt. "Okay, I ready," she said.

Careful to walk slowly so as not to stir dust up on her shoes, she crossed the street toward the diner. The little boys stopped running and watched her with large black eyes and open mouths. Crow smiled, touched her cornrows. She knew she looked beautiful. At the door, her hand shook just a little, but she lifted her shoulders, grasped the knob, and walked inside. There was music blaring from the jukebox. Blues. Little Jimmy Walker's harmonica rang out to greet her. A good sign. Taking a deep breath, Crow inhaled the heavenly aromas of fried chicken, crowder peas, barbecue sauce. Her stomach growled, and she shoved her fist into her midsection. No time to think about food now. Looking around the room Crow saw that the wooden floor was swept clean, the six metal tables were covered with bright red oilcloth, and the chairs were neatly tucked in beneath the tables' sides. The counter, too, was wiped clean. Jars of pickles, pigs' feet, baby corn, and pickled okra stood in a row in front of the metal cash register. Behind the counter she caught her reflection in the spotless mirror. She guessed the café-style door led to the kitchen. "Hello? Hello?"

The door swung forward and a large man, wearing a long white apron stained with barbecue sauce, mustard, and ketchup, walked toward her. His voice was deep. Pleasant. "We're closed. Forgot to put the sign out. Open again at five sharp."

Crow's heart hammered. Another affirmation of her destiny. He hadn't locked the door or put the sign out. "Are you David Jefferson?" she asked. Of course he was. She recognized him from the picture.

"Yeah, I'm him, the owner."

Crow looked away. A fly buzzed over the lids of the jars and settled on top of the register. She looked back at her father. "I don't want to eat. I came to see you."

He wiped his hands on the cloth he held and drew his brows together. "Oh? Well, I'm not hiring any more help. Only need one waitress and that's my wife."

His wife! Crow hadn't once thought about his having a wife. And it came quickly to her that he would have children, too, maybe a daughter, another daughter. The room was quiet now. The music had stopped. "No, I don't want. No, I came to . . ."

He shifted his weight from one foot to the other. He stared at her. His smile vanished. "You are . . . are you? . . ."

Did he recognize her? "Yes, my name is Sharmaine Jefferson, but I'm called Crow, and what I hear tell is you give me that name yourself."

He dropped the cloth, walked to the counter, and stood beside the register. "Crow?" His voice sounded as rusty as the word must have been to him.

Crow reached into the bodice of her dress where she'd pinned her money, and brought out the little folded square of newspaper. She held it out to him. "I saw this in the Zebulon paper. They don't usually print out-of-town news, but it was in there cause your mayor's sister lives in our town."

He took the paper from her hand, but he didn't look at it. "You're Crow?"

"All growed up now, of course."

"Of course," he repeated. Pulling out a chair at the nearest table, he sat down quickly, as if his legs might collapse. He looked up at Crow, still standing beside the counter, then motioned her to the chair across from him.

At the table Crow, avoiding his eyes, stared down at the shaker filled with salt and rice kernels. She fingered the glass pepper shaker. "I know you wasn't expectin to ever see me again, but . . ."

"No, no I sure wasn't." He unfolded the paper, and looking down at his picture beside the mayor, he smiled. "You saw this, huh?"

"Uh-huh. We thought you was in Natchez. But then I read about your diner, and I thought I'd take a run over here, see if you the same man used to be my daddy."

"Natchez. Well, I was there years back. A long time ago. Seems like another life now. It was so long ago."

"Yeah, Mama told me the story bout how you was runnin from the law." His lips tightened and she hurried on. "But you hadn't done nothin really. Wasn't your idea to rob that place. You was drunk and didn't know what you was doin."

His face muscles relaxed; he reached beneath his apron and took out a pack of Pall Malls and a box of Red Ball matches. "That's the truth." He offered her a cigarette and lit it for her. Then, sitting back in his chair with rings of blue smoke circling his head, he told her of the years of flight from one town to another, working for white men who cheated him of his pay. He had intended on going back home someday until he heard from a man he met in Tylertown that Tee Wee had married and moved. And then he had decided to bury the past in his head, if not in his heart. He stubbed out his cigarette in the tin ashtray. "I wanted to come back for y'all. Lord knows, I wanted to, but sometimes it's best to just let go of things. Give up on what you wanted and start over on something new."

Crow couldn't believe what he was saying. "Give up? I don't give up on what I want. Never. It ain't best. If you want somethin really bad, you do whatever it takes to get it. You wait if you has to, but you don't quit tryin for it. Not if you want it." He hadn't really wanted it; that was it. He didn't care enough.

"Crow," he said in a gentle voice. "My Crow. You're still a little ole gal. You don't know about the world and how it beats you down. Beats you quicker if you are a Negro. You got a lot to learn."

Crow shook her head. "That ain't right, neither. I ain't lettin nobody beat me down. White, black, yellow, or red, it don't matter. I fight for what I want." She stood up. "And I'll get it. I'm here ain't I?"

David looked up at her. He slapped his hand on the table and laughed a deep rolling thunderous laugh. "You right. You are most definitely here. How'd you get here anyhow? I didn't see a car out front."

"Walked and hitched. It was hot out there."

David looked at the big rotating fan across the floor. "Not too cool in here, neither. Want something to drink?"

Crow finally smiled. "You got any food left? I ain't ate, and I got money to pay."

David grinned. "I believe I owe you a dinner; just wait till you taste my ribs."

The ribs were delicious. Crow licked the thick, rich barbecue sauce from her fingers and said, "You cook near as good as Mama."

David smiled. "She doesn't do ribs like me." Then he asked Crow about everyone on Parsons Place, and after she had described their lives, he nodded. "I'm glad Tee Wee found another man. You tell her I'm happy for her. Tell her I think about her."

"No! You and me will be a secret. I may tell her someday, but I don't know how she'd feel about me comin here, and I ain't needin her permission." She looked toward the door. "I got to go. Man that dropped me off gonna give me a ride back."

They stood at the door, and after a moment David reached out and pulled her to him. He held her close and whispered, "I'm glad you found me."

Crow stiffened, then relaxed into his arms. "Me, too," she said. "I always knew I'd find you someday. I knew it."

As she stepped into the street, he called out to her. "Crow? Crow, you ever need anything, you let me know. I know I can't make all those years up to you, but you know where to find me now."

Crow grinned and waved. "Yeah, I found you and I ain't gonna lose you again."

—

SHE FLAGGED DOWN the driver of the truck that would bring her home and sat silently beside him. As she watched the streets of Flower fade from view, she placed her hand over her heart where she had pinned the slip of paper bearing her father's address. She had a real daddy now. Closing her eyes, she saw his brown arms lifting her up into the blue sky. "Coo coo, Daddy," she whispered.

Chapter 23

*O*N THE MORNING OF HER EIGHTEENTH BIRTHDAY, RUTHIE slept late. The phone had been ringing all morning, and each time she heard the shrill bell, she covered her head with her pillow and drifted back into sleep. Now she opened her eyes and lay listening to Tee Wee's voice coming from the hallway. "Okay, I'll tell em you RSVP yes to the party and you sorry you didn't call earlier. I writing it down. Good-bye." She slammed down the receiver and, Ruthie heard her say, "RSVP, XYZ. Why they got to put that on the invites they sent out? I got enough to do in my kitchen without runnin out here to this telephone every fifteen minutes."

Ruthie yawned. She had stayed up past midnight studying the packet she'd received from Mississippi State College for Women. In less than two months she would pack her new plaid bedspread and matching curtains into her mother's old trunk and drive away from her family, her friends, the room where she'd slept all her life to begin a new life in Columbus, Mississippi.

What are you going to major in? was the question she'd been hearing over and over ever since she had turned in her blue cap and gown to Mrs. Westin behind the high school auditorium stage. She had graduated first in her class, and as valedictorian, she delivered a speech about ships and horizons and rough waters, and now she had no idea as to what direction she should sail her own boat. Her mother wanted her to be a teacher. "If your husband dies, you can always get a job teaching in an elementary school," she'd said the night before.

All during dinner her parents had gone on and on about her career, her future, *her* life, like it belonged to them just because it was their egg and sperm that hooked up one night. When Ruthie had said that she'd thought about training to be a nurse and then going to Africa or South America to be a missionary, her mother had visibly shuddered and said, "Nonsense. You'll get married, have children, and stay right here in Mississippi where you belong."

Ruthie threw back her covers and slid her feet into her slippers. She wasn't going to worry about the future today. Today was her birthday, she had a new dress to wear to her party, and Dimple had volunteered to do her hair in a fancy twist.

Tee Wee told her she'd have to eat cold cereal for breakfast. Every burner on the stove held a boiling pot and the oven was working on a turkey. When Ruthie said she wasn't hungry anyway, Tee Wee turned back to the sink where she was washing greens. "Okay, it's your stomach that's gonna gripe later on. I ain't got time to mollycoddle you with all this cookin for the party tonight."

Ruthie took a banana from the bowl on the table. "I'm sorry you're having to work so hard for my party."

Tee Wee wheeled around. "Oh lordy, I forgot to say happy birthday. I ain't mindin the work. Just worryin to get it done on time. Happy number eighteen."

"Thanks, Tee Wee. I guess I'm a legal woman now."

Tee Wee laughed. "Sure is. You done hit the big number. You go make yourself pretty. Crow comin down to help out for your party, and your mama's gone to town to pick up some surprises for you."

Ruthie knew what the surprise was. She was getting the rest of the luggage set her family had bought for her graduation. Her mother believed in matched suitcases, matched panty, bra, and half-slip sets, brush-and-comb sets, and shoes and purses dyed exactly the same shades. Ruthie wanted a gold cigarette case, but she knew she wouldn't get one. Her mother would have a fit if she knew Ruthie had been smoking for nearly a year now. Dimple had taught her how to inhale, blow smoke out of her nose, make smoke rings and even French curls. Ruthie didn't like to remember what a hard time she'd had learning. The first time she'd smoked nearly a half a pack of Lucky Strikes, she had vomited on the driveway in front of Dimple's house. But she had been determined to be cool like Bette Davis, Ava Gardner, and Kim Novak, who waved cigarettes as they talked and blew white clouds into the air at dramatic moments. And now Ruthie could do all those things. She would throw her head back and watch the spirals of smoke drifting away from her pouting lips and she'd feel sexy and powerful and, most of all, very very mature. She loved to watch Dennis smoke. Slumped against the door of his Ford, with hunched shoulders, he cupped his cigarette in his palm like James Dean and Sal Mineo. Exhaling blue streams, he would stare out the windshield looking into the dark woods where they parked as if he saw something out there that made him feel sad and helpless. Then Ruthie couldn't resist reaching across the seat to touch his face, to turn him toward her, to cover his face with her kisses.

The phone rang again. "I'll get it, Tee," she said, tossing the banana peel into the garbage can. "Probably another RSVP."

It was Dimple saying she was ready to do her hair anytime. "Great!" Ruthie said. "I'll see if I can borrow Browder's truck and, if His Highness lets me, I'll be right over."

The door to Browder's room was closed. Ruthie eased it open and peeked in at Browder, who lay on his back, legs splayed wide on the bed, one hand resting on his white briefs. She stared at the bulging mound beneath his fingers. Dennis wanted her fingers on that spot on his body, and she imagined herself tiptoeing across the room, placing her hand beside Browder's, feeling . . . Her face grew warm and quickly she backed out of the room. Turning eighteen was making her crazy; she had to get control of her thoughts. "Keys," she said aloud. "Get the keys and go to Dimple's." They were hanging on a nail beside the back door.

Tee Wee called out from the kitchen. "Where you off to?"

Ruthie fixed a smile on her face, then turned around. "Oh, I'm going over to Dimple's to get my hair put up. If Browder wakes up, tell him I'll be back in an hour."

Tee Wee leaned against the kitchen table, arms folded over her big chest. "Huh, I spect he won't be outta dreamy land in no hour. That boy can sleep the longest. J. P. is up with the chickens every day." She looked down at the flour-covered table. "He still missin Memphis somethin fierce, though."

Ruthie dropped her hand from the doorknob. "I know. Poor J. P. How's Icey doing? She's been so quiet since she came back to work last week."

"Oh, she be better each day, I reckon. Ain't crazy no more, but the sorrow's got hold of her still and seem like she can't shake it none. Thinks Memphis dying is her fault somehow. I reckon that the way with mamas. I know I felt like that bout Ernestine when she first left all those

years ago. And now look what happen. She got a teaching job, two children, a new man, and in her last letter I read she gonna be comin over to
here for a visit fore too long in their new car."

"I hope she comes before I leave for school."

"She might. I'm sure gonna miss you when you leaves. Ain't gonna
be nobody to get me books to read."

"You can get your own now. We'll go down and get you a library
card before I go. And I'll write to you, so you'll have more letters to
read."

Tee Wee looked away and then waved her arm toward the door.
"You get on with your day. I got to get on with mine."

Even though noon was still hours away, the truck's steering wheel
was too hot to touch. Ruthie rolled down the windows and waited for it
to cool. She was so happy that Dimple had called. It seemed to Ruthie
that Dimple was wired with a higher voltage of the life force than the
other girls she knew, and just being around her made Ruthie feel electri-
fied, too. They had become friends two years ago when Dimple worked
at Gillis' Drug Store, where Ruthie and Catherine hung out after school.
Dimple had just broken up with Troy, was dating Gerald White, and in
the past year had gone through stormy relationships with four other
men. Now she was going out with Walt Powers, the manager of Magnolia Printing where Dimple worked as the secretary and bookkeeper.

Ruthie started the truck and pulled out onto Enterprise Road. She
was especially happy that Dimple would be coming to her party because
her mother had invited some of her dull friends. She felt good about
standing her ground and insisting on inviting Dimple after her mother
had given her the raised-eyebrow, turned-down-mouth look. She and her
mother argued so much lately. After each disagreement, her mother's entire body would sag and she would suddenly look old and tired. Then
Ruthie would become even more angry because she would feel guilty for
being the cause of her suffering. Why couldn't her mother hide things
better? Why did she have to parade her disappointment in her daughter
for everyone to see? Ruthie gripped the wheel tighter. Because she
wanted everyone's sympathy, that's why. She acted like there was something terrible wrong with her; like she was going to die, and, Ruthie
knew, that if her mother found out what she and Dennis were doing
when they parked, she probably would die from shock. Ruthie turned
the radio up louder. "Sixteen candles," she sang. She would have eighteen candles, and she wasn't going to let her mother ruin her birthday.

When she turned into the Butlers' drive, she noticed how badly the house was in need of repair. The yellow paint was cracked and peeling, a rusted drainpipe had come loose and was leaning drunkenly off the side porch, and weeds grew in every crack in the front walk. Dimple's father had run off with a woman from Tylertown when Dimple was only four, and her mother had never remarried. She might not need a man, Ruthie thought, but the house sure did.

When Dimple opened the front door, she said, "Shit, I messed up a nail. Come on in." Her red hair was wrapped around pink sponge rollers; she wore pink pedal pushers, a polka-dotted blouse, and tennis shoes. "So, how's it feel turning the big legal numero?"

Ruthie grinned. "Not bad."

Dimple, flapping her spread fingers up and down on either side of her body, looked like a bird frantic to fly. "Come on in the kitchen. I got the bobby pins and stuff laid out on the table."

Ruthie followed her across the white linoleum floor to the small dinette set wedged in beside an old safe, which held some cracked china and plates that looked like the ones people threw pennies in at the carnival.

Dimple raked a brush down Ruthie's long brown hair. "You doing the hundred strokes every night like I told you to?"

"Uh-huh. And I'm trying that new freckle vanishing cream you told me about, but it isn't working. I tried the lemon juice mixture, too, but every time I go out in the sun, ten more spots pop up." She looked up at Dimple's creamy white skin. Peaches and cream, everyone called her complexion.

"Well, you're cute as a button. I wouldn't worry about a few brown dots. Besides, it's your birthday, and your hair is gonna be gorgeous in a twist. I might even put some beads or little rosettes in if I can find them. What color is your dress?"

"Black." Dimple yanked her hair. "Ouch. It's low cut. I hid it from Mama. She's gonna die when she sees it."

"I'm wearing a green sheath, low cut, too, satin material that cups my butt."

"That'll drive Browder wild. I think he still has a crush on you. I'll never forget that Christmas program when he forgot to sing because he was looking down your dress."

Dimple laughed. "Yeah, that was a scream. I knew he was looking, so I leaned forward and jiggled them a little every now and then."

"I wish I had your nerve. I could never do that in church. I'd feel like

God would come right down through the roof and snatch me up to throw me into hell." The memory of the night she'd had the vision of Jesus on the cross came rushing back. She shivered. "I know Jesus has appeared before sinners to try and save them."

Dimple reached over her shoulder for a bobby pin. "You believe that, don't you?"

"Of course, don't you?"

Dimple frowned. "Well, one time I did. Now I don't know. Seems like an awful lot of bad things happen to good people, and then there's all this judgment about what's a sin. I mean, who told the preacher that wearing a lot of makeup makes Jesus mad? I don't think Jesus cares one whit cause I think He was just a man like everybody else."

Ruthie lowered her head. "Oh, Dimple, don't say things like that. Mama would say that's the Devil trying to win you over through thinking instead of feeling your faith."

"Well, all's I know is I have murdered nobody, stole, or cheated, and people say I'm going to hell. I think they're just jealous cause I have a lot more fun than they do."

Ruthie laughed. "Well, that last part is true. Mama thinks taking cakes to the nursing home is fun." She looked around the small room, noting the Farm Bureau calendar, the wooden rack where mugs dangled haphazardly from their handles. There were dirty dishes in the sink; on the stove she could see the black iron skillet, a white layer of fat floating on top. A mousetrap lay beside a twenty-pound sack of cornmeal. If her mother was right and cleanliness was next to godliness, then Dimple and her mother were both headed to a fiery fate. She felt Dimple's warm fingers against her skin as she pinned the fine strands at the nape of her neck. If only she could feel the way Dimple did, then she and Dennis wouldn't be having so many fights. They'd had a horrible row on their last date.

After the Saturday double feature, they had driven out to the deserted lane beside the Wainwright Place. Dennis parked his Ford beneath a sycamore surrounded by maples, but the shade afforded no relief from the heat. Ruthie had gotten out of the car to walk beneath the canopy of variegated shades of green leaves overhead. Lifting her arms out from her side, she spun around until she fell dizzily against the trunk of a maple tree. "I wish I could see into the future," she said, walking back to Dennis, who was spreading a quilt on the ground beside the car.

"I'll buy you a crystal ball, and you can gaze into it and see us getting married."

"Do you really think we will?" Ruthie said, kneeling beside him on the edge of the quilt.

Grasping her shoulders, he pulled her down. "I know it."

Snuggling against his chest, she had thought how lucky she was to be his girlfriend. Her hand lifted to his cheekbone, and with her finger, she traced the pattern of lines around each eye, his nose, and finally his mouth. He rolled on top of her and kissed her lips. "Mmmm, I love the taste of you," he said.

Ruthie opened her mouth to his tongue. Dennis slipped his hand beneath her skirt and stroked the inside of her thigh. When his hands moved higher, she knew she would soon be lost and that was when the fight began. The same fight they had nearly every time they parked. Dennis saying that if she loved him she would go all the way, Ruthie begging him to understand that she was afraid, that God would punish them for this sin.

"Hey." Dimple tapped her cheek. "Wake up. I'm nearly done. You've been so quiet. Something bothering you?"

Keeping her eyes on the box of pins, Ruthie said, "Yeah, kind of. Dimple, when you first started, you know, having er, doing stuff with boys I mean . . ."

Dimple's fingers stilled in her hair. "You mean having sex?"

"Well, going all the way Dennis calls it."

"Yeah? What you want to know?"

"You didn't feel, well, guilty? Scared? I mean didn't you worry just a little bit about it being a sin?" She quoted her mother, " 'An act reserved for the marriage bed'?"

Dimple patted her hair, pulled out the chair on Ruthie's right, and sat down. "Ruthie, the honest-to-God truth is I never really thought about it. First time, I was just fifteen and it seemed like such a natural thing to do. You live on a farm. Look around at the cows and pigs and goats. We are animals just like them. We're just cursed with bigger brains to know when people are trying to control us, trying to make us live the way they live so they can feel better about their own bad choices. I listened to my body, not the preacher or people like your mama. My body said, 'This feels right, Dimple.' And, Ruthie"—she was nearly laughing—"all men say the same thing that my body said. Easy for others to make you feel guilty about something they all want, too. You think your mama doesn't like to wrap up in that big old antique bed with your daddy?"

Ruthie blushed. "I don't know. Maybe." She was remembering the time she had walked by the closed door of her parents' bedroom. She had impulsively turned the knob, peeked in, and seen her father's naked body rising above her mother's. His head was thrown back, her mother's arms were around his shoulders, her nails digging so deeply into his flesh that tiny drops of blood were visible on his back. Shuddering with unnamed fear, she had quietly closed the door and stood in the hall breathing so loudly she was afraid they would hear her.

Ruthie gripped the kitchen table and pushed the memory from her mind. She wasn't going to spoil her birthday.

Dimple stood up and held a pink plastic hand mirror in front of Ruthie's face. "Forget all that and look at this hair. You're gonna be the most beautiful eighteen-year-old in all of Lexie County."

Ruthie took the mirror and saw a light winking out of her eyes, a light that she hadn't seen before. "Tonight I may be beautiful. But beautiful or not, I know one thing for sure."

"What's that?"

"I'm going to have fun, capital F-U-N."

Chapter 24

ICEY DIDN'T WANT ANYTHING TO DO WITH THE BIG BIRTHDAY party. She didn't feel like watching a bunch of white people flit around the yard like strutting chickens with puffed-up feathers. She didn't feel like hearing Miz Parsons say, "Icey, I believe the punch bowl may need refilling; would you see to it?" Or worse, "Icey, run and get a tissue, an ashtray, a bowl." She stood beneath the water oak holding a stack of blue-and-white-checked tablecloths she was supposed to spread over these ugly plywood tables to fool people into thinkin they was at a dining room table. She looked up to the tree branches where Deke had hung little paper lanterns that was supposed to look like lights. And at her feet sat washtubs dressed up in striped towels that would hold ice and cold drinks. "White people is so worried about how everythin looks," she said aloud. Unfolding a tablecloth, she shook it out across the table, then moved to the next one.

Icey kicked one of the washtubs beneath the tree. She was hot as a firecracker. Pulling a handkerchief from her apron pocket, she mopped her face. That Glory, she thought, she oughta be out here doin this, stead of me. But no, she got herself a big job down to Johnny Moore's store sweepin out cigar butts and wipin up tobacco juice off'n the floor. When Icey jerked a loose thread from one of the cloths, it slid off the table and landed in the dirt. She put her hands on her hips and mimicked Glory's prissy voice, "Glory savin her money to leave here and go somewheres where she can get herself a better life. Like this here life ain't nothin." Stooping over, she picked up the cloth, and gave it a vigorous shake. As it floated down to the table, so did her spirits. Maybe Glory be right, she thought. Since that day in the hospital when she'd realized she would never hold her baby Memphis in her arms again, all her thoughts had centered on how she could have prevented his death. A mama who don't know where her six-year-old son is at night ain't no mama at all, she said to herself. And Tee Wee ain't no better than me. Her J. P. out there leading Memphis in the dark. She shook her head, "No, it ain't nobody's fault, ceptin mine. I am the one being punished for the beds of pleasure I made without bein married. I am the one who did them things for the gold in my mouth."

"Icey?" It was Crow, sashaying across the pasture.

"Yeah? What's you want?"

"I'm coming to help out. Mama said to."

Icey took in Crow's switching hips, her breasts bouncing freely. She looked like a Jezebel, and Icey knew for sure that, if she wasn't one already, she would be soon enough. She'd seen the way Crow would sidle up to men. The way she'd hum and twist around when she knew she was being watched.

Crow's eyes swept the tables. "Cloths are hanging down too low on one side just about every table."

Icey cocked her head to the side. "Look fairly even to me."

Crow began straightening the cloths. "Well, it won't to Miz Parsons. You know she's liable to show up with a yardstick to measure these here drops."

"You right bout that." Here was one thing she and Crow were in complete agreement on. Butter wouldn't melt in Tee Wee's mouth when it came to the Parsons, but Crow, she weren't nothin like her mama. "I got other stuff to see to; you can finish up here," she said to the top of Crow's bent head. She looked over at the house; she didn't feel like listenin to Tee Wee brag about her food right now.

She followed the path to the barn where Deke was fixing the broken combine, then, changing her mind, she veered away and walked along the fence line. Here was where Memphis had taken his last steps and said his last words. But not to her; she hadn't been with him. She had been up at the house, trying to convince Tee Wee she wasn't no thief. She lifted her head to the white-hot sky. "The sorrows You give me, Jesus. How am I to bear these burdens You done laid on my shoulders?" She never cried anymore, but she felt the weight of an ocean of tears sitting on her chest. When Deke would try to make her smile with his silly jokes and songs, she never laughed. And when he reached for her in the night, her body wouldn't respond to him. She couldn't remember now how once she'd loved his big shoulders, his long legs, the rippled layers of muscle running down his stomach and across his back. She shook her head to block out the sight of his big pole nudging at her thigh. The last time Deke had tried to make love to her, he had lifted her arms and placed them across his shoulders, but she held them stiff, fists clenched at the wall behind him, and she had rolled away and turned on her side to avoid seeing the pain on Deke's face.

Icey walked all the way to the Grahams' cornfield before retracing her steps toward home. She climbed the sloping hill on the edge of the Parsons' property and stood for a moment surveying the land stretched out before her. From here Parsons Place looked like a tiny play farm set. The two tenant houses with yards swept clean, the big white house, the gray weathered barn could have all been placed by some child's hand to stand neat and orderly within the boundaries of the fences that held the cows and horses, goats and pigs. Looking beyond the barn Icey could see the pond, the woods, the furrowed rows of vegetables in the garden. *"The tomatoes!"* She was supposed to pick tomatoes for the party, and onions, and peppers, too. Tee Wee would be furious with her for holding up her cooking. She ran toward the garden.

Icey was right about Tee Wee's mood; all of the party preparations had put her in one of her red hazes. When she found the two tomatoes Icey had mashed into pulp with her hurrying hands, she had bellowed like the Parsons' old white-faced bull.

Now Icey sat at the kitchen table tying little red bows around the vases of gardenias, marigolds, mums, and snapdragons. Her thick fingers fumbled with the tiny satin ribbons, and she felt like throwing the vases at the wall.

Tee Wee had calmed down some, and now she said in a phony, pleasant voice rising above the water running over the tomatoes, "Did you see Ruthie's hair?"

"No, I ain't seen nobody this day cept your Crow who wanted to tell me I ain't doin a good job with them table coverins."

Tee Wee turned off the faucet. "Well, Dimple Butler put it up in a twist and put some of them red flowers in it. It looks so pretty."

Icey snipped another piece of ribbon from the cord. "Hmmph, that Butler gal! I reckon she know all the white beauty secrets, but she ain't got no husband yet."

"That true. But I hears she got plenty to choose from." Tee Wee, slicing the tomatoes, nicked her forefinger. "Ow! I reckon the Parsons want my blood, too, for this here party," she muttered.

Icey thought Mrs. Parsons wouldn't care if she bled a bucket as long as her silly bows got tied, but she held her tongue, not wanting to add to the fire blazing in Tee Wee's eyes. She returned to the topic of Dimple. "Ain't gonna be nobody wantin to marry Dimple Butler. Why buy the cow when you can have the milk for free? Ruthie best watch out hangin round an older gal like her, sayin Lord knows what. Ruthie be givin free milk, too, if'n she keep listenin to Dimple. Both them lily-white gals gonna wind up with big bellies and no man."

Tee Wee stomped over to the table. "You shush up. Ruthie a good girl." She leaned closer. "Besides, who you to be callin the kettle black, you ole ashy skillet?"

Icey could feel the pain from her chest running up to her throat, the muscles of her face tightening. "You right. I sinned and the Lord made me pay for it."

Tee Wee's face was stone. "I tired of hearin ever bad thing that happen in life is your fault. You just wantin people to feel sorry for you is all."

"Shut up; you don't know nothin bout me."

Tee Wee backed toward the stove. "Now don't go gettin your tail over the dashboard. I ain't mean to upset you none."

"Here lately, just the sight of you upsets me," Icey shouted, waving her arms and knocking over two vases.

Tee Wee smiled. "Oh, so it's me causin you all your misery?"

Icey mopped the spilled water with her apron. "I want you to quit talkin bout me. Stay outta my business. Tend to your own. You think you so perfect. You oughta look at your own house. See that girl of yours; Crow is the Devil with black eyes." As soon as she heard herself, Icey wanted to take the words back, but she knew it was too late.

Tee Wee stood paralyzed at the stove. After a long moment she said in a tone Icey had never heard before, "What you mean—the Devil?"

"I ain't mean nothin. I don't know what I'm sayin half the time."

Tee Wee picked up a wooden spoon and shook it in front of Icey's face. "You know. You tell me. *Now.*"

Icey backed toward the door. "I ain't sayin nothin." Spoon held shoulder-high, Tee Wee marched across the kitchen floor. Keeping her eyes on Tee Wee until she felt the screen door against her back, Icey turned and fled down the back steps. She stood beside the pump house, her breaths coming in short gasps, until she saw Tee Wee's great bulk hurtling down the steps toward her. In her purple apron, huge brown arms stretched out, her tongue thrust forward, she looked like a giant bug about to devour its prey. Icey was the prey. Running across the yard, she told herself that she had lost a lot of weight and was faster than Tee Wee would ever be. But Tee Wee's wrath was propelling her like high-octane gasoline, and before Icey had gotten to the camellia bushes, she caught up to her. Tee Wee's spoon crashed down on her left shoulder. *"Ow! Stop. You hurtin me,"* she yelled. She turned and held up her fists like a boxer; Tee Wee dropped her spoon and landed the first slap on Icey's cheek.

Icey grabbed Tee Wee around the waist and they fell to the ground, both screaming now, rolling over each other's flailing legs. Tee Wee grunted as Icey sank her teeth into her upper arm. Punches and slaps rained on stomachs, faces, butts, and broad backs. When Icey tasted blood, she wasn't sure if it was hers or Tee Wee's.

Neither of them heard Luther's yells over their own. "Y'all gone crazy. Here now. Stop it. Git back, Tee. Icey, move away." Grabbing Icey from behind, he dragged her a few feet across the ground. When Icey looked up at Luther, blanched pale with horror, she thought for a moment that he was a white man. Behind him Tee Wee scrambled to her knees. Blood poured down her face from her right eyebrow. Her apron was hanging down her back, and one sleeve of her dress was torn away. She held her stomach and moaned. Icey lifted her hand to her swollen cheek; her eye felt puffy, and her dirt-streaked arms were tinged pink. She began to cry. "We is both bad hurt, Tee."

Tee Wee began to wail, too. "Oh, God forgive me, Icey. What has we done?"

Luther looked down at his wife. "You done gone crazy, that's what you done."

Icey crawled over to Tee Wee. She grabbed her arm and pulled them both to their feet. Then, turning to Luther, she spit on the ground. "You stay outta this, man. We ain't crazy. We knows what we feel. We felt like fightin, huh Tee?"

Tee Wee squared her shoulders and stretched her neck high. "Yeah, that's right. We got too much to do, we both upset, and a fight just makes you feel good sometime."

Luther shook his head. "That's the dumbest thing you ever said, Tee. That beat all you ever said." He pushed his hat back on his head. "And that go for you, too, Icey. I ain't knowin what this here all about, but I knows one thing and that is I hope I don't never understand it." Luther pulled his hat down and walked back toward the barn.

Icey slid to the ground and Tee Wee slowly eased her damaged body to sit beside her. They sat in silence for several minutes, the space between them heavy with emotion. Icey turned to Tee Wee. "You still mad?"

Tee Wee didn't look at her. "Some. I reckon I'll get over it."

"Me, too. Let's just forget all that was said this here day."

Tee Wee let out a long deep whoosh of air. "I want to. I'll try."

The two of them looked across the lawn to the tables wearing their checked cloths, to the paper lanterns hanging above them. "Look right pretty, don't it?" Icey said.

"Sure do," Tee Wee said. "And them cloths all looks straight to me."

Icey cocked her head sideways, "No, they still whaumpy-jawed on one side."

Tee Wee laid her head against Icey's. "No, they straight." She lightly butted Icey's head. "It's your eye that's whaumpy-jawed. It's swelled up like a goose egg."

"Well, your face got a big knot on it."

Tee Wee chuckled. "I reckon we ain't neither one gonna be none too pretty at the party."

Icey laughed. "What we gonna say to Miz Parsons when she sees us all beat up?"

"I'll just tell her the same thing we told Luther. We needed to fight to feel better."

Icey put her arm around Tee Wee's shoulder. "You know, I'm thinkin you might be right bout that. I believes I do feel better."

Tee Wee hesitated a moment, then reached for her hand and squeezed it. "Me, too, Icey. Me, too."

Chapter 25

RUTHIE SAT HUDDLED ON HER BED HUGGING HER OLD DOLL Josie, rescued from a shelf in her closet. Josie's painted pink cheeks had faded to a light dusting of color, most of her eyelashes were missing, and her cloth body was lumpy and stained. Holding her offered comfort, but Ruthie needed reassurance that no childhood treasure could give.

This morning she and Tee Wee had found her mother writhing in pain on the bathroom floor. She was clammy, her face white as paper. After helping her to bed, Ruthie had called Dr. Matthews, who was in her mother's room now. Each time she had heard her mother's frightened voice rising above the quiet murmurs of the doctor, Ruthie buried her face in Josie's stomach. Why hadn't she, her father, or Tee Wee insisted that she see a doctor before now? During the past weeks her mother had exhibited all the signs of a serious illness: loss of appetite, stomach pain, bowel trouble, and she had lost fifteen pounds.

The door to the bedroom opened; the doctor's voice was louder now. "Monday, I'll schedule the tests and we'll take a look inside, see what's going on."

Ruthie waited until she heard the front door close and then tiptoed down the hall to her parents' room. Her mother lay on her back, glassy eyes focused on the ceiling fan above her. Her fingers moved against her chest as if they held clicking crochet needles. "Mama?" Ruthie stepped into the room. "Can I get you something?"

Her eyes shifted to Ruthie at the foot of her bed. "No. Nothing." Turning onto her side, her back to the door, she curled into a fetal position. Ruthie waited. She wanted her mother to say something reassuring, something that meant their lives would return to normal soon. But she buried her face into her pillow and said, "Turn out the light."

Back in her room, Ruthie raised the window and lit a cigarette. She wished her father were home, but he had gone to the livestock auction in Jackson. Browder was working in town and wouldn't be any comfort anyway. She wanted Tee Wee.

TEE WEE KNEW Mrs. Parsons was hiding her illness, and on the night of Ruthie's birthday party, she had known that she couldn't keep her secret much longer. The party had turned out so nice, too. Mrs. Parsons had told her and Icey to stay in the house because she didn't want everyone seeing their swollen faces, so Crow had served Tee Wee's beautiful cake. Crow had surprised her mother by dressing up and acting happy that she was to be the one to wait on all those white people. Each time she returned to the kitchen for dishes, she delivered short reports on the party. "That Missy Jordan is makin a fool of herself over Browder," she told them. "Dennis and Ruthie are sneakin kisses at their table." After she and Icey had cleaned up the big mess in the kitchen, they had found Mrs. Parsons on the porch, arms tucked into her body, her face contorted with pain.

As she stood on the front steps watching the doctor's fancy sports car turn onto Enterprise Road, she thought that he didn't look old enough to be doctoring a doll. She had seen Ruthie with that old doll of hers this morning; she'd best go see about her.

She found her in her room stubbing out a cigarette in her stolen ashtray. Fanning the smoke away, she lifted her eyes to Tee Wee's face. "Is she going to die?"

Tee Wee sat down beside her on the window seat. Holding back her tears, she said, "It's most likely cancer. Just today I seen the Angel of Death over her bed. The Lord callin her."

"She can't leave me," Ruthie whispered.

Tee Wee took her hand. "Go on; let it out. We cry now. That's all we can do."

Ruthie rested her head on Tee Wee's shoulder. "How will we get through this?"

"The Lord will see to it. He will give us strength. He don't give nobody a burden they can't carry. I reckon I know that. I seen it plenty of times." She managed a small smile. "Besides, once I seen that angel over

Lester's bed when he had the measles, and that old angel just flew off to some other bed, an old old person's bed most likely."

"You don't have to lie. I'm not a baby. I have to face what comes."

"Yes, honey. That's the truth. We all got our crosses to bear in this world, and you gonna have to carry yours, too." She stood, looking down on Ruthie's wet face. "Now I got to see to my peas. You put on a smile for your mama."

MRS. PARSONS FELT BETTER after taking the medicine the doctor had left for her. She didn't eat any dinner, but she shuffled into the living room to watch *The Loretta Young Show*, and she smiled when Ruthie produced the long-lost Josie from behind her back. "Oh, I had nearly forgotten about her. You acted like she was alive when you were little."

Ruthie grinned. "Yeah, she was great company, agreed with me on everything. And she knows all my secrets and hasn't ever told a one of them."

"We all need someone to tell our troubles to," her mother said in a childlike voice.

When Loretta opened the door to the stage set, with skirt swirling around her ankles, Ruthie watched her glide gracefully into her make-believe living room where she stood smiling into the camera, welcoming everyone to the evening's performance. Ruthie wished life mirrored the plots of the show's stories. No matter what crises she faced, Loretta always triumphed over them. If Loretta had cancer, she would be cured by a handsome doctor who would hold her in his arms and they would live happily ever after. Looking over at her mother's pale face, she thought about Tee Wee seeing the angel over Lester's bed, and a surge of anger rose up inside her. She wanted comfort, not superstitious nonsense. Angels didn't hover over beds; they didn't come to take people away, and her mother wasn't going anywhere except to the hospital for a few tests. But then the image of Jesus on the cross in Pisgah Church came to her mind, and she knew that the spirit and physical worlds did merge. She knew it firsthand.

After her mother returned to bed, Ruthie went out to the porch swing and sat staring at the crescent moon. Why had this happened to her mother? Why now? Ruthie wished she could take back some of the words she had said to her when they had last argued about her career. She didn't care about college or what she majored in. She cared about her mother and Dennis. And thoughts of him tangled with worries of her mother until she felt her brain was plaiting into knots.

She squeezed her cheeks between her palms. It had been six weeks now. Six weeks ago Ruthie Parsons had lost her virginity. She was ruined, a sinner, and it came to her now that her mother's illness was the punishment God had delivered for her own sins.

Ruthie pulled a cushion from the chair beside her and nestled back against it. Her thoughts traveled back to the fateful night of her birthday party. Before the guests had arrived, she had stared, disbelievingly, into her mirror. She was transformed! Her new push-up bra gave her cleavage; Dimple's hairstyle made her look older, and the makeup she had borrowed covered nearly all of her freckles. She had told Tee Wee she was an old fusspot when she had said that Ruthie was asking for trouble in that dress.

But Tee Wee had been right. Trouble was brewing, churning around her as she ate her cake, opened her presents, and danced with her guests. Trouble was whirling like a tornado, and she hadn't felt even the stirring of a breeze. It began when Dennis, his checks flaming, had accused her of flirting with Charles Day. Ruthie had tried to laugh it off. "It's my birthday," she said. "I can do whatever I please."

They were dancing to "Love Me Tender," and, as Elvis sang, "Never let me go," Dennis pressed his hand hard against her back. "You're sure not trying to please me."

Ruthie cuddled into his body, played her fingers up his neck. "I'm sorry. You know I love you; I'm just having fun. Maybe I got a little bit carried away."

"Okay," he said, but he hesitated before his body relaxed into hers. And so the storm was quiet, but the tornado was still hovering over her unsuspecting head.

All that night Ruthie hadn't felt like herself. She was more like the person she wanted to be, but her new personality was like wearing shoes that looked good but pinched your toes. She should have refused when Dennis suggested they take a walk after the guests had left, but she had taken his hand and rubbed her bare arm against his as they walked toward the pine grove beside the house. As she watched Dennis gathering straw for them to sit on, Ruthie leaned back against the trunk of a pine and gazed across the pasture to where the silver half-moon cast jewels of light across the pond. She remembered the day she had knelt on this exact spot and watched Crow and Browder lying in the cattails. She had been so young then, hadn't known what their feelings were. What if Browder and Crow were still . . . She pushed the thought away. No, they were just kids playacting the plots of movies. She herself had acted in a couple of Browder's shows. But then hadn't she seen Browder's eyes following Crow around the yard all night? What was going on between them? She might never find out. Browder kept his thoughts and feelings to himself, and you couldn't eavesdrop inside someone's head.

Dennis pulled her over to the straw bed. "What are you thinking so hard about?"

"Nothing."

"Not me? Who then?" His smile wasn't natural. "Old Charles?"

"No!" Ruthie yanked her arm away. She hated Dennis when he was like this, and she suspected now that, when he had gone over to his car several times, he had been sneaking some Jim Beam into his glass of Coca-Cola.

"Okay, sorry. Let's forget it. You look so beautiful tonight." When he kissed her, her suspicion about the whiskey was confirmed. In the moonlight filtering through the tops of the pines, she examined his face as though she were seeing him for the first time. His cleft chin was his most interesting feature. She liked to put her lips to it and feel the uneven skin caress her mouth. In his acorn eyes there were little flecks of green that darkened when he was angry or passionate. She kissed his prominent nose that curved up slightly on the end. "You're beautiful, too," she said.

He lifted her hands and pressed his lips to her wrists. "You're supposed to say I'm handsome like Rock Hudson."

Ruthie shivered. She felt like someone else. "Do you have any booze left?" she heard herself say. Dennis stared at her. She knew she had shocked him, and she laughed. "Well, I'm eighteen now; don't I get a celebration drink?"

Dennis ran to the car and returned with a half-full bottle. After the first swallow, her throat burned and her eyes watered. She had wanted to like it, wanted to get drunk just to know what it felt like. "It tastes awful," she said, taking another swallow.

Ruthie decided later that the night would have ended differently if she hadn't been such a fool about the booze. She felt all soft, fuzzy, languid like she had been asleep and was just waking up. When the bottle was nearly empty, Dennis tossed it aside and rolled on top of her, nudging her legs apart with his knees. "I love you. I love you, Ruthie."

"No, don't," she murmured, lifting her hips to him. And then his fingers were inside her panties, and she reached up and pulled him down. "I love you, too," she said.

Ruthie walked to the edge of the porch and gripped the railing. She would never forget the feel of her black dress as it slid down her legs, the cicadas' taunting cries, the smell of whiskey and pine resin. She remembered Dennis' teeth biting into her breast, his naked body larger and darker than she had thought. She remembered the moment of pain she felt inside as he pushed his way into her, and the feeling afterward as she quivered and held him to her. She remembered, too, the blood that Dennis had wiped away with his briefs, proof that she was a virgin no more.

God had seen it all, and God knew that what was in her heart wasn't repentance, but only fear. She may as well admit to herself that she wanted to do it again, that her breasts tingled at the thought of his mouth on them, that a knowing ache had begun that she was powerless to control. She was bad bad bad, and now God was punishing her through her mother's illness. It was all her fault. She would burn in hell. "Mama, I'm sorry. Mama, don't leave me. Please, God, don't take her away from me."

Chapter 26

HE NEWS OF HIS MOTHER'S ILLNESS JOLTED BROWDER LIKE an electrical current. His daddy had told him that the tests showed a cancer in the colon that had already spread to the kidneys and would continue its march through his mother's body, destroying cells like boll weevils eating up cotton. Her body would be just as ravaged as a field of withered brown plants. "But what about treatment? Can't those stupid doctors do something?" he had asked his father.

"Too late. This type of cancer is hard to contain, nearly always fatal." His father's voice was as emotionless as if he were reading from the *Farmer's Almanac*. They were sitting on bales of hay in the barn where Browder's daddy had told him there was work to be done. But there was nothing to be done in the barn or for his mother. "Your mama knows, but she wanted me to tell you. Said she didn't have the strength."

"Does Ruthie know?"

"Uh-huh. She was with her when the tests came back." His father sighed, looked up to the rafters of the barn as if searching for letters to form words for him. "Your mama wants you to keep on with your job, act normal. Be easier that way. She don't want to talk about it." He shifted his weight, lifted his straw hat and raked his hand over his thinning hair. "Reckon you can do what's needed?"

Browder felt tears stinging his eyes. He chewed his lip. He wasn't going to cry in front of his daddy. He didn't want him; he wanted his mother's soft arms. "I'll do whatever Mama wants me to."

His father nodded, then slapped his arm. "Awright then. You keep going to your prissy job and keep your mouth shut."

Browder felt his fists curling. Why'd he have to end the conversation like this? He had thought they were equals, bound by the terrible news. But his daddy was already walking away from him, dismissing him now like he was one of the hired hands.

"Bastard," Browder whispered. He left the barn and went out into the open field where the air was fresh and the scent of the grains wafted through the tall grass. Sitting on the ground, he wiped the tears from his face with his shirt. Why couldn't his daddy respect him? He was making good money now as Mr. Ruggleman's assistant. *Prissy job*—the words reverberated in his head. What was so prissy about running errands for an important lawyer? He carried valuable documents over to the courthouse; he did go for the coffee and sometimes the secretary Miss Davis made him take out the trash when the building janitor wasn't around, but he was a part of a big successful law office. Why couldn't his daddy see that?

Browder lay back and stared up at the sky. Dark clouds were forming, but there hadn't been any rain in weeks, and he knew these fast rolling ones wouldn't bring any relief. He closed his eyes. Tomorrow was payday. Tomorrow he would have twenty-five dollars for Crow. He smiled. She probably hadn't believed he could earn that much so soon.

On Saturday Browder's emotions traveled the entire range of his capabilities as a human being as he searched for Crow. He found her in the pasture picking a red clover bouquet. Pretending not to see him, she lifted her arms, swung her body full circle, and tossed the clover over her head to let the wine-colored blossoms fall haphazardly on her dark hair. Browder ran to her. "I've got the money," he said.

She turned to face him. "Twenty-five?"

Browder nodded. His heart was pounding like a jackhammer on concrete.

Crow's lips spread into a lazy smile. "Eleven o'clock tonight. The barn." Smiling broadly then, she waved her fingers and walked away.

Browder stood watching her sashay past him. She's happy because she's going to get the money, he thought. Not because of me.

At supper that night, he was the last one to take his seat. He looked over at his mother, who was lifting an empty fork to her mouth. Beside her Ruthie's head was bent to her plate. This was so stupid, everyone acting like his mother was okay. At the head of the table his daddy ignored his wife's feeble attempt to eat. He turned to Browder and frowned. "So how was your day, son? All worn out from running errands back and forth across Second Street?"

Browder pushed his forearms forward on the white cloth, hunching down over his plate of ham, yams, peas, and tomato slices. He curled his hand backward and scooped peas onto his fork. "Didn't work today, Daddy; it's Saturday."

"Oh, that's right. Just being a dumb farmer, I forgot it's golf day for your country club set." His father lifted his glass in a toast to Browder.

Browder's mother bowed her head. "Could we talk about something else? This arguing isn't good for any of our digestions." Browder looked over at his mother. Her skin was nearly transparent, and he envisioned the dark cancerous growth bulging out inside her. He fought down his panic.

His father's voice was loud and arrogant. "We're not arguing. I'm just stating a fact. Country people work for a living, and this son of mine don't know what real work is."

After dinner Browder was working hard on looking good for Crow. He showered and shaved the patches of blond stubble from his face. In front of the medicine cabinet mirror, he ran his palm over his face, smooth as a varnished baseball bat. He thrust his chin forward, squinted his eyes. He wanted to look dangerous, mysterious; he wanted to look like a man women couldn't say no to.

Missy Jordan sure wouldn't say no to him. He remembered her pale face, her limp hair, her watery eyes looking up at him when he'd danced with her at Ruthie's party. He wasn't going to have to settle for her, because he had the money to buy the best now.

Browder opened his closet, pulled out a solid blue shirt. He looked good in blue; at least that's what his mother said. So now here he was nearly twenty years old and practically a virgin. He wasn't sure if he could count that one time with Crow beside the pond. He knew for sure he hadn't done what other guys at school described. But tonight would be different. Tonight he would do it all.

That night, leaning against the tractor, he wondered if Crow was sitting in her house laughing at him as he waited in the barn like a fool. "Damn you, Crow! You better show up," he said aloud.

"Or what you gonna do, Browder?" Crow walked into the dim light and stood with her back against the rough wood of the door.

"Crow! I been waiting a long time."

She laughed. "Not that long. And don't you think I was worth waitin for?" Crow moved away from the door and spun around the barn, arms extended from her sides. She was wearing a full-skirted black cotton dress, and, as she turned, the folds of the dress flared and billowed out around her legs. The dress was cut low, scalloped across her breasts. Browder could barely breathe. He sucked in some air. She smiled at him. "Did you bring the money?"

"Damn!" Browder walked toward her. "Do you have to spoil this before we even say hello?" He reached into his pocket. "I got the money. Here."

Crow took the roll of bills and stuffed them in her skirt pocket. At least she didn't count it, Browder thought. He followed her eyes around the barn. She wrinkled her nose. "Smells like oil and engine grease. Let's go outside."

Was she just putting him off? Browder felt a knot of anxiety rising in his stomach. She had the money; what if she just walked away? He hurried to her, took her hand, and said, "Okay, let's go to the pond. That's your favorite place, isn't it?"

Crow shook her head. "No, let's go to the woods. There's a full moon, and somebody might see us at the pond."

Crow led him to a felled pine tree. She lay back on the rough bark, balancing her body on the large rotten trunk. Her skirt fell to the ground and Browder knelt on the hem, pinning her down. Crow lifted her arms above her head. "Are we gonna playact some picture you saw at the show? Are my arms tied up like this?" She crossed her wrists.

"That was kid stuff. We're not children anymore."

Crow pulled on her skirt and sat up, drawing her knees against her chest. "You right bout that." She looked over at him, and in the moonlight filtering through the tops of the pines, Browder watched her face soften. She was really looking at him as if she had never seen him before. "You growed to be a pretty good-looking man . . . for a white boy." She rolled off the log sideways onto Browder's lap and they fell backward onto the ground.

Crow flipped over onto her stomach, and, looking down at him, she leaned forward so that her lips were only inches above his. "Do you think I growed into a pretty woman . . . for a black gal?"

Browder's lips were trembling to kiss hers, but he looked into her dark eyes. "Crow, you are beautiful for a black woman, a white one, yellow, green. You know it, too. You knew it when you were twelve."

Crow fell onto her back. "I know I'm prettier than that dough girl, Missy, you was talkin to at Ruthie's party."

Browder looked over and saw the mischievous grin Crow was wearing now. "You noticed?" She was grinning wider, nearly laughing. Browder was stunned. Crow was admitting she had watched him at the party. And if she had, there was a reason. Maybe she wasn't baiting him this time. And it was as if a tiny beam of light had been turned on somewhere inside him, and he could feel it snaking its way through his entire body so that it seemed he wore a string of blinking Christmas lights inside. Had he ever felt this happy in all his life? He lifted himself and propping his body on his elbow, he lay on his side facing Crow. "I already told myself I would never settle for someone like Missy. It's you or nobody, Crow. I hope you aren't teasing me about this. If you are, it's not funny this time. Are you? Are you joking?"

CROW HAD BEEN TEASING; Browder was so easy to trick. After she left Browder frantically pulling on his clothes to get back to his room before his father woke up, she had sprinted across the pasture listening to the music of crinkling bills inside her pocket. He had paid her in fives and ones and the weight of the fat roll of money felt wonderful. She stowed her cash in her hiding place and then lay on her cot unable to sleep. She had never felt so awake as she tallied her future. If Browder kept his job, say four more meetings with him before he had to go back to school, then she would have $125 for her time. Add a couple of wedding and funerals, wasn't that old Mr. Bentley about to die? Add the little bit she earned from the Parsons, and she would have enough to leave this hateful place. She crossed her arms behind her head. Where would she go? She would go to Chicago, get a job singing in a blues club. She knew she was good enough; all she needed was some decent clothes to wear on stage.

Closing her eyes, the image of Browder's face looming over her as she lay on her back in the pine grove reappeared. She hadn't been lying about his looks. He had filled out some, and his hair didn't spike up all over his head like it had when he was younger. She remembered his words. "You're beautiful . . . exciting . . . mysterious . . . can't get enough of you." She had to admit she liked all those compliments.

Luther was snoring now, and his whistling and grunting was loud enough to penetrate the two closed doors between them. Crow pulled her pillow around her ears to block out the sounds. What would Luther say about her and Browder? She didn't care a rat's ass what he thought.

As a matter of fact, she wished he did know she wasn't bowing and scraping to the Parsons like all the rest of the coloreds around here. Rules didn't mean nothing to her. *Taboo, forbidden, dangerous*—those words were red capes for her to charge at like a bull with sharp horns. She would ride Browder's pole any time she felt like it. And, turning over on her side, she burrowed into the covers; she remembered the helpless look on Browder's face when she told him she wouldn't meet him again until he had twenty-five dollars in his pocket. She almost considered reducing her price just to see him go all wobbly and weak-kneed over her again.

Chapter 27

"COME ON, BOB." J. P. LOOKED BACK AND SAW THAT BOB TWO was never going to be as obedient as his first dog. The puppy followed Icey more often than anyone else, and J. P. knew that she didn't even like Bob, who was lying on her porch, head down, with eyes targeting J. P. that said *Call me till you're hoarse, but I am staying right where I am.*

J. P. threw a stick at the dog. "Shoot, Bob. Don't you wanna go down to the barn with me? We gonna see some squirrels on the way, and maybe a rabbit, or a possum." Bob cocked his head as if seeming to consider this information, and then slowly rose from his position and ambled down the wooden steps to his master. "That's a good boy." J. P. patted his head. "Come on now. Let's see what Deke's doing down to the barn."

The double doors of the barn were open on both sides and sunlight streaked through the open space where Deke squatted beside the garden tiller. He was wearing faded overalls with no shirt and brown work boots with broken laces; around his forehead he had tied a black handkerchief to absorb the sweat that poured from his hairline. His large muscular arms wrapped around the tiller glistened as he lifted the heavy equipment to turn in on its side. "Is it broke?" J. P. asked, as he skipped across the dirt floor to stand beside Deke.

"Nope, just needing some sharpening and adjustment. You takes care of your tools and machines, they ain't so quick to break on you. That's a good thing for a boy to learn—to take care of his possessions. Hand me that grinder, J. P. You be my helper today."

J. P. looked around to determine which of the objects strewn around

Deke was the grinder. Finally he chose a long file and held it out. Deke laughed. "We be a long time sharpening with that little ole thing." He dragged the grinder toward the tiller blade, which J. P. saw he was far too small to lift. "You want to learn the names of tools." He held up a wrench and named it. "Wrench, and this one you can adjust. See?" He twisted the silver wheel on the tool. "Make it fit the bolt you want to loosen or tighten."

J. P. squatted beside him, and Bob took this as his cue to trot out of the barn toward the house where Icey was hanging sheets on the clothesline. "Darn that Bob. He always wanting to be with Icey."

Deke wiped his hands on a green rag. "Yeah, and she don't care for him much. I reckon he missing his mama and think Icey make a good substitute."

J. P. considered this. "Do dogs know the difference between men and women?"

"I reckon they can tell by the different smells of humans."

"You think Bob knows who is colored and who is white?"

Deke reached over for his quart jar of water, unscrewed the metal lid, and took a long swallow. "Probably so. Dogs can see in black and white they say."

"You know lots more than my daddy."

"That ain't true, J. P. Your daddy know a lot more about farming than I do. Not just crops, but hogs, cows, mules. He can help a foal into the world better than any vet."

J. P. rubbed his nose. "I don't want to be no farmer. Crow says I'm gonna go to a white school and learn about how to cheat people outta their money."

Deke grabbed J. P.'s arms and turned him toward him. "Crow got a lot of ideas gonna get her in trouble. Don't you be saying such about going to no white school."

He was hurting J. P.'s arms. He winced before asking, "How come?"

Deke loosened his grip but didn't let go. "You too young to understand. But you got to keep your mouth shut, especially round whites."

J. P.'s heart quickened its beat against his green-checked shirt. He was always saying something he shouldn't. Seemed like his mouth would open and words would just fly out like insects and he was powerless to stop them from swarming out into the world. "Mama told me that already, and not to look up, neither."

Deke nodded. "That's right. You a smart boy, way smart for your age, and I reckon you can understand more'n most." He squatted down to look straight into J. P.'s wide eyes. "You see, bout four years ago, there was this little girl name of Linda Brown. She was a few years older than you and she lived in a state called Kansas. This girl was black and she wanting to go to a white school, and when she found out she couldn't, her folks hired a great man, name of Thurgood Marshall, to try and get people to see that she had the right to go to that school."

"So what'd he do?"

"Well, he won the right for her to go, but see, this law was supposed to be for all black children. You have the right, law says so. That's what Crow is talking about. But it ain't worked out the way it suppose to. Folks down here ain't obeying that law."

Deke laid his hand on J. P.'s knee. "I don't want you to get hurt." He was quiet for a moment and then said, "Here's what happened last year. There was some more coloreds was gonna go to another school up in Arkansas, and the white people still tried to keep them from it. You can get hurt, killed even, if you don't do what white people want you to." Deke looked away. His eyes traveled to the slanted rafters above them. "I knew a man didn't know when to keep his mouth shut. Klan hanged him."

J. P. looked up at the rafter overhead and he saw that man, swinging from a rope, his chin on his chest, his tongue lolling out of his open mouth. He hadn't known he could be hanged for those words that ran out of him. His knee trembled beneath Deke's hand. He whispered, "What'd he say?"

Deke's eyes shifted to his face. "Said I shouldn't be scaring little boys who got to get up from here and go find his dog fore Icey beat him with her broom."

"Okay, I'm gone," J. P. said, and leaving the barn, he ran toward the Parsons' backyard. Stopping to throw chinaberries at the guinea hen who scratched for worms in the ground beneath the tree, he wished for the thousandth time that Memphis would come running up to play with him. "Ain't nobody to play with round here," he told the speckled back of the bird. "My dog won't even play with me. I'm gonna run away and be on the *Gillette Cavalcade of Sports*. I'll knock out Floyd Patterson with one punch, and I'll be crowned heavyweight champion of the world." He shook his fists over his head. "Ladies and gentlemen, J. P. Weathersby, the champ of all time." Dropping his hands, he scissored his legs, jumping left, jabbing the air with his right hand, then left, a triple punch, delivering an uppercut to his imaginary opponent.

His mother came out of the house. "What you think you doin, boy?"

J. P. dropped his fists. "Nothing."

"Did I tell you to get a bucket and pick some pole beans?"

"Yes'm, but you didn't say this morning."

Tee Wee sat on the steps. "Come over here." She yanked him close to her with a rough jerk, then patted the top of his head. "You feelin lonesome?"

"Uh-huh."

"Been down at the barn with Deke?"

"Uh-huh."

"Deke don't need you worryin him none when he workin."

J. P. leaned against his mother's soft body. He smelled flour and bacon in the folds of her dress. "Have you seen Bob? I got to find him."

"What you so fidgety bout? Somethin botherin you?"

J. P. felt his mother's eyes boring into his. She knew how to look right through the holes into his head. "It ain't nothing. I been talking to Deke is all."

Tee Wee held his face in her hands. "Talkin bout what?"

J. P. tried to wiggle away, but she held his cheeks together so tightly, he knew he had fish lips. "Let go, Mama." She did, but her eyes held him. "He was telling me that a man he knew was hanged cause he didn't keep his lips buttoned up. And he said I got to be more careful talking bout going to a white school someday." He didn't want to cry, but he felt his throat closing up. "Mama, I don't want to get hanged."

She grabbed him, held him so tightly against her chest that he could barely breathe. "Shush! You ain't gonna get hanged. Ain't nobody gonna touch a hair on your head long as I'm alive. Deke oughta be ashamed tellin you lies like that." Tee Wee looked back at the screen door and lowered her voice. "We talk more later. You get on over to the garden and pick them beans."

Her hand flew back and smacked his butt hard enough for it to sting. As J. P. ran toward the garden, he wondered why his mama was like that. One minute she was kissing him all over and the next she'd slap him hard as she could. Halfway to the garden, he stopped and turned around. He had forgotten the bucket to put the beans in.

After getting the pail and banging it against his leg hard enough to bring tears to his eyes, he opened the gate to the garden and sauntered down the rows of tomatoes, peas, squash, okra, and finally the pole bean stalks. They were twice the height of J. P., and he decided he'd just pick off the bottom where the beans hung in heavy clusters. Bottle flies buzzed around his head as he picked, and he constantly swatted at them as his bare feet inched down the row. When he reached the middle of the row, where he knew he could no longer be seen from the house, he sat down beside his bucket. Something was wrong with everybody, and he couldn't understand inside his head what was going on outside of it. One thing wrong was Mrs. Parsons was so sick. Ruthie told him she would go to heaven to see Memphis. He wanted to see Memphis, too, but he didn't want to go to heaven. What he wanted was for Memphis to come back. It seemed like the more he wanted something, the less chance there was of it happening. Right now what he wanted was for this bucket to fill up with beans without him having to pick them.

At five o'clock the cows began to come up, and J. P. sat straddled on the fence watching their approach. Kelly came up with her calf J. P. had named Spider. His father wouldn't milk Kelly, but she came with the others to the feeding trough where Luther was mixing oats and grain with his shovel. He looked up at J. P. "Open that gate and let em come on."

J. P. hopped down and lifted the latch on the gate. He slapped the rump of each cow as she walked into the lot. "Suppertime. Suppertime," he called to them. When Spider followed his mama into the lot, J. P. closed the gate and ran to the little tan calf. He was the exact color of the camel he'd seen in his Bible storybook. "Hey, Spider," he crooned into the calf's neck as he stroked his head. Kelly looked back at J. P. as if to warn him against any further closeness to her newborn. Backing up, J. P. danced across the lot to the trough where Luther was milking one of the Jerseys. The milk rang melodiously into the tin bucket, quickening in rhythm as the cow's milk came down into her bag. J. P. clapped in unison with the streams of milk.

"Stop it, son, you scaring the cows." Luther didn't look at him, but he frowned. "You oughta know better than to do that."

J. P. dropped his hands and rubbed his toes in the dirt. "Sorry. Daddy? You reckon Deke could fix an airplane engine if one landed here in the field and was broke?"

"Ain't no airplane gonna land in this field."

"But what if one did? You reckon Deke could fix it?"

Luther's hands slowed, but he continued to pull on the Jersey's teats. "No, I don't think a airplane engine is nothin like a tractor. Deke don't know nothin bout airplanes."

J. P. leaned against Kelly, who had nudged her way to the trough. "Bet he does. Bet he can fix anything there is in the whole world."

Now Luther's hands were still. "You think a lot of Deke, don't you?"

J. P. heard the warning tone of his father's voice. He backed into Kelly's side pushing her rear quarters at an angle. "Yes sir."

Luther looked at him with dark, sad eyes for a long minute. "Deke's a good man. I'm glad you his friend, him losin his own boy, he needin another one around. Go get the strainin cloth; we bout done with this one and ready to pour it out."

J. P. ran to the house for the cheesecloth, and on his way back, flapping the cloth in the air, he knew Deke was right. His daddy couldn't sharpen a tiller blade, but he sure did know a lot of other things. When he reached the lot, he saw Luther standing beside the far fence; he held his milking stool in one hand, the pail of milk in the other. His eyes were staring out across the pasture in wonder as if he had seen an airplane landing there. "Daddy," J. P. called out. "Daddy, I got the cloth; I'm ready to help you with the milk."

Chapter 28

RUTHIE EASED HER MOTHER'S CAR ONTO THE SHOULDER beside Carterdale Road and lit a cigarette. She had volunteered to make the trip into Zebulon to fill another prescription for her mother chiefly because she needed a respite from Parsons Place. The business of dying demanded that every activity be logged in a ledger, accounts had to be tallied, the smallest remark edited with red pencils. Tee Wee monitored her eating as though she were the patient. "You needs to keep up your strength for the comin days," she had told her after Ruthie had pushed away her plate of fried eggs this morning. But how much strength did she need to sit with her mother who now hardly ever left her bed?

Ruthie tossed her cigarette out of the window and rested her head back on the seat. Nearly every afternoon she sat in her mother's bedroom on the chair where her father hung his pants, and she would search for something interesting to say to her mother. But it seemed that her mother had already begun to leave her and was no longer concerned with her daughter's life. Ruthie's eyes stung with tears. She knew she shouldn't feel sorry for herself; she shouldn't be focused on herself. Her mother was the one dying, suffering with the pain that drained her energy and daily faded the light in her eyes that would soon be snuffed out by a covetous Jehovah who demanded the return of her soul.

Ruthie banged her hands on the steering wheel; she couldn't help the resentment she carried inside her. It was her last summer before college. She should be going to town to buy new clothes and a bedspread for her dorm room. She felt cheated.

She dropped her hands and reached for the ignition key. She had to get going. She would be missed, questioned about taking so long to run errands. Everyone except Browder was on a time schedule. Browder! She hated him. Mama wouldn't smile for anyone, but let him come into her room for a five-minute hello, and she perked right up and pretended she was suffering from a cold that was a little bit annoying. He didn't help her to the bathroom, run for pills and juices and a crochet needle that had been lost for months. No, and Browder didn't tell anyone where he was going on the nights when he slipped out of the house smelling like he'd been swimming in a vat of Old Spice.

When she arrived in Zebulon, Ruthie, lost in her thoughts, drove past Cooks' Pharmacy and had to circle the block to park. After picking up the bottle of painkillers and loading the chicken scratch in the trunk, she decided to stop by the Movie Star lingerie factory where Dimple had just been hired as the bookkeeper. She had quit her job at Magnolia Printing when she and Walt broke up. Dimple was sure to be a good antidote for the blues.

She was sitting behind her small desk filing her nails when Ruthie stuck her head in through the partially opened office door. "Hey, you got a minute?"

Dimple grinned. "Got an hour. Slow as molasses in January around here. Orders for panties are way down. You'd think everyone in the state is going bare-assed beneath their clothes." She tossed the nail file into the wire OUT basket. "So, what's up?"

Ruthie pulled the typing chair over to Dimple's desk and sat down. "Nothing much. I just had to get out of the house. It's like living in a hospital." She bent her head. "I guess I shouldn't say that."

Dimple blew a raspberry across the desk. "Poot. I couldn't stand it even for one day. It's normal not to want to be around sick people." She leaned forward, and Ruthie could see the two milk-white mounds of her breasts rising out of a green lace bra. "You need to have some fun, kid. I'll bet you haven't had a date since your birthday party."

"Dennis comes over some, but not often. He's working at the Goodyear store to earn college money."

Dimple rose and stuck her leg out to straighten the seams of her stockings; then she tucked her white blouse in around the wide black belt that cinched her waist. Ruthie guessed that this was a ritual that occurred each time Dimple left her desk. No one would ever catch her with a hanging slip strap or baggy hose around her ankles.

Dimple leaned back against the metal filing cabinet. "Are you going to Catherine's party? It'll be the last one before all of you kids go off to seek your fame and fortune at school or whatever."

"Yes, Dennis and I plan to go, but right now everything's so up in the air with Mama and Dennis' family not having enough money to send him to college, I just don't feel like I can enjoy it." She dropped her head into her hands and spoke softly through her fingers. "I dread going really. Dennis and me, we . . . well . . ."

"Y'all having problems?"

"No. Yes. I love him, Dimple. I thought someday we'd get married, but now I don't know. I thought you and Troy Greer would marry, and then Walt." She shrugged her shoulders. "Who can tell what will happen. I guess only God knows the outcome of us all."

Dimple opened and slammed a file drawer. "Ruthie, that's such shit. You think God is sitting around on some cloud saying to Himself, 'Today Dimple Butler is going to get laid by Harry Rutledge and I'll let them get married next month'?"

"Well, not like that, but I do believe He has a plan for our lives, and if we aren't good people, He will change our path to punish us."

"And I think you punish yourself enough without needing any help from Him."

ON THE DRIVE back home Ruthie thought about how different her relationship with Dennis was from Dimple's and her lovers. While Ruthie was helplessly being driven by her fears, Dimple was comfortable in the driver's seat, taking her men wherever she wanted them to go. She was an unrepentant Delilah, seducing her lovers into surrendering their strengths to her. Brother Thompson had preached a sermon about Samson's weakness and Delilah's power, quoting scripture from Judges. He said that Samson was bold before men and weak before women. But weren't all men? The preacher's voice had boomeranged around Pisgah's walls when he had warned the men, "If you fall asleep in the lap of your lust, you will wake up in the hands of the Philistines." He had described Delilah, quoting Proverbs: "Honeycomb lips and mouth smoother than oil." Delilah was a bitch. But when Ruthie had seen the movie, she had been seduced by Delilah, too. She had thought that she wanted to be Grace Kelly in an ice-blue gown that swirled like a pinwheel as she glided down a curving staircase; but when she had seen the chiffon veils, the coin headdress, the seductive breastplates Delilah wore, Ruthie could see how Victor Mature would choose her over Grace any day. And even after Samson was blinded, turning the huge grinding stone, when Delilah came to him, Ruthie could tell he still wanted her. That was the lap of lust. Maybe she was more like Samson than Delilah. She remembered Brother Thompson saying that Samson fought the Lord's battles by day and disobeyed the commandments by night. She understood Samson; she was Grace Kelly in the day and Delilah at night.

When she arrived back at Parsons Place, Ruthie put all thoughts of Dimple and Delilah out of her mind as she entered her mother's room. "Got your pills," she said.

Her mother held out her hand for the bottle, read the label, and then nodded. "Did you get my embroidery thread?"

Ruthie stared at her. "Mama, you didn't say to."

"I did, but as usual, you weren't listening. Thinking about boys and parties and your own needs." She tossed the pills across the bed. "I understand. It's no fun to have a sick mother in the house." She pulled the sheet to her neck. "I'm going to take a nap."

Ruthie wavered for a minute before going out. She wanted to explain that she did care, that she wasn't an unfeeling person, but her mother's words had come perilously close to the truth and she wasn't sure that she could defend herself. "G'night," she said as she switched off the light and threw her mother's face into darkness.

After dinner, as Ruthie was walking down the hall to her room, her father called out to her from the living room. "Come in here; we need to talk."

Ruthie sat on the couch across from her father's chair. She fingered the white doily on its arm.

"Is Mama asleep?"

Ruthie nodded. They both knew that she wouldn't sleep long on sheets that would grow damp with her perspiration and have to be changed soon. Her father looked older and sadder than she had ever seen him. The lines in his face seemed to have deepened since morning. "What's the matter?" she asked.

He took his time, lighting his cigar, holding it up and staring at its glowing tip. He laid the cigar on the smoke stand and leaned forward. "It's about Mama and what's going to lie ahead in this house. Your mama needs you." He held up his hand as if she were going to interrupt him. "I know we have Tee Wee to help, but there are certain things she can't do for your mama that you can."

"Like what?" Ruthie wanted to know.

"Like being here at night for one. If I have to go to auction or see to a sick animal, or whatever, I need you to be here to stay with her."

"Oh." Ruthie's mind was swimming now with whirlpooling thoughts of never having a date again, being chained to her mother's bed, never attending a party. But she was going to college soon, and she comforted herself with that thought.

As if reading her mind, her daddy, lifting the cigar and puffing on it, blew out a cloud of blue smoke, then said, "I know you're planning on going to the W, but we'll just have to wait and see on that. You can't go off with your mama dying."

Ruthie knew her mouth had fallen open in dismay for a cry of *No* that she had not uttered. In an instant her entire future was jeopardized.

"I know how much you love your mama, but we have to face the inevitable now. It's time," he whispered in a gentle voice. He pulled his handkerchief from his back pocket and wiped his nose and eyes.

Ruthie was paralyzed. Should she go over and hug him? Daddy hadn't ever cried in front of her that she could recall, and she wished he wouldn't now. She bowed her head, hating herself for her earlier selfish thoughts. Mama needed her, and Daddy needed her, and that was all that really mattered. She didn't know what courses to take anyway; she wasn't ready to begin studying for a career that had no name.

"I'll do whatever you need. I want to spend as much time with Mama as I can before, before . . . you know." She looked down at her fingers poking through the crocheted doily.

"Okay. That's settled then." He rose and turned on the television set. His eyes locked onto the *Gillette Calvacade of Sports* announcer, dismissing her from his thoughts. "Check on your mama before you go to bed," he said.

On her way to her mother's bed, Ruthie ran into Browder in the hall. He had never looked happier. His clothes were wrinkled, his hair uncombed, his tennis shoes covered with mud, and his eyes were filmed with a dreamy mist. Smiling, he walked around her, closed his bedroom door, and called to her. "Night, Ruthie. Sweet dreams."

Ruthie stuck her middle finger up. "Asshole," she whispered, as she entered her mother's room. She was sleeping peacefully, so Ruthie went to her own room, stripped out of her blouse and shorts, and lay on the bed in her bra and panties. She hated Browder. How come he got to go and come as he pleased? And where had he been anyway? She thought of how he had looked in the hall, like some lovesick puppy. He *was* in love; she just knew it. But who with? Missy? Ruthie frowned. She didn't seem her brother's type. She blew her bangs out of her eyes. The whole day she had felt she was wandering through a maze not knowing what to expect from anyone. Faces passed through her mind: She saw Dimple, Dennis, Browder, Daddy, and Mama. And what about all the coloreds on Parsons Place? What was behind those smiles and frowns; what were the words that formed in their heads that they never spoke? She remembered how as a child she had sat on the trunk in the little space beside her parents' bedroom listening for clues to live by. She had learned early that people say things in private that sometimes are exactly the opposite of what they say in public. And in a way, she was happier that this was so. She didn't really want to know Daddy's feelings; didn't want to see his pain. Mama's was enough. Ruthie's eyes filled up again. How could she carry both of their sufferings and her own? It wasn't fair. She had wanted to be an adult for so long, but now she wished she could turn the calendar back, she would still be a virgin, Mama would be healthy, Daddy would be talking about the farm, and Browder would act like a normal brother instead of a moody half-wit.

Ruthie searched for her cigarettes in her purse and lit one with her new lighter. Raising the window, she sat on the chintz-covered seat, blowing smoke out through the screen. The cicadas' songs were harsh and loud, and Ruthie was irritated by the racket. "Shut up," she called out. "Go to sleep and leave me in peace." She opened the screen and threw out her cigarette, then slammed the window down. The words came into her head: *The peace that passeth all understanding.* Everything is past understanding, she thought. And *peace* was just another meaningless word like *virgin* and *forgiveness.* If only she could piece her hymen back together and replace it in her body. If only she could dissolve the cancer inside her mother's stomach. If she could do these things, then she could forgive herself and love God again.

Chapter 29

SNUGGLED DOWN IN THE FOLDS OF ICEY'S DRESS, BOB TWO closed his eyes and dozed in the summer heat. Icey moved her index finger behind his left ear. "Sweet baby, sweetums boy," she crooned. "Don't you be tellin nobody bout me feedin you scraps when I come home to dinner. It be our secret, now, you hear?" She smiled at the dog. He seemed to understand her and was never offended by her harsh commands when J. P. was around. A dog can keep a secret better than a human, she thought, and her mind turned to her own inability to keep one. If only she hadn't told Tee Wee what she guessed about Crow.

She was waiting for Tee Wee and J. P. to return from town where they had gone to sell eggs, cakes, and pies. When Icey had asked Tee Wee to buy red thread for her, Tee Wee hadn't even tried to act like this would be a big favor. No, Tee Wee wasn't herself since she had blabbed out what she thought about Crow. But what was the truth? Did Tee Wee know? Icey turned the questions over and over in her mind like sand in an hourglass. First she thought yes, each grain a clue as to what was true, then she would tip the glass over and examine those grains that said she was wrong about Crow. She lifted her hands to her head. It was too much to think about. She'd get a terrible headache if she kept it up.

When she saw Tee Wee's Ford snaking up the drive, she dumped Bob Two to the floor and nudged him with her foot. "Git away," she said. She waited until the dog had settled beneath the oak tree, then waved and walked toward the car. "Sell much?"

Tee Wee opened the door and eased her big stomach from under the steering wheel. Sweat was pouring down her face, and her sunken eyes held no light. J. P. was grinning. "Mama let me do all the door knocking and I sold out in two hours about. We was hot, though." He wiped his hands down the front of his overalls. "We got your thread. Mama was gonna forget it, but I'm the one remembered and say, 'We got to get Miz Icey thread fore we go home.' " J. P. spotted Bob and slapped his hands on his thighs. "Come on, boy. Hey, there."

When Bob didn't move, Icey frowned. He was gonna give away the secret if he couldn't act no better than that. "So you makin good money sellin in town, Tee?"

Tee Wee slammed the car door. "Some. Ain't gonna be buyin no Cadillac car no time soon."

"Well, we thinkin of gettin a television set for Christmas. I reckon you got enough saved for one, too." She walked beside Tee Wee toward her house.

Tee Wee patted her chest where she kept her money stuffed in her bra when she was in town. "This ain't near enough for somethin like that."

"You could get one on time," she said, following her inside.

Tee Wee wheeled around and glared at her. "I ain't owin nothin to nobody. We ain't like you and Deke always wantin somethin you can't wait to get."

Icey put her hands on her hips. "Well, Miz High n Mighty, we smart enough to get things while we young enough to enjoy em. You wait too long for something, you too old to know how to use it."

Tee Wee reached in her bag and pulled out a spool of red Coats thread. "Here, take it and go home. I got chores to do fore I pick up Masie and Lester at the show."

Icey took the thread. "I goin," she said. Her body was going limp and her head was just beginning to throb. She was gonna have that headache after all.

Back in her living room she wondered why she and Tee Wee had to act like this. She knew she couldn't help it, but Tee Wee ought to try harder. After all, she was suffering still over her baby, Memphis. And Crow was a grown girl, not a child. And she wasn't sweet like her babies. Icey picked up her worn Bible and ran her fingers over the gold lettering on the cover. Jesus didn't judge. He let that old whore Mary Mag Lean wash and dry His feet. And there was that verse about "Let he who is without sin cast the first stone." Icey bowed her head. "Lord, I most sorry for thinkin bad bout Crow. I know You punishin me already for my sins and I ain't needin to go adding to what You already got on me. But Tee Wee, she make me think bad thoughts. Why she got to care if I get a television set and say mean things to me? And then I got to say mean things back to let her know she thinkin wrong. I just tryin and tryin to save that woman's soul, but You give me a heavy burden, Jesus, when You give me Tee Wee for a friend. Amen."

Icey laid the Bible back on the table where she displayed it for visitors and stood up. Her head felt like a ball was bouncing inside it, but headache or no, she had to cook up some greens to add to what they had left from yesterday. Before she reached the kitchen, Deke came in and, grabbing her from behind, his arms wrapping around her waist, bit her ear. "Your man is home early today," he whispered.

Icey pulled away. "How come you home fore dark?"

"Mister Parsons told me to go on home and 'spend some time with the wife,' " he said, imitating his gravelly voice. "He gettin a little soft since Miz Parsons been down sick."

"Yeah, she don't seem to care bout things much, neither. I accidentally hit that hall mirror with my floor polisher handle and it cracked some and when I told her bout it, she didn't even blink. Said she didn't like seein herself in it no ways."

Deke went to the sink and picked up the Lava soap to scrub his grease-stained hands. Drying them on the dish towel, he stuck his tongue in the corner of his mouth and grinned at her. "So, what about we make some time for loving since we got some free?"

Icey didn't answer. She looked at him leaning back against the sink. He was still a good-looking man. He wore no shirt beneath his overalls, and his smooth light brown skin was speckled with tiny drops of water that sparkled in the dim light. She felt a desire rising within her, but she crossed her arms. "Who gonna cook supper? Glory ain't home yet to help none, so I ain't got no free time like you." She nodded toward the bucket of greens sitting on the table. "Besides that, I got a headache. Tee Wee give it to me." When she moved toward the bucket, Deke caught her arm.

"Supper will wait and I know the best headache remedy in the world." He was smiling. His pink tongue rolling over each word stirred an ache inside her. Icey opened her mouth to say no, but he kissed her before the word could escape. With a grunt he lifted her into his arms, and, closing her eyes, she listened to his footsteps on the floorboards as he carried her to their bed.

Lying in bed, she kept her eyes closed. She heard the thud of his boots, the rustle of his overalls being pulled down his legs. She felt the weight of him on the bed and then on her body. His hands were lifting her dress, and now she thought of how long it had been since she'd wanted him, and was she sure that she wanted him now? When she felt his skin brushing against her, she knew that she did. And she smiled up at him realizing he was right as rain about that headache remedy.

AFTER HELPING ICEY wash up the dishes, Deke left the house to go into town with Luther. They wouldn't come home drunk again, Icey was sure of that. Deke wasn't about to do anything to get her riled now. Earlier he had shouted "Praise the Lord" three times during their lovemaking and Icey had taken this to be a sign from Jesus. And so, when Deke was lying quiet beside her, a happy look of contentment on his face, she had leaned up on her elbow and poked her finger in his chest. "Deke, you hear what you been sayin?" He had tried to pretend he didn't, but she had him. "You praisin Jesus for your blessins. You thankin Him for me, your good woman." Deke had tried to avoid her eyes, but she had gripped his chin and jerked his head toward her. She said the words slowly and carefully, and with each word, she squeezed his jaw a little tighter. "It is time for you to join the church, get baptized in the river, and be born as a Lamb of God."

Now Icey felt a tinge of remorse that she had used his pole to make him promise to be baptized, but the Lord works in mysterious ways, she told herself, and this way was the only one she knew would work for sure. When she began licking the rim of his ear, he agreed to take the Christian plunge into the Tangipahoa River.

After dinner she decided to go over and tell Tee Wee the good news. Tee Wee didn't answer her knock, but J. P. came from around the house and told her that Mama had gone down to the Parsons' to check on Miz Parsons cause Ruthie had come up and said she was having a bad spell and couldn't nobody but Tee Wee make her feel better. Icey stood for a moment wondering if she should go down there, too. She was feeling a little jealousy over Tee Wee's summons, but after imagining giving up her evening to sit in a sickroom, she decided she was glad she didn't have any effect on Miz Parsons' body.

She tried to wait up for Tee Wee so she could tell her about Deke, but she nodded off in her rocker. Tee Wee's voice startled her awake. "Poor

poor Miz Parsons," she wailed. "That woman sufferin some bad. She askin for me and don't want nobody in the room ceptin me. I been down there over two hours, tryin to ease her some."

Icey rubbed her eyes, stretched her arms over her head. "That too bad. I would be some mad if'n I had to stay down there all that time with no pay."

Tee Wee climbed the steps and eased down on the top one. "Wouldn't take no money if they said to. I love her. You do what you can for folks you love."

Tee Wee was right about that. Icey liked Miz Parsons all right, but she couldn't say she loved her. She couldn't say she had ever loved a white person. But Tee Wee did love all the Parsons, and she knew Ruthie and her mother loved Tee Wee. Maybe Ruthie loved her, too. Sometimes she acted like she did. "Well, she gonna die, Tee Wee. Ain't nothin in this world you can do bout that."

Tee Wee wiped her hands on her apron. "I know. There be so many sorrows in the world we can't do nothin about. Mister Parsons say tonight God bein stingy even with the rain, givin it to others and not to us who need it so bad. I believes we'd all feel some better if'n it would rain."

Icey nodded. "Yeah, the other night when it came a cloud and thunder boom out and a crack of lightnin went down next to the pigpen, I thought it would pour down, but it never did. Seemed like God teasin us."

"We can't question the ways of the Lord."

Icey was happy to hear this, since it was proof that she had been right about the way the Lord had shown her to get Deke to join His flock. "Speakin of the Lord, I got somethin wonderful to tell you, Tee." She wished Tee Wee would shift her body around more so that she could watch her face when she told her the news.

"What that?"

She couldn't miss this opportunity to witness Tee Wee's surprise, so she left her chair and went to sit beside her on the steps. "Deke gonna be saved on Sunday."

Tee Wee's expression was a huge disappointment. She wore a look of puzzlement, her brows drawn together, her lips pursed "What you mean *gonna* be saved? You can't decide that. The Spirit got to come into you. You got to get filled with the Spirit in your body. You can't be saved by thinkin."

Icey felt her headache coming back. Resting her elbows on her knees, she pressed her index fingers on her temples. "Oh, no. He already got filled with the Spirit, but he wasn't at church when it happen."

"Where was he?"

Icey began makin wider and wider circles with her fingers. "Well, he was . . . he was uh, he was in his home which is often filled with Spirit which come to us cause of me readin the Bible so much."

Tee Wee leaned in toward her. "That right? Well, tell me more, sister. Where exactly was he and how did it all come about?"

Icey's head was pounding like a sledgehammer against steel. What in the name of Jesus was she gonna hear herself say now? "I was readin the Good Book, readin loud and fast, and he was sittin there listenin to the gospel pourin from my mouth, and I seen this stream of words, golden words, a gold chain comin from inside me right toward Deke. The little golden letters went straight into his left ear." Icey dropped her hands from her head and she waved her fingers across Tee Wee's face and then pointed to her ear. "Like this. Then Deke's face just shined, shined like it was gold, too, and I waited, still readin loud as I could. Deke he shoutin 'Praise the Lord' over and over." Icey felt calmer now saying one truth, and, licking her lips, she went on. "Then he jump up and his body start wigglin like a calf being roped, him kickin and twistin ever which way." Icey stole a glance at Tee Wee and was satisfied to see that her eyes were wide, her mouth slack, her tongue half out of her mouth. "Finally, he fall to the floor, still as a corpse, and I walk over and lean down, and I see little gold threads just like the thread you brought me today, only gold, comin out of his right ear. They stream over to the Bible and go into the letterin on the cover." Icey folded her hands together as if she was praying. "I know then my Deke done been saved and on Sunday he gonna go to the river and walk into the bosom of Jesus cause he already been filled with the Spirit."

Tee Wee didn't say anything for a long time. Her eyes rolled around as if she were seeing Deke and Icey and all that she had described. When she stood up to go home, she said, "Icey, that story got to be told at meetin on Sunday. Deke got to get up and tell it to all the brothers and sisters. Ain't nobody ever seen nothin like that and they all be wantin to hear every word bout this. I know Deke be wantin it to hurry and be Sunday so he can testify in God's house."

Before her words had fully registered in Icey's brain, Tee Wee had walked across the yard and was standing at her screen door. "Good night, Icey. Tell Deke we sure happy for him and can't hardly wait to hear him talk on Sunday."

The bang of the screen door was like a shotgun explosion in Icey's head. She looked around her porch expecting to see her skull scattered in fragments across the gray boards. Slowly she reached up and felt the roundness of her head. She inched her way to the door with her eyes closed, and, once inside her house, she fell facedown on her bed. She breathed in the stale odors of their lovemaking and, clawing at the sheet, stuffed the cloth in her mouth. She drummed her feet against the mattress. Jerking the sheet from her mouth and slapping her head and face over and over, she screamed, "Icey, Icey, now look what you done. Icey, Icey, when Deke find out what you said, he gonna kill you fore the sun rise tomorrow."

Chapter 30

CROW WALKED DOWN ENTERPRISE ROAD AND TURNED OFF onto the gravel lane that led to the Kepper Place. Each time she came here now she thought of poor J. P. watching Mr. Kepper shoot his dog. Long before Bob was killed, Moses Jones, who lived in the Keppers' tenant house, had told her that they treated their colored help like they weren't human. The first time Crow had agreed to trade her favors with Moses for cash, he repeated a conversation he had overheard between Mr. Kepper and his wife. "He say he could train me like a monkey to act just like a human. We ain't nothin but work animals to him," he had said, pulling down the straps of his overalls, revealing his scarred body. The scar that ran from his rib cage around his left side was the result of being gored by the Keppers' bull. The other scar was smaller, but positioned dangerously close to his manhood. "That one I got when Mister Kepper knocked me facedown on a plow point for not makin the row straight." Crow traced the patterns of the scars with her fingertips, and then she asked for the five dollars he had promised for the one afternoon.

Mr. Kepper was partially right about Moses' animal instincts; in bed, grunting and rooting and snorting, he resembled a wild pig. But Crow liked him even though she was sore and bruised from that first time. His ears were too large, flopping out from his head like a small elephant's, but his eyes were emerald green, his woolly hair the color of russet fall leaves, and his skin reminded her of the coffee milk she had drunk as a child.

As Crow neared the tiny shack, she wiped her face on the hem of her dress and smoothed it over her hips. She had promised Moses she would come last week, and then had postponed the date when Browder came up with the twenty-five dollars she had charged him. "You gettin somethin good cheap, Moses," she said, as she pulled open the screen door and walked inside.

Moses was drinking from a jug of corn liquor, and Crow wrinkled her nose when he kissed her. "That stuff smells bad," she told him. "Go wash your mouth out with some bakin soda."

He frowned. "You ain't complained bout my breath none before, and I takes a drink ever time you come."

Crow shrugged. "Maybe it somethin you ate, but I ain't doing it till you cleans up your mouth." She sat on the broken porch chair waiting for him to go to the well; there was no running water in the house. She remembered the sweet taste of mint when Browder had kissed her, and she smiled knowing he must have spent at least an hour spiffying hisself up for her.

Moses returned and Crow allowed him to undress her and carry her to the pallet where he and his three brothers slept. Both of their families were all at meeting, and Crow now wished she were there, too. It was stifling lying on the rough wool blanket and her toes kept catching in the big hole at the bottom of it. Moses was sweating heavily and she tasted the salty drops as they fell into her mouth. He was heavy, too, and she stared up at the rough rafters overhead, rising away from her suffocating body. Browder had carefully held himself with his hands on either side of her head, and he had said "sorry" at least three times when he had bumped his mouth on her shoulder. Plus, she reminded herself, she had earned a lot more for less misery than she was feeling now. When Moses stood up, Crow looked away as he pulled on his overalls. "You want some hooch now?" he asked her. "I could go for a swig myself."

"No, I got to get home, told Mama I had a headache and I better be lookin like I got one when she come home." She rose and dressed, tucking the five ones inside her bra. She walked over to the table where Moses sat with his jug. "I'm goin now."

Moses grabbed her wrist. "What's your hurry? They ain't gonna be back from meetin for a long time. They baptizing Deke down at the creek."

"I know. Icey told Mama a whopper tale about him gettin saved and then later admitted she was lyin. Mama loved that." She turned away. "But it don't matter what time they get back. I ain't watchin you get fartfaced drunk."

Moses stood up and followed her to the door. As she started down the steps, he called after her, "Two weeks. I got some extra work over to the Whittingtons'; I'll have five again after that."

Crow stopped and turned back to him. He was smiling, preening like a peacock. "No, that was our last time. I ain't comin back."

Moses was shocked. "Why, baby? Wasn't I good?"

No you wasn't, Crow thought, but what did she care what he thought. "I made up my mind to quit with you is all. Ain't no more to it." She turned around and sprinted away before Moses reached the steps.

On the way home Crow stopped to watch a huge blue heron as it rose up from the Keppers' pond. Flapping its wide wings, it sailed gracefully over her head. "Beautiful bird," she called to it. "I am gonna go to where you flyin to." She stood watching the bird until it disappeared behind the tall pines in the distance. "I can disappear, too. Fly out of everybody's sight." I ain't got to lay down with stinky men like Moses to do it, either, she thought. I'll get enough from Browder to go to Chicago, sing the blues with Little Walter and Howlin' Wolf. Rising to her toes, and holding her arms over her head, she spun around and bowed to an invisible audience whose thunderous applause rose all around her.

BROWDER DIDN'T HAVE twenty-five dollars. He had saved only ten from his paycheck the following Friday. "That's all I got, Crow," he told her. "I don't make but twenty-two a week, and I got expenses."

Crow backed away from Browder's truck. "I reckon you'll have to forget it then," she said. He had just returned from work and Crow, knowing Friday was payday, had been waiting beneath the oak tree for him.

Browder loosened his tie and dropped his hands to his thighs. "Couldn't we work out something, like a time payment plan maybe?" His voice was squeaky, pleading like a young boy's asking his mama for a toy.

Crow reached out and grabbed the tail of his tie and yanked it. "What you think I am? A remittance man?" She smiled, enjoying this game.

Browder wasn't smiling. He pressed his lips together and took a step toward her. She could feel his breath on her face. "Please, Crow, all I been thinking about since last Saturday is you. I swear I'll pay you the rest when I get it."

Crow turned and walked to the tree, leaned back against the rough bark. "You been thinkin bout me, huh?" He nodded. "You thinkin how good I was to you?" He smiled. "You ain't studyin bout that Missy gal no more?"

"Christ, no. I told you I can't stand her. Don't even say her name to me."

Crow watched his face redden and thought how good it was feeling to know she could best a white girl who would give it to him for free. "Well, let me consider this a minute." She held her hand to her face, index finger tapping her cheek. "Hmmm, by my figurin, I believe you is fifteen dollars short. That's a lot of money to owe."

"Yeah, but I told you . . ."

Crow held up her hand for silence. "Now, if I was to cut the time in half, say instead of from eleven to dawn, we meet at twelve and get finished by three in the mornin, then I could reduce my price."

She nearly giggled watching Browder trying to calculate hourly wages in his head. His brows knitted together like a squeezed accordion. "Would that come to ten dollars then?"

Crow did laugh then. "I reckon it's close enough. You want to meet at the pond at midnight tonight?"

"Yeah. I'll be there, twelve sharp."

"Okay, then," Crow said pushing herself away from the tree. She flipped his tie as she walked past him. "Bring the money."

After supper Tee Wee asked Crow to clean up the kitchen because she was going down to help Ruthie get Mrs. Parsons settled in for the night. "Why you got to go?" Crow asked. "Can't Miz High n Mighty Ruthie tend to her own mama?"

Tee Wee stood with her hand on the door. "Yeah, but Miz Parsons like to have me cream and rub her legs. They so dry, and Ruthie ain't got strong hands like I does."

"They ain't payin you extra for all that rubbin, are they?" She didn't wait for an answer. "I wouldn't do nothin for them without pay. They white, and they can afford to raise your wage."

Tee Wee's eyes were sad, her shoulders slumped forward. In a quiet voice she said, "I don't need no money to help out somcone I care for, Crow. Sweet Jesus didn't ask for no money to heal the sick, and He expect us to follow His way." She opened the door, and, without looking at Crow, she called back into the house. "You clean up that mess; you done been paid with a full belly. I'll be back directly." She slammed the screen door and Crow listened to the heavy tread of her big feet as she stomped down the front steps. She turned to the dirty plates and pans scattered around the kitchen. "My belly is full of you, Mama," she yelled. "And I had enough of it."

She quickly finished the cleanup, and, heating a pan of water, she stripped off her clothes and washed her body with a bar of Pears soap she had stolen from the Parsons' bathroom. In her bedroom she took a long time deciding what she would wear for her meeting with Browder. She wanted to look perfect tonight; she wanted to see him go weak-kneed again at the mere sight of her.

She gave him an extra hour, and it was four-fifteen when she slipped back into the house. Luther rose at four-thirty to milk, and Crow was worried he might be up already. The whistling sound of his snores reassured her, and she slipped past Lester and J. P. on their pallets in the living room, and entered her room, tiptoeing over Masie who was smiling in her sleep. As Crow pulled on her nightgown, she thought about Browder's white white hands moving over every inch of her body. He had surprised her tonight when he had asked for instructions in what he called "lovemaking." None of the men she had been with had ever worried about pleasing her, and she hadn't known that sex could be a two-way road. In the dark room Crow imagined the sun beginning its ascent into the sky, exchanging the stars and moon she had lain beneath for a blue canvas to paint with bright light. She longed for the night to return. In the moonlight she fantasized that she and Browder were silver people, not black or white, but only different shades of pure sterling.

As the word *silver* lingered in her mind, Crow jerked upright and covered her mouth with her hand. She couldn't believe herself. She had forgotten to ask Browder for her payment! That son-of-a-bitch owed her money. Crow lay back down; she would get it first thing tomorrow morning. "He'll have it," she said to Masie's back. "He knows better than to cheat me."

Browder not only had the money, he delivered it to her early the next morning. Tee Wee and Icey had gone into Zebulon, and Crow was laying out her clothes to attend Calinda Jones' wedding that afternoon. Calinda was paying her six dollars to sing two songs, and even though Crow hated "Because," she had agreed to take the job. When Browder knocked on the door, Crow answered it in her nightgown. "You up early."

Browder grinned. "Or very late. I didn't sleep at all, and I feel great."

Crow walked out onto the porch and stood with her back to the screen door. "I don't feel tired none, either." She remembered her money then. "Browder, you—"

"Didn't pay you," he said, taking her hand and placing the bills on her palm. "I'm broke now, and I don't care."

Crow folded the money without counting it. "So what's a broke white boy do on a Saturday?"

Browder lowered his head. "First I got to go into town and refill Mama's prescription. She's in terrible pain, Crow, and she tries to hide it from me."

"Yeah, Mama said she had a bad night when she checked on her this mornin." Crow stared at her bare toes. "I'm sorry for y'all. I would hate it to be my mama lyin in bed sufferin." Crow realized that this was true. What would she do without Tee Wee to drive her nuts every day? She guessed Browder would miss his mama, too, even if she was a royal ass sometimes. You had to love your mama no matter what. She lifted her eyes to Browder; his face was contorted with a grimace that told her he was trying to stifle his emotions. "Maybe she'll get better," she said, knowing this wasn't so and a dumb thing to say.

Browder shook his head. "Daddy said there's no hope. Cancer is too far gone, just eaten up her insides." His voice grew louder. "I wish I didn't have to go back to college; I hate the thought of leaving her in a few weeks." He looked into Crow's face. "And I don't want to leave you, either."

At his words, Crow felt a stirring inside that made her feel weak and confused. She realized that she didn't want him to go. Must be that the cash bull won't keep giving. That was it. She would miss all his money. But then she heard herself say, "Since you got your mama's troubles and you got to go back to school, and you broke, too, maybe I could let you meet me again and you can owe me."

His jaw dropped. "You mean it?"

Crow smiled. "I must be goin crazy, but yeah, I do. Tonight at eleven. On credit. The pine grove." Browder was speechless, staring at her as if she were an exotic bird instead of the Crow he knew. "Now go on and get your mama's medicine; I got to get ready to sing for a weddin at Mount Zion."

As Crow stood on the porch watching Browder trot across the yard toward home, she felt the crisp bills against her hand. She looked down at the folded square she held. "I am crazy," she said. "Just flat outta my mind lettin Browder make me feel sorry for him. Well, I said I'd meet him and I will, but this is the last time he's gonna get it for free. I ain't gonna be no charity that takes care of white boys with dyin mamas."

Chapter 31

HEN RUTHIE TOLD DENNIS THAT SHE MIGHT NOT BE GO-
ing to MSCW after all, he was elated. "That's great, baby," he said. "I
don't think I'm going to be able to swing tuition until next year, and now
we'll both be here together."

"But Dennis, the reason is Mama's going to die. I don't feel like celebrating about it." They were sitting on the swing on the Parsons' front
porch. It was time to go in, but she wanted the comfort of Dennis' arms
around her just a little longer.

Earlier Ruthie had endured an interrogation from Dennis' mother,
Mrs. Wardlaw, who had invited her to dinner, which wasn't nearly as
good as the meals Tee Wee prepared for them, and she and Dennis had
hurried away from his doting mother and sullen father as soon as they
could. Tonight was the first time Ruthie had been the one to suggest they
park and make love before going home. Sex had become the lifeline she
clung to that kept her from sinking farther into the abyss of misery into
which she had descended now that her mother was dying.

Ruthie stood up, checked the zipper on her skirt, and smoothed
down her hair. "We can talk about this tomorrow. I've got to go in.
Daddy may still be up."

"I'll call you," Dennis said. "I love you."

She kissed him. "I love you, too."

Her father was in bed, but Browder was tiptoeing down the hall.
"Where are you off to at this time of night?" Ruthie asked.

"None of your beeswax and don't tell nobody you saw me, okay?"

Browder waited for her answer. When she didn't respond, he said, "Please. Promise?"

Ruthie heard the desperate tone in his question. She didn't want to get him into trouble; the Parsons' family didn't need any arguments right now. "Okay. I won't say anything, but you better be careful. You might get caught since Mama doesn't always sleep all night anymore."

"I know, I know. Thanks, Ruthie," Browder said as he hurried toward the door.

RUTHIE COULDN'T SLEEP and was sitting in her rocker reading the Bible when she heard Browder returning. She looked at the clock. Four-thirty! Where had he been all night? He wasn't going to volunteer to tell her; that was certain. She closed her book and ran her hand over the pebbled texture of the cover. She had prayed and read for hours, hoping for comfort and understanding. She had fornicated, that was a definite sin; that God slew His enemies was also a fact. But Memphis and her mother weren't enemies or sinners, and why did God have to make fornicating so pleasurable and hard to resist? She had believed Jesus' words in Acts 11: "Ask and it shall be given you; seek, and ye shall find; knock, and it shall be opened unto you." That just wasn't true. Ruthie had asked and sought and knocked all night and God hadn't heard any of her cries for help. In fact, she felt more confused than ever, and she was glad that today was Sunday so that she could attend church. If He wouldn't come to her room, maybe He would show up at Pisgah Church.

But Ruthie didn't go to church after all because her daddy ordered her to sit with her mother while he went to visit his brother over in Tylertown. Ruthie tried not to show her disappointment. Catherine had asked her to come over later and help plan her party. Now she would have to stay home instead. She heated the leftovers that Tee Wee had cooked the day before, and then, stacking the dishes, she went into her mother's room. She looked better today; she was sitting up reading the *Saturday Evening Post.* "How you feeling?" she asked, taking her customary seat on the chair drawn up beside the bed.

"Better today. I slept good, and I even ate a little oatmeal earlier this morning." She patted her hair. "I wish I could get my hair washed, though. It feels just awful. Do you think you could do it?"

Ruthie wanted with all her heart to say no, but she forced a smile. "Sure I can. Let me think how we could do it without too much trouble."

Ruthie managed to wash her mother's hair while she sat on a straight chair beside the bathtub. By the time she had rinsed the suds out, both of them were soaked, and a pool of water surrounded them. "Uh-oh," Ruthie said when she dropped the towel in the water. "Hold on, Mama. I'll get another one, and I'll get you a dry gown." As she dried her mother's hair and helped her into her gown, she held back her tears. Her mother was like an infant now, and she heard herself baby talking to her. But Mama didn't seem to mind. When Ruthie led her to bed, she was as docile as a lamb following its mother.

After Ruthie rolled her mother's thinning hair on sponge rollers and fitted the dryer cap over her head, they were both exhausted. "Can you lie down with the cap on?" Ruthie yelled into her mama's ear. No, of course she couldn't with the hose attachment in her way. Ruthie propped pillows, fluffed and positioned them, and was satisfied that her mother was as comfortable as she could be under the circumstances. She returned to the bathroom to clean up the mess they had made. She caught her reflection in the mirror and saw her mother's eyes, her father's hair, her nose that Mama said was exactly like her aunt Shirley's. I am pieces, not whole. Fragments of them all, but not fitted together into anything unique or special, she thought, as she wiped up the tile floor with a towel. She wanted to know more about her mother, her family. There wasn't much time left for asking questions, only a month, or week, or maybe a day before her mother's lips would be silenced forever.

Her mother fell asleep while her hair dried, and when she woke up, she was crying. Ruthie leaned over, turned off the dryer and pulled the cap back from her ears. "What's wrong?"

Her mother's tears rolled across her face and pooled in her ear. "Wet. I peed the bed. I didn't feel it, couldn't . . ."

Ruthie stared at the wet sheet her mother lifted. What should she say? "Well, I guess, we'll have to, uh, get you up."

Her mother's eyes turned cold. "Of course you will. Do you expect me to lie in urine?"

"No, I . . ."

"Then get some sheets. Don't stand there staring at me like an idiot. Get going."

Ruthie ran to the linen closet and pulled out the sheets. Her eyes were stinging, but she wasn't going to cry. She didn't mean to bark at me, she's just upset about peeing on herself, Ruthie told herself. But she could have said it nicer. I'm not an idiot.

When Ruthie's mother was settled back in bed in a dry gown on clean linens, she held up the hand mirror and examined her hair. She patted the curls Ruthie had fashioned around her ears. "It's not quite right, but it doesn't look too bad, does it?"

"I think it looks good, Mama. I'm proud of my hairdo."

Her mother lowered the mirror. "Well, I don't think you should go to beauty school. Maybe Tee Wee can fix it tomorrow."

Ruthie snatched the mirror from her. "If you don't need anything else, I have some things I need to do in my room," she said, walking away from the bed.

"I want some apple juice before you go. And something to eat. I don't know what. Let me think. Is there any pie?"

"Sweet potato." Ruthie heard the impatient tone in her voice.

"No, I don't want that." Her mother turned on her side, her back to Ruthie. "Never mind. I don't want to bother you. I'll wait until Browder or your daddy comes home. They won't mind. You run on."

Ruthie ran to her room and fell on her bed. She burrowed into her pillow muffling her cries. She hated Mama. "She loves Browder and Daddy and Tee Wee," she said. "But not me, not me."

She had said those words to Tee Wee the day before after her mother had snapped at her. When Ruthie had pulled out a yellow nightgown from her closet, her mother had acted like a two-year-old throwing a temper tantrum. "I told you I wanted to wear the green one. Not yellow! I hate that gown. Can't you do anything right?"

After exchanging the gowns, Ruthie had gone into the kitchen where she fell into Tee Wee's arms and sobbed. "Mama hates me."

Tee Wee had stroked her back. "No, your Mama loves you more'n life itself."

"But she's so mean to me."

"She's in pain, honey. Folks in pain don't act like theirselves. It's the hurtin and them pills she takin ever four hours. Her mind ain't right sometime. She lookin at you, thinkin of herself, wishin she was going to a party like you, wishin she was gonna live longer, not be in pain. She can't help it none. She don't want to hurt you."

"Well, she does. Especially after I see how nice she is to Browder and Daddy."

Tee Wee hugged her tighter. "Baby, it's always the daughters that bears the sufferin of the mothers. You'll see someday when you has your own girl."

Ruthie wanted to believe Tee Wee. She wanted to believe her mother loved her, that her irrational behavior was caused by her pain and the medication she was taking, but she couldn't help feeling the way she did.

She slid off the bed and knelt beside it. "Dear God, I need Your help. Please do something. Send a miracle. Make her well. If You heal her, I'll stop fornicating. I swear it."

Just before she fell asleep Ruthie remembered that Browder had been out all night. He had to be meeting someone, and if it was Crow and Tee Wee found out, going to hell would be better than what she'd do to him.

ON THE FOLLOWING SUNDAY, sitting in his parked truck half a mile down Carterdale Road, Browder wasn't worrying about going to hell or Tee Wee, or even his mother at that moment. He was happy. He couldn't believe his life had changed so quickly and dramatically. Now that his dream had come true, it was hard for him to believe it, and his moments of elation were sprinkled with nagging doubts and fears. What if Crow suddenly changed her mind? What if she were playing a cruel joke on him?

They were meeting in daylight for the first time. Crow had suggested it, saying Sunday afternoons were boring and she might as well spend this one with him. Too excited and happy to stay in the house any longer, he had left thirty minutes early. He wanted to get away from the long faces, the smell of the sickness, the doom that blanketed everyone. Alone now, he couldn't help smiling, couldn't hide the thousand-watt bulb inside him.

After Crow arrived fifteen minutes late, opening the door to the truck and sliding in without an apology for her tardiness, Browder drove to the cemetery and parked beside the graves. Crow turned to him with a puzzled look. "We gonna do it here?"

Browder grinned. "A long time ago I came out here and told all these dead people my secrets. I wanted to come back to let them know how things turned out."

Crow slapped his arm. "You're plumb crazy."

"Maybe. Come on, get out. I'll introduce you to my ancestors."

As they strolled across the cemetery, Browder pointed out his relatives' graves and told her the stories he knew about each of them. As they walked toward the O'Neals' plot, Crow broke away from him and ran up to a small tombstone that was a tiny concrete lamb. She stooped to read the inscription. "Lucinda Jackson, born December second, nineteen forty-one, died March thirty-first, nineteen forty-two." She looked up. "This one's a baby, didn't even live a year."

"Yeah, there are lots of babies buried out here. My grandma had three born dead."

Crow turned away from the small tombstone. "Why'd you bring me here? I hate thinking about dead babies. This ain't no fun."

"I'm sorry. I didn't think about the babies. Lots of these people were old old when they died."

"Will your mama be buried here?"

He had forgotten about his mama. She wasn't going to be one of the really old ones. "Yeah, I guess. We got a plot over there." He pointed to the grave sites on the far side of the cemetery.

Crow tapped his cheek with her palm. "Come on. Let's don't talk about the dead no more. Let's do somethin to feel good." She grinned. "I'll bet I can think of a way to get you smilin again."

They lay on a quilt beneath the trees away from the graves but in view of them. Browder thought that Crow was more beautiful than ever with the sun spots filtering through the trees dotting her skin. After their lovemaking, Crow lay in the crook of his arm with her eyes closed, and Browder took a deep breath before he asked the question that had been in his mind since their first time. "Crow, how many men you been with?"

Crow didn't open her eyes. "Four."

"Did you do the same things with them that we do?" He kept his eyes on her face, but her expression didn't change.

"Some. Not all."

Browder squeezed his eyes shut and then opened them before he said, "Did you feel the same with them? Were they better than me?"

Crow opened her eyes and raised up on her elbow. She started to smile, and he knew she was thinking about teasing him, but she leaned over and kissed him. "No, I hated them. None of them cared nothin bout me, just they own selves."

Browder could hardly believe how wonderful he felt now. "I please you then? I make you feel good?"

Crow licked his ear and whispered, "You the only one who ever made me come."

He couldn't help the words that fell out between them. "I love you, Crow."

Her eyes swept across the graves. "Don't go thinkin you more than what you are to me. I ain't stayin here no matter what. Not for you, not for nobody. I can't."

Browder's heart felt like a stone. He tried to keep the fear out of his voice. "Is that what the money's for? To leave Parsons Place?"

"Yeah. To take off and be somebody. I got plans, Browder. Big plans for my life, and you got to go back to school." She spread her arms out. "All this, it's just fun. Ain't nothin more to it."

Browder rolled onto his stomach and buried his face in his crossed arms. "It's more to me. I love you, Crow."

Crow stood up and pulled her dress over her head. She tugged at the end of the quilt. "Get up. We got to go. Mama will be yellin for me to do somethin."

When he started the truck's motor, Browder sat with the sound of the engine rumbling in his ears. With his hand on the shift lever, he turned to Crow. "You still gonna meet me? You're not leaving yet?"

"No, I can't go nowhere right now cept to the shitty little tenant house on your daddy's land." She pulled the skirt down over her knees. "I like you all right, Browder. I like a lot about you that I didn't used to. I reckon you know me bout as well as anybody does. You're lucky to be a white boy with money, even if you ain't real rich." She ran her hands across the dashboard to his. "You growed up easy, and you can't probably understand how it is for me, and I know that, and I ain't carin if you do. But I like what you say to me and I like ridin your pole, and I ain't ready to quit no more than you."

Browder nearly cried with relief, but he managed to shift the truck into reverse and drive them home.

After that day, all he could think about was that Crow would leave someday. He imagined walking to her house, finding Tee Wee on the porch, crying, saying her daughter was gone. And the possibility of her going only made him more desperate to be with her, to imprint his body on hers to make himself permanent somehow. He could tell she felt the same. Her suggestions for places to meet and things to try became more and more daring. It was like being on a circus trapeze swinging higher and higher, hanging from his knees, and then his toes. Beneath him there was no net, and the knowledge of what would happen if they fell served only to goad them both into taking foolish risks.

One night Browder smuggled Crow into his bedroom after she had insisted on seeing where he dreamed about her. He had waited for her at

Mount Zion Church, crouching in the bushes, remembering how he had gotten drunk at Icey's wedding, and how beautiful Crow had been that day. When Crow came out of the small wooden church, he waved her over to him, and they made love just yards from where Tee Wee and Icey placed dishes on folding tables for dinner.

As the weeks passed and the prospect of returning to Ole Miss loomed like a threatening thunderstorm over him, Browder told himself that he would be able to bear being separated from Crow. When he sat beside his mother's bed, he avoided looking at her sallow skin, the dark circles beneath her dull eyes. He ignored the feel of her loose skin falling away from her bones when she lifted her arms to him. He told himself that everything would turn out okay, somehow. He and Crow would be together for the rest of their lives, his mother would live until Christmas, maybe even next summer. He convinced himself that he was born under a lucky star that would protect him, and he held on to Crow and his fantasies, desperately hoping that he was destined to star in the movie with the happy ending.

Chapter 32

EE WEE WOKE IN THE MIDDLE OF THE NIGHT; SHE HAD BEEN crying in her sleep. She pushed up onto her elbows and looked over at Luther, who was curled onto his side. It was just a bad bad dream. But this dream, she knew, was one of them that hangs around in your mind like a nagging job you got to do, like clean out the chicken coop, and every time you look at it, your heart sinks, cause you know the mess is still there and it won't go away. And this dream was a foretelling one. Miz Parsons was gonna die, and, just like in the dream, Tee Wee would be standing over the coffin looking down at her lying there in a blue nightgown. She shivered, squinted at the windup clock beside her bed. Four-thirty, nearly time to get up. She eased her feet to the floor and headed for the kitchen.

She did her best thinking while cooking. As she put the coffeepot on the stove and poured buttermilk into the bowl to mix biscuits, she began to take an inventory of her children. Ernestine and the older boys doing fine. Well, Rufus was a worry, couldn't hold no job long. And Lester, what was gonna become of that boy with no more book learning than he had. Masie, too early to tell, Tee Wee decided. She was a hard worker anyway. Then there was J. P.—Tee Wee frowned. J. P. was a worry; he still was missing Memphis something fierce, and seem like he was over with Deke more and more. Luther was always too busy to pay much attention to him. Then, stirring vigorously, Tee Wee turned her mind to Crow, the one she worried about the most. She stopped stirring and looked up at the ceiling. What was it Icey had called Crow that started their fight?

"The Devil with dark eyes." Tee Wee had pushed it out of her mind, but now she saw Icey's face as she said the words again. There had been a knowing in that face. She sprinkled more flour in the pan and began kneading and patting the dough. And where had Crow been that day she went off without a word to anyone? When she'd come prancing in that night, she said she had been visiting some school friends who moved to Liberty. But Tee Wee didn't believe that for a minute. She slapped the biscuits against her palm, rolling them into balls and throwing them down onto the baking pan. She was gonna find out what that girl was up to. She knew something else Crow didn't know she knew. She had found the money in her hiding place a long time ago. A brief smile flickered on her face. Well, there was one way Crow did take after her: Tee Wee herself had a new hidey-hole stuffed with bills right here in the kitchen. She looked up at the farm picture on the wall; behind it was where she'd carved out a square hole just large enough to stick her hand in. Not even Luther would guess there was more than five hundred dollars behind that sweet picture. She wasn't telling him about that money because it was money she had saved from selling her cakes and pies in town, from butter she'd churned, and from selling the eggs that the chickens she fed laid. Tee Wee knew that Crow's money had come just as hard. She made some singing at weddings and funerals, but she couldn't exactly say where Crow had gotten so much. One thing was certain though: Tee Wee understood that cash meant the same to both her and her girl— freedom. One day she would open her own bakery; white folks were getting lazier by the day, not wanting to bake for themselves, paying others to do what they didn't feel like doing for themselves. She put the biscuits in the oven and closed her eyes. She could see her little shop, its clean white counter laden with coconut pies, red satin cakes, wedding and birthday cakes lined up to tempt people into getting lazier and lazier. Everyone said Ruthie's birthday cake was a work of art that tasted like heaven. She wondered what Crow had planned for her money.

"Tee Wee?" It was Icey, calling from the front door.

"You finally up? I already got my biscuits in."

Icey came into the kitchen. "It's early. You must of couldn't sleep, neither."

The dream came back to her now. "No, had a nightmare bout poor ole Miz Parsons."

Icey pulled out a chair and sat down. "I dreamed of Memphis again, got up, and saw your light was on. You got any coffee?"

Tee Wee reached for the pot on the stove and poured the hot black brew into her least chipped cup. "My dream told me Miz Parsons gonna be in the ground before Labor Day. She gonna go fast. I feel it in here." She punched her stomach.

"I don't see how we be able to stand another funeral. We will all remember this here year as the bad bad one."

Tee Wee poured another cup of coffee and sat across from Icey. "That the truth."

"I reckon Ruthie's boyfriend a comfort to her. I sees him over there a whole lot."

Tee Wee set her cup down hard, splashing coffee onto the table. "That Dennis Wardlaw! He pesters that gal somethin terrible. He up to no good, too. I knows that."

"Well, of all the Parsons, Ruthie got the most horse sense. I reckon she can handle him. Now if'n the table was turned and it was Browder, I'd say look out. He ain't got the sense God give him. Him home all these weeks and got a piddlin job runnin errands at the courthouse. I ain't seen him help his daddy at all."

Tee Wee rose and took the biscuits out of the oven. "Perfect," she said, setting the pan on the table for Icey's admiration. "Mister Parsons don't want his help. Don't think much of him near as I can tell. That boy got a lot to learn, too."

Icey watched Tee Wee lifting each biscuit with a knife onto a plate. She was hungry. "Yeah, he stay away from his daddy. He disappears round here just like Crow."

Tee Wee's back stiffened. "That reminds me. What you said bout Crow that day, bout her bein the Devil? What you meanin by that?" She hoped she sounded calm.

"Tee, I told you. I ain't mean nothin." Icey's voice wavered.

"You know somethin I don't know. We is both mamas. If your Glory was in trouble, I'd tell you. We is sisters in this life, and we help each other out in the bad times. I help you after Memphis passed; it's your turn now."

Icey ducked her head. "Oh, Tee, I true speakin when I say I don't know nothin. I just see things make me think I might know."

Tee Wee moved to stand in front of Icey. "Things like what?"

"I really don't want to say. You might come at me with that knife. You know that sayin that the bearer of the bad news is the one that gets her head chopped off."

"I ain't choppin no heads, unless you don't tell me what I want to know."

"Okay, it's just this. I seen Crow with that Moses Jones, Joe Wells, a lot of mens. I be an experienced woman in that way, and I know what a gal is askin for by her hips swingin a certain beat. I thinkin a gal ain't rode the pole don't look at mens like she do."

Tee Wee's eyes filled with tears before Icey finished. She felt sick and weak. She stumbled over to her chair and covered her face with her hands. Icey was right. She'd known all along. She hadn't seen what she didn't want to see. An image of Crow appeared in her mind. She saw her at Ruthie's party, her yellow skirt swishing, mouth open wide, eyes following the men around the yard. She had known, but she'd blocked out the truth just as she had done with so many things. She spoke through her hands. "Go on, if there's more. Let's hear it all."

Icey was whispering now. "Ain't no more . . . ceptin . . . well . . . it ain't just Negro men. I seen her lookin at a white boy, too."

Tee Wee let out a low moan. And he's got money, she thought to herself.

Icey patted Tee Wee's hunched back. "I sorry. I didn't want to say none of this. I wish I could take back everythin I said. I wish I could keep my old big mouth shut." She leaned down to look into Tee Wee's face. "You hearin me?"

"I hear. Ain't your fault. I thank you for tellin me the truth." She sat up and grabbed Icey's forearm. "Don't say nothin to nobody else. Nobody. I ain't tellin Luther none of it."

Icey rubbed the red spot on her arm. "My lips is sealed tight as a cannin jar lid."

TEE WEE WAITED a week. For seven days she spied on Crow. She spent a lot of time alone by the pond. She would lie on the bank, sit with her hands around her knees, sit so still Tee Wee would think she was asleep, but then she'd throw her head back and look up at the sky. But she wasn't always alone. She spent a lot of time with Browder. At night Tee Wee lay in bed listening to the floorboards creak, the door hinge squeak, and once she followed Crow out to the barn where Browder was standing in the moonlight holding open the door. After watching Crow slip inside, Tee Wee had trudged back up to the house to lie on her bed, her body stiff as an embalmed corpse. When she heard Crow return, hot tears spilled out of Tee Wee's eyes, and she stuffed her pillow into her mouth so as not to awaken Luther with her pain.

After these seven days of spying, Tee Wee sat on the swing on the Parsons' porch waiting for Crow to come home. She had decided to beat her. She had spanked all of her children because she believed in the old saying, *Spare the rod, spoil the child.* Tee Wee knew beating Crow was a risk; she was nearly twenty, she could run away, she could fight back. But something told Tee Wee that Crow would run when she wanted and not until she wanted. Tee Wee wasn't scared of getting a few bruises, and strong as Crow was, she wasn't anywhere near as big as her mother.

Crow had been asked to drive Mrs. Parsons to the doctor today because no one else had been available. Although Icey said she could drive good, Mrs. Parsons had said she'd rather Crow take her. Tee Wee figured she had seen Icey driving up and down the driveway, running over flower beds, rocks, and little pines that now wouldn't ever produce any cones.

At the foot of the drive Tee Wee saw a car slowing. It was the new mailman in a gray truck. After he pushed a stack of mail into the box, Tee Wee left the swing and walked down the drive thinking that maybe she had a letter from Ernestine.

There was news from Ernestine, and Tee Wee returned to the swing to read it as fast as she could. When she had finished, she laid the unfolded letter down on her lap and sighed with disappointment. Ernestine had written that she wouldn't be coming home. "Mama, you remember the boycott led by Dr. King over here that gave us the right to sit where we want on public buses? Well, our cause is just begun and looks like it's going to be a long fight. The Klan over here is doing a lot of night riding, and we are all scared to leave our homes. You know how bad I want to see y'all, but these aren't good times to be a Negro traveling across Alabama and Mississippi." Tee Wee put her hand to her chest. She could feel her heart thumping. Was Ernestine and them babies in danger? Why'd she have to go get mixed up with them people over in Montgomery? "The cause," Tee Wee said out loud. She was all for it. It would be wonderful for her babies to go to the white folks' school, to have the right to go anywhere without worrying about a sign saying NO COLOREDS. She knew she was equal to any white woman, truth be told, above many of them. Yes siree, plenty of things needed changin, she thought, but not if it means the Klan gettin hold of my babies. Ernestine ought to be thinkin more bout her children, keepin them safe. Tee Wee lifted the letter and dropped it back in her lap. Then she thought, Ernestine *is* thinkin bout her babies, wantin them to have a good education, wantin them to have what the white children got for nothin ceptin havin been born with pale skin. She shook her head. It was all so confusing. She'd heard Mr. Parsons talking to his friends about niggers getting uppity. But she'd also seen Miz Parsons frown when he talked like that. What was in their hearts was the question Tee Wee wished she knew the answer to. Best to let sleeping dogs lie; you wake em up suddenly and the sweetest mutt just might take a bite outta your hand.

Mrs. Parsons needed Tee Wee to help her to bed and it wasn't until late afternoon when she had the chance to find Crow. She was sitting beneath the oak tree with her bare feet propped up on the seat of her chair, painting her toenails a deep maroon.

"That a right pretty color," Tee Wee said sweetly. She would catch her unawares.

"Can't tell till it dry. Ruthie gave it to me, so it's probably the cheap stuff."

Tee Wee pulled her chair close to Crow. She watched her long fingers hold the tiny brush, dip it into the bottle balanced on the chair between her feet. "Who you been visiting over to the Kepper Place?"

Crow's feet hit the bottle and it fell over on its side. "Now, look!" Crow yelled. Wiping at the spilled polish with the head rag Tee Wee handed her, she settled back in her chair. She looked straight into Tee Wee's eyes. "I ain't been to the Keppers'. Why did you ask that?" Her voice was hard, controlled.

"I hear tell you been out visitin a lot of houses round here." Crow was silent, but her hand stilled on her foot. "I got to thinkin bout them visits. You know what I think?"

"I know you gonna tell me."

"That's right. I'm gonna feed you what I been chewin on all day." Leaning forward, she placed her hands on either side of Crow's chair, so that she was trapped. "First thing come to my mind is, Crow don't tell where she goes half the time. Now where is that gal, I'm sayin all the time. Where she got off to she don't want nobody to know? Second thing I think is, How come Crow don't have no callers to the house? Most gals her age have callers; they go to the show. Lots of girls her age are married by now." Tee Wee could feel Crow's anger welling up. She gripped the chair tighter. Crow might head-butt her in the stomach to get away. She was ready. "Reason Crow don't have no callers is Crow don't want none. No, she don't, and you know why?" Crow was twisting her tongue in her mouth like she used to do when she was a little girl. "The reason is Crow is gettin money for her body." She was shouting now. "Crow is no better than them whores at Burglundtown Bar." She spread her feet, ready for Crow's first move. She lowered her voice. "Crow don't care how her mama raised her, she don't care bout sinnin, she don't care bout nothin. All she care bout is money." She tried to see into Crow's face, but her head was still bowed. "The worst of all is she takin money from a *white* boy." Tee Wee was out of breath. She hadn't said nearly all she wanted to say, but she didn't feel she had the wind in her to go on.

Minutes passed and Crow didn't move, didn't speak. Finally, she lifted her head. "Mama?" Tee Wee heard the sorrow in the word. She was so surprised by this that she let go of the chair. Crow still didn't try to get up. Please, Lord Jesus, let her tell me I'm wrong, Tee Wee prayed. Make her give me a reason for bein in that barn. Make me ask forgiveness for judgin my baby wrong. When Crow looked up, in her face Tee Wee saw the pain that she knew could only be felt by a daughter admitting the ugly truth of herself to a mother who believed it and could never believe it. And Tee Wee saw in her face the loss of her innocence that was Tee Wee's own loss. She fell to knees, took Crow's face in her hands, kissed her on the lips, as tears raced down their cheeks. "Oh, Mama," Crow cried. "It was the money. I wanted his money. I wish I hadn't let him do all them things, but he said I was pretty, he made me feel good. He'd do anything I wanted. I didn't mean it to go so far. I didn't want . . ." She buried her face on Tee Wee's shoulder. "He loves me, Mama. I think he'd marry me if he could."

Tee Wee pushed her away. "Who?"

"Browder."

"*No!*" she yelled. "No, not him." But Crow didn't hear her words; jumping up and overturning her chair, she fled across the yard toward the pond.

Tee Wee sat watching her dark shadow merge into the fading light surrounding her, then bent her head to her chest. To allow a white boy to fall in love with her! She had never once considered the possibility of such a thing. The white world was a closed world to all coloreds, and now Crow had gone through a forbidden door. Tee Wee pulled herself up onto her chair and sat breathing in the strong smell of rotting vegetables that wafted across the yard. In the distance she heard one of the Parsons' horses neighing softly, mournfully. She swatted a mosquito on her neck. Oh, she had heard of mixed couples, as they called them, up north. Maybe there were some in the South she just hadn't heard about. If there was a black man who went with a white woman, the Klan would make sure he didn't have no pole to use on another one. Tee Wee sighed. Crow was headed for trouble. Closing her eyes, she leaned back and remembered the birth of her daughter. She thought of Crow's father and pictured David throwing his child in the air; she saw him holding her, rocking her, calming her quivering body when she threw a tantrum. "Oh, David," she whispered into the night. "You couldn't tease her outta this. Crow be like a mad dog runnin toward a shotgun. And ain't nobody gonna stop her from destroyin herself."

Chapter 33.

CROW WAS LATE AND BROWDER WAS WORRIED. STANDING ON the west bank of the pond, he looked up to the constellations that had moved to their summer positions, where he could now make out Lyra and Vega clearly. When he and Crow met at the pond, they would lie on their backs and he would point out the star that he had wished on. He wouldn't tell her what his wish was yet. He would wait until the time was right and then tell her his plan for them. He couldn't continue believing his fantasies anymore; he was prepared to take a step into reality. If Crow wanted to leave Parsons Place soon, he was prepared to go with her. He couldn't leave while his mother was still lying in her bed dying, but afterward, after what was going to happen was done, then they would go wherever she liked. He could get a job doing something somewhere.

Browder paced back and forth on the bank. It was nearly one. Crow wasn't coming. Something was wrong. He could feel it in his body; nervous tingling sensations in his hands, traveling up his arms. He drew in a long breath to calm himself. What could have happened? Browder looked over at the tenant houses. Maybe Crow was still at home. Maybe she needed him.

As he jogged across the pasture, he replayed their last meeting in his mind. Last Saturday they had climbed to the hayloft, and on the sweet-smelling hay Crow had made a bed for them. Lying naked beside her Browder found the courage to ask her the questions that tormented him in his bed nightly. Who were the men she had been with before him? Where did she plan on going?

"Ain't tellin names. I already said I hate them all." She turned on her side to face him. "When I get the money to leave, I plan on ridin the train to Chicago. Or maybe Harlem. Probably Chicago, though. Lots of the greatest blues singers are there, and I can sing as good as any of them." Crow ran her hand down his stomach. "What does it matter to you? Let's don't waste any more time talkin. I got to go back and do my chores fore dark."

Browder caught her hand. "It matters to me. Everything you do matters."

When he approached the Weathersby house, he saw that there were no lights on; they were all asleep. But Crow would be up, wouldn't she? Peeping in the kitchen window, he saw dirty dishes sitting on the tiny table. Tee Wee wasn't one to leave cleaning up until morning. Something wasn't right. Just then he heard movement behind him and wheeled around.

Crow put her finger to her lips. "Shhhh," she whispered, motioning him away from the house. He followed her to the rotting car shed, where Luther's old truck was parked beneath the sagging tin roof. Crow leaned back against the tailgate.

"Where the hell have you . . . Crow! What happened?" In the moonlight he saw that her hair was sticking out in wild knots, her eyes were swollen, her ebony skin had turned to ash.

She shook her head back and forth. "Can't."

Cupping her chin, Browder stared into her eyes. "You have to tell me. What is it?"

Crow pushed away from the truck and stumbled against him. He caught her and carried her in his arms to the base of the oak tree, where he sat holding her until she grew calm. He kissed the top of her head. "I'm here. No matter what it is, I'll help you."

"You the one needin help. Mama knows about us."

Browder thought his heart might disintegrate in the flame that rose up within him. "Oh my God. What's she gonna do? Will she tell my daddy?"

"No, she ain't gonna risk your daddy throwin us off the place."

"I wouldn't let that happen."

Crow looked at him and shook her head. Her old look of disgust for him returned. "You ain't got no say-so round here."

Browder knew fear was showing in his face and he wanted to be brave. He spoke in a loud voice. "Well, what's she intend to do then?"

"Nothin. She ain't gonna do nothin. It's me that will save you."

"What do you mean?"

"I been sittin out here thinkin. I was gonna wait and tell you tomorrow when I had it all straight in my head, but since you here, I'll go on and say what I been turnin over in my mind." Crow straightened her shoulders; she was talking faster now. The ghost of the scheming Crow Browder had known for so long was taking over her body, and Browder felt another kind of fear rising. "I got to go away."

Browder grabbed her. *"No."* He realized now that he had known what her words would be before she said them.

"Yes, it's the only thing to do. You know I was plannin on it anyhow. I just ain't got enough money to go as far as I want."

"Crow, I'll follow you. I was waiting to tell you, but look, after Mama dies, I'll come to you. Anywhere. I'll get a job and we can be together."

Crow spit on the ground. "I ain't needin no white boy doggin my tracks. You stay away from me. I don't want you. Can't you understand plain English words?"

Terrified he was going to cry in front of her, Browder ground his teeth. "I thought maybe you loved me. I mean what all we been doing, you didn't ask for any money."

"Shit, Browder, you dumb as you ever was. You think women don't enjoy ridin poles? I was just havin fun. That's all it was. I tried to tell you; you wasn't listenin."

Browder rose and turned his back to her. Her words were like wasps stinging him from head to toe. He wondered if he could withstand such pain. "Where will you go then?"

"To where my daddy lives."

Browder turned back to her. "Your daddy! I didn't know you knew him."

"Didn't, but that day I was gone, I went to where he lives. He's a big shot, got lots and lots of money." Crow bowed her head, avoiding his eyes. "He, he and me, we hit it off fine."

Browder stared down at the top of her head. Something was bothering him, but his pain was in the way of his understanding. He stalled, walking around the tree, stumbling over the roots that the darkness hid. Reaching up, he pulled a leaf from the tree and shredded it. His mind flew to the many films he'd seen about lying women. Crow was a good actress. He had taught her himself, hadn't he? When he'd come full circle around the tree, he stopped and placed his hands on Crow's shoulders, felt her stiffen. "So if you're so happy about going, how come you been crying over it?"

Crow turned her head toward her house. "Mama, Luther, J. P., even the brats. It ain't easy to leave your family." Her eyes brightened with what Browder knew was a bigger lie. "Mama beat me, too; she said she's not gonna stand for no white boy messin with her gal. You lucky she didn't come after you with Luther's shotgun and hunt you down like a rabbit. If I was you, I'd stay clear of Mama for a long, long time."

She was turning him away from her tears and trading into his fears. He suddenly felt tired; too heavy with an exhaustion that made him wonder if he would be able to walk across the pasture home. Crow was an opponent he could never beat. He would only know what she wanted him to. In defeat, he whispered, "When are you going?"

"Tomorrow. When I plan to do somethin, I do it."

"Well, that's true. I know that much about you anyway." He thought about pulling her up, kissing her, forcing her to lie with him one more time, but he knew that would only happen in the theater. And it came into his mind that picture shows were made for fools who were dumb enough to believe any lie. Within him there rose up an intense hatred for Alan Ladd and John Wayne, for every actor who said phony lines, and every actress who faked love, and he loathed every movie director that had sold him false dreams. He wasn't going to say the last line of the farewell scene. He couldn't.

Browder turned away from her and ran, stumbling over the field in the darkness toward the white silent reality of his home. In his room he closed and locked the door. Leaning against it, he looked around his room. It looked like a movie set. He had everything a college boy should have, everything except the one thing he wanted. And, pushing away from the door, he lunged toward the dresser and swept everything on it to the floor. He pulled at the white curtains until the rod gave way and they crashed to the floor. He smashed his violin against the nightstand. After he pushed the mattress off the bed, he fell onto it, and lay there panting for breath.

His father banged on his door. "What's going on in there? You woke us all up."

"It's okay, Daddy. I was trying to move some stuff. Things fell and broke."

"Well keep it down. Your mother's sick, you know."

He lay listening to his father's footsteps retreating down the hall. He was too exhausted to think now; his mind was as empty as a scarecrow's. As he closed his eyes, he saw Crow's face as he had seen it earlier in the moonlight. Her full lips, her swollen, dark eyes. "Crow, I love you," he said. "I won't give you up." And feeling the determination of his words, Browder uncurled his body, rolled onto his back, and spread out his legs. "Someday, Crow. Someday I'll find a way to get you back."

Chapter 34

As RUTHIE, SHOES IN HAND, TIPTOED DOWN THE HALL toward her room, she passed by Browder's door and saw that his light was still on. She stood with her hand on the knob, but then walked on toward her bedroom. After the night she had heard all of the commotion in his room, Browder had barely left it. He had quit his job in Zebulon, saying he wanted to spend more time with their mother, but Ruthie suspected that Crow's leaving Parsons Place was the true reason for his melancholy. He wouldn't talk to her, and she really wasn't sure what she would say to him anyway. "Cry and you'll feel better"? "Have sex with someone and you can forget everything else for a while"?

Sex was the antidote for her own despair, wasn't it? And she had lost herself in it tonight. After leaving Catherine's party, she and Dennis had driven to their parking place near Jackson Road, and there Ruthie had abandoned every modicum of modesty, allowing him to do things to her body that she had never imagined.

She avoided looking at herself in the mirror as she undressed. Safe in her bed, she pulled up her covers, and then threw them off and walked to her rocking chair where she sat stroking her doll's faded pink cheeks. "Josie, Josie, what am I going to do? How could I have let Dennis do those things when I'm not sure I truly love him?" Pressing her palms against her cheekbones, she moaned aloud. "I'm awful. Dirty. Sinful."

"*Ruthie.*" It was her father's voice, and the panic in his cry chilled her. Running down the hall, she glimpsed Browder in his white jockey shorts dashing toward the telephone. When she reached her mother's room, she saw her father in its center, frantically kicking his feet into his pants.

"Daddy?"

"She's going. Get Tee Wee. Get the car. Get, get, get somebody," he yelled, jerking his pants up to his waist.

Ruthie wanted to see her mother, but she was too frightened to go farther into the room. She ran back to her own room and threw on the wrinkled dress she had worn to the party. By the time she had found her shoes and run outside, Browder and her father were carrying her mother to the car. Ruthie watched them lay her mother's thin body onto the backseat. She was chalk white, her mouth was a black circle, she looked less lifelike than Josie. "I'll get Tee Wee and meet y'all at the hospital," she said.

AT THE HOSPITAL Ruthie paced the tiled floors with military precision. She marched down the left side, turned to the drink machine, trooped back up the right to square back to the left again. Browder, Tee Wee, Luther, and her father sat in black vinyl chairs beside the drink machine. "Ruthie, sit down. You're driving us nuts," Browder said, as she passed by his chair.

"Okay, okay." She sat on the chair beside Tee Wee, who was whispering with closed eyes. Ruthie touched her arm. "You praying?"

Tee Wee opened her eyes. "Yes, I askin Jesus to give your mama more time on this earth. We all needin time to say our good-byes."

Luther leaned over and touched Tee Wee's shoulder. "Jesus is callin her to live in heaven where she won't feel no more pain. When He ready to take her, He will."

"That's right." Tee Wee nodded. "But I needin to tell her somethin fore she go. I need . . ." Her voice broke and she shook her head.

Ruthie rose from her chair. She couldn't sit; she just couldn't. With each step, she chanted her own prayer. "Don't take her yet. Don't take her yet. Don't don't don't." When she turned and saw Dr. Matthews coming down the hall, she ran to him. "How is she? Can we see her?"

His voice was soft, filled with compassion. "Her blood pressure is dropping fast. A few hours left at the most. We're putting her in a room now. You can see her soon."

Minutes later, when she entered her mother's room, Ruthie clamped her hand over her mouth to keep from crying out. Her rubbery legs weren't going to hold her up. She held on to the wall. Her father, Browder, Luther, even Tee Wee seemed like strangers she barely knew. Their faces contorted with grief were the countenances of a thousand people in hospital rooms, and their words seemed stupid and irrelevant to Ruthie. Let them keep the vigil; let them believe that her mother was listening to them, caring about what they had to say. Her mother wasn't going to be happier in heaven. She wanted to stay on the Parsons Place with the people she loved, with her figurines, her crochet.

She thought no one noticed when she left the room but minutes later, standing on the hospital's porch, she heard Tee Wee's voice. "I thought I might find you out here."

"Is she gone?"

"Not yet. Don't you want to be there, baby?"

"No. I said good-bye."

"You been a good daughter, Ruthie. She was some proud of you."

Ruthie wanted no part of Tee Wee's comfort. "Well, she wouldn't have been if she had really known me. But she didn't want to know me, and now I'm glad."

"Ruthie! Stop it, child. What you saying?" Tee Wee gripped her arm.

Ruthie jerked away and ran down the sidewalk. "Go away. I want to be alone. I don't need you to take care of me. Just go." She didn't look back until she reached the street, then turning right, she walked down the centerline of Delaware Avenue. She stopped and listened for Tee Wee's footsteps, but she heard only the wind scraping a piece of cardboard down the street. What if her mother had known that while she was dying her daughter was having sex with a guy maybe she didn't even love? While she was doing those shameful things, her mother had said her last words, seen the last faces before she slipped into a coma. Maybe if she had been there, Mama would have said something important to her, would have said she loved her. But Ruthie hadn't been there when it mattered. Lost in her pleasure, she hadn't given her mother one thought. How could she go back in there, stand beside her mother's bed, and pretend she was a good daughter? No, she wasn't going to be a hypocrite.

As she passed by the dark houses neatly lined on Delaware, she imagined the people inside them who would be awakening soon to go to work, to eat breakfast, to drive to the stores, to live tomorrow as an ordinary day. But Ruthie's day, she knew, would not be routine. She would be motherless. On the corner of Delaware and Third, she looked up at the facade of the gray stone Catholic church. God could save her mother if He wanted to. If He were in there, could she persuade Him to heal her mother? She remembered the warm eyes of the priest, Father Mac Something. On the day she had sat in his office, he had said that miracles do happen, but he hadn't believed she was chosen, was given the stigmata. The priest was wrong. She shouldn't have listened to him. Jesus *had* spoken to her when she was ten; she was sure of it. He would hear her prayer now if she would believe in Him, if she were stronger in her faith, if she made a great sacrifice to prove her sincerity. Slowly she walked across the street toward the church. The building rose up in the dim moonlight like a haunted castle, and when she pushed on the heavy wooden door, she almost expected a ghoulish creature to usher her inside. The door wasn't locked, and Ruthie now thought this in itself was a miracle. Slipping inside, she closed the door behind her. She had never been inside a Catholic church, and she felt like a stranger touring a foreign land as she passed the font, the red votives, the statues standing in the recessed windows. Her eyes were drawn immediately to the ten-foot cross and the porcelain Christ stretched in agony before her. Slowly she crept down the aisle toward Him. The exotic scent of incense hung heavily in the air, and Ruthie wiped her perspiring palms down the sides of her dress. The statue was centered on the wall over the white, lace-covered communion table, where Ruthie halted and lifted her arms from her side. "Here I am," she whispered. "Help me." Her voice sounded hollow and distorted as the sounds she made lifted to the high vaulted ceiling. Sinking to her knees, she looked up into Jesus' face. His eyes were closed, red streaks depicting trickling blood ran down His forehead, and Ruthie touched her own brow remembering the pain she had felt there so long ago. She folded her hands and lifted them up to her forehead. "Please don't take my mother. I'll do anything You want. Anything."

Staring at the cross, she waited for a sign, but God had abandoned her. She was a sinner, not a saint. She rose and slowly backed away from the cross. "I understand," she said. There was no bargaining with Him. God was taking her mother from her, and she would pay for her sins. Ruthie bowed her head. "Thy will be done," she said.

THE NEXT MORNING Ruthie waited until eight o'clock to call Dennis. Her mother had died at five and was lying at Quinn's Funeral Home on a porcelain slab having her blood drained into a trough. She and Tee Wee would take her funeral gown over in an hour or so, but first she had to see Dennis.

Ruthie borrowed Browder's truck and drove as recklessly as she had ever driven down Carterdale Road. When she pulled into the high school parking lot, she saw Dennis' green Ford on the side of the big cream-colored building. He sprinted over to the truck. "Sorry about your mama. Come here, baby. Let me hold you."

Ruthie fell into his arms, and they stood in the parking lot, swaying like a mother rocking her child. But Ruthie had never felt so old in all her life. Looking up into Dennis' face, she thought that he was the child. No future really. He wasn't that smart or ambitious. He drank too much. He would go to fat like his father one day, and he was spoiled, too. Always getting what he wanted from his parents, from her, from all the girls he'd made love to before her. No, he wasn't good husband material. She wished his arms weren't so comforting. She let go of him.

"What can I do?" he said. "When's the wake?"

Ruthie leaned back against the truck door. "Wake will be at six. Haven't got all the arrangements made yet. I'll let you know." His eyes were darker than ever; his mouth looked soft like it did after they'd made love. "Dennis, you love me?"

"You know I do."

"I want to get married."

"Married?" Dennis thrust his head forward like a chicken about to peck a worm.

"We weren't going to college this fall anyway. You said you didn't know if your grades would be good enough to get in."

Dennis rubbed his hands up and down his thighs. "Yeah, but, but if I, if we, got married, I mean I don't have a real job yet. Where would we live?"

Ruthie took his hands and placed his palms on her breasts. "Feel that. That's my heart beating so hard you can feel it all across my chest. That's how much I love you and want you." Dennis didn't move his hands, but he was still frowning. "Think about the good things, not the problems. Every night we'd be together. No more 'I don't want to go home.' No more sneaking around. We could make love in a bed every night."

"Sure, that'd be great, but still, Ruthie. I think this is some kind of re-action to your mama dying. You might feel different after a while."

She covered his mouth with her hand. "No, I won't. It's . . . it's . . . we were meant to be together." Dennis dropped his hands to his side. He opened his mouth, but he didn't speak. "Dennis, we can live with Daddy. He'll be lonely with Mother gone, and Browder will be going back to school. Daddy needs me, and you can be a big help to him around the farm. He'll pay you. You'll see. It will be perfect." She smiled at him and leaned forward, kissing the hollow of his throat.

When Ruthie saw his jaw relax, his lips go slack, she exhaled a long breath. She had won. She'd done it. Dennis pulled her close and kissed her cheeks, her eyelids, her nose, her mouth. "I love you," he whispered over and over.

She lifted her face to the gray cloud sailing above her. She felt nearly happy. After she was married, she wouldn't be a fornicating sinner, and she would be a good Christian for the rest of her life. She tried to look behind the clouds, far into the heavens where she believed He sat in judgment. "Satisfied?" she whispered.

Chapter 35

ISGAH CHURCH WAS FILLED WITH MOURNERS. FOLDING CHAIRS from the Sunday school rooms had to be brought in for extra seating along the aisles and against the back wall. On the first five pews the Parsons and their numerous relatives sat with white shirts, faces, and hands dotting the line of black suits and dresses. They looked like rows of domino tiles about to collapse. In the back of the church the Negro mourners formed a chain of zigzagging hats—the men holding theirs in their laps, the women wearing theirs high on coiled hair. Tears cascaded down the cheeks of all of them, leaving white trails through the makeup of the women and creating shiny seams on the faces of a few men. The perfumed air was stifling even though standing fans had been set up in the corners of the church. All of these cloying scents, from the thirty-five wreaths, the talcum-powdered and perfumed bodies, the candle wax, and the various soaps, shaving lotions, and, in the case of Mr. Talbot, insecticide he had used on his gardenias earlier in the day, combined to form a dense cloud which the whirling fans could not disperse.

When Miss Wilda began pounding "Amazing Grace" on the yellowed keys of the relic upright piano, the quiet murmuring of the congregation subsided to silence. In front of the wooden railing of the altar, the half-open casket, its occupant visible in profile, rested on its bier, and Ruthie sat between her father and Browder on the first pew, her eyes on the profile of her mother's unnatural face. The embalmer, Joe McCord, had tried to create life in Mrs. Parsons' chalk-white face by overuse of rouge and pink powder, which had only made her look more dead than she already was. McCord had covered her hardened body with the blue negligee set she herself had chosen. Her folded hands wore the rings Mr. Parsons would remove just before the lid of the coffin was closed and sealed forever. On the polished mahogany the blanket of red roses resting on the bottom half of the casket tipped precariously toward the mourners.

Icey and Tee Wee, divided by Luther sitting on a broken folding chair, could barely see the coffin. Both of them held white handkerchiefs to their faces and wore their hats dipped forward so that their flowing eyes were nearly hidden. J. P., sitting on Tee Wee's left, leaned out to see Deke, who sat on Icey's right. When Deke smiled at him, J. P. leaned out farther to say something to him, but Tee Wee jerked him back into his seat with such force that the chair bit into his back, causing him to cry out. His mother slapped his arm and gave him a glaring frown that kept him silent and still.

In the center rows, friends and more distant family sat craning around each other's heads to see the Parsons, the coffin, and Preacher Thompson, who sat in his chair behind the pulpit. Dimple Butler with her head bowed moved closer to Troy Greer, who had called her the night before and offered her a ride to the funeral. On the aisle Dennis, wearing a navy blue blazer over gray slacks, leaned out to keep his eye on the back of Ruthie's head.

When Brother Thompson rose from his seat, Ruthie's teeth began clicking together, and she dug her nails into her palms. The funeral heralded the closing of the coffin, and Ruthie wasn't ready for her mother's face to be covered by the white satin lining of the coffin lid. She closed her eyes, imagining looking up in the darkness of the rectangular box, seeing nothing in a black void, unable to scream, unable to move.

As Icey listened to the preacher's words, she thought that he wasn't near as good a speaker as Brother Dixon. Although she didn't remember much about Memphis' funeral, she did recall her preacher shouting out God's love, hollering loud enough for her to feel it. Waving his arms and pushing the Spirit out to her, he had made Icey feel Jesus was with her. This pale man looked so tired and frail that she figured if the Spirit tried to enter him, he'd just fall down in a gray heap of funeral suit. But as she listened to his words, she admitted that he did have a lot of nice things to say bout Miz Parsons. He talked about how she loved to do good works down at the old folks' home, and how she loved her family so much. That was all true. He didn't mention how before she got sick she used to be so picky about her house and her fancy whatnots and all. But ain't none of us perfect, Icey thought. Cept Memphis, she corrected herself. He was perfect, not like that J. P. squirming on his chair over there.

J. P., who up till now had been still as a crane on the pond bank waiting for a fish to surface, was itching something awful. Tee Wee had stiffened his shirt collar with white boiled starch until it stood up high on the back of his head and tickled the curls around his ears. He snaked his hand up, keeping his elbow in, and scratched his neck. Then he gave a vigorous rub to the back of his head. He wasn't but seven years old and here he had been to two funerals already. He wondered how many more he'd be going to by the time he was ten. White funerals wasn't much, he decided. He didn't know any of the songs, and no one stood up and clapped to the music, or danced, or sang along with the skinny lady who stood by the piano. The white preacher said a lot bout Jesus calling Miz Parsons home, and he wondered if her and Memphis were in the same house. Did white and black people live together in heaven, and if they did, did they have the same water fountains and bathrooms? J. P. crossed his ankles and swung them gently so as not to hit the chair legs. And was Jesus Himself white or black? All the pictures in the Parsons' house showed him to be white-skinned with light brown hair. He had seen a few where Jesus looked more like a dago, though, with darker skin and curly black hair. The misery he felt in his dress suit and stiff shirt took his thoughts back to himself. He was sleepy and hot, and with heavy-lidded eyes he gazed at the dust motes in the rays of sunlight streaming across the room until finally he slumped against his mother's upper arm and sank into sleep.

Tee Wee felt J. P.'s weight against her body, and, moving her arm, she encircled him and laid his head on her breast. My baby, she said to herself. My last child. The one that gonna make me proudest. She licked her fingers and smoothed down J. P.'s hair. She had helped fix Miz Parsons' hair at the funeral home. Her beautician had got it too puffed out on the sides, and when Tee Wee had brought the negligee set with Ruthie, she had grabbed the comb from Miz Nunnery and settled Miz Parsons' hair down on her head. It was her right. After all, it had been her who had sat with her that last night in the hospital. She had watched her go out peaceful, had seen her spirit fly right out of her body; it circled once round the room, and then went out the small window facing Magnolia Street. And Tee Wee's grief had been lessened by witnessing this leaving. Miz Parsons had opened her eyes, said her grandmama Miz Bell was coming for her, and just before she'd died, she said to Tee Wee, "Mamaw

Bell is here now." Tee Wee hadn't seen her, but she believed she was there cause the room filled with light and smelled like calla lilies, which was Miz Bell's favorite flower. Now Tee Wee wished she could comfort Ruthie with that story. She intended to tell her at the wake last night, but Ruthie had been surrounded with people, and Mr. McCord told Tee Wee that it was best for her to stay in the back of the room in the shadows where she wouldn't be so noticeable to the Parsons' guests. "Ruthie like my own daughter," she had said to Mr. McCord, but he had ignored her and gone off to hand Mr. Young a pen to sign the guest register. My daughter, she said to herself. Where is my Crow? She hadn't heard a word from her in the six long weeks she had been gone. Tee Wee wiped her wet eyes; she wished Crow was here. She wished she knew if she was all right. What if she died? Would anybody know where her mama lived? Tee Wee squeezed J. P.'s body closer to her. No, Crow be all right, she thought. Crow always know how to take care of herself.

Browder was thinking of Crow, too. He held her in his thoughts as an antidote for his pain. Like the askew flowers on his mother's coffin, pictures of Crow in his head helped him avoid reality. He picked a white thread from the knee of his black pants; he had pretended he was dressing for a date with Crow, and instead of this hard pew, he imagined that he was sitting on the soft grass beside the pond. The flowers didn't fit into his fantasy, but he kept his eye on them from time to time; in case some action was needed, he would be ready to save the day. He hadn't been fully successful in denying his mother's approaching death. The specter had entered the house in the form of the smells of disinfectant, acrid medicine odors, and another scent that reminded him of the rotting leaves on the floor of the woods. Since Crow had left, he had stayed mostly in his room, leaving only for calls of nature and food, but still he hadn't been able to escape the constant sick sounds of the house: the hurried steps, the moans, the sobs of Tee Wee, louder each day. On the day of his mother's death, he had lain on her bed, fitting himself on the sheet atop the imprint of her body. Sucking in the stale air of her disease, he felt his body slowing, slowing down so that he felt his skin dissolving against his bones. Then he had cried. Cried for her and for Crow. Cried because it was as it had always been. He was powerless, a puny man without control of even a small piece of space in the world. His helplessness angered him, and he fought the desire to destroy his mother's room as he had his own. Now he sat with his jaw clenched, teeth grinding. He pulled himself back to the pond where Crow danced among the cattails. She had come home, she told him. She loved him and no one else. She didn't give a damn what anyone said about them. Browder nearly smiled. The image was so detailed and clear that it seemed more real than this room, and for a moment, he felt the joy of dreaming of a future that he knew could never be.

AFTER THE BURIAL, Tee Wee had no time to think about anything except her duties. She began by putting out the best china, silver, all that stuff Miz Parsons never used, on the dining room table. The fried chicken, chicken pie with rice, and the pork chops she put on the sideboard, the desserts on the lace-covered card table in front of the window. The most important job, and the most difficult one, was to keep track of who brought what for the funeral meal. Icey was supposed to help with this and the dishes, but she was nowhere in sight. Tee Wee sighed, looking down at her small pad. She'd written "coernut pie, Miz Roggers; pound cake, Miz Dunkcan; lemen merang, Miz ? had on blue blouse." And if her job wasn't hard enough, people kept coming into the kitchen asking, "Tee Wee, do we have butter for the rolls?" or "Auntie, is there sugar anywhere?" "Butter. Sugar," Tee Wee muttered. "Can't any them white folks think for they self? Butter in the icebox where everybody keep it, and sugar in the bowl where it always at."

"Where what is at?" Icey entered the kitchen from the back door.

"Sugar. Folks like to drive me crazy. Where you been? I needin help."

Icey removed her hat and laid it on the table. "Had to go home for a minute. Had to. Couldn't help it."

"Hurmp," Tee Wee snorted. "I reckon you ain't give no thought to what's all to do round here." She grabbed up a bowl of butter beans. "Here, take these in to the table. My feets done run more'n a horse's at a race."

Icey took the dish, and slowly, bowl wobbling and sloshing juice, she turned toward the dining room. "When you find out how come I late, you gonna understand it," she called back to Tee Wee.

Probably Deke got saved in the outhouse this time, Tee Wee said to herself. Ever since Icey had confessed to making up her story about Deke's getting the Spirit, Tee Wee hadn't trusted a thing Icey told her. "Anybody lie bout the Spirit, lie bout anything," she had said to Icey when she'd told her the real story. She knew Icey would never have told the truth had she not been scared of Deke's finding her out. When Icey returned with a mysterious smile, Tee Wee ignored her. She wasn't gonna ask her nothin.

In the living room Ruthie sat beside her father on the couch. She had walked Dennis to his car and told him she wanted time alone now with her family. They would keep their plans a secret; this wasn't the time to announce their intentions. Oh God, what was her father's reaction going to be when he found out about her and Dennis? She looked over at him. He sat with a plate Aunt Sarah had fixed him in his lap, and, although he held his fork poised over his food, he hadn't eaten a bite. The smell of the food was making Ruthie sick again, and, rising, she headed for the front door. She leaned over the porch rail, hoping she wasn't going to throw up in the azalea bushes, but after a minute the fresh air calmed her waves of nausea and she leaned back against the post supporting the rail. I am damaged, she said to herself. That was the word her Aunt Ola had used ten days ago when Ruthie had overheard her talking to Aunt Sarah. She said the Wilkerson girl, who had been thrown from her horse, was damaged when her hymen was ruptured. Her aunt's words fell over her like rocks, weighing her down. "No man will want her now; she isn't a virgin." Ruthie folded her hands and prayed. "God, I know you took Mama to punish me; please don't take anybody else. I'm going to marry Dennis. God, please please, forgive me."

BROWDER SAT IN a corner in the living room watching his father. He looked like a very old man with stooped shoulders, his hair flecked with gray, his chest caved in, and his long legs splayed out before him looking limp and too weak to support him. Why couldn't his father have been the one to die? Why did it have to be her? Browder wanted to get away from these people, but every time he stood up someone hugged him and blocked his path. Better to sit here until they were all gone. No, better to return to the pond of his mind. With Crow. He'd told himself he would find her, but he hadn't even tried. He knew it was useless. She wouldn't be found unless she wanted to see him. But she did love him. He was sure of that. David Jefferson. David Jefferson. That name was one he'd never forget. One day he'd find David Jefferson and then he'd find out about Crow. He hated him, too. Hated him for abandoning her and for taking her in, if he did. Maybe she'd lied about that, also. Browder managed to thread his way through the crowd to the kitchen with only two condolence pauses. When Tee Wee turned and saw him, she shot him a mean look, the same look she'd been giving him ever since she'd found out about him and Crow. He hadn't spoken to her once because he was a little afraid of her, but today he knew his mother would want him to do what was right. He cleared his throat. "Uh, Tee Wee?"

She lifted a plate of pears topped with dollops of mayonnaise. "What you want?" Her voice was harsh with no trace of sympathy for him.

He had intended to offer some sort of token for a reconciliation. He was going to say something about how his mother would want them to be friends. But Tee Wee's stony, closed face warned him away. "Nothing," he said.

"Then get on out of my kitchen."

"Mama wouldn't want us to have hard feelings," Browder ventured to say.

"No, you right. But your mama would have died of a broken heart stead of cancer if she'd of known what you done."

She was right. But Tee Wee hadn't told anyone, he didn't think. Not even Icey, who was treating him the same as she always did. "Thanks for not telling Mama."

Tee Wee slammed the pears down on the kitchen table. "Didn't do it for you. I didn't tell cause of her. Don't be thinkin nothin else. You worse than nigger trash. You think you so high above us colored, but you ain't." Rage welled up inside her now and she thought that she might slap him if he didn't go away.

Browder read this last thought and ran for the back door. He should have told Tee Wee he loved Crow; it wasn't just sex, but she would never believe him. He was nigger trash to her and always would be. When he reached the bank of the pond, he called out across the muddy water, "Crow, Crow, come back. Come home."

IN THE KITCHEN Tee Wee set the pears on the table. Her anger directed her thoughts toward a dark future. Miz Parsons was gone now, and she was the one who made Mr. Parsons treat all the Negroes on his place fair. She had heard rumors that his daddy had beaten a black man for stealing a hoe, and there was all that business about him killing Johnnie Wilks because Johnnie had caused his mule Dolly to fall in a ditch and break her leg. Ole Mr. Feke Parsons said it was an accident, but everyone believed

Parsons had killed Johnnie in a fit of rage. She remembered the old man yelling at her, telling her to get her black ass moving. What if Mr. Parsons turned out like his daddy now that his wife wasn't around to protect them? Tee Wee sat down beside the table and stared at the pears. She thought about her life here on Parsons Place. Ruthie would be going away to school, the sight of Browder made her insides coil up into a knot, and long as he was around, Crow couldn't come home. She smashed a pear with her fist, and as the mayonnaise oozed over the sides of the pale pulp, Tee Wee considered leaving Parsons Place. They ought to get away before trouble happened. She looked out the window at the parched ground. But how and where? They didn't have enough money to leave, owed Mr. Parsons four hundred dollars still. Luther's dream of buying his land was a joke. Mr. Parsons wasn't gonna sell nothin to coloreds. Tee Wee dropped her head in her hands, and great racking sobs tore out of her. She cried for Crow, for J. P., for Luther and herself. She cried for all the sorrow she'd kept inside her every time she cooked a meal in this house. And she cried for Miz Parsons, who had her share of sorrow, too. But death had taken her from her pain, and there was no escape for the Weathersbys now. Tee Wee stood up, and, picking up the damaged pear, she popped it into her mouth and ground her teeth on it.

In the dining room Icey was enjoying herself. She had tasted nearly every dish on the table and sideboard. This was the best funeral spread she'd ever eaten. And she wasn't the only one thought so. She had given out Tee Wee's recipe for blackberry cobbler, the secret to Tee Wee's sweet corn bread, and had made up a list of the ingredients for her corn casserole. She wasn't exactly sure about any of the recipes people asked her for, but she enjoyed the attention she was getting from the Pisgah ladies who kept complimenting her on her cooking. She picked up the empty butter bean dish and went back to the kitchen for a refill. Before she had taken two steps on the linoleum, she saw Tee Wee's bulging mouth and was about to tell her to save some food for the guests when she saw that she was chewing like a starving yard dog. Then she looked up and saw the wet cheeks, the pained expression in Tee Wee's eyes. "What's happened?" She wasn't just crying over the dead, she was sure of that.

Tee Wee swallowed the pear. "Icey, I'm scared."

A wave of fear splashed against Icey's chest. If Tee Wee was afraid, there was reason for her to be, too. "What of?"

Tee Wee wiped her hands on her apron. "The future. What gonna happen to all us colored here with Miz Parsons lyin in the Whittington Cemetery?"

Icey bit her lip. She didn't understand. "What you mean?"

"You ain't studied on this but I has. We might get kicked off the place, Mister Parsons might not treat us good without her; lots of things can change now. Your skin is black; you ought to be thinkin bout what that mean now."

Icey looked down at her arm as if she were seeing its color for the first time. "I knows I black same as you. This is stupid talk. Ain't nothin gonna happen. You sat up with Miz Parsons too long; your brain ain't runnin right cause you just plumb wore out."

Tee Wee pressed her lips together and then said, "I been tired all my life, worked since I was a little girl, and reckon I be workin tills the day I fall dead. All I wantin is for my babies not to have to work hard as me and don't look like I can help em much."

Icey nodded. "We all work hard, but Tee, you got to look on the bright side. Ever cloud have a silver linin, darkest before dawn, uh—"

"Shut your mouth, Icey. None of that mean nothin to us. You ain't got one good reason for me to believe things gonna be okay."

Icey clapped her hands together. "I do, too. It my surprise I was gonna tell you. I'm gonna have another baby, Tee. That be a reason. This little one," she patted her stomach, "be the reason for me."

Tee Wee stared at Icey's hands. For once, maybe Icey was right. Maybe there was a reason to hope. Maybe them clouds of Icey's did have silver bottoms. And tomorrow it was supposed to rain. She smiled. Picking up the plate of pears, she held them out in the space between them. "Don't eat all these fore you carry them in."

Icey took the plate. "I won't. I ain't hungry a bit."

Part Three

1968

EE WEE SLID HER PORCH ROCKER AROUND TO FACE ICEY'S house, settled into it, and crossed her hands over her stomach. She could hardly wait to see the expression on Icey's face after she heard the big news. As she rocked, she watched two squirrels chase each other around the oak tree until they disappeared into the canopy of leaves overhead. Although it was only May, it seemed like August, and Tee Wee hoped Icey would hurry up and come out so that she could go back in and sit in front of the little table fan Luther had bought at a junk sale.

She didn't have to wait long. Icey's door slammed, and Icey, wearing her new gray-and-white maid's uniform, stepped out onto her porch. "Hey," Tee Wee called. "I got good news to tell."

Icey looked over toward Tee Wee's chair. "You best tell it fast; I got to get to work. Miz High n Mighty be lookin at the clock when I comes in the door."

Tee Wee turned her head so that Icey wouldn't see her smile. She pulled on her long face and tried to sound sympathetic. "I know. Your life is some hard these days, and I do feels for you. And havin to wear that outfit is nothin but an insult to you."

Icey smoothed the skirt over her hips. "I think I look nice in it, and it say to people I am a professional maid. Not just a house nigger. Your girl Masie stay in the Parsons' kitchen and don't have no special uniform." Icey strolled across the yard and mounted the steps to Tee Wee's porch. She cocked one hip. "I reckon I should be glad she be the new cook, though; I done lost a lot of pounds eatin her vittles. Deke said I ain't never looked better."

Tee Wee glared at Icey. She was still a huge woman, but Tee Wee had to admit she looked good. And she knew that she herself had put on at least ten more pounds since the change of life had come to her. Remembering her menopausal state, she wiped her brow with her hand. She would ignore the comment about Masie's cookin because she had to agree with Icey on that. Masie hadn't taken after her mama. Rufus was the only one of her young'ns who could cook anywhere near as good as her.

Icey sat on the adjacent rocker and crossed her legs to show Tee Wee that she could; Tee Wee's bare feet were spread as wide as the chair itself. Tee Wee wiped her neck and held out her wet palm. "Well, you ain't had the change come down on you like me. I suffer so with it, and I know that's why I gained a little weight."

Icey drew up her shoulders. "Pshhh, I got the change all right. Got the sweats worse'n any you could imagine."

Tee Wee decided to let that go. She was anxious to get to her news. "Guess who called me on the tel lee phone this morning."

"I ain't got time to guess. Just tell me who."

Tee Wee smiled. Icey wasn't gonna go nowhere till she found out her news. "Well, it were last night. I was just gettin my nightgown on to go to bed. You know I have to get to sleep early now that I'm a store owner." She paused to savor the words *store owner*. She could hardly believe this fact was true, but exactly one month ago she had signed the rent lease and opened The Camellia Bakery on Front Street in Zebulon. All those years of saving butter and egg money, doing without new clothes or fancy bric-a-bracs like Icey bought, had paid off. And each morning when she unlocked the shiny red-painted door to her bakery, she felt like she was opening the pearly gates of heaven.

"Speakin of which, ain't you got to get to your store? How come you ain't left already? Is them cakes and pies not sellin?"

"Oh no. Business is good, real good. I don't open Mondays till ten. I sell so much on the weekend, I take Mondays easy."

"Well, you gonna tell me who called or not?"

"Crow, Miss Sharmaine Jefferson. That's who. And she is comin for a visit. Comin to see her brother, J. P. Weathersby, get his high school diploma on Saturday."

Icey stood and walked down the steps. "Well, it's about time she remember who her folks is. I feels sorry for you, Tee, havin two daughters who don't never come see bout their mama. I hopes my little Hilda don't grow up to go off somewhere and forgit her mama."

Tee Wee had to think for a minute on how to reply to this. It was true that Crow hadn't come home in ten years, and Ernestine had only visited once in the last eighteen. But they both wrote letters and called; she felt she was still a part of their lives. She wasn't gonna let Icey ruin her good mood with her bad mouth. "They ain't forgot me; they just busy makin their mama proud," she hollered toward Icey's retreating back.

Tee Wee hurried inside, grabbed her fan, and carried it to her dresser. If she didn't stick her face near the whirring blades, she would sweat so much that her powder would cake on her face. She applied a coat of purple lipstick and blotted her lips on a piece of toilet paper. She had begun wearing a little makeup last week, thinking that when you deal with the public, you ought to look your best.

Icey's reaction to Crow's coming had disappointed her; she had to be just filled up with envy that Tee Wee's daughter was a singing star now. But no, butter wouldn't melt in that gold-toothed mouth of hers. As she drove into Zebulon in the battered used truck Luther had bought fifth or sixth hand, she admitted to herself that she was a little nervous about Crow coming home. She really didn't know her anymore. Tee Wee thought back ten years to the day Crow had left. She remembered how surprised she had been to learn that David Jefferson owned a restaurant in Flower, Mississippi. At first, she had been angry that he had another life, another woman, but she was glad that Crow had found him so that she had somewhere to run to. David had saved her from Browder. And she reckoned Crow owed him her music talent, too. She smiled. Lord, he could sure play that harmonica he used to carry everywhere in his shirt pocket.

Tee Wee parked on Front Street and sat for a moment admiring the cream-colored building that held her dreams. Dennis Wardlaw, Ruthie's husband, owned it, and Tee Wee was sure it was Ruthie who had talked him into renting it to her. The building was a small rectangle, narrow across the sidewalk, running eighty feet back for the salesroom and kitchen. Above the red door, a gingerbread man held the sign that read, CAMELLIA BAKERY. As she passed by the plate-glass window, she admired the cakes and pies displayed on footed glass plates surrounded by the artificial greenery Ruthie had given her. After unlocking the door, she flipped on the light, illuminating the glass showcase where sugar cookies, tea cakes, banana and raisin breads were aligned in neat rows. She was early. There would be plenty of time to bake some cakes and a pie or two.

As she mixed flour and creamed butter her thoughts wandered like the Tangipahoa River around the lives of her children. Most of them were doing well now. Rufus got into trouble still, but his wife and young'ns had helped settle him down some. The last time he had spent a night in jail was when he got caught wearing a three-piece double-breasted suit a white man had brought in for dry cleaning at Colonial Cleaners where Rufus worked. He had been found out because he left a movie ticket stub in the pocket of the suit. Tee Wee shook her head. If you gonna be a criminal, you got to be smarter than Rufus. Ernestine was still over in Alabama teaching school. Paul and his wife had given her four fine grandchildren; Masie, well, she was planning on getting out of the Parsons' house soon. Tee Wee held her wooden spoon over the mixing bowl and frowned. She hadn't heard from Lester in more than a month. He hadn't written to his twin Masie, either, and both of them were worried his luck had run out over in Vietnam.

When she heard someone knocking on the front window, she peeked out the back room and saw J. P. He signaled to her to unlock the door.

"What you want, J. P.? I got bakin goin on here." Tee Wee's face wore a frown, but inside she felt a wave of absolute joy that this handsome boy was her son. He was wearing his best blue jeans and a forest-green shirt, starched and ironed so that he looked to Tee Wee like a mannequin in a store window.

He smiled, showing all his straight white teeth everyone commented on. "Daddy dropped me off, but I need the truck to run some errands and then get back home. Can I have the keys?" He was already behind the glass case helping himself to a tea cake.

Tee Wee snatched it out of his hand. "You ain't gonna eat up my profits, J. P. You got cookies at home." She blew on the tea cake and placed it back in the case.

J. P. was doing push-ups against the counter. Tee Wee pulled him away and with a cloth wiped his prints from the glass. "What errands you got that's so important?"

"I need a new shirt to wear under my graduation robe, some socks, underwear."

"Where you gettin the money for all this?"

"I borrowed some from Daddy, and I'm gonna pay him back next week."

"How you gettin money to pay him back?"

J. P. reached for the keys beside the cash register and dangled them in front of her. "That's the other errand." He grinned. "I got a job interview at Larry's Used Cars."

Tee Wee didn't smile back. "Boy, what you mean? You ain't no car salesman. You ain't even got a car for yourself."

J. P. headed for the door. "It's not a selling job. I'll be washing, waxing, cleaning up, stuff like that. Maybe doing some mechanic work. I don't know till I talk to him."

"You ain't no mechanic," Tee Wee said, following him across the floor.

"Deke taught me some. I know more than Daddy about changing oil and replacing filters." He kissed her cheek. "Thanks for the truck. I gotta go."

"J. P., don't go takin no job until you know what all's involved," she called out as she watched him running across the street, tossing the keys in the air. "Oh Lordy," she said, closing and locking the door. "A used-car salesman, and how he think he gonna get to that job? I reckon Mr. Car Salesman Larry ain't gonna give him no car."

The cake batter was lumpy, and Tee Wee snatched up the wooden spoon and whipped it around the bowl with fury. J. P. didn't need no new shirt, probably could get by on the socks, too. And underwear, who was ever gonna see his underpants? Then she smiled. Her baby boy was something. He was different from her other sons, always asking the why and how come of things. Seemed like he just cared more, too—about other people, about all this civil rights business, about the war over in Vietnam. Tee Wee sighed. She wished she understood more about that war Lester was fightin in. She couldn't tell nothin from the news she read. Some folks was sayin we got to fight to save them people from the communists, and other folks was sayin we going to Canada, ain't gonna fight in a war that we shouldn't be in. Tee Wee added a cup of chopped nuts and watched them bob around in the batter. Lester hadn't cared about the right or wrong of the war. When he had gotten the draft notice, he had acted nearly happy about it. He wanted to see the world, be a hero, shoot at something besides squirrels and rabbits. What did he know? Too young to know sheep shit from shinola. She stopped stirring and looked up, remembering lines from the few letters she had received. "Mama, I sure miss your cooking. Sometimes I dream I'm eating your chicken n dumplings and collard greens and I wake up so hungry I can't hardly stand being here no more." He wrote about the fungus on his feet, the jungle heat rising in steam after a rain. He said his best friend had lost both of his arms and begged the company medic to let him die. Lester said he couldn't tell a friend from an enemy, and he thought about how they'd joke at home that all black people look alike to whites. Tee Wee poured the batter into the springform pan and a few tears dropped on top of the yellow batter. She wiped her eyes and slid the cake in the oven. She had read Lester's last letter over and over. He had written in pencil on lined tablet paper. His platoon was out on patrol; they were lost; the Vietcong had silenced their radio with a bullet. He was more scared than he had ever been in his life. "Mama, if I don't make it back, give my watch to J. P. Masie will probably feel my death if the Lord takes me."

Tee Wee prayed over the apples she peeled. "Sweet Jesus, take care of my son, Lester. Don't let nothin happen to him." She picked up her paring knife and chopped the apples into bite-sized pieces. She wasn't gonna think on no more bad things. This was a week to celebrate. She hadn't gotten the chance to tell Icey that J. P. was going to get an award for having the highest marks of any student in the senior class. And now Crow would be riding the train down from Memphis. My cup sure enough runnin over, Tee Wee thought, as she rolled out the pie dough and fitted it onto the plate.

After taking the cakes and pies out of the oven, Tee Wee went to the front of the store, unlocked the door, and turned the CLOSED sign around. "The Camellia Bakery is open for business," she said. "Get your pocketbooks and come on in here with em." She looked out onto the street; there weren't many people out and about yet. Tee Wee needed to sell the cookies and other sweets in the case before they went bad; she hated to reduce prices or, worse, feed the stale leftovers to her family. She walked back to the cash register and hit the key to open it. She loved the ding it made, and she loved to look at the rows of green bills. There were a lot more ones than tens, fives, or twenties, but Tee Wee was feeling more prosperous than she ever had. She wasn't gonna fail in this. There were too many lazy white folks in the world who would keep her register dinging.

When the door opened, she looked up and saw Mrs. Gardner, a tall, big-boned lady who bought something nearly every week. As she closed the door, she took a deep breath. "My, it smells heavenly in here. What's good today, Miss Weathersby?"

Tee Wee stood silently behind her cash register. She had heard right. This white woman had called her *Miss* Weathersby. Her hands trembled and her eyes filled with proud water as she moved to her spotless glass case. "Red velvet or German chocolate cake. Either one will melt in your mouth," she said, lifting out the just-baked cake filled with nuts and tears.

Chapter 37

ON FRIDAY MORNING J. P. STOOD ON THE SMALL WOODEN PLAT-
form outside the Zebulon depot. He looked up at the clock over the
door. Eleven-fifteen. Crow's train was due in at eleven-thirty, and Mr. An-
gley, the ticket seller, had told him it was running on time. Smiling, he
patted his neatly clipped Afro thinking that Crow would be impressed
that her baby brother had grown into a good-looking man. He had considered wearing his new white shirt, but decided to save it for the graduation ceremony tomorrow. Tomorrow! It seemed like it wasn't ever going
to get here. It was his big day, his day to be honored, to get presents, to
begin his adult life. "Come on, train," he whispered as he sat down on
the ladder-backed bench beside the door. Polished by the pants, dresses,
and coats of thousands of passengers, the bench's varnish was faded and
smooth to his hands as he ran them up and down the slats. When a white
couple came out onto the platform, he rose and walked down the steps
to join the group of blacks standing on the graveled space near the
tracks. He passed by a fat woman in rose-colored house slippers cradling
a heavy shopping bag, two barefoot children lagging pennies against the
tracks, and a group of ragtag black men laughing at some story an old
toothless man was telling.

Standing alone farther down the track, he told himself that he wasn't
like them. On Monday he would begin working at Mr. Larry's car business, and in the fall he was going to Tougaloo College where he planned
to study the law. He believed in Dr. King's dream and he remembered his
words, "We are called to be a people of conviction, not conformity." As
he thought back to the night he had heard the terrible news of Dr. King's

assassination on the radio, a wave of sadness mixed with anger washed over him. He had been visiting at his best friend Ray Simmons' house. As they sat on the couch and watched Mrs. King and her children mourn on the television set, both of them had cried as if they had lost their own fathers. Ray had predicted that Negroes would riot in protest, and he said they should get some guns or knives themselves, but J. P. had reminded him that Dr. King was against violence. "Education will be our weapon," J. P. said, imagining himself booming out these words from a podium to a sea of black faces.

The quickening of the crowd, raising their voices and shuffling their packages, told J. P. that the train must be in sight, and, leaning out, he saw the face of the black engine rushing toward them. When the shrill whistle blasts began as it reached the Pearl Street Bridge, J. P. bounced on his toes. He felt exactly like he had as a kid when he had spotted the train carrying Santy Claus coming toward him. But this train was bringing Crow, and like Santa, she would come with a gift inside her suitcase just for him.

When he saw her stepping down the metal foldout steps in black high heels, J. P. stood for a moment, unable to believe his eyes. Crow had changed. She looked rich and important. As she came toward him, he watched the crowd parting like the Red Sea before her. All his former confidence in her approval of him vanished like morning fog. He looked down at his scruffy tennis shoes, one with a broken lace, and wished he could sink into the ground. "J. P.," Crow called. "Is that you?" Her long arms encircled his back, her skin was soft against his cheek, and beneath her picture hat her eyes shone out at him. "When did you grow up to be so handsome?"

J. P. shrugged. He had no idea what to say to this fancy woman. "Hey, Crow," he said. "The train was on time."

Crow laughed. "Yeah, will miracles never cease. Let me get my suitcases before somebody steals them," she said, turning to the porter unloading the baggage onto the gravel. With his eyes on her swaying hips in the tight black skirt, J. P. followed the swiftly moving long legs he remembered sprinting across the pasture. He grinned. What was Mama going to say when she saw her glamorous daughter?

When he parked in front of the bakery, J. P. saw Tee Wee's face at the window. She flapped her arm in a wave, swung open the red door, and ran out to the truck. After grabbing Crow in a bear hug that lasted for a long time, she held her away from her. "Crow! You look like a movie star. Just wait till Icey sees you; she gonna fall over green as a turnip leaf with envy."

As J. P. stood on the sidewalk listening to the music of their voices, he felt he would burst with happiness. Then the two women he loved most in the world pulled him inside the warm, sweet-smelling bakery, and his eyes filled with thankful water as he slipped one of his mama's delicious tea cakes into his mouth.

J. P. could tell Crow was nearly as surprised by her mama and the bakery as Tee Wee was by her glamour. She wandered over every inch of the store and came to stand beneath the picture of the house with the red barn that had hung over the table in their kitchen. "I remember this. I used to stare up at that house, hoping I'd have one like that someday." Crow laughed. "I could afford it now, but I live in a little apartment, not much bigger than our old house."

"What's your place like?" J. P. asked, imagining purple velvet drapes, brass chandeliers, and heavy mahogany furniture set on fine Oriental rugs like the houses of the rich he had seen at the picture show.

Crow laid her pink handbag on the counter and sat on the stool behind it where J. P. usually perched. "Oh, it's just a typical apartment: kitchen, living room, bedroom, bath." She leaned out and squeezed his forearm. "It's a lot bigger than most apartments and the bathroom has a counter to put your things on. The sink and tub are pink."

Crow wasn't going to appreciate the small bathroom addition to their house Luther was so proud of. But not having to go outside in cold weather was pure luxury to all the Weathersbys. "We got a bathroom now," he said.

Tee Wee nodded. "Crow knows that. I wrote her about it years ago when Luther put it in." She turned to Crow. "What you don't know is J. P. is gonna get an award tomorrow for the student makin the highest grades in his class."

"Mama!" J. P. yelled. "I wanted to tell her myself."

Crow leapt off the stool and hugged him. "Wow! Congratulations. I'm so proud of you." She squeezed his face between her hands. "I always said you were the smartest of all of us."

J. P.'s face flushed with pleasurable heat. Crow was acting like he, instead of her, was the celebrity in the family. "Thanks."

"Ain't this somethin, though? Jesus has sure been good to us," Tee Wee said. She wanted to close the store and go home with them, but she would have to stay until all the graduation cake orders were picked up. She hugged Crow against her breast. "I'm so glad you came home. Been a long long time since you walked off down Enterprise Road."

"I haven't forgot," Crow said softly. "I remember everything."

On the ride home, J. P. quizzed his sister about her life in Memphis. When he asked about the stars she had met, Bo Diddley in particular, she smoothed her skirt across her thighs. "No. I did see Lena Horne perform one night though. She's incredible, J. P. I wish you could've been there with me."

Lena Horne wasn't somebody J. P. was living or dying to see, but he tried to sound enthusiastic. "Me, too." Then, seeing that Crow's head was turned toward the fields of plowed red earth, he fell silent. This Crow wasn't the same one who had chased the little kids around the yard, yelling at them. She wasn't the sister who slapped him once for saying he wished he'd been born white. Of course, he had been only seven when she left; maybe his memories of her weren't realistic. He tapped her arm. "Remember my dog Bob Two that Deke found in the woods and brought home to me?"

Crow smiled. "Yeah, he still living?"

"Uh-huh. He's old, but he still gets around, eats like a horse."

"Mama looks old, too. I guess she must be fifty-something by now." Crow's eyes darkened. "Everything and everybody changes, nothing stays the same, that's for sure. And you should be glad of it, J. P. Don't look backward, just go forward. Things are getting better for blacks. When I first got to Memphis, I couldn't even sit at a table in some of the nightclubs I was singing in."

"Well, it might be better in Memphis, but down here we still got to watch our step. A lot of white folks in Mississippi were celebrating instead of mourning when Doctor King was assassinated."

Crow nodded. "I know, but no matter what they think and feel, they can't stop us now. Law says they got to give us our rights." She pinched J. P.'s arm. "Matter of fact, I got a surprise for you that is going to make a big difference in the way people around here see you."

J. P.'s heart somersaulted. "What is it?" He was thinking maybe Crow was going to buy him a car. Wasn't she rich now and couldn't she afford a sports car?

"Not telling yet. You have to wait." Crow leaned over and rubbed his Afro. "But you're going to be surprised, really really surprised."

It had to be a car! J. P. slapped the steering wheel and honked his horn as he turned into the Weathersbys' drive. "Here we are. We're home, Crow."

Chapter 38

ON FRIDAY AFTERNOON THE CLOUDS OVER PARSONS PLACE MUSH-roomed over the sun, diffusing the light and casting a pall over the pasture where Crow walked on her way to the pond. This morning when she had followed J. P. into the house, she was surprised at how faulty her memories of her home had turned out to be. The house was smaller, darker, and shabbier than she remembered, and the tiny bathroom addition with its tiled floor and shiny porcelain fixtures was like an ugly woman wearing a beautiful dress that only served to emphasize her unattractiveness. In her old bedroom, changing into a pair of shorts, as Crow looked around at the iron bedsteads, she remembered the makeshift cots and pallets scattered across the room that had vanished like the voices of the girls who had lain on them. Lifting the rag rug, she searched for the loose board that had covered her hiding place, but it had been nailed down.

Crow tried not to show her relief when J. P. said he had to go back into town to talk to Mr. Larry about his new job. As she stood on the porch watching the truck bump down the drive, she welcomed her solitude, needing this time alone to balance her seesawing emotions. When she had flown from here ten years ago, Crow had carried with her the smell of the farm: a collage of manure, rotting vegetables, pesticides, the rank odor of unwashed dogs, and the scent of the rich earth, which had been her cologne all these years. And it was these aromas that overwhelmed her, bringing her past to the present, and both anger and sorrow welled up inside her.

She had headed for the pond; it was a magnet drawing her to scores of memories. When she reached the bank, she saw that a new wooden pier extended twelve feet out over the muddy water. Two Christmas trees had been thrown into the shallow water, and their brown dead branches stuck up like ghoulish skeleton hands. Tossing a clod of red clay into the water, she watched the ripples spread, and then, sitting on the hard-packed ground, she drew her knees to her chest and wrapped her arms around her legs. She felt in need of comfort, for what she didn't know. All Crow was sure of was that from the moment she had stepped off the train she had lost something of herself and now she tried to summon the lost parts. Lines of songs ran through her head. "Don't care bout nothin but my baby. Fish gotta swim; birds gotta fly. I gotta love one man till I die." Love. She sang so many songs about love and desire and passion. People in love and people wanting love listened to her voice drifting out from their radios and record players, and she manipulated their emotions, keeping her own under tight control. Crow gazed across the pond to the cattails and saw herself there lying beside Browder. She remembered the timbre of his voice whispering words that lingered still in her mind. She didn't want to think of the past. Hadn't she less than three hours ago told J. P. to look to the future?

But here at the pond the past was more tangible than her apartment in Memphis, more relevant to her identity than the albums that bore her voice. As she walked out onto the pier, Crow felt once again the losses she had mourned here: her father, Memphis, Browder, even Caddie, the cat she had buried on the far bank. But she was nearly thirty now, a grown-up woman with little resemblance to that girl who had run to this sanctuary. When she reached the end of the pier, Crow sat on the warm boards and dangled her feet over the dark water. She remembered a movie in which the passage of time was shown by the pages of a calendar turning quickly to the future. It was as if the ten years since she had left had been torn away as easily and swiftly as the years of that calendar, and all the changes she had affected in her new life seemed inconsequential here on Parsons Place. "I shouldn't have come home," Crow said out loud to the murky water. "I don't belong here anymore." But as she stood and turned back toward the bank, she knew that a part of her had never left.

Crow told herself the reason her feet took her in the direction of the Parsons' house was that she wanted to see Masie. Her mother had written the news that Browder had married Missy after his father had died more than seven years ago, but no image of Missy came to mind, except that of a pale girl with watery eyes. Crow's feet dug into the soil as she walked toward the Parsons' barn. Browder's marriage meant nothing to her. She had had several proposals, and if it weren't for her career, she might be happily living with one of the many black men who adored her.

She frowned. Her relationship with Browder had been a mistake, and because she had made very few errors in her life, every misstep rankled permanently in her mind. But if she hadn't run from that mistake, she wouldn't have been in Flower that day to meet Winston Brown, and although she knew for certain that she would have gotten to Chicago or Memphis on her own, Winston had accelerated her timetable considerably.

Crow had saved the tips she received in her father's restaurant and all the money she earned singing in Flower at every wedding, funeral, and festival, but she had calculated that it would take nearly a year for her to have enough to go to Chicago to begin her career. Rooms were expensive; she would need better clothes, a warm coat, and extra cash for buying hooch to trade for the opportunity to sing with a band at a club. She didn't know how she knew, but she was certain that she would be a star, a star like Bessie Smith or Billie Holiday, bigger than either of them, and she wasn't going to drink liquor or shoot horse. She would be smarter than they had been.

And then one Saturday just before closing the diner, Winston Brown had entered Crow's life and changed it forever. It was nearly eleven and the tables were wiped clean except for one where two couples lingered drinking coffee. Crow was standing with arms stretched across the jukebox, swinging her hips, singing along with Ray Charles, B4, "I Got a Woman." She didn't hear the door open, but when the song ended, she turned and saw him sitting at a table watching her with a big smile on his white white face.

When Crow walked to his table, he kept his smile. "You have a beautiful voice." He spoke in a peculiar accent that she had never heard before.

"Lots of folks tell me that," she said, taking in his pin-striped suit, gold watch, and ruby ring.

His green eyes, the color of the wild ferns that grew on the floor of the woods back home, swept over her. "You're a lovely girl, too."

Crow was suspicious of this dandy man. She wasn't looking to make money on her back anymore. "You wantin somethin to eat or you just here for the view?" She placed her pencil on her pad and waited.

He laughed. "Food," he said. "I'm famished. Motored down from Memphis this morning."

As he ate two fried pork chops, he told her that his name was Winston Brown, he was from England, now owned a recording studio in Memphis, and was traveling to New Orleans. After he left that night, Crow hadn't expected to see him again, but one week later, he returned and sat at the same table, daintily eating ribs with a knife and fork. He asked Crow to sing another song for him, and after she had sung every Bessie Smith song on the jukebox, he told her that her voice had a distinctive quality like no other he had heard. "Come back to Memphis with me; I'll make you a star. I promise," he said.

Crow hadn't said yes that day; she wasn't sure she trusted this peculiar Englishman. He might be a con man or some kind of nut. Winston had thought she was hesitant because of her fear of his making advances to her, and, looking down at his fried eggs the next morning, he said in a low voice, "I prefer men. You needn't worry about being pestered by me."

Crow sank into the chair beside him and laughed. "I thought so first time I saw you. But if you was expectin payment from me, that wouldn't be a reason to say no." She looked over his head at the other tables occupied with black workingmen in coveralls and khakis. Breathing in the smell of burned bacon and fried potatoes, she wiped the sweat from her upper lip. Her eyes traveled over Winston; he wore a gray blazer with a maroon emblem over his right pocket, a silk tie, gold rings that wouldn't turn his fingers green. She stuck out her hand. "It's a deal. I'll take a chance on you. Even if this don't work out, I can't be no worse off than now, I guess."

And it had worked out. Better than Crow could ever have imagined. But her doubts had remained for several months while Winston battled with tight-fisted club owners, dubious disc jockeys, blaring horn players, and drummers overpowering the sounds of sweet harmonicas. It had taken nearly a year for her to get a gig on Beale Street, and another half year before her records were played on stations like WTIX in New Orleans. But then her career gained momentum like a train clicking on steel tracks across open prairie. Smooth and fast. Riding on that fast train, she had rushed toward her first album, her first hit in the top forty, and finally she had been one of the few blacks to be photographed and interviewed for a layout in *Photoplay* magazine.

Crow looked down at her dirty toes sticking out of her sandals. She grinned. No one around here would believe she had worn a pair of shoes that cost nearly a hundred dollars for that picture in *Photoplay*.

As she walked on toward the Parsons', she saw Icey across the yard yanking sheets off the clothesline. Before Crow reached the house, Icey turned and waved. "Hey," she called out. "I heard you was comin home."

"Yeah, just got in this morning."

"I reckon you seen your mama already?"

"Yes, at the bakery." Crow smiled when Icey drew up her shoulders. She hadn't changed at all, still jealous of Mama. "I hear Masie is working in the kitchen now, and I thought I'd come say hello."

Icey smiled, her gold tooth glittering. "Yeah, she in the kitchen all right. Burning something most likely."

Masie was crying in the kitchen. Icey was right; she had burned the rice and it had stuck in Missy's best pan. Wiping her tears, she hugged Crow and told her that she looked beautiful. She knew she looked awful. Sitting at the kitchen table Masie told Crow that she was taking a secretarial course, and as soon as she got her certificate, she was quitting this job. Missy Parsons was "the most unhappy person in the whole state." It was because she and Browder hadn't got any babies to fill up the empty rooms in their house. "I think she's even jealous when a cow drops a calf," Masie said. When Crow asked if Browder wanted a baby as much as his wife, Masie said that she reckoned he did, but he didn't let on to folks how he felt. "He is sure a good uncle to Ruthie's little girl, Annie Ruth. Always taking her someplace, buying her something. He loves her to death. And she dotes on him, too."

On the way home Crow tried to imagine Browder with a little girl, but all of the pictures in her head were ones of him as he had looked when he was nineteen. When she stopped to admire a pipevine swallowtail with blue-green hindwings sailing overhead, it occurred to her that the beauty of the butterfly emerged from a poisonous caterpillar like those that had stung her more than once. As she spun around to trace the swallowtail's flight over her left shoulder, Crow saw him. Browder was watching the butterfly, too.

She caught her breath; she could run away from here before he turned and saw her. But her sandals may as well have been stuck in cement, and she stood helplessly as he came toward her. Browder was more handsome than she had remembered. His blond hair was long now, parted to the side with one lock falling across his forehead. He seemed taller in his jeans, worn low on his hips. Crow waited, and when he raised his eyes, she met the blue of them with her dark ones.

"Hey," she said. "I'm back."

Browder's face reflected his shock. "Crow? Crow," he said. Then, relaxing the muscles in his face, he smiled. "I didn't know you were home."

"Just got here. Came for J. P.'s graduation ceremony."

Browder moved sideways to align himself with the shadow the sun cast before her. "Y'all must be real proud of him. Masie said he's going to go to college."

His voice was deeper. Pleasing to her. She had turned down dates with a lot of men because she couldn't abide their scratchy tones. She met Browder's eyes as she lifted her long hair and released it to cascade across her shoulders. She was glad she had straightened it and hadn't given in to Winston who said an Afro would look good on her. No wigs; no Afros; no braids anymore. She knew what straight men liked. "Yeah, we're going to have a lawyer in the family someday."

"And you. You're a big star now. I've heard you on the radio. You always were a good singer. I remember you singing when—" He broke off his sentence, dropped his hand, and looked down at the soft grass.

Crow waved his words away. She could handle this better than he could. "Yeah, well. It beats scrubbing floors in a white person's house." Then she heard herself saying, "If I hadn't run away from here, it might be me instead of Masie scrubbing your wife's pots." She bit her lip. That wasn't what she wanted to say.

He dug his hands into his pockets, lifting his shoulders. "I'm glad you made it. I'm happy for you." He grinned then, the old smile she remembered now. "I tell people I knew you when you were just a little girl playing in the dirt around here."

Crow wiggled her toes in her sandals. "I still got dirt on me, but I'm not a little girl anymore." She wanted to touch him; his smile stirred an ache inside her. The warning bell rang in her head, the one that always pealed when she was nearing shallow waters hiding dangerous rocks. "I got to go," she said.

His hand shot out and grabbed her wrist. "Wait. How long will you be here?"

"Just a day or so. I've got a recording session next week." She felt the pressure of his fingers on her skin. "I gotta go." She didn't look at him; she wouldn't risk any more of herself. "Bye," she called, and before he could answer, she pulled away and ran across the pasture, her sandals cutting white ribbons through the cloth of green land.

Chapter 39.

ROWDER WATCHED CROW SPRINT ACROSS THE GRASS UN-
til she turned up the fence line and he could see her no more. He was
breathless, his heartbeats skittering like drumming fingers. He told himself that his body was only reacting to the surprise of running into her,
the unexpected. Crow was a childhood playmate, a girl he'd had an ado-
lescent crush on. Nothing more. The past was the past. He was married
now. Happy. He loved his wife. Bending over, he placed his hands on his
knees and rocked like a runner after a race. "Dammit! Why'd you have to
come back?" he said.

He straightened up. He had work to do, and he'd better get on with
it. He needed to check the barbed wire around the pole butter beans.
Even though it was early in the season and the beans were only flowering
now, he wanted to make sure that last year's mistake wouldn't happen
again.

As he walked across the pasture, he took out his handkerchief and
wiped the back of his neck. He thought back to the loss of his eighteen
Jerseys last summer. When they had wandered into the garden and dined
on his butter beans, the sharp stems of the beans had punctured the
cows' intestines and gas had formed so that their bellies had swelled like
giant balloons. Shaking his head, Luther had stuck a knife in one corpse
and ignited the escaping gas with a match. "Your daddy knew better," he
had said to Browder. Luther hadn't said anything when Browder's cotton
had been attacked by boll weevils, nor when he had planted two acres of
sweet potatoes in red clay that would not allow them to be nourished.
Browder slapped his thighs with his handkerchief; it was bad luck that

one year there was too much rain, another year too little. Dickie Webber at the Merchants Bank had called him twice last week about his overdue payment on the last loan. He had already sold Luther twenty acres for cash money, and now he was tapped out again.

God knows he had tried to be a good farmer. He'd read farm journals, enrolled in the classes the county agent taught, and consulted the *Farmer's Almanac* every year before planting. But none of the measures he took to improve himself had helped him become the success his father had wanted him to be. His heart had never belonged to this land he walked across. He had wanted to be a film producer. Had even taken a few drama classes at Ole Miss, but his daddy had refused to pay for an education toward an "impractical pipedream."

When he reached the fence, Browder shooed away the crows dining on his early tomatoes. Covering his ears against their noisy cawing, he thought of Crow again, her dark eyes, her long legs, the curve of her neck when she lifted her hair.

Looking out across the rows of his wilting plants, he thought back to the battle he had fought to overcome his grief over Crow's leaving and his mother's death. He had returned to school hoping that it would be a panacea for his unhappiness, but the distance from his home only increased his feelings of loss and he had sunk into an even deeper depression. He looked for solace in the theater in Oxford, but the silver screen was tarnished for him now. Every celluloid heartache was his own, each love affair belonged to him and Crow, and all of the deaths in the stories reopened the wound of his isolation. He skipped classes and stayed in his room most nights, until one afternoon his roommate coaxed him into going to a party in Columbus at Mississippi State College for Women.

Browder had forgotten that Missy Jordan was a freshman at MSCW, and when she came over to him at the party, he could barely believe this girl was the same one who only months before had annoyed him at Ruthie's birthday celebration. The new Missy had lost her former pudginess. Her blond hair flipped around her shoulders and the blue of her eyes matched the tiny blue flowers in her blouse perfectly. She was lovely. Browder asked her to dance. As he held her in his arms, he allowed himself to compare her to Crow, and the ache returned, but then he felt Missy's fingers rim his ear and she whispered, "Let's get out of here." When he kissed her later that night, he knew that he had found someone to fill the cavern Crow had carved in his heart.

Browder asked her to be his wife on the day of his graduation. They would live in Columbus until Missy was awarded her teaching degree at MSCW, and then they would drive out to California. With his business degree Browder thought that maybe he could get into some facet of the movie business where he could meet people who might open the door for him to follow his passion for films. But then that fall his father had had the stroke, and Ruthie had telephoned him at the finance company where he was working and begged him to come home to Parsons Place.

Lifting his hoe, Browder chopped away the Johnson grass that threatened to choke the beans, the squash, and the staked tomato plants. He worked mindlessly, stopping only to sip from the canteen hanging from the fence. It was nearly dinnertime when, filthy and exhausted, he slung his hoe across the wheelbarrow and headed toward home. He hoped Masie had cooked something good for a change.

Missy was waiting for him on the back steps. "Masie quit today. I'll have to cook supper, and I'm having my period on top of all that."

Browder stopped at the outside faucet to wash his hands and arms. As the water trickled over his forearms, he dreaded the evening stretching before him. Missy's barrenness was the source of all of her misery, and each month when her panties stained red overnight, she was filled with bitter disappointment. Shaking the water from his arms, Browder walked to the steps. "Don't worry, honey. We'll find another cook. How come Masie quit?"

Missy crossed her arms. "She burned the rice and ruined my best stainless pan."

Browder propped his foot on the steps. He would let her tell it all although he longed to get into the shower, have something cool to drink. "So then what?"

"I don't know. I told her she was going to have to pay for the pan; she said something smart, and then . . . then I guess I just lost my temper and before I knew it, she was throwing her apron in my face and running out the back door." Her voice rose higher. "I didn't mean to upset her. Now I don't know what we'll do about dinner."

Browder sighed. He wanted a beer, that shower, and a good dinner that was not simmering on the stove. "Maybe Icey could cook."

"Icey! I'd have fired her the first week we moved in here if your daddy hadn't made you promise not to."

Browder pulled open the screen door. "Going to take a shower. I'm beat."

As the hot water cascaded over him, Browder thought about the

promises he had made to his father. Those promises his daddy had ex-
tracted from him had changed his life, and he wished for the thousandth
time he hadn't succumbed to the old man's wishes. But he was dying,
and Browder had sat in the chair beside his hospital bed listening to his
labored breathing, his raspy voice. "Son, I know you never took to farming. Disappointed me time and again. Maybe I was too hard on you, but I
thought you'd toughen up, learn to love the place as much as me." Then
his father had stretched out his hand, and when Browder took it in his
own, he felt bound to his father's wasted body. "Promise me. Promise
me, you'll keep the place. Luther and Deke have promised me they'd
stay on and help you. I can't leave this world knowing someone else will
live in the home where I brought your mama as a young bride. It's your
legacy; promise me you'll make it yours for your children."

Browder stepped out of the shower and wrapped a towel around his
waist. Wiping steam from the mirror, he stared at his reflection. He had
wanted to pull his hand away, run away from his father's hospital bed. He
had wanted to shout, *No, I don't want Parsons Place. I won't do it.* But he
hadn't said those words; he had seen the hope shining in his daddy's eyes
and he knew that his father loved him, had always loved him. "I promise," Browder said.

In the bedroom that had been his parents' Browder tossed his towel
on the floor and lay across the bed. He counted the teardrops in the
fancy crystal chandelier Missy had insisted on buying last year. Twelve,
thirteen, fourteen, second row, fifteen, sixteen. . . . Rolling over, pulling
the spread over his bare legs, his thoughts ran backward to Crow. He saw
her in the hayloft, wriggling out of her sundress with a wide grin on her
face. He thought of the day they had made love at the cemetery. He
squeezed his head between his hands. No, he wouldn't open himself up
to those memories. God knows he had enough to worry about between
the bills and Missy's unhappiness.

In the beginning when Browder had told Missy that in his father's
will Ruthie had been given cash and insurance money and him the
headaches of running the farm, she had seen Browder as a landowner,
she his beautiful bride in his castle. As he lay on the bed listening to the
pots banging in the kitchen, Browder thought about how hopeful Missy
had been that first year. Luther, Deke, Tee Wee, and Icey had all been relieved when he told them that he would follow his parents' wishes that
they be allowed to continue to rent the tenant houses and retain their
jobs. Life on Parsons Place was nearly idyllic. Browder took his bride to

the picture show on Saturdays, ate lunch with her parents after church on Sundays, and Missy would often follow him to the fields where she made the onerous scraping of cotton less detestable by admiring the curve of his arm, the breadth of his shoulder, the muscles that flexed as his hoe bit into the earth. At night they had lain in Browder's parents' antique bed, simultaneously reaching for each other. Lovemaking with Missy was vastly different from how it had been with Crow. He couldn't understand Missy's reluctance to make love during the daylight hours, and she had cried and hid her face in the pillow after he had forced his head between her legs. He felt a tenderness toward Missy he doubted would ever have been possible with Crow. He couldn't stay mad at her when she cuddled beneath his arm, whispering about the fat babies they would have. She twirled her hair around her index finger when she was worried; she sprayed perfume on the sheets that smelled like violets.

Browder lifted his head. Something had burned in the kitchen, and, as the charred smell wafted into the bedroom, he heard Missy's angry voice. *"Dammit."*

He went to her and wrapped her in his arms. Crow would be leaving soon. Missy was his wife in sickness and health, for better or worse. He ate the overcooked vegetables and burned biscuits and told Missy that they were good.

Chapter 40

S SHE SHOOK CORNFLAKES INTO ANNIE RUTH'S BOWL, RUTHIE decided she would take J. P.'s gift out to him this morning. He could wear the gold monogrammed cuff links at the graduation later today.

"Annie Ruth, time to eat," she yelled into the den over the sound of the Saturday-morning cartoons.

Annie Ruth, wearing a green satin dressing gown that Ruthie had discarded, sauntered into the kitchen, fanned the full skirt around her chair, and reached for her spoon. "Can we go to the show today?" Nine-year-old Annie Ruth was addicted to movies and planned on becoming an actress when she grew up. When she had told this to her uncle Browder, he had winked and said the love of films was in her blood.

Ruthie poured milk into a glass and handed it to her daughter. "No, we cannot, but how would you like to go out and visit Hilda? Icey called and invited you, and I thought we could take J. P.'s gift out to him at the same time."

"Cool," she said, swiping the milk that dribbled down her chin. "Is Daddy coming?"

"Saturday is his busy day. You know that."

Annie Ruth's shoulders slumped and her dark eyebrows drew together in just the way Dennis' did when he was unhappy. Shoving her bowl to the center of the table, she swirled her hair around her face. Ruthie was sure she was copying the performance of an actress on television. "Can we go see Uncle Browder's new calf while we're out there?"

"I don't see why not."

After breakfast while Annie Ruth was dressing, Ruthie wiped the countertops and rinsed the dishes. She was looking forward to seeing her brother. In the last couple of years their visits had been sporadic. There was always something preventing them from spending time together. Ruthie volunteered at the hospital, was a room mother for Annie Ruth's class each year, and there was always an errand, a dentist appointment, ballet classes, and all the detritus that came with the life of a Realtor's wife. Ruthie threw the sponge in the sink. Annie Ruth deserved more time with her father, too, but most nights she went to bed without a kiss from her daddy.

She turned to the table where the newspaper lay opened to the real estate ads. There was Dennis smiling at her above the photos of the houses he had listed. He hadn't changed all that much in the ten years they had been married. In fact, he was even more handsome as he approached his twenty-eighth birthday. She wished she wasn't so thin, wished she was more fashionable. Dimple was continually offering to do a makeover on her, but something always kept her from going through with it. She knew she couldn't part with her long hair that cascaded nearly to her waist, which Dimple said made her look like a hippie or a flower child. "Get some daisies and stick em on your head and you'll be ready for the move to the commune," Dimple had said.

Ruthie tossed the newspaper into the trash can and hurried to the laundry room. As she pulled the clothes hamper over to the washer, she winced with pain. Her shoulder was still sore from the last fight she and Dennis had had two days past. Afterward he had apologized for yanking her arm too hard. He was sorry, it was the booze, he had told her, that and his anger over losing the listing to that Peevy agent. It was always the liquor that caused him to hurt her. As she dangled Dennis' black sock over the machine, she thought back to the first time it had happened. She had just learned that she was pregnant with Annie Ruth, and Dennis had opened his new office and was working late at Wardlaw Realty nearly every night. That night Dennis was later than usual when he staggered into the bedroom holding his briefcase closely to his chest. He had lost a sale and wouldn't be getting the commission check they were counting on. When Ruthie, wanting to comfort him and lessen his worries about money, had offered to ask her father for a loan, Dennis had flown into a rage. "You and your daddy think I can't support you. You think all you Parsons are better than me, better than everybody."

Ruthie was already backing away from him. "No, I just thought with the baby coming and all . . ."

He grabbed her then, pushed her against the dresser, and then threw his briefcase at her. The hard corner edge of the case bit into her stomach and she cried out, *"The baby!"*

Immediately, Dennis' face registered horror over what he had done. He dropped to his knees, pressed his face into her stomach. "Oh my God, I'm sorry, honey. I'm sorry, little baby. I didn't mean it."

And Ruthie had sunk to the floor and cried with him, rocking him in her arms crooning to him as if he were her unborn child. "Shhhh. It's okay. We're okay. You didn't mean to. I know I know I know."

Ruthie stuffed the remaining clothes into the machine, spun the dial of the washer, and pushed it in. He never meant to hurt her. He loved her. When he was sober, he was a good husband and father to Annie Ruth. He tried hard, but each time something went awry, with every disappointment, lost sale, whatever occurred, Dennis reached for the bottle instead of her. The scenario of that first night had been repeated so many times, she felt as though she was on a carousel where the same painted horses rose and descended over and over, always returning to the place they had stopped before. Each time she thought about leaving Dennis, asking for a divorce, she thought of a reason not to. There were so many reasons to stay: Her child needed a father, divorce was a sin, she had promised God she would be a good wife to him, it was her duty as a Christian to help him. She loved him. But did she love him? He was the father of her child, her lover, the only man she had given herself to. But when he came home drunk, she feared him and her heart turned to stone.

The washer had filled and Ruthie pressed her palms down on the vibrating lid. She would have to remember not to favor her shoulder when she visited Tee Wee. It was hard enough to listen to Dimple's suspicions about Dennis, and although she denied her accusations that Dennis was responsible for her occasional bruises—"I'm accident-prone, just clumsy as a new puppy"—she knew that Dimple wasn't fooled. Dimple would never understand why she stayed with Dennis, and probably Tee Wee wouldn't, either. She had made a promise to God, and she meant to keep it. How could she leave Dennis? He was her husband, and Paul had written the Lord's command in I Corinthians: "Let not the wife depart from her husband. The wife is bound by the law as long as her husband liveth."

When she heard Annie Ruth skipping down the hall, she turned to her. "I'm ready," Annie Ruth said. "Let's go to Uncle Browder's."

Ruthie held Annie Ruth's hand out to the side. "And you look so pretty in those pink shorts. I'll get my purse and we'll be off."

When Ruthie passed the Weathersbys' and pulled into the Parsons' rutted drive, she felt a familiar pang as they slowly bounced up the gravel road. She loved her old home, but she was glad she and Dennis had moved into town. After their father had died, Browder offered to sell them land to build on, but Dennis didn't like the country, and now Ruthie was glad because she could never hide her secrets living out here.

Browder and Missy were going into Zebulon to buy a new bedroom suite, but he told a frowning Missy that they could go later in the day and ushered Ruthie and Annie Ruth to the cow lot. After he led the little red calf away from her mother's side, Annie Ruth stroked the calf's head. "What's her name?" she asked.

"Don't have one. What you want to call her?"

Annie Ruth cocked her head and examined the calf's angular face. "Mmmm. It's a girl?" Browder nodded. "Well, how about Rebecca? Mama just read a book to me about a girl named Rebecca on a farm."

"Rebecca it is. Probably shorten it to Becky, though. That be okay?"

"Yep." Annie Ruth rubbed her nose against the calf's face. "You're so cute; I love you, Becky," she crooned.

After the calf was returned to her anxious mother, Annie Ruth ran toward the tenant house to play with Hilda. "Stay in the yard. I'll be there in a minute," Ruthie called after her.

"I will. Bye, Uncle Browder. Thanks for letting me name Becky."

Browder leaned back against the fence, resting his elbows on the top rail. He smiled at Ruthie. "So, how's tricks at your house?"

"Tricky."

"Dennis selling a subdivision of houses today?"

"Who knows? Missy seems kinda upset, Browder. Maybe I'd better go."

"No. She'll get over it. Had a bad night, Masie quit, and Missy started her period again." He was smiling, but his voice sounded phony and forced.

Ruthie walked to the fence. Looking into his eyes, she noticed the network of red veins surrounding his pupils. "Browder, I wish God would bless y'all with a baby."

"And I wish God would bless you with a husband who didn't drink so much."

Ruthie looked down at her tennis shoes. Dennis' drinking binges were common knowledge in the small town of Zebulon. "It's not so bad.

It's just when he has problems at the office. Some weeks, even months he comes straight home sober as a judge."

He squeezed her shoulder. "If you say so." He stared into her eyes as though willing her to share her secrets. "But if you ever need to talk, I'm here."

Ruthie turned her head away. "I know. Thanks."

When the giggles of Annie Ruth and Hilda on the tire swing drifted across the pasture, Browder's eyes darted around the tenant houses, and Ruthie wondered if he was hoping to see Crow. She put her hand on his arm. "Crow's back. Did you know?"

Browder wiped his mouth with his hand. "I saw her yesterday."

Ruthie felt her heart would stop. "Browder, be careful."

He lifed his brows. "Careful of what? She become a mass murderer?"

She held his forearms, pinning them to his side. "Browder, I don't know how you feel about Crow, but I know there was something, just what I don't know, but something, between you two. I've always thought that her leaving here had to do with you in some way." Ruthie dropped her hands. A whip-poor-will called; a truck roared past. She held her breath, waiting for him to respond.

"Little Ruthie, my baby sister. You were always following me and Crow around like a shadow. I knew you saw things, but I guess I thought you were too young to understand what was going on."

"I didn't understand then, but now I think I do."

"You know, it feels kind of good to have you know. I mean to have you to talk to about it. There's never been anyone." His mouth turned down into a sad smile. "I really loved her. It wasn't just sex. I loved her, Ruthie." He ducked his head and in a low voice said, "But that was a life-time ago. We used to meet"—he swept his arms around—"everywhere. The barn, the woods, the pond. I thought she loved me back then."

"What happened?"

"Tee Wee found out and wanted to drive one of those long kitchen knives of hers into my heart. Crow wanted to go anyhow." He pinched his nose with his fingertips. "I don't know. I never knew what she really thought."

Ruthie took his hand. "And you haven't seen or talked to her in all these years."

Browder shook her off. "No, I swear. I've been faithful to Missy. I would never hurt her. I'm not like . . ." Ruthie tried to cover his mouth, but he pushed her hand away. "Not like Dennis."

"No!"

"I'm sorry. I shouldn't have said that."

When he held out his arms, she came into them. He rocked her like a child, kissing her hair, stroking her back in little circles as Tee Wee had when she was a girl. "It's okay, Ruthie. I'm here. Let me help you. You need help."

She pulled away. "I have God's help; He's all I need," Ruthie said.

Chapter 41

ICEY SAT ON THE COUCH IN HER LIVING ROOM DROWNING IN terrible waves of jealousy. She stood up, peeked out the window at Crow and J. P. sitting on their steps, and sat back down. Tee Wee had invited Icey's family over for barbecue after the graduation, and she didn't think she could stand eating one rib of that family's pig. She'd choke on it for sure. All morning the Weathersbys' house had been a beehive of activity. Hilda and Annie Ruth had run in and out of her house buzzing about J. P.'s blue gown, Tee Wee's big cake that had a tasseled hat made out of icing on it, Crow's fancy suitcases filled with stuff that smelled better than gardenias. She ought to go over there and have a look for herself. She rose and then fell back to the couch. No, she wasn't up to it.

Looking around her room, Icey cataloged the improvements she had made. She had a window air unit now, and the Weathersbys were still sweating. Last week Icey had brought home a lava lamp that had made Tee Wee's eyes pop and, best of all, her daughter was going to a white school. Hilda is smart as a whip, Icey said to herself. And she'll know more than all of Tee Wee's young'ns put together when her graduation day rolls around.

She stood up and began to pace. She felt better; she had no reason to be jealous of Tee Wee really. Her true aggravation stemmed from the knowledge that Tee Wee had been sneaky all these years, hiding things from her best friend, getting herself an education without saying one word. She remembered the years when Tee Wee brought Ernestine's letters over for her to read. When she'd stopped bringing them, Icey had thought somebody else was reading them to her. She hadn't suspected the truth, that Ruthie (who, it turned out, was just as sneaky as Tee Wee) was teaching Tee Wee out of white schoolbooks. Icey looked up at her new light fixture, a wagon wheel with a bulb in the middle. There's another reason for Tee Wee to be jealous of me, she thought. Okay, so what if Tee Wee could read, keep records at the store. The store. That bakery was the burr in her butt. How had she gotten the money for all that cooking equipment? And Tee Wee and Luther owned a few acres of the pasture on Parsons Place now. How come Deke hadn't made enough to buy some?

Then there was Crow. Who'd have ever thought she'd be wishing Crow was her daughter? She was nothing but a slut when she left here, Icey said to herself, but look at her now. She went back to the window and saw that Crow was swinging on Hilda's tire. She ought to go out there and tell her to get her skinny butt outta her swing. She sat back down; she didn't feel up to talking to Crow. Icey wiped at the perspiration that had formed along her hairline. The air conditioner wasn't helping much with her hot flashes, which were much worse at night. The change of life made most white women crazy, but Icey felt as sharp as ever. Of course, Tee Wee, who was noticeably sweating more now, might be losing some of her brain power from the body changes. She wouldn't be able to have any more children, but she had known Hilda would be her last when she had her in Tee Wee's car.

Icey shivered, remembering that day that was both awful and wonderful. She and Tee Wee, Glory, J. P., two of Rufus' kids, and Lester were on their way to the show to see a Shirley Temple picture when her water broke and she'd had the big contractions that pushed little Hilda into the crowded car among the dangling legs, knees, and elbows of the passengers. Tee Wee had driven off into Mr. Hatten's hay field, screaming, "Oh Lord, Lord, Lord" all the way. The kids were shouting so loud, she hadn't even heard Hilda's first cry. Maybe that was why Hilda was so different from all the rest of her children. Even Tee Wee admitted that Hilda had the sweetest smile of any child in Mississippi. And everybody loved her soft musical voice, her big brown eyes that were fringed with thick curly lashes. She was a beauty inside and out.

Now Icey decided to go to that barbecue. Crow wasn't nothing compared to Hilda. She would dress her in that little white piqué short set Ruthie had given her for her ninth birthday. She looked back out the window at Crow and J. P. with their heads together. What was so all-fired interesting that had J. P. still as a fence post standing in front of Crow?

———

J. P. WAS WAITING for Crow to give him his graduation present. Ever since she had arrived home, she had tormented him with delays, and now she promised him the wait was over. When he had learned that his present was hidden in the house, he could barely hide his disappointment knowing now that he wouldn't be driving the car he had been dreaming of. He said good-bye to the shiny red Triumph, the big black Caddy, even the small yellow Volkswagen he had been driving around in his head. He squared his shoulders; he was a man now. He reminded himself that it was better to pretend that you got what you wanted than to mourn what you didn't have. He had overcome many heartaches with this belief, and he had now convinced himself that Crow would give him something even better than a car.

J. P. whistled to Bob Two, who was pacing in front of Icey's door. The dog looked over at him, and then lay down, pushing his back against the screen. Long ago J. P. had caught Icey feeding Bob, and now little Hilda was feeding him, too. Well, he was going away to college, so it was best that the dog had them to take care of him. J. P. looked back at his mama's door; Crow was taking a long time getting his gift. He swung his arms around, threw a few jabs at the porch rail. He was too excited to stand still any longer.

Finally, Crow returned with her hands behind her back. "I got it. Pick a hand."

J. P. groaned. "Come on, Crow. Let me have it."

She laughed. "Okay, okay. Here it is."

J. P. stared at the blue envelope. All she was giving him was a card? "Thanks," he said, taking it from her. He knew his voice registered his disappointment, but he couldn't help it. When he opened the card, a check fell to the porch floor. Picking it up, he looked first at his full name, John Paul Weathersby, on the top line. Then he saw a three and zeroes. Two, no three, and then the dot. He squeezed the paper tighter. "Three thousand dollars?"

Crow laughed again. "You'd think it was three hundred thousand."

J. P. looked back at the word *thousand*. He had never before seen it written on a check, and he stared at the zeroes. Suddenly he understood that this was *his* money. "This will buy a car, a great car!" he yelled.

Crow shook her head. "Whoa, horse. There's a string attached to this money."

He thought about throwing her down and choking her. It was a mean trick. The lump in his stomach rose to his throat.

When Crow looked at his face, she put her arm around his shoulder. Her voice was soft. "J. P., my gift isn't this money; it's what this money is going to do for you."

J. P. pulled away. "Okay, what's this check gonna do?"

"It's going to buy your future. It's college money."

"I already . . ."

She stopped him. "No, it's not for Tougaloo or any other Negro college. This is tuition money for Ole Miss, the University of Mississippi. I want you to have the best education you can get, same as a white boy." Crow's voice swelled. Her hands were on his shoulders. "You've got the grades to get in. I called Ernestine and she knows people in the NAACP who have the connections for you to be accepted. I want you to go right on through law school there. You could be the next Thurgood Marshall, J. P."

J. P.'s mind was empty. He had never thought of going to a white college.

Crow pulled him down to the steps and sat with her thigh against his. "Listen, J. P., James Meredith paved your way to go five years ago. It's your turn. I don't want you to be a nigger lawyer getting divorces or writing house contracts for poor black people. I want you to have the best, be the best. You get a degree, get affiliated with the NAACP, and you can fight for all of us to have the best. There'll be a lot of court cases coming in the next years, especially here in the South. We need young men like you."

J. P. stared at Crow's red toenails. His dream was to be a lawyer, to fight civil rights cases, to become a famous orator like Dr. King, but he had seen himself doing all this among his own kind. There were no white faces floating around in his dreams. He didn't want to go to school with white people. Crow could take back this check. He wasn't going to some school where nobody wanted him. "Crow, I'm not a James Meredith. I didn't even go to a white high school. They only integrated the elementary schools here so far, and a lot of the white families put their kids in the new private school so that they wouldn't have to sit in desks beside little black girls like Hilda."

Crow's eyes turned into hot coals. "Listen to me, J. P. You are not like Rufus or Paul or even poor Lester, who's out there in some swamp in Vietnam toting a white man's gun. You are like me. We don't bow to anybody, and we don't let anything get in our way. I want something, I go after it. It doesn't matter what I have to do to get it."

J. P. looked away from Crow's angry face. Her words pierced him, and he felt ashamed of his cowardly heart. "Yeah, but it's easier for you."

That was the wrong thing to say. Crow was shouting now, outraged. "*Easy*? Easy? You think I got where I am without workin for it? Ha, a field nigger got it easier than me some days."

Crow was out of control now. She sounded more like her old self, less polished, less careful with her words. He shook his head. "Wait, I didn't mean that." He heard his tiny child's voice. He didn't want Crow to think less of him. What she thought about him mattered more than anything in the world. "I want to go, but I'm scared."

Crow pulled him close. "We all scared sometimes, but fear can be a good thing. I learned that early. You can use it to see ahead. That way you always know what's coming before other people. You look at your fears and you'll be ready for anything."

J. P. felt the strength of her arms around him. He repeated her words in his head. "You can use it to see ahead." He saw the future clearly. He saw that life was like a boxing match. It would throw its punches, maybe knock him down, but he was going to rise before the referee counted to ten. The knot in his stomach was still there; it would most likely stay there for a long, long time. But every time he felt it, he would think of his big sister's words. He touched Crow's cheek with his lips. "If I'm going to go to a white boy's university, I reckon I'd better go get my robe on to receive my black boy's diploma."

Crow held up her wrist and read the time on her gold watch. "Oh my God! It's nearly time to leave. Where's Mama?"

Chapter 42

EE WEE LIFTED THE FOREST-GREEN TURBAN FROM HER HEAD, wrapped it in tissue paper, and placed it in the bottom drawer of her dresser. Today the hat had been her crown. When she had opened her eyes on this graduation day and seen the sun rising over the field, she had thanked Sweet Jesus for giving her good weather for the barbecue. And He had just kept right on blessing her until the last rib was eaten, and everyone in the house but her had fallen into their beds with happy memories of this day. As she hung up her dress and pulled her night-gown over her head, she thought about the times when there hadn't been enough to eat, when she had worried that her children's lives would be as hard as hers. Tee Wee draped Luther's pants over the chair. He was still wearing his socks and shirt when he had fallen sideways across the bed and immediately begun to snore loud enough to wake the dead. When she leaned over him and pinched his nose, he didn't move. Drunk as a skunk. Well, she was too keyed up to sleep anyway.

In the kitchen she flicked the wall switch and blinked against the strong light. She was a little dizzy herself from all the celebration drinks she'd consumed. She looked around at the mess. Dirty dishes covered the counter and table, a pile of wrapping paper and ribbon was heaped on the floor, and cigarette butts, wadded napkins, a mountain of rib bones stuck out of the heaping garbage can beside the door. She waved her arm over the room. "I get to you in the mornin," she said. "Ain't gonna worry tonight." Turning off the light, she left the mess to sit on the couch where she relived the events of the day. She couldn't remember a day in her life as fine as this one. The grand opening of her bakery was nearly as wonderful, but she had been too anxious to enjoy it fully.

Her worries had been small today. The barbecue was excellent, the tender meat shredding off the pork bones. The potato salad had just the right amount of mayonnaise, and her cake was as light and heavenly as any ever made. She frowned. Icey hadn't complimented her on one dish, even though she had eaten three pieces of cake. She didn't help any, neither. When Tee Wee had come outside carrying a big bowl of beans, she had seen Icey sitting in the lawn chair with a sour puss, and after everyone emptied their plates, she was still sitting there with her butt roosting on that seat.

When Tee Wee plopped down on the lawn chair beside her, she bumped Icey's chair. "Look out! You gonna turn me over," Icey said.

Tee Wee inched her chair sideways. "This turned out to be a fine party, didn't it?" She looked around the yard at all of their children and grandchildren running like flitting bees from one house to the other.

Icey burped softly. "Food was all right. I reckon I ate more'n I should, but seem like this change of life makes me hungrier than usual."

"Yeah, me, too. I can't resist my sweets down at the bakery."

She watched Icey's sour puss draw up like she'd eaten a quince. "It ain't just the eatin. I got so many body problems with the change. I don't reckon anybody has ever felt it more than me. I just so sensitive to my innards."

Tee Wee swatted a mosquito from her face. "You don't know nothin. I sweat so much at night I wring water outta my nightgown . . . and sheets."

"Well, Deke said he believed, if he couldn't hold his breath, he might drown lyin beside me. It seems like I can feel my womb curlin up at the edges like burnin paper."

"Just curlin? Mine twists and jumps like a buckin horse. I feel like I'll fall to the floor sometimes. But I stay on my feet, business is so good down at the bakery."

Icey's teeth clicked. "I'm glad to hear it. Of course, when it gets hotter, people won't eat as many sweets as they do in cool weather."

Tee Wee raised up higher in her chair and smiled. "I thought of that. I'm gonna make Jell-O desserts and lemon icebox pies. I'm getting a churn ice cream maker to make peach, strawberry, blueberry, blackberry, all kinds of ice cream, and sell it cup or cone."

Icey pushed herself out of her chair. Tee Wee didn't want her to leave before she heard J. P.'s big news. "Did J. P. tell you what Crow gave him for his present?" Icey's stricken face told Tee Wee that she didn't want to know this. "She gave him a check for Threeee Thousand Dollars," Tee Wee said as slowly as she could talk.

Icey sat back down in her lawn chair. "Three Hundred?"

"Thousand. It's for his education. He won't have to work and go half time to a Negro college now. He's going to Ole Miss in the fall."

"The University of Mississippi?"

"That's the one. Where Browder went and where the United States government says blacks are to be made welcome." Tee Wee looked across the yard to where Luther and Deke were talking with Crow. She stood with her hands in the back pockets of her blue shorts, her legs splayed wide, rocking from side to side as she talked. This was her baby girl who had three thousand dollars to give for a present.

"How'd she get that kind of money, Tee? What she doin up there in Memphis?"

"You know how. She's a famous singer. I played her records for you on J. P.'s phonograph."

Icey shook her head. "I just didn't realize little ole records cost that much."

"It ain't how much they cost; it's how many they sells. And she makes money singin in hotels and fancy nightclubs, too."

"Well, I'm glad none of mine wanted to be in show business. I wouldn't want none of my young'ns in them clubs. That don't sound like a good life at all."

Tee Wee smiled. Icey was down for the ten count; she would deliver the last blow now. "None of your children got Crow's voice, and none of them got three thousand dollars to give for a graduatin present."

Icey stood up. "Hilda, get off of that swing. It's time to go home."

Remembering how Icey had dragged Hilda by her upper arms into the house, Tee Wee leaned back against the couch and grinned. Probably right now Icey was sitting over there trying to make Hilda memorize a song to sing next time she came over. She picked up the graduation program from the table beside her. There was J. P.'s name with a star next to it. In the speech he had given to his class, he talked about how their futures was rising like bright stars. He had quoted from Dr. King's "I Have a Dream" speech, and there wasn't a dry eye in the cafeteria where the ceremony was held. Tee Wee had felt then that nearly bout every one of her dreams had come true. Her family filled an entire row of seats, and they were all dressed in their best. She admitted Crow outshone them all in her elegant red suit and ostrich-feather hat, but she was proud of them all. Even Rufus had worn a suit, and he had assured his mama that it was his.

Rising from her chair, Tee Wee could still hear Luther's snores erupting from the bedroom, but she was tired and thought she could sleep now. Shoving him over, she lay down and then felt the tears rising in her chest again. She remembered her mama saying, "Laugh before breakfast, cry before bed." Happiness and sorrow were always so closely knitted together within her. Life was a series of beginnings and endings: bassinets and coffins, diplomas and wills, one going, another returning. She felt it all. Turning on her side, she cried again with both pleasure and pain.

LYING IN BED next door Icey felt like crying, too. She fanned herself with the edge of the sheet and poked her finger into Deke's ribs. "How come we ain't got enough money to buy our piece of the Parsons Place? Is Luther getting more pay than you?"

Deke opened his eyes. His voice was deep and slow; his words slurred with the whiskey Luther had shared with him. "No, we make the same wage, which ain't much. Luther made extra money on his crops. I told you from the start I wasn't no farmer, and our corn didn't make much last year, cotton got weevils, you know that, and your five rows of peas barely made enough to feed just us."

"Well, that may be," Icey said, wiping the sweat from around her hairline with her fingers. "But he didn't make enough for Tee Wee to buy all that for the bakery, too."

Deke turned on his side, his back to her. "Tee Wee saved her money. You started spending the money when you got that gold tooth in your mouth and you ain't stopped at a store without coming out with a bag of something since."

Icey sat up and pulled her nightgown over her head. It felt like a lead sheet laying on her stomach. "Deke, did Luther tell you Crow give J. P. three thousand dollars?"

"Uh-huh."

"You think it's true?"

"Uh-huh."

"You think he's really going to Ole Miss?"

"Uh-huh."

Icey lay back down. "You think we ever gonna be able to buy this place and get enough money so's I can quit workin for the Parsons? Masie's quit already. Did I tell you she's moved into town with our Glory? You reckon we could move there, too, someday?"

Deke's snore told her that she was going to have to figure this out on her own. If Memphis hadn't died, he'd be graduating next year and he would be a lot smarter than J. P. He'd go to some white college up north. No, she wouldn't want him to go that far away. She had heard they didn't even have grits up in those states. Well, he could go to Ole Miss, too, but he would be the president of the class, or maybe a big football star. Them football players make lots of money. Yeah, while J. P. was sittin in some little cubbyhole office, listenin to people's problems, Memphis would be out runnin free in front of a stadium full of people cheerin and callin out his name.

Icey wiped at the tears running down toward her ears. Memphis wasn't gonna play football; he was gone and God just kept on making her life hard and helpin Tee Wee's get easier and better. She looked over at Deke. He was a handsome man. Hadn't gotten all wrinkled and saggy like Luther. There was one blessing: Deke was still a good lover. She couldn't stand to be married to a man whose pole went permanently limp like she suspected Luther's had. She knew for a fact that Tee Wee was lyin when she said she was tired from Luther's pesterin. She was tired from draggin her big butt around that bakery day after day.

Icey clenched her fists and hit the mattress. She was sick to death of housecleaning for white people. She had had it with "yes'ms" and "no'ms" to every white face around here. Civil rights was just a joke to people like her, even to Deke, who had told her his opinion that Bobby Kennedy was gonna be president and make people treat them better. "That rich boy don't care nothin bout us," she had said to Deke. "He ain't even gonna get elected cause no white person in Mississippi gonna put an X by his name on ballot day." But Deke was a dreamer always thinkin there was a savior. He told her lots of folks would vote for any Kennedy, including some white southerners. She hadn't ever voted, too scared to go down to the fire station among all those arrogant faces. She rolled over and stroked Deke's back. She might go this year. Deke could be right about that Kennedy boy. Some things were better now. Hilda was going to the integrated school, had a white teacher, good books. She even got to ride the school bus and sit anywhere she wanted to. And J. P.

was going to Ole Miss. She bit her lip. Why'd she have to go thinkin bout him again? She had circled right back to her misery. She wasn't gonna think about that no more.

She closed her eyes, hoping for release from her thoughts in sleep, but visions of Crow swaying on red-painted toes popped in her head. She heard Tee Wee saying, "Peach, blueberry, blackberry." She opened her eyes. "Everybody and everythin changin. I can, too, but how?" She lay awake for a long time, plowing ideas over and over in the field of her mind. Exhausted, she finally fell asleep and dreamed of sitting in a pasture of red clover surrounded by babies, fat and brown. When they parted their lips to speak, she saw a gold tooth in every mouth.

Chapter 43

ON THE MORNING AFTER GRADUATION DAY, THE WEATHERSBYS were suffering terrible hangovers. J. P. was in the bathroom vomiting into the bowl. Tee Wee had a headache, and Luther's hands were shaking so much the cows' tits were spewing milk everywhere but in the bucket. Crow had never felt better.

"It was a wonderful day yesterday," Tee Wee said to Crow, as she slid a plate of fried eggs across the table to her. "Look like you the only one didn't tip the bottle too many times."

Crow nodded. "I'm careful about booze; it's a weakness that has toppled too many singers." She fell on her eggs, forking large bites into her mouth, chewing as she talked. She hadn't eaten in a month what she had consumed in these past two days. "Can I have J. P.'s eggs, too, or are you gonna eat them?"

Tee Wee laid J. P.'s runny eggs that had sent him, pale and sweating, to the toilet beside Crow's empty plate. "You got a good appetite this mornin."

"Yeah, I don't eat like this normally. I have to watch my weight. When I get back to Memphis, I'll be eating salads for a long time."

"You is skin and bones, girl."

"Mama, I'm not. Besides I have to fit in my evening gowns and they show every little bump on my body."

Tee Wee frowned. "So when do you go back?"

Crow lifted her head from her plate. "Tomorrow. I got a recording session to do."

Tee Wee sat down in the chair across from Crow. "I was hopin you could come down to the bakery and meet some of my customers."

Crow shrugged. "Guess I'll have to catch them next time." She looked down at her plate to avoid her mother's sad eyes. Her recording session wasn't until the end of the week; she could change her train ticket. A part of her wanted to stay longer, but her instincts told her to run. "Maybe you could come up to Memphis some weekend. See one of my shows. You've never been to one."

Tee Wee nibbled on a piece of ham. "No, I never been to Memphis, either. It ain't far from there to Ole Miss, is it?"

"Sixty or seventy miles, I think. Yeah, J. P. could come up, too. I could show y'all the sights. You know Elvis Presley has a home there." When she saw her mother's face lighting up, Crow felt an urgent need to get out of the house fast. She didn't want to become the tour guide for their lives. She wasn't going to be responsible for making them happy, and she damn sure wasn't going to feel guilty for having something better for herself. She had done what she came for, seen J. P. graduate, given him his chance. That was all she owed them. She stood up. "Think I'll get dressed and go walk off some of this food."

After she changed into her shorts, Crow met Icey and Hilda in the front yard on their way to church. Hilda's big eyes were focused on Crow's straight hair. She patted her cornrows tied with plaid ribbons. "Mama said you are filthy rich."

Icey grabbed her hand. "Hush up, Hilda. Where your manners?"

Crow laughed. She squatted down and lifted the hem of Hilda's pale blue dress. "You must be rich, too, to have a beautiful dress like this."

"Mama sewed it," Hilda said. "She makes all my clothes now that we got a Singer sewing machine that cost a lots of money."

Icey's face softened. "Yeah, Deke bought me that machine for Christmas last year when he seen how good I am at sewin. I even made him a Sunday suit." She looked back at the closed door of her house. "Which he ought to be wearin right now on his way to meetin instead of them overalls he got on in front of the television set." She jerked Hilda's arm. "We got to get down the drive. Our friends is pickin us up. Look like your mama ain't goin to thank the Lord for her blessins today."

"No, they all got hangovers from the party. I guess the Lord will just have to understand."

When they were halfway down the drive, Icey turned back and yelled to Crow, "Tell your mama I'll pray for her. I sure will."

Crow walked to the side of the house and saw that someone had planted mums and gladiolas along the wall. The shades of red, yellow, lavender, and salmon blooms brightened up the gray boards of the house, and Crow breathed in their perfume. In the old days there wasn't time for weeding flower beds, but now the earth around the plants was freshly hoed. J. P., I'll bet, Crow thought. He was the one special spark rising out of the darkness of her past. She walked on to the hog pens and stood staring at a sleeping pregnant sow lying in the straw. Crow wondered if the pig dreamed of a litter of sons and daughters. Her dreams weren't ever going to include any brats of her own.

When she reached the field of red clover, Crow lay down on her back and watched a buzzard circle the far side of the pasture. Must be a carcass over there to feed on, she thought. Out here in the country the cycle of death and birth seemed more immediate, nearly tangible. While the cries of the sow's newborns rang out across this field, a hawk would circle overhead searching for prey. Gazing up at the fingers of wispy clouds, Crow remembered how she and Browder would name them as if they were constellations. When two clouds united into one across the blue canvas sky, Browder would tell her God was painting a marriage. Crow laid her hand over her chest and felt the steady beats of her heart against the thin yellow blouse she wore over her white shorts. She lowered her hand to her bare midriff. Her stomach was flat, her thighs firm. She felt in touch with her body as she hadn't in a very long time. In Memphis she constantly worried about her weight, her skin, the condition of her hair. It was as if her body parts were separate, unconnected, like a doll's that you could pull off, fix perfectly, and put back together. Here her body felt whole and complete. If she raised her finger, its movement ran through every muscle and tissue from her toes to her forehead. She thought of the lines of the skeleton song, "Hip bone connected to the thighbone." She felt connected. Then why was she so anxious to leave? She saw his blond hair, his china face, his hands tanned and nearly hairless, and she knew the answer.

Crow plucked a crimson clover and twirled it between her fingers. When she got back to Memphis, Browder would recede from her mind like the moon from the morning sky. But the moon would rise again, and she knew she couldn't control her heart any more than she could stop the rotation of the planets in the sky. Fly away, Crow, fly, fly fast away, she chanted like a mantra in her head. But she waited in the pasture, hoping Browder would find her there.

—

BROWDER WAS SEARCHING in his suit pockets for his tithing envelope to drop into the collection plate at Valley Hill Baptist Church. He missed attending Pisgah Church, missed seeing Ruthie and Annie Ruth, and his old buddies, but Missy was Baptist, and Baptist she would remain. At least the songs were nearly the same in both religions, and as he passed the silver money dish, his voice rang out, overpowering everyone's on his pew. During the long sermon, Browder's thoughts turned to Crow. He wished she hadn't come back, was grateful that she had, wanted her in his arms, wanted to forget her. He looked over at Missy, who sat with her eyes fixed on the cross behind Brother Bickham's head. In her blue-and-white-striped dress with matching pillbox hat, shoes, and purse, she looked as coordinated as everything in their house. She was mad at him, but he didn't know why. Last night she had cried for more than an hour and had spoken to him in monosyllables all morning. When she bowed her head, he knew that she was praying for a child, and he wished God would listen up. He had endured the humiliation of the fertility tests and sat listening to the arrogant specialist suggest that Browder wear boxer shorts rather than briefs, that Missy have a glass of wine before sex. He was sick of thermometers, extra pillows, whispered prayers at the worst times. Half the time when he and Missy made love, he felt like he was being watched by the doctor, her mother, and even Missy's sister, who had given Missy a catalog of herbal remedies.

When the service was over, Missy met her parents in the back of the sanctuary and told them that she didn't feel up to their routine Sunday dinner. Browder sighed with disappointment. Even though he didn't like having to listen to Missy, her sister, and Mrs. Jordan prattle on every Sunday about nothing, Mrs. Jordan was a good cook, and now he'd have to eat burned leftovers for dinner.

After greeting a few of Missy's relatives and friends he couldn't avoid, Browder drove Missy home, where the floodgates opened in their bedroom.

"What's wrong? What are you so mad about?" he asked, ripping off his tie.

Missy pulled her dress over her head and sat on the bed in her slip. "You know. And now I know the reason we haven't gotten pregnant. God is punishing one of us."

Browder's confusion was complete. "Huh? What are you talking about? What sin is one of us being punished for?"

"Adultery," she whispered.

Browder felt a shock going through him like an electrical current. He couldn't believe Missy had cheated on him. When and with whom? He wouldn't have been more surprised if she had said she had taken a trip to Mars. "How did you? Who?"

"Browder, I found out about you and Dimple Greer yesterday when we went into town to buy the bedroom suite," Missy said, and then burst into tears.

She told him that, after he had dropped her off at the furniture store, she had run into Dimple, and somehow Browder's humiliation at the Christmas program at Pisgah so many years ago had popped up in their conversation. Dimple had laughed about his fascination with her breasts and said how funny it was to her that he had married the girl who helped him remember the lines to "O Holy Night." Browder agreed that Dimple lacked good judgment in bringing up the scene, but he didn't see how that meant he was screwing her now. Then Missy told him that Dimple had said that Troy had made several trips to Texas to buy cattle, and that during one of those trips, Browder had stopped by and fixed a flat on her Cadillac and had sat in her kitchen drinking beer. "How could you?" Missy said, clenching her fists.

Browder confessed that he had gone inside with Dimple, had stayed more than an hour, had accepted a beer in payment for his labor. "But I didn't touch her; I played with the boys. I held the baby, not her."

"*The baby!* It's probably your baby, not Troy's. She had my baby. And now I'll never have one because you, you, you sowed your seed on another row."

Browder shook his head. His anger evaporated. This was what had Missy so upset. It always came back to the same reason. She might forgive him for sleeping with another woman, but she could never absolve him from the crime of holding someone else's baby. His words were slowly and softly spoken. "Missy, that's crazy, and you know it. I have never been unfaithful to you, and God knows I wish we had a child, but we don't, and maybe we won't ever. But the reason isn't because we're being punished and it isn't because I'm screwing Dimple Greer."

On the drive home from church he had planned to flee from Missy and her inexplicable anger. He had felt drawn to the pasture as if it were a magnet pulling him there, to where he had known somehow that Crow was waiting for him. Looking down at Missy's tear-streaked face, Browder saw her pain and knew that he couldn't leave her. He lay on the bed and pulled her down beside him. "I love you," he said. "Only you."

Chapter 44

J. P. WAS SECRETLY RELIEVED THAT CROW HAD TO GO BACK TO
Memphis on Monday morning. He was ashamed of his eagerness for her
to leave, but he didn't feel he could take much more of her nagging him
about his future. At the train station this morning he had decided Crow
was one of those people who fed you good advice, but then kept on
stuffing you with it until you couldn't digest any more.

Now J. P. was on his way to his first day of work at Larry's Used Cars,
and he was much more excited about this job than he was about going to
school. You didn't get a paycheck at the end of every week at school.
When he saw the big white sign with red-and-black lettering that said
ENTRANCE, he turned into the shell driveway and parked in front of the
small white house that was the office.

J. P.'s new employer, Mr. Larry Martino, wasn't much taller than J. P.
who was five feet, six inches, and his skin was only a couple of shades
lighter than his. He was an Italian, but most people around Zebulon referred to him as "The Dago." His brother, Sal Martino, ran a fruit and
vegetable stand on North Fifth Street, and it was rumored the two brothers were "connected." He was nine years old when he had heard this sup-
position, and he had thought it meant they had telephones. Mr. Sal's eyes
were as blue as Frank Sinatra's, but Mr. Larry's dark eyes and wavy blue-
black hair gave him a dangerous tough-guy look that had convinced a lot
of women to buy a car from him.

Mr. Larry strode across the car lot to J. P.'s truck and yelled, "Move it.
You park around back." He pointed to the right side of the office. "And
don't park near the faucet; we'll need that space. Wait for me back there."

"Yes sir!" J. P. said too loudly. He wanted everything to go perfectly on this first day, and here he had already made a mistake.

When Mr. Larry came around the building to where J. P. waited beside the faucet, he held a set of keys with a white tag attached to a length of string. "Okay, J. P., you ready to get to work?"

"I'm ready for anything," J. P. said.

Mr. Larry motioned for him to follow his fast walk around to the front of the lot. "Cars are like women, J. P. The ugly gals don't go to the prom, and the ugly cars don't get driven off the lot. The pretty girls who got flaws don't get married, and the pretty vehicles with blemishes don't get sold. Now, women cover up their flaws with powder and paint, and we got our makeup for the cars, too. Up north where I come from we use Bondo on rust spots, then paint over it. After a while the paint bubbles up, and you can tell you bought a rusted-out fender, but it lasts long enough for the car to find a lover. Down here, we just got to cover up scratches and such, buff out what we can." Mr. Larry held up the keys. "You start with that old brown 'fifty-nine Dodge parked on the back row."

J. P. liked the way Mr. Larry talked. "Yes sir, I'll get her to the prom and down the aisle, too."

Mr. Larry clapped him on the back. "That's the ticket. You're the detail man."

It took J. P. nearly four hours of rubbing before he felt satisfied that he had transformed the Dodge. During that time he had seen Mr. Larry drive off the lot in a white Chevy Impala with red leather interior, a black Hillman with fancy hub covers, and a two-toned cream and brown Buick Century with a woman who seemed more interested in Mr. Larry than the car. Mr. Larry had come back several times to show J. P. how to do his job and to inspect his work. He had pointed to a small bit of chrome on the rear bumper. "Missed a spot here." With his pocketknife, he flicked a clod of dirt from a tire rim. J. P. didn't mind his boss being a stickler; he was a perfectionist himself.

J. P.'s next transformation was a red Volkswagen exactly like the yellow one he had dreamed about. Mr. Larry told him to finish it quickly because it would sell fast. As the afternoon sun beat mercilessly on the chrome of the car, J. P.'s eyes stung with sweat and he thought longingly of the ham biscuit Tee Wee had packed for his lunch. After he vacuumed the VW, Mr. Larry opened the office window and stuck his head out. "You can take a break now, and if you park them cars ten feet to your left, you can wax them in the shade. Might be cooler there." He closed the window, but not before J. P. heard him laugh and say, "Dumb nigger."

As he ate his biscuit, J. P. thought about Mr. Larry's assessment of him. He ought to quit. He imagined walking into the office, saying, *I'm too smart to work for you* or *You think I'm so dumb, how come I'm going to Ole Miss?* But then he thought about Saturday. Payday. He wanted that check. Tee Wee had made him put Crow's three thousand in the bank, and he wasn't allowed to touch a nickel of it. But how could he work for a man who ridiculed him? Crow had told him to stand up to people who gave him a hard time, but she was talking about students, not his boss.

After lunch J. P. drove the VW beneath the tree and began applying the wax using the circular motion Mr. Larry had shown him. He was much cooler now; should have thought of it himself. He *was* dumb. Squatting beside the front tire, J. P. worked across the front bumper, applying the white paste, taking care that he didn't miss the tiniest spot.

When Mr. Larry opened the window again, he said, "You're doing a good job, J. P. Fine work on these beauties. You're my detail man."

J. P. flapped his cloth against his leg. He wished he didn't feel so proud. But Mr. Larry seemed all right to him at this minute. This job was gonna work out fine. Just fine.

By quitting time, J. P. had transformed four cars into sure sellers. He looked down at his good plaid shirt and best jeans and saw that they were ruined. Tomorrow he would dress more appropriately. He would also be a lot faster on the waxing. As he drove the truck around to the front, Mr. Larry held up his hand for him to stop. He walked over to him. "Seven-thirty sharp tomorrow. You did a good day's work. You not a slacker; I saw that. You keep up the good work, and maybe I'll teach you some of my secrets about the car business. You got an eye for a good car already."

J. P. grinned. "Yes sir. I'll see you tomorrow, seven-thirty on the dot."

After supper that night J. P. rubbed his sore arm muscles with liniment and went out on the porch where his daddy sat whittling on a stick. "Can I borrow the truck?"

"What you needin it for?" Luther asked, without breaking the rhythm of his cuts.

"I thought I'd go over to Ray's house, tell him about my first day."

Luther spit into the yard. "You do all right?"

"Yeah, I reckon. Mister Larry said I got a knack for the car business."

"Well, you be on time tomorrow." He lifted the stick, turned it as if he were figuring out what he had made. J. P. couldn't see anything but a hacked-up stick. "Okay, you can take the truck. I ain't goin nowhere cept to bed."

"Thanks, Daddy," J. P. said, jumping off the porch. "I won't be late. Bye." He waited for Luther to say good night, but he had already turned back to his stick, studying it as though he were a sculptor about to whittle his masterpiece.

On the drive out to Ray's, J. P. thought about his father. He couldn't help comparing him to Deke. If Deke were his father, J. P. was sure he would have asked him a lot of questions about his first day at Mr. Larry's. His daddy was more interested in what the hogs did all day. But at least he had a father; Ray's papa had bled to death after the Cottons' Jersey bull had pinned him against the barn with his horns. Two years ago Ray's mama had married her brother-in-law, Pepper Simmons, who was the cook at the McCoglin Hotel, and Ray didn't like his stepdaddy much.

Ray told J. P. his folks had gone to the show in town, so they could drink a couple of beers out on the porch. After handing a Falstaff to J. P., he picked up his fedora from beside the rocker. "New one today. Check it out." He pointed to the center of the brim.

Nearly every inch of the hat was covered in bottle caps. Most of them were beer caps, but there were soda pop caps, too. Ray had fastened them to the hat by prying out the cork in the cap, then reinserting it after he stuck the sharp metal edge through the hat. "Dixie," J. P. said. "Thought you had one already."

"Yeah, but it come off somewheres. You ought to get you one of these started. I got plenty of extra caps I could give you."

"No, a hat will mess up my hair," he said, stroking his Afro.

Ray jabbed his arm. "You need to hide your ugly head under a hat."

When J. P. told Ray about his new job, he saw the jealousy in his eyes. "Man, you fell into the butterfat for sure. You get to drive all them cars?"

"Well, I just move them around on the lot, but it takes finesse to line them up perfectly. Mister Larry is hard to please." He sat his bottle on the porch floor. He didn't like the taste of beer, but he always accepted one so that Ray wouldn't think he was a sissy. He stood up and said, "I got to be getting home to bed. Got to get up early for work tomorrow."

Before he fell asleep J. P. lay for a long time staring at the oval water stain on the ceiling. In just a few months he would be lying in a strange bed far away from home. He laid his hand on his chest and felt his heart muscle beating fast against his palm. Did he really want to go? He could stay right here on Enterprise Road, continue working for Mr. Larry, learning to like drinking beer with Ray. They were so different and yet they had been friends for a long time, and J. P. believed that somehow Ray understood him better than Crow ever would. He had heard it said that opposites attract when two unlikely people fell in love. It could be like that with friends, too. He and Ray saw in each other what they lacked in themselves. J. P. wished that he could trade his mortarboard hat for a bottle cap fedora, but he closed his eyes and just before he fell asleep, he admitted to himself that he was never going to like beer.

Chapter 45

TEE WEE NEEDED A NAP; SHE WAS WORN SLAP OUT. SUNDAY was supposed to be a day of rest, but she had been as busy as a bee in an acre of gardenias. She had cooked for the dinner at church, washed six loads of clothes and hung them out on the line behind the house, sewed up three rips in J. P.'s shirts he tore up down at that car lot, and plucked three chickens the dogs had killed. She went into her bedroom and lay down on the bed without taking off her dress. The room was too warm, the fan was broken, and, as she tossed on the bed, sweat formed around her hairline and dripped between her breasts. It would be cooler on the porch; she might fall asleep in the rocker.

She had just settled in and was beginning to doze off when she heard Icey's shrill voice. "Tee, hey *Teee.*"

Through the slits in her half-closed eyes, Tee Wee saw Icey's square bare feet planted in front of her chair. She sighed. "Hey, Icey. I was near bout asleep."

Icey dropped onto the chair beside her. "Oh, sorry. I just wanted to talk to you about somethin. Haven't had no chance to say much with all the goins-on round here lately."

Now Tee Wee felt happier about seeing Icey. "Yeah, been a lot of cheerful tears at my house. I don't believe you saw J. P.'s cuff links Ruthie give him. Twenty-four-karat gold. I read it off the back of them."

"He showed me them. Real nice. It's good he'll have some nice things to take to school. Gonna need all the help he can get going to a place where he ain't goin to be all that welcome." Icey rocked faster. "I come over here to talk about somethin important."

An alarm went off in Tee Wee's head. Icey was wearing her *I-know everythin-bout-everythin-in-the-world* look. Well, she might as well get it over with, find out what Icey had on her pea brain. "What's that?"

Icey's eyes lifted to the tree in the front yard, and Tee Wee could tell she was reciting a speech she had memorized. "It's like this. You are doin real real good down at the bakery now. You got a good business goin, and word gettin around now and so you most likely gonna get even more customers." Tee Wee nodded, trying not to grin too widely to show her pleasure at Icey's praise. But Icey wasn't looking at her; she stayed focused on the tree. "So you are my friend, and I'm startin to worry about you cause you are like a sister." Tee Wee frowned, wondering what in the world she was up to. Icey had paused to catch her breath, but now she gave a big heave, chest rising, and she continued. "Now, if you get more business than you can handle down there, what happens? What happens is you start to run out of cakes or pie or whatever, and Miz So-and-So gets mad cause she wanted that cake for her company comin, and you can't cook that cake and Miz Other-So-and-So's pie and that school-teacher wants cookies for the party and you only got two hands." Tee Wee was beginning to feel dizzy. "Then they all get mad and quit comin." Icey shifted her eyes to Tee Wee's face. She appeared to be finished with what she wanted to say.

"Well, Icey, I guess that could happen, but right now I got plenty of everythin. I try not to make too much so it don't go stale if I don't sell it."

"Okay, but you lookin at right now. I'm lookin at the future. You got to look ahead, Tee Wee. That's your big flaw. You don't see things comin like I do."

Tee Wee was still confused about what point Icey was trying to make. She smelled a rat and it was leaning over her chair arm right now. "So what you sayin?"

Icey's face was so close she could see the little downy hairs covering her chin. "I'm sayin you need help." She let out her breath so suddenly Tee Wee felt a blast of air on her face. "You need me."

So this was what all this jabberin was about, Tee Wee thought. Icey wanted to work in the bakery. Why do I need her? I need her like a baby needs colic, like a dog needs the mange, like a pig needs a crystal glass to drink out of. She would tell her the day she hired her would be the day she turned white. Icey's knuckles were already white, and Tee Wee saw that she was so tense that her eyebrows had come together to form one straight line across her brow. Why would Icey want to allow her to boss her around day after day? She should just say, *I don't need you* and end this crazy conversation right now, but she saw fear in Icey's eyes. Something was bad wrong. She sighed. "Icey, you not happy down at the Parsons' no more?"

Tears formed in Icey's eyes. "I hate it, Tee. That Missy Parsons is picky picky, and she's a witch. Didn't Masie tell you she called her a good-for-nothin nigger?"

"Masie said she quit because she got a good job down at the court-house doin filing in the office. She got her papers from the secretary school she went to."

"Well, no matter what she told you, I know she quit cause of the meanness of that woman. Missy don't like Negroes. She accuses me of stealin every time she loses somethin. Then, when I finds it for her, she don't even say she's sorry."

"I know how she is. I used to work there, too, remember?"

"Yeah, but she's worst now. Gets worst with every day she don't have a baby. I think she's crazy, Tee. Browder, he don't see it, but I do."

"So, you want to quit and get another job. Hey! What about Ruthie? She don't have no help in the house, and I know she ain't up to snuff on housework."

"I don't want to clean white people's houses the rest of my life. I want . . . I want to be somethin better."

"And I'm it?"

Icey shook her head. "Well, not exactly. What I was thinkin is this. You might be needin help later on and I could do all the things except the actual cookin. I could even help with that. I'm as good a cook as you. But also, and this is the wonderful idea I got, I could sell things in one of them showcases you don't need."

"I don't have but one case."

"But you could buy another one."

"What would you sell?" Tee Wee felt as if she was putting her foot over the top of a well, about to fall hundreds of feet through darkness into ice-cold water.

Icey was trying not to smile, but her eyes were sparkling. "Sewin! You know I can tat doilies and remember that doll dress I made Hilda out of milk filters? I got lots of ideas for such stuff. I can make animals with button eyes out of yarn. Oh, I have so many talents you ain't even seen. And people come in to get their little girl one of my dolls, they'll buy a cookie from you while they decidin." Grasping the arm of Tee Wee's chair, she stopped her rocking. "What do you think? Isn't that a great idea? We would be"—her voice slowed and rose dramatically—*"partners."* Before Tee Wee could speak, Icey hurried down the steps. "You takes your time thinkin on this. You'll see what a good plan this is."

Tee Wee rose and went back to her bedroom. It didn't seem so hot now. In fact, she felt a chill coming down on her body. She lay back down. She would see Icey every day, all day. She would have to tell her no, but how did you tell Icey no when she was set on you telling her yes? She was worse than a dog with a steak bone; she wouldn't ever ever let it go. Closing her eyes, the word *partner* rang like the church bell over and over in her ears.

When she heard the pounding on the door, she realized she must have finally fallen asleep. She had been dreaming of something unpleasant, but she couldn't remember what. Slowly she made her way to the door.

The two white men on her porch were the ones in her dream. Only in the dream their faces were covered with camouflage scarves, and they had stepped off a black train, which Tee Wee knew meant death. They didn't have to tell her Lester was dead.

Just minutes after the marines left in their official car with lettering on the side that blurred in Tee Wee's vision, Masie passed them in her red Pinto at the end of the drive. Now it occurred to Tee Wee that Masie had been coming every day for the past four days with an anxious look about her. She had known her twin was dead. "Mama," she yelled, running toward her. "Mama?"

Tee Wee nodded. "He's kilt. Body ain't here yet. Comin on the train from Jackson." She tried to sit down, but her legs seemed to be locked at the knee. "Luther. Go get him. And tell Icey." She staggered inside and fell onto the couch, a near corpse herself. Her chills were back. Her teeth clicked and she rocked back and forth so violently, she moved the couch across the bare floor until her legs were wedged into the coffee table. When Icey rushed in, she shoved the couch back against the window with Tee Wee sprawled across it, and Tee Wee could think well enough to be amazed at her sudden strength. She was talking to her, tears streaming down her face, she was slapping her arms, squeezing her cheeks. She heard her say Memphis' and her own name several times. By the time Luther arrived solemn and quiet, standing over her with his arms out, she could finally hear herself begin to cry for her son.

She lay on the bed listening as Luther dialed the telephone over and over. She wondered how many numbers did it take to count death. She remembered hearing Walter Cronkite or Dan Rather say that there were a lot more black soldiers dying in the Vietnam War. Only a few of them were officers; their status in the military hadn't changed much since World War II. Lester was just one more dead nigger lying in that faraway jungle. The marine with so many colorful ribbons on his chest had told her that Lester was a real hero, would be getting a medal. Posst hummusly, whatever that meant. She thought now how odd that those bars the men wore on their chests should be so pretty. What color would Lester's medal be? She hoped blue; that was his favorite color.

When Luther came in and sat beside her, he lifted her hand and said, "Crow will ride with him. She said on the phone that she'll take the same train and ride with him. He won't be alone."

His voice broke and she felt the weight of him on her chest. She stroked his head, patted the flat space between his shoulder blades. "Poor Luther," she whispered. "You loved him like he was your own blood. Poor dear old man, my husband, Luther."

$\mathcal{W}$HEN CROW RETURNED TO MEMPHIS AFTER LESTER'S FUNERAL, she felt like a guest in her own apartment. On the afternoon of her arrival she wandered from room to room as if she were seeing the sectional couch, the brass bed, the photos of herself in the hall for the first time. In the kitchen she sat on a bar stool, leafing through the stack of mail Winston had left on the counter. Mostly bills, two fan letters, circulars and advertisements. She dropped the envelopes into a pile and swept them onto the floor. She was angry and sad and confused, and she wished she could erase her visit to Mississippi as easily as she deleted mistakes on her tapes in the recording studio. But there was no cassette large enough to record the mistakes she had made after she escorted her brother's body home.

At Lester's funeral Crow sat with the choir facing her family, who filled the first three rows on both sides of the church. All of her brothers and sisters had come home with their wives, husbands, and children whose names Crow couldn't remember. Looking down the row to where Masie sat, Crow thought of all the times she had baby-sat the twins, wiping their running noses, swatting their brown butts, chasing them around the yard. How could Lester be lying in a coffin covered with roses? He was only twenty-two; he was supposed to have decades of time for singing, dancing, laughing, and loving.

Crow sat with her eyes narrowed at Brother Dixon as he strutted in front of the casket raving about the golden chariot that had taken Lester to live in the bosom of Sweet Jesus. She heard all of the "amens" and the "hallelujahs," and she watched her mother leap to her feet crying out, "My boy, my boy! Oh Lord, take care of my boy." Crow dug her nails into her palms. Lester didn't want a chariot; he wanted a sports car. He didn't want to live with Jesus; he wanted to live with flesh-and-blood people. If Lester was looking down on them from Gloryland, then he was plenty pissed to be so misunderstood.

When it came time for Crow's solo, she rose and lifted her arms, fanning her robe out in white triangles. She was a performer again. Tee Wee had chosen the gospel song "Where the Soul Never Dies," which Crow had sung many times before. She began in a low, mournful tone. "To Canaan's land I'm on my way, Where the soul of man never dies; My darkest night will turn to day." Crow walked to the casket, laid her hand on the rounded lid, and sang the chorus andante. "Dear friend, there'll be no sad farewells, There'll be no tear-dimmed eyes; Where all is peace and joy and love, And the soul never dies." She sang on about the rose that bloomed, the love light beaming, deathless sleep and everlasting joys. Crossing her hands over her breast, she held the last C note until her lungs were nearly collapsed. When the congregation applauded, Crow forgot where she was and bowed to her fans.

At the grave she sang "I'll Live in Glory" with less feeling. Her tolerance for these shouting mourners had been stretched to its limit, and when the United States Marine Corps got into the circus ring, she wanted to grab one of their guns and shoot them all. It wasn't enough that Lester was riding golden vehicles, walking on golden streets. He was a hero, too, fated to die willingly in a swamp halfway around the world so that his mama could take the folded triangular flag from the picture-perfect marine's white-gloved hands. She wouldn't go back to the house for the funeral feast. They could eat their fried chicken and blackberry pie without her.

With her high heels in her hand, Crow walked down the blacktop road away from the graveyard and the dead. It was the first day of June, a sunny day with a cloudless sky. It would be the perfect day for a picnic or a swim in the Amite River. It was an inappropriate day for burying young men. Her body felt stiff and cramped like a squeezed accordion; she needed to stretch out every muscle from her neck to her feet. Quickening her pace, she jogged for half a mile to the Taylor Place, where she tossed her shoes on the grass and wriggled out of her shredded hose. With the hem of her pink linen dress, she wiped the sweat from brow and neck and sank to the ground, where she sat watching the dragonflies swooping across clusters of buttercups and black-eyed Susans.

She didn't know how long she had been sitting when she saw a green truck pass by and then reappear to stop on the road in front of her. Browder stuck his head out the window and called to her. "Crow, get in. I'll take you home."

She shook her head from side to side. "Go away. Leave me alone."

Browder got out of the truck and stood on the pavement. "Crow, come on. It's late."

Looking to her right, she saw that the sun had turned pink in the western sky. The mourners would be packing up their dishes to go home now, and she would have to leave here, too. She picked up her shoes and slowly made her way across the road to the truck. After she opened the passenger's door and slid onto the seat, she rested her head against the warm window and closed her eyes. When she opened them again, she saw that they were on Enterprise Road now, nearly home. She touched Browder's arm. "Not yet; I'm not ready to go home."

"But, Crow, they're all worried about you. I promised Masie I'd find you and bring you back."

"Then nothing's changed; they were always looking for me."

Browder slowed the truck. "Where to, then?"

"I don't care." She sat up straighter. "No, I know where. I want to go to the Whittington Cemetery, where your people are buried."

When Browder parked the truck, Crow got out and meandered around the grave markers. "Remember when we came here before? You showed me all your dead relatives, told me a lot of their stories. I didn't have a dead brother then."

Browder walked behind her. "I didn't have dead parents then, either. Mama and Daddy are over there."

She walked to where he pointed, and stood looking down at the Parsons' marble stone. There was space in the plot for two more graves. "Will you be buried here, too?"

Browder dug his hands into his pants' pockets. He shrugged. "Haven't thought about it. It's hard enough to plan living."

"I guess Lester was making plans for living, too, but he didn't get to carry any of them out," Crow said, turning and walking away from him.

Browder caught up to her. "None of us know when our time is going to be up."

"No, no, we sure as hell don't, do we? I thought a twenty-two-year-old would live at least another year or so. I thought Mama would die before him, her and Luther and Icey and Deke. Ernestine. Me. Shouldn't we have died first?"

Browder said nothing. There wasn't an answer, and she didn't expect one. Like her, he would be thirty this year. How much time could either of them count on? They had reached the woods beside the graves, and Crow was surprised to see that the trees she had remembered as spindly saplings were now as tall as towers bearing sturdy wide branches. "Everything's grown up a lot. Changed. Did you see Ernestine? I wouldn't have known her; she's old now." She sat down and leaned her back against the nearest pine. "I wonder if I'll get deep creases around my eyes like her. Course we got different daddies. But I already got a few gray hairs to yank out every month or so." She looked up at Browder, who was standing as stiffly as the marines at the grave site. "How will you see your gray hairs in all those blond ones?"

"Maybe I got some already." He walked to her and held out his hand. "Let's go."

Crow's jaw shot out; she shook her head. "No. Not yet." She looked up at him. "Just a little longer. Please?"

Browder sighed and sat down beside her. "You gonna be okay, Crow? You're worrying me, you know."

"Why?"

"I don't know. You're just not yourself, different." She saw the concern in his eyes, bluer now as the late-afternoon sun shot its last light across his face.

"You don't know me well enough anymore to know if I'm the same or not."

Browder smiled. "Yes I do. I know you better than anyone."

Crow wanted this lie to be true. She wanted to believe that there was one person in this world who understood her, who knew her secrets, her dreams, and even her shortcomings. She longed for that one other human being who comprehended everything about her and accepted and approved of it all, and for the first time in her life she acknowledged her loneliness. She turned to Browder, took the points of his shirt collar in her hands, and pulled him to her. "Love me. Love me like you used to."

"I can't," he said. "We can't. Must not . . ." And then "Dammit, I want you, Crow." His mouth met hers and his arms were encircling her.

She fought death with her mouth, her teeth, her nails on his back. She battled her loneliness scissoring her legs across his, holding him against her breasts as if she could split open her chest and draw him inside so that her heart itself would beat in unison with his. When they both lay exhausted, the ground growing cold against their skin, she cried, at last releasing the waterfall of tears she had dammed earlier. She hadn't ever cried in a man's arms, and she gratefully let all of her grief pour out into the vessel he offered now.

When she was quiet, Browder kissed her hair. "I love you," he said. "I have never stopped loving you. I know that now."

Crow said nothing. She longed to trust him, believe that he was her lifeboat she could crawl into whenever she was tossed about in rough seas, but now she was clearheaded and the old doubts began to resurface. "What about her?"

"Missy?"

"You love her, don't you? If you do, how can you love me?"

Browder covered his eyes with his palm. "I don't know; all I know is that I don't want to lose you again."

Now, as Crow picked up the mail scattered on the floor, she thought about all that both she and Browder had to lose. She must lose her past, regain her life here. Pay these bills, buy food for her empty refrigerator. When the wall phone in the kitchen rang, she knocked over the bar stool and jerked the receiver from the hook. It could be Browder.

It was Winston reminding her that she was supposed to be at the Benton Hotel at six o'clock to do the dinner show. Had she forgotten? Was she okay? Did she find her mail? Crow answered his questions, checked the clock on the stove, and saw that she had less than an hour to get dressed. She hurried down the hall to the bathroom, throwing her clothes against the walls as she ran.

When she felt the shock of the hot water cascading down her back, she lifted her face to the hard spray. She thought of the lines from the musical *South Pacific*, "I'm gonna wash that man right out of my hair." She would wash Browder out of her hair, her body, and her thoughts. "Ain't nothing good gonna come from loving you," she sang as she reached for the soap and scrubbed her skin until it burned. After she stepped out of the shower, she wrapped her hair in a towel, and, with her forearm, she wiped the steam from the mirror. When her face began to appear, she saw that she was crying.

—

WHILE CROW WAS singing to her audience, Barbra Steisand sang to Browder in the Palace Theater. *Funny Girl* wasn't funny, and he hated musicals, but Missy was enjoying herself, smiling at last. It had taken a dictionary of words for him to convince her he wasn't having an affair with Dimple. But now he *was* an adulterer, a sinner, a cheat. He felt like a carpenter with no tools. He knew he should try to repair the damage, but he lacked the resources to rebuild the relationship. There were too many holes and burned-out places to even know where to begin to patch things between him and Missy. He couldn't do it. He wasn't sure he wanted to.

Staring unseeing at the screen, Browder's thoughts drifted to Crow. After they left the cemetery on the day of Lester's funeral, Browder had driven Crow to the bottom of the Weathersbys' drive. They hadn't exchanged more than a few words on the way there, and he had no idea what Crow was thinking as she sat huddled against the door in her wrinkled and grass-stained suit. When he stopped the truck, she looked out the window as though she didn't know where she was. He touched her thigh. "When will I see you again?"

She opened her door. "Go home to your wife, Browder. I'm leaving day after tomorrow and I won't be coming back."

Leaning across the seat, his words drifted out from the open window. "You said that before, Crow. You'll come back, and I'll be waiting for you."

That night sitting across from Missy at the kitchen table, eating the hamburger she had fried into a hard ball, Browder realized the enormity of what he had done. Missy picked at her potato salad with her fork, took a small bite of meat, and then looked up at him. "Do you still love me?"

Her words were darts hitting his chest. "Of course I do," he said, wondering if this were true. Crow had just said that he loved his wife and he hadn't denied it, so he must still love her.

"You don't think about Dimple and wish you were married to her and had all those kids?" She twisted a blond curl over her ear around her finger.

"No, never." He ran his hands across his knit shirt. He had changed out of his suit pants, stuffing them into the laundry hamper for Icey to find on washday. He saw the irony of defending himself against her accusations of the right act with the wrong woman. "Missy, you got to believe me. All I did was change her tire. What did you want me to say? 'No, my wife won't let me help you; call somebody else'?"

Missy pushed her plate away. "No, I guess you did have to. She's just so . . . so . . . you know . . . sexy." Her face crumpled like a wadded tissue. "I'm not desirable. Men don't look at me the way they do her."

Browder wanted to cry for her. This truth softened him and he hurt for her honest appraisal of herself. He didn't know what it would be like to be a woman who couldn't compete with women like Dimple. He lifted Missy's chin and wiped her tear-streaked cheeks. "I look at you that way," he had said, hoping that this was true.

When he heard people talking Browder realized that Barbra had finally quit singing and he could go home. Missy squeezed his arm. "Wasn't it wonderful?" she said.

Browder tried to return her smile. "Yeah, wonderful is the word."

Chapter 47

ITH HER RING FINGER RUTHIE DABBED CONCEALER AROUND her eye and smoothed it out to her cheekbones. She cocked her head, allowing the fluorescent bathroom light to fall on her face, and was confident that she had done a good job; no one at Pisgah would be able to see the shiner once she applied powder.

She went down the hall to Annie Ruth's bedroom made cozy with white shelves filled with stuffed animals, a miniature doll collection, and beautiful illustrated books. The pink gingham curtains and matching ruffled spread were custom-made and had cost a fortune, but Ruthie had been determined that her daughter should have a perfect sanctuary from the turmoil in her home. Annie Ruth wasn't in her bedroom, and Ruthie hurried to the kitchen where her daughter, dressed in her yellow cotton dress, stood barefoot on a chair that she had pulled up to the cabinet. "It's time for Sunday school. What are you doing, honey?"

Annie Ruth turned around. "I was just looking," she said in a tiny scared voice.

"Looking for what?"

"Nothing." She got down and stood hanging on to the chair back.

"Is something the matter?"

Annie Ruth dropped her hand from the chair. "I was looking for Daddy's bottle." She raised her eyes to her Ruthie. "I was going to pour it out."

A flash of heat rose up inside Ruthie. Annie Ruth must have heard their fight last night. "Oh, baby," she said, pulling her to her chest and stroking her hair. She was stiff as wood against her. "It's okay. Really. It's okay. Daddy's not here; he took the bottle with him."

"Where is he?"

"Daddy went to spend the night in a motel. I'll bet he'll be home after we come back from church." She tried for a smile and accomplished a halfhearted spread of her lips. She didn't tell her she had already called the Colonial Motel and found out he was in Room 124 passed out on the bed with the door open. "Maybe we'll go somewhere fun later. Maybe the park. Would you like that?" Annie Ruth didn't answer. She gave her the look she wore when she was telling a story about some dumb kid at school. Ruthie didn't know what else she could say to help her feel better. "Well, go finish dressing. We'll be late."

In church Ruthie prayed with her eyes fixed on the cross behind the pulpit. "Please help me. How can I stay with my husband when my baby girl is suffering? I've tried so hard to help him, Lord, but You've given me a burden I can't carry." She bowed her head, remembering the day five years ago when she had packed hers and Annie Ruth's suitcases, determined to begin a new life, a life without fear. And what had God done but send Dennis home early sick with the flu, begging her to stay, crying for forgiveness. No, God wasn't going to release her from her promise; He would continue throwing up roadblocks to keep her from escaping this marriage that He expected her to honor.

Ruthie tried to listen to the sermon, but the Reverend Fortenberry might as well have been speaking in French or some other foreign tongue. Her mind was like snarled yarn, and she picked at the knots, trying to untangle her thoughts. She had been so happy yesterday when she stopped by the bakery to buy a chocolate cake. Dennis had been coming home early, and sober, for several weeks. He had promised to take Annie Ruth to the Jackson zoo the next weekend, he wanted to attend Pisgah Church with them on Sunday, he loved it when Ruthie wore her hair down like a sun-streaked wave flowing over her, he had said.

At the bakery Tee Wee's face lit up when Ruthie told her that Annie Ruth was going to be in her first ballet recital. Tee Wee twirled Annie Ruth around beneath her big arm. "A dancer! Look at you. Graceful as a little swan." She winked at Ruthie. They both knew her short chubby legs were never going to nimbly pirouette across the stage.

"Have you got a chocolate cake left?" Ruthie asked.

"You know I do," Tee Wee said, pointing to the display case. "How y'all been? Haven't seen much of you since Lester's funeral." The light in her eyes dimmed and she dropped her head. "That plant you brought out is still pretty. Thank you again for it."

Ruthie hugged her. "We're fine. It's you I'm worried about."

"No. I'm awright, just goin on, you know. Can't do nothin else. Life is for the livin they say. Got J. P. to think bout now. Gettin him ready to go off to school. That boy is full of hisself these days."

Ruthie laughed. "He's got a right to be, going off to Ole Miss." She looked at her watch. "Got to go. Dennis is coming home early and I'm planning an extra-nice dinner."

Tee Wee frowned. "How you two doin? He ain't drinkin so much?"

Ruthie took the white cardboard box that held the cake Tee Wee gave to her. "He's fine. We're all fine. I've told you over and over there's nothing to worry about. God looks after His flock. You don't have to be our shepherd."

"Maybe not. But sometime Mr. Dennis seem more like a wolf than a lamb. Put your billfold up. You ain't payin for a little ole cake I made so easy."

Dennis had loved the cake, but while Ruthie was washing the dishes, he'd gone out to his station wagon where he had secreted a bottle of bourbon in the glove compartment. After she finished cleaning up in the kitchen, Ruthie put Annie Ruth to bed and then went out to him. He was leaning against the car swinging the nearly empty bottle in his hand. "Wanna talk to you bout something," he said.

Ruthie crossed her arms. "Time to come in."

"No. I'll come in when I get good and goddamn ready." He set the bottle on the concrete and walked over to her. Dennis told her that the payment for his business loan was overdue. He wanted Ruthie to sign over the trust fund her father had left for Annie Ruth's college. "I'll pay it back," he had said, kissing the tip of her ear. "It's just till I get that big deal I'm working on with Ted Willow."

Ruthie had refused him, saying that Annie Ruth's education was too important to risk, and suddenly she was on the carousel again returning to the ugliness of her marriage. Like so many times before, Dennis' insults turned to the Parsons' snobbishness; Ruthie was unwilling to help him because she thought she was too good for him. "You care more about those stupid niggers out on Parsons Place than you do me." When she saw his fists curling, his jaw tighten, she backed toward the steps. "Dennis, *no*," she screamed. He caught her before she could reach the safety of the house. "You're the reason I get drunk, bitch," he yelled as his fist struck the bone below her left eye. Ruthie pushed him and when he fell onto the concrete, she escaped into the house and locked the door. "It's your fault, your own fault," he shouted before staggering back to his station wagon. From the kitchen window Ruthie watched him back across the lawn before his taillights disappeared. "Don't let him kill anyone, God," she said, reaching for the ice pack she kept in the freezer.

After church Ruthie drove home with a knot of fear in her stomach. Annie Ruth was quiet, her face ashen. Ruthie reached across the seat and patted her thigh. "You look pretty in yellow." She should have taken Annie Ruth to Icey's or Browder's. If Dennis came home, she didn't know what might happen.

When she turned the corner of Delaware onto her street, she saw Dennis' station wagon parked on the driveway beside their white brick Spanish-style house. "He's home," she said to Annie Ruth, hoping she didn't detect the quiver in her voice. "Daddy's home."

She found him sitting on the patio with a glass of orange juice in his hand. Ruthie slid back the glass doors and went to the wrought-iron table, where she saw a wrapped gift lying beside Dennis' listing book. Passing behind him, she sat on the patio chair across the table. "We were at church." She nodded to the house. "I sent Annie Ruth in to change clothes."

Dennis looked terrible. He looked much older than twenty-eight with big puffy bags rising beneath his red-veined eyes. His hand shook when he lifted his glass to his lips. He pushed the gold paper with the royal blue ribbon to her. "Peace offering."

She looked down at the gift, but her hands remained in her lap.

Dennis slid the box closer. "Please? Ruthie, forgive me. I'm so sorry. I never meant to hurt you. It was the booze, worrying about money. I'll kill myself before I hurt you again." He held up his palm. "I swear it. Open your gift. Please?"

She tore the wrapping from the velvet box and then lifted a string of pearls up to the light. Their pink tint told her these weren't the cultured pearls that she normally wore. "Dennis. They're beautiful," she whispered.

"Early anniversary present. I bought them last week and planned to save them for the big day, but I thought now was a better time."

Ruthie opened the clasp and put them around her neck. "Thank you. I love them, really really love them." His sad eyes were breaking her heart.

Dennis put his glass on the table and came to her. He pulled her from her chair and held her, kissing the top of her head. "I don't know what I'd do without you. I love you so much. Forgive me?"

The tears broke through and she clung to him. She rubbed her cheek against his T-shirt, her soft blanket that soothed her earlier fears. She wanted to believe him. Maybe this time, this time . . . "I hate it when we fight," she said, burying her head into his shoulder.

When they heard Annie Ruth sliding the door back. Dennis wiped his eyes and smiled at her. "Hey, kiddo. How was church?"

"Fine," she said. Her eyes lifted to Ruthie's face, asking her was everything between them going to be all right now. When Ruthie nodded, she hesitated, but then moved closer and allowed Dennis to wrap his arms around her.

Ruthie stared over their heads across the lawn to where a humming-bird hung in the air drinking sugar water from the feeder. It darted up and down, the beat of its wings so fast they were nearly invisible. She heard Dennis promise Annie Ruth that he was going to take them to church every Sunday morning from now on. Ruthie wanted to believe him. She needed to believe that he would be here, that he could make her happy. She raised her hand to her throat and felt the hardness of the pearls against her palm. Whether Dennis kept his promises or not, she wouldn't forget that beneath the luster of these pearls she wore the dark bruises of her marriage.

The next morning as Ruthie was getting into her car to pick up Annie Ruth, Dimple turned her Cadillac into the driveway. "Hey, girl. Got time for coffee?"

Ruthie shut her car door. "Sure. I was just going out to Parsons Place, but I don't have to go right away."

Dimple was an entire bouquet of flowers in her red, blue, yellow, and green pantsuit. As she walked across the drive, she pushed plastic yellow sunglasses through her straw-colored hair to rest on top of her head and pointed to her hair. "What do you think? Thea at Price's Beauty bleached it yesterday. I wanna see if blondes have more fun."

Ruthie stood awestruck. "It's . . . it's different," she said. "Does Troy like it?" Dimple's beautiful skin had turned sallow beneath the yellow and white curls.

She laughed. "Loves it. Says I should've been born blond." Following Ruthie into the kitchen, Dimple sat at the round maple table and lit a cigarette. "Mind if I smoke? You quit, didn't you?"

Ruthie reached into the cupboard for an ashtray. "Yeah, I'm over that stage of trying to look mysterious or sexy or whatever I thought I looked like when I was eighteen." She sat the ceramic dish on the table. "Where are your kids?"

Dimple had begun giving birth six months after her marriage to Troy seven years ago. After the four boys she had finally produced the baby girl whom she was grooming in the cradle to wear the Miss Mississippi crown one day. "Mama's got em." She blew out a cloud of smoke. "Except for Davie; he's at a friend's house."

As Ruthie made fresh coffee, she felt lighter and happier now. Dimple's robust humor filled the kitchen, and she thought how fortunate she was to have a friend like her.

"Saw your sister-in-law eyeing a new bedroom set the other day. She's a sourpuss, isn't she?"

Ruthie sighed. "Poor Missy. If only they could have a baby."

"Poot, sky's the same color whether you're standing under it with a crowd or by yourself."

Ruthie poured the coffee and brought the cups to the table. "No, you're wrong, Dimple. I know for sure a baby would help . . . some anyway."

Dimple pushed away the sugar bowl and cream pitcher. "Got to take it black. I'm on a diet again." She patted her stomach. "I can't lose the weight Yvonne put on me." She surveyed Ruthie's body. "You look good. I bet you eat anything you want, too."

"I don't have time to eat once school starts. There's always something that has to be done for Annie Ruth's class, and now it's so hot I don't feel like eating much."

Dimple stubbed out her cigarette and lit another one with a gold lighter in the shape of a cow. "So you gonna be a martyr room mother again? I told the boys there wasn't a snowball's chance in hell I would go down to that sweat-smelly school and get ordered around by a bunch of old-maid crones. I don't see how you stand it."

"It's not that bad. Most of Annie Ruth's teachers are really nice."

Dimple rocked her head from side to side. "Nice, nice, nice. Everybody is sooo nice. When are you going to quit trying to be nice and do something for yourself? You're a goddamn slave to Dennis, Annie Ruth, Pisgah Church, and that hospital."

Ruthie was stung by her sharp words. "You don't have to raise your voice."

"Sorry, I always get worked up after I been reading Gloria Steinem.

But, Ruthie, you're worse than a man pleaser; you're an everybody pleaser. And"—she tapped her cigarette hard against the ashtray rim— "you aren't as happy as you pretend to be. I know how things really are between you and Dennis. Look at me, Ruthie."

When Ruthie lifted her face beneath the light hanging above the table and saw Dimple draw back in horror, she knew the concealer she'd applied hadn't done its job. She held her hand up to Dimple's open mouth. "Don't say it. It's nothing really. Just banged myself on the corner of the cabinet."

Dimple slammed her mug down on the table, splashing coffee onto the white napkin. "That again! Bullshit! That's such bunk. He did it; I know he did. You think God wants you to be some kind of martyr whose purpose in this world is to suffer? Ruthie Wardlaw, you are gonna wake up one day when you're an old shriveled-up lady and say to yourself that you spent so much of your whole life worrying about what God wanted you to do that you forgot to live it. Or worse, Dennis is gonna go too far someday and you won't have a life to live."

Ruthie's face was flaming. Dimple's accusation had struck far too close to the truth. What right did Dimple have to say these things to her? She ought to tell her to get out of her kitchen right now. "Listen," she began.

Dimple held up her hand. "No, I was out of line. I'm sorry. It's just that I worry about you and Annie Ruth, too. I care about you, honey. You're really the only friend I've ever had. I'd die if I thought I'd hurt you."

Ruthie's anger evaporated. Poor Dimple needed a good friend as much as she did. She leaned over and hugged her. "It's okay. Don't worry. I know you mean well, and, Dimple, really it's not as bad as it looks. I'll be just fine. I promise."

Chapter 48

. P. BACKED THE 1960 BLACK MERCEDES INTO THE SHOWCASE
spot on the front of the lot. He had become an expert driver, parking
cars into small spaces, lining them up so that their fronts were as straight
as a plumb line. When he had returned to work after the funeral, he had
felt guilty about enjoying his job, but he couldn't help loving driving the
fancy cars he dreamed of owning someday. Over the last few weeks he
had learned quite a lot about the car business. He learned how to detect
rust spots beneath paint jobs and identify transmissions that were only
going to last a few hundred more miles. He was surprised at how many
people tried to pawn off lemons on Mr. Larry, but his boss was too sharp
for most of them, although occasionally he would shake his head and tell
J. P. he paid too much for a car. "I let my emotions get into that deal," he
said to J. P. when he bought a black GTO from a college student that had
been driven way too hard. Sometimes Mr. Larry would pass his mistakes
on to his customers, but usually people who bought at Larry's Used Cars
got good value for their money.

Most of Mr. Larry's trade was built around serviceable vehicles like
midsized Fords, Chevy trucks, and Dodge sedans, but Mr. Larry couldn't
resist driving home the red '61 Corvette he had seen at the auction in
Baldwin, Mississippi. Now J. P. walked to it and began to lovingly polish
every inch of its shiny chrome to perfection.

Mr. Larry came out when he was done. "Man, that's a pretty little
gal, ain't she?"

"Yes sir. How much you going to ask for her? I think I'll buy this
beauty and take her home."

"J. P., this car needs a blonde with big old blue eyes in the passenger's seat. You too ugly to drive it."

Laughing, J. P. wiped the sweat from his bare chest and threw his plaid shirt on without buttoning it. He would drive the sports car if only around to the front lot to park it beside the Mercedes.

When J. P. returned to the office, Mr. Larry was sitting at his desk heaped with *Blue Books*, Bill of Sale forms, automobile magazines, and piles of loose papers. He looked up at J. P. and said, "Could you stay late today and mind the store for me?"

"You mean by myself?" He tried to look solemn so that his face wouldn't reveal his thrill.

Mr. Larry smiled. "Well, I reckon you know enough now to hold down the fort. The little woman is after me to take her down to the coast for the weekend and wants to get an early start. I hate to close up early on a Saturday when we get so many lookers." He crossed his hands behind his head. "So, how bout it? Think you can handle it?"

"Yes sir," J. P. said too loudly. He lowered his voice. "What would you be expecting me to do while you're gone?"

"Well, don't take no bad checks." He chuckled. "You just sit in here, answer the phone. If somebody wants to take a test-drive, tell them I'll be back on Monday. You got the price list, tell them you've seen me come down from time to time." He stood up and reached across the desk to the key board. "You know about the keys, all of em's got tags. About six o'clock, unless you got customers, lock em up and then"—he handed a key ring to J. P.—"you use this key to lock the office and this one to lock the gate when you leave."

J. P. nodded. "Little one's office, bigger one is the gate. I got it."

"Okay, guess that's about it. Any questions?"

"No sir. Don't worry. I won't leave until six or the last customer has left."

Mr. Larry stood up. "I know that, boy. I ain't worried about that. My big worry is keeping that woman of mine happy for a couple of days."

J. P. didn't move from the spot where he stood until he saw Mr. Larry's big maroon Mercury pull out into the street. Slowly he walked around the small office as if he'd never been there before. He admired the trophies Mr. Larry had won for drag racing in his early days. He typed a few nonsensical letters on the old Underwood upright typewriter on the small metal table. Easing into the desk chair, he picked up the phone. "Yeah, Bob. I need three grand on that old Pontiac," he said to the dial tone. He shuffled the stacks of papers on the desk, making sure to put them back in the proper order. Then, leaning back in the chair, he crossed his hands behind his head.

By two o'clock when no one had come by, J. P. began to feel drowsy and turned on the radio, drumming his hands on the desk to the beats of the music. But the music only intensified his longing for something, anything, to happen. In the doorway, he leaned against the frame as he had seen Mr. Larry do while he watched customers wandering around the lot. When two women drove up in a beat-up Studebaker, J. P. ran out of the office. "Afternoon, can I help you ladies?" he asked.

A black woman in her sixties wearing a navy blue gabardine dress got out of the car and said, "My daughter and I need a bigger car for our family. Where's the manager?"

"Mister Larry, the owner, is out today, but I will be happy to assist you with any questions you may have." He saw the woman taking in his appearance from top to bottom. His shirt was stained with grease and his blue jeans were streaked with dirt. "I also keep the cars clean, and I apologize for my appearance," he said, sticking out his hand. "J. P. Weathersby, at your service."

The woman stared at his hand. "When will the manager be back?"

"Monday, ma'am."

"Oh." She turned to her daughter. "Charlotte Ann, let's go. We'll come back when the real manager is here."

J. P. kept his smile plastered on his face as he watched the two women drive away. Waving good-bye, he said, "You old bat. I hope your car falls apart on the way home."

At three o'clock J. P., looking out the office window, saw a battered truck pull into the drive. It was Ray, who would be impressed that he was the boss this afternoon.

When Ray came into the office, he tilted his bottle cap hat back on his head and grinned at J. P., who sat with his feet propped on the desk. "Hey, my man. You the boss around here?"

"Sure enough. Come on in. I guess I could work out a deal for you, old friend."

Ray's eyes were shining. "I can't believe this. You runnin this place?"

J. P.'s arm swept the room. "You see anybody but me?"

Ray examined every object in the room. When he lifted the trophies,

J. P. warned him to be careful not to drop them. He took Ray out on the lot to show him all the cars he had washed and waxed. Even the cheapest, oldest car, a Plymouth DeSoto, was a step up for Ray. After J. P. had shown him everything he could think of, even the hose he used to wash the cars, Ray turned to him. "Say, J. P., you got the keys to all the cars?"

"Yeah, but Mister Larry said to tell people to come back on Monday to test-drive."

"I just want to hear the engine on that Corvette. Let's crank her up. What would be the harm in that?"

J. P. shrugged his shoulders. "Nothing. Wait here. I'll go get the keys." When he returned Ray settled into the driver's seat of the Corvette.

"How do I look, brother?"

"You're too ugly to drive a beautiful car like this," J. P. said, recalling his repartee with Mr. Larry.

Ray revved the engine. "Barroom. Hear that, J. P. That's a lot of horses under that hood." He opened the passenger's door. "Get in. Feel the vibrations of this baby."

J. P. jackknifed his body into the bucket seat. He sank back into the leather and inhaled. "Smells good, too, even though it's not new."

"Yeah, but the best thing about this car is how it feels going down the highway at eighty, ninety miles an hour. We could take it out. No one would find out."

When he heard the shrill bell ringing, J. P. got out of the Corvette. "Telephone. I'll be right back." An older male voice was on the line. He wanted to know how much his 1960 Buick was worth. It had seventy-five thousand miles on it, but all of them were miles to and from church. Did J. P. have a *Blue Book* handy? J. P. said that he needed more information to give him a fair estimate, but he looked through the *Blue Book* to see what ballpark they were in. The old man spoke slowly and couldn't hear well, and J. P. had to repeat the information, but he never lost his patience. He was enjoying the trouble the old man caused him. It made him feel authentic.

When he hung up, he glanced out the office window and saw the Corvette pulling out into the street. J. P.'s heart caught on fire. He ran to the door. *"Ray,"* he screamed. *"Ray,* come back." Ray lifted his hand and waved as J. P. raced across the lot. He grabbed the door handle as if he could hold the car back with sheer desperation.

Ray patted the seat beside him. "Get in. I'll take you for a little ride."

"No." J. P. gripped the silver handle tighter. "We can't. Back up into the lot."

"I'm goin, with or without you. If you're not comin, get off the door." He pressed the accelerator, revving the engine.

J. P. loosened his grip. It would be better to go, make sure he didn't hurt the engine by doing something stupid. Ray wasn't used to driving a car like this. "Okay, okay, but just around the block." He opened the door and sank down on the leather seat. "Once around and then back to the lot."

Ray had already shifted and was moving down Chestnut before J. P. finished his sentence. At the end of the block, he turned right.

"No, Ray."

"Come on, J. P. This beauty ain't for block-cruisin. We gotta get out on the highway to really feel these horses." He floorboarded the gas pedal and J. P.'s head snapped back like he'd been punched. The knot of fear in his stomach wasn't going to go away until they parked this car back in its place, and he cursed himself for giving in to Ray. Why did he have to be such a big shot?

When they reached Highway 51, Ray rolled down his window and propped his elbow on the door. "Man, look at us, J. P. We needs sunglasses is all."

J. P. couldn't help smiling at the picture that suddenly formed in his head. This was the car of his dreams. Maybe someday. He'd get a law degree, make a ton of money. Then someday would be that day. Maybe . . . Suddenly, he caught a flash of a blue Mustang pulling out of the side road, the red light hanging just ahead. *"Watch out,"* he yelled, stomping his feet against the floorboard.

Ray lifted his feet, too, frantically jamming his shoes down on the clutch and the accelerator. J. P. saw Ray's mouth opening, heard his scream, and then he saw a triangle of blue metal crashing through the windshield.

How many moments later, he never knew, he looked up at the sky and saw that clouds had appeared and God was crying over him. He wiped the water from his face and saw that his tears had turned red. Rolling onto his side, J. P. looked across the ground at a junk pile, red and blue and black and a piece of a doll lying beside it. It reminded him of Josie, that old doll Ruthie used to have. This doll's eyes were wide, questioning. J. P. lifted his head. He could hear sirens, people screaming in the distance. The doll didn't move. He crawled toward it. When he reached the pavement, something pierced his hand, and he lifted it off a sharp-edged bottle cap. Just before a black veil closed over him, he recognized the doll. She was a pretty white girl, named Judy, who loved his mama's tea cakes.

WHEN SHERIFF DAVIS and his deputy, Ed Graves, appeared at the foot of J. P.'s hospital bed on Sunday afternoon, Tee Wee was guiding a straw in a glass of grape juice to J. P.'s mouth. His arm was encased in a plaster cast from just below his shoulder to his wrist; a bulky white bandage protruded from the left side of his face, and the skin beneath his eyes was puffy and bruised. He had been crying with both physical and mental pain ever since his mother had told him about Ray and Judy Willow. He couldn't believe that they were dead. He remembered his mother's prayers, pain, but little else.

The sheriff called his name out in an official-sounding voice. "John Paul Weathersby. You were involved in an accident yesterday. I need a statement from you."

Tee Wee set the glass of juice on the tray beside the bed. "He got a concussion, head injury, a broken bone, lots of stitches. He can't be filling out no report."

The sheriff pointed to the tape recorder in his deputy's hand. He spoke slowly and loudly as if she were deaf or too slow in the head to follow his words. "Mother, the two victims are dead. He's the only one who can tell us what happened." Tee Wee slid past the tray table and moved behind them to the other side of the bed, where she stood holding on to the IV pole like a sentry with a pike protecting her boy.

Sheriff Davis took her seat and sat looking at J. P. silently while Ed Graves set up the recorder on the tray. He opened his steno tablet and clicked his pen against the paper. "Now let's see. John, from what we can make out so far, you and the Simmons boy was driving a red Corvette. That right?"

"Yes sir," J. P. whispered. He was scared of this man. He hadn't ever talked to the law except for Sheriff Patterson, whom he remembered puking on the ground after he'd run over Memphis. Deke had said to steer clear of uniformed men because they were always looking for a reason to lock up a black man. He looked over at Tee Wee for support, but her eyes showed fear greater than his own.

"The other car was driven by Judy Willow, a blue Mustang. You remember that car?" J. P.'s heart thumped against his sore ribs. He did remember, the flash of blue, his calling "Watch out" to Ray. He recalled the feel of the floorboard against his feet as he tried to jam on invisible brakes. When he didn't answer, the sheriff went on. "Now we know you tried to stop, long skid marks on the pavement, but you was going too fast to get stopped before you hit that Mustang." He smiled then. "A fine sports car like a Corvette; it don't want to do the speed limit, does it? It just cries out to be driven fast. How fast was you going, John?"

J. P. felt the wind rushing into his face. He saw the trees on the side of the road blurring into green streaks, the dotted white lines connecting into a single strip on the road before them. "I don't know, sir," he said. "Maybe eighty, ninety."

The sheriff nodded. "So that teenage girl didn't have much of a chance, did she?"

J. P.'s eyes filled with tears. "No sir. Ray didn't have a chance, either."

Tee Wee leaned forward, took his hand, and squeezed it hard. "It's all right, honey. Don't get yourself upset again. Ain't good for your stitches and healing." She looked over at Sheriff Davis. "Ray and J. P. been friends since they was little boys."

"I got just a few more questions and then we'll take the statement," the sheriff said. "Now, John, you and me both know that Corvette didn't belong to either one of you boys. I found out it is registered to Mister Larry Martino. Did Mister Martino hand you two niggers the keys and say, 'Go drive my car a hundred miles an hour on Highway Fifty-One until you hit somebody'? Did he say that?"

The atmosphere in the room had turned so heavy it was almost palpable. J. P. smelled his own sweat mingled with the odor of blood and disinfectant. The sheriff's words, "two niggers," hung in the air between them. He lifted his bandaged head from the pillow and turned to the man. "No sir, but I worked for Mister Larry, and he left me in charge. He trusted me to handle things while he was gone, and I . . ." He dropped back to his pillow, "And I let him down I reckon. I shouldn't have let Ray talk me into driving that car. I should have had better sense."

The sheriff closed his pad. "Yep, hindsight is always sharper than foresight with you coloreds." He stood up. "I'm sorry for you, boy. I heard you was one of the intelligent ones, but I guess you ain't so smart after all."

J. P. stayed three days in the hospital, during which time both Ray and Judy were buried. Tee Wee attended Ray's funeral and sent a sympathy card to the Willow family. She told J. P. she added his name to the card because she knew he would want her to. Nearly all of J. P.'s friends and family members came to visit, and his room became the noisiest one on the hall. He liked his nurse, Miss Cornell, who was Ruthie's friend. She teased him about all the girls lined up the hall waiting for a kiss from him. J. P. tried to laugh at everyone's jokes; he tried to pretend he was happy to see all of them, but the truth was he wanted to be alone. He was bothered by the sheriff's daily visits to ask him more questions about his statement. He had told him everything he could remember. During his second visit, Sheriff Davis began to talk as though it had been J. P. who was driving the Corvette. J. P. corrected him. "No sir, Ray, he was driving. I was sitting in the passenger's seat."

"Now, John, you've already said that you was the one driving, and Homer Wells says that when he got to the scene with the ambulance that you was lying on the left side of the pavement. Your friend was over in the grass off the shoulder."

J. P. was stunned. He hadn't said he was driving, had he? He didn't know why he was on the pavement; he remembered the pain in his hand, the color blue, something else, but that was all. "No sir, I wasn't driving. You misunderstood what I said."

The sheriff took out his pad, leafed through the pages. "Right here I'm reading what you said. 'I shouldn't have let Ray talk me into driving that car.' Got it on tape."

J. P. felt his heart melting into his stomach. "That isn't what I meant. I meant I shouldn't have let him talk me into letting him drive."

The sheriff had closed his notebook. "You might as well stop lying; it ain't gonna do you no good to lie."

"I don't lie." He knew his voice was too loud and sounded like he was talking back to a white man. "You just ask anybody who knows me. I am not a liar."

The sheriff stood up and smiled. "Oh, I'll ask around, John. I already spoke to Ray's stepdaddy, and he says you boys were always up to something, stealing his beer, going out to honky-tonks." He walked to the door. "You mull over this situation, boy. You think on it some more. Next time I come maybe you'll tell the truth."

When J. P. told his mama what the sheriff had said, she had been strangely silent. He had expected her to burst out with a bushel basket of angry words, but she shook her head and pinched her brows together, and said, "I'll speak to your daddy and Deke about this. Don't say no more bout it to anybody else, you hear?"

J. P. stopped talking about his worries, but they gnawed at him like the big rats in the barn. Every time he tried to think of something else, the sheriff's words would sneak around his thought and eat at him. He remembered that the sheriff had called Judy and Ray victims on one of his visits to his room. If there is a victim then there has to be a victimizer, and it was beginning to look like the sheriff had decided it was him.

On the day of his release from the hospital, J. P. eased his cast through the hole Tee Wee had cut in his shirt. He was excited about going home and seeing Bob and getting to sleep in his own bed again. Even though Tee Wee had brought most of his meals to the hospital, the food was sure going to taste better when eaten at home. When the door to his room opened, J. P. called from behind the curtain. "I'm ready. You got the wheelchair, Mama?"

It was Sheriff Davis who pulled away the drape and walked to his bed. "I see you looking better today. Bout time to be released and go home, ain't it?"

"Yes sir, doctor said I can go soon as my mama comes for me."

"You getting up and walking around now?"

J. P. couldn't understand this solicitous inquiry, but he nodded. "Yes sir, I still get a little woozy, but I can get to the bathroom all right."

"Them pain pills will make you dizzy. You probably be off them fore long."

J. P. had been prepared to tell the sheriff that he could prove he was honest if he'd just give him the chance, but now he was confused by this turn of conversation.

The sheriff took out his steno pad. "I got one more piece of the pie to clear up here, boy. You said, and I'm reading, 'I worked for Mister Larry, and he left me in charge. He trusted me to handle things while he was gone, and I let him down.' You remember saying that?"

"I do, and I still feel bad about letting him down." J. P. lowered his eyes to the signatures and funny lines his family had written on his cast.

"Mister Larry Martino was down at the coast with his bride last Saturday afternoon, and he gave you the keys to lock up the cars and the office."

"Yes sir."

Sheriff Davis leaned closer to him. "But he didn't tell you that you could use those keys to steal a car off his lot, did he?"

It took a minute for J. P. to understand the implications of this question. This man thought that he wasn't planning on bringing the car back. His mouth was dry and he licked his lips over and over trying to speak, but no words came.

"You say you feel bad about it; I reckon that will be some comfort to Mister Martino when he gets that wrecked car back." Sheriff Davis turned toward the door.

"Wait," J. P. called. "Ask Mister Larry about me. He'll tell you. He knows I wasn't stealing that car." He breathed more normally now. The sheriff might not believe him, but he would believe Mister Larry.

The sheriff opened the door. He motioned with his head and then his deputy, Ed Graves, came into the room. "I already talked to Mister Larry, boy. He says you stole that car; he sure didn't give it to you. He was surprised you turned out to be a thief, but he said he should have known better than to trust your black ass."

J. P. went cold, and when he saw the silver handcuffs Ed Graves had unhooked from his belt, he felt his bowels wanting to move. He held on to the rail on his bed when the sheriff advised him of his rights. He was charged with automobile theft and vehicular homicide, and he was not going home; he was going to the Lexie County jail. J. P. had never been in a police car, and he was surprised by the wire between the seats, the missing window handles. The strong body odors that permeated the backseat of the patrol car made him nauseous, but it wasn't until he breathed in the stale, rancid air of his cell that he spewed vomit onto the cement floor.

Chapter 49

ITTING STRAIGHT AND HIGH BEHIND THE WHEEL OF THE truck, Tee Wee drove slowly down Enterprise Road toward town. She was on her way to the jail to visit J. P., and her heart felt as heavy as a fruitcake. Troubles came in threes for the trinity, the Father, Son, and Holy Ghost. First it was Lester, next came the accident, and now J. P. was in a jail cell without no bail. She had begged God to break His rule of the threes, but He hadn't, and now it was up to Crow to get J. P. out of jail and back home where he belonged.

Luther was the one who suggested she make the call to Crow. Last night after she had ladled gravy onto his pork chop, she had pushed her own plate away. "I can't eat nothin, knowin my boy is layin in that cold cell," she had said to Luther. "We was so happy. Seem like J. P.'s graduation was yesterday and we was all rejoicing. Now everythin is wrong, and it seems like nothin gonna ever be right again."

Luther got up and knelt by her chair. "Tee, you ought to call Crow, get some money for a good lawyer. That one the court give him ain't no good. Crow's got the money, she loves J. P., and she'll want to help out." He pulled her to her feet. "Call her up. Right now. She'll see to it."

Tee Wee smiled. "How come you get so smart all of a sudden?"

He reached over, picked up his pork chop, and took a big bite. "It's the fat. Oils your brain to run faster. You should of ate."

Tee Wee turned onto Highway 24 and crept along unaware of the line of traffic behind her. She needed time to think before she saw J. P. It seemed like she couldn't think good for herself no more. Her mind wound around like a spinning tire stuck in the mud, and she couldn't get started toward anywhere. Even her prayers were nonsensical. "Help us. Help me. Where's Lester? Tell me what You done with my boy. Make that lawyer Crow's bringin be smart. Don't let Icey tear up nothin at the bakery."

The phone call to Crow had been a hard one to make, but she had dreaded asking for a favor from Icey worse. After closing the shop for two days, she had known that she would lose all her business if she didn't find someone to run it for her. She hated owing Icey, and she was worried that once she got her big butt behind the counter, she'd be hard to get rid of, but there wasn't anyone else she could ask. Icey had surprised her, though, hadn't asked any questions, hadn't said a thing about paying her back. She had hugged her and said, "I glad to be able to do somethin, Tee. You can count on me."

When she reached the outskirts of Zebulon and passed by Mr. Larry's car lot, she had a mind to turn into his drive to try to talk some sense into him. J. P. had thought so high on him, said he was a good man to work for, but look where that thinkin had taken him. Now Mr. Larry was telling the sheriff and anybody that would listen that J. P. had stole that car and drove it like a weapon to kill that girl. Tee Wee gripped the wheel tighter. She was so mad at the lies. White lies. All her life she had been told that a white lie is a little lie that ain't so bad, but the definition of *white lie* had changed in her mind to mean words from white mouths that got bigger with each tellin. Wouldn't do no good to speak to Mr. Larry. He wasn't going to listen to a word out of her mouth. She pressed on the accelerator and sped on toward Magnolia to the county jail.

Tee Wee didn't see how her baby would survive in that filthy cell. He wasn't eating, not even his favorite peach cobbler Tee Wee had brought him still warm from the oven. In his oversized jail outfit, with his Afro growing out wild, J. P. was beginning to *look* like a criminal.

As Tee Wee pulled into the parking space in front of the jail, she prayed again. "I'm countin on Crow and Icey, Lord. It's come to this. Don't You be foolin me with them two." The morning dew had left wet spots on the sidewalk, and she walked slowly up the steps, carrying her basket of food and the bag with J. P.'s change of underwear.

Donnie Quinn was bringing a cup of coffee to his desk when Tee Wee opened the door to the outer office. He was a college student studying criminal justice, and Sheriff Davis had given him an office job for the summer. He set his cup on the counter and stuffed his shirt down into his pants. "Morning, Tee Wee. What you got good today?"

Tee Wee had had the presence of mind to bring her culinary skills to her son's aid, and the entire workforce at the county jail had enjoyed slices of cake and pie and muffins filled with plump blueberries. She set her basket on the counter and lifted out a sack of sugar cookies. "Here you go. These taste good with that coffee."

Donnie picked up a cookie, bit into it, and rolled his eyes. "Delicious." Without looking into her basket and bag, he unlocked the door that led to the cells. No one worried that she had buried a hacksaw or a weapon in her basket of sweets. "Your boy didn't sleep last night," he said in a low voice as they walked down the short hall lined with cells. "Nobody did; Rusty Smith got thrown in number two, drunk and wild as a bobcat. Hollered like one all night."

When they reached J. P.'s cell, Tee Wee looked through the bars into the small chamber. There was a sink, a slop jar, and two cots chained to opposite walls beneath wooden shelves. The concrete floor was wet and streaked with green mildew and the smell of feces and urine and fear lay like a fetid cloak over them. This was her son's home now. She tried to smile. "J. P., I brought you some things."

He was sitting on the dirty mattress ticking of his cot. The bare skin of his side showed through the large rip in his shirt that had been cut to accommodate his cast, his eyes were dull and sunken, but he was smiling as he stood up and came toward her. A phony smile for me, Tee Wee thought, as she entered the cell. "Hey, baby," she said. She pinched his upper arm. "You got to eat, boy. You gettin to be skin and bone."

"It's hard to eat in here. Smells so bad, all the food starts to smell bad, too."

Tee Wee sat down on his cot and patted the spot beside her. "I got good news."

"They dropped the charges?" His tone told Tee Wee he wasn't being serious.

"No, baby, but that might come true fore long." She smiled as broadly as her heavy heart would allow. "Crow is comin and bringin a smart, white lawyer with her."

"No, Mama! Not Crow. I didn't want her to know. I told you that. She's gonna be, she's, she's . . . I didn't want. When is she coming?"

"Soon as she can. Tomorrow maybe. I know you wanted to keep it from her, but it's in the paper." Tee Wee stood up. "Besides, she's your sister, and she be the only one with enough money to get you out of here. You need her. I does, too." Her chest heaved; she wiped her hands down her dress before reaching inside her bodice to pull out a tissue to wipe her damp face. "I can't help you. I ain't got the money. You know that."

J. P. shrugged his shoulders, lifted his palms in the air. "I'm sorry, Mama. You're right. I'm ashamed. Crow was counting on me going to college and now . . ."

With her hands on his shoulders, Tee Wee looked into his eyes. "You are goin to college. You done nothin to be ashamed of. All of us is proud of you. You our A student; you gonna be *somebody*. You hear, J. P.? You listenin to your mama?"

J. P.'s eyes filled with tears. "I'm listening. I just got to believe it is all."

As she walked toward the bars, Tee Wee said, "Your bones is healin fast, and skin cuts, too. Mend your mind now. It's up to you; can't nobody do that for you."

CROW'S TRAIN WAS LATE, and Tee Wee leaned out over the track to see as far toward Summit as she could. Crow had called her with the news that she was stopping in Jackson to pick up Tyler Powers, the white lawyer she had hired. He would prove that J. P. was being railroaded because he was black and registered to attend Ole Miss. Tee Wee had told Crow she didn't think maybe that was true. It was Mr. Larry saying he stole the car, and the sheriff believing that J. P. was driving. All that and the fact that the Willow family owned the Movie Star lingerie factory and was big shots around Zebulon. Tee Wee liked that J. P.'s new lawyer's name was Powers. That was a good omen. She shifted her black patent purse to her left hand, rubbed a spot on it with her finger. Her hat felt crooked, and she reached up to straighten it. She was wearing her graduation outfit because she wanted to look her best for this city lawyer who was coming to save her son. But whatever Mr. Powers thought of her really didn't matter. All that really mattered was him getting her boy out of that filthy jail.

When the yellow orb of light appeared beneath the concrete overpass and the train's shrill whistle blew, Tee Wee looked up to the blue sky. "Thank You, Sweet Jesus. I know You be bringin salvation to us all."

Crow's bright angry eyes scared her. Her voice was louder than usual, her shoulders squared in her navy blue suit. "Mama, this is Mister Powers, J. P.'s new lawyer. He wants to be taken to the jail right away to confer with his client."

Tee Wee blinked as the tall white man held out his hand for her to shake. His blond hair was caught back in a ponytail fastened with a green rubber band. He wore bell-bottom pants and an open-neck shirt that was unbuttoned to expose the big gold medallion that lay on his curly white chest hairs. He couldn't have been more than thirty years old. This was the man who held her son's future in his brown briefcase. "Please to meet you," she said, frowning at Crow. Mr. Powers pumped her hand like he was drawing water from a well. "I reckon you want a place to stay at. There's a Holiday Inn out on Delaware. You want me to drive you to it?" she asked.

Mr. Powers looked bewildered. "You own a car?"

"Truck," Tee Wee said.

"Oh, well, that will be fine. I was under the mistaken impression you didn't have transportation." At least he talked like a lawyer even if he didn't look like one, and she thought to herself that Crow must have laid on the *pore-ole-Mississippi-niggers* routine. "Oh, we got wheels, ain't much, but we get around," she said with a shake of her head.

Powers wanted to see J. P. right away, and when Tee Wee pulled up in front of the jail, he leapt out of the truck before she'd turned off the engine. "I'll need an hour, and I'd like to talk to him alone this first time. Call for me at"—he checked his silver watch, which looked like a dog chain to Tee Wee—"eleven-thirty."

Tee Wee and Crow sat in the truck watching him stride up the walk with one hand in his pocket. Tee Wee jerked her head over to Crow. "What was you thinkin? He don't look right to me. Looks like a hippie and they don't go over none too good round here."

Crow laughed. "I wish you could have seen your face when we got off the train."

"Ha ha. This is your brother's life we're talkin bout. Ain't no time for laughin."

Crow's smile vanished. Her voice was sad and heavy. "I know that, Mama. I want to see him so bad that I can hardly stand to wait until Powers gets through talking. I know he looks like some draft dodger without a penny, but, Mama, he's a real successful lawyer with a big firm in Washington, DC. Don't let his looks fool you."

"Why'd you tell him we was like church mice?" On the drive to the jail Mr. Powers had talked like he thought they had no electricity or inside toilets.

"Thought it might make him fight harder for J. P. He's one of those white do-gooders who believes he's got a calling to lift the downtrodden blacks up into the whites' cushy world."

Tee Wee chuckled softly. "Well, I reckon I wouldn't mind bein raised up some." Her voice took on a serious tone. "Do you think he can help J. P.? Is he good enough to beat that Lowell Gatlin, who's bent on puttin J. P. in Parchman Prison?"

"He's good enough. Lowell Gatlin got the DA's job because he had money. Doesn't mean he's smart. Powers is smart, graduated from Harvard."

"Is that as good as Ole Miss?"

She laughed. "Better, Mama. A lot lot better." She stood up. "Let's get out and walk. I need some exercise."

Tee Wee opened her door, put her foot down to the pavement, then hesitated. She looked back at her daughter's beautiful dark face. "Crow. Crow, thanks for comin. Thanks for helpin out your brother. I don't know what we'd of done without you."

Crow smiled, waved her arm in dismissal. "He's my baby brother, Mama. I love him; I love all of you."

Tee Wee met her on the sidewalk. She couldn't remember ever hearing Crow say she loved them. Putting her arms around her daughter, she hugged her tightly. "My little flyaway bird. I thank the Good Lord for sendin you home."

Chapter 50

FTER HER MOTHER LEFT TO CHECK ON ICEY AT THE BAK-
ery, Crow sat on a bench outside the jail to wait for Powers. She drew her
compact from her purse and squinted at her reflection. She still couldn't
believe all that had happened since Tee Wee's phone call on Thursday
night. Crow had barely recognized her mother's voice spilling out her
fear and grief. "I'll get a good lawyer," Crow said to her. "They'll lock
him in prison and throw away the key if you let that court-appointed
idiot try the case."

When Crow phoned Winston, asking for help, he told her that his
friend Powers was her man. He was a civil rights advocate, passionate,
smart, and successful. An hour later Winston called Crow back and told
her that Powers could meet her in Jackson to take the train down to
Zebulon. "I'll cancel the rehearsal session tomorrow and hold off on
booking any engagements until I hear from you. I wish there was more
I could do to help. I know how highly you regard your little brother,"
he said.

Crow wrapped the phone cord around her finger. "Yeah, he's special.
He was the one I was counting on to make something of himself. I hope
to God your friend can get him out of this mess. You don't know how it
is down there, Winston. Blacks are always found guilty."

After she hung up the phone, Crow turned out the lights, changed
into her nightgown, and lay across her bed on her back. She drew her
hands down the soft nylon to her stomach. Was there another human being lying here with her? No, she couldn't be pregnant; she wouldn't allow

it. With her fists, she pummeled her abdomen. "Come on, come on, Granny Red. For God's sake, let me start my period tonight."

She fell asleep on top of the covers and woke at four shivering with cold in the air-conditioned room. Huddling beneath her spread, she closed her eyes, but she couldn't go back to sleep. She cupped her breasts with her hands. They were sore and enlarged, but that didn't mean anything, did it? Swelling occurred with her monthlies, didn't it? She was panicking over nothing. So her period was a little late; that happened sometimes, but not to her, and not this late. What if she were pregnant? What would she do about it?

Crow sat up and turned on the lamp beside her bed. She and Browder hadn't used any protection, but she hadn't been worried about it. There had been other times when she hadn't used anything with her past lovers, and she had thought that maybe she was sterile. She hadn't cared if she was. Snotty-nosed young'ns were part of her past, and she didn't need any of them in her future. She tucked her hands beneath her arms and rocked. Oh God, what else could happen? Lester and J. P. and now maybe a half-white baby. Fear was washing over her, running through her veins like ice water. She raced to the bathroom where she vomited into the bowl until her stomach was empty, and afterward, she lay on the yellow bath mat with her knees drawn to her chest. If she were pregnant, she would have an abortion; she knew several musicians who had arranged them for their girlfriends. There was plenty of time, and she had the money to pay for a good doctor to do it. She rose to her knees and, holding on to the tub, pulled her herself up. She would go back to Mississippi, see J. P. through whatever happened, and then by the time she returned, maybe she would have started her period. She stared at her drawn face in the mirror. There was no use lying to herself; she was carrying Browder's child.

Crow had returned to bed and lay facing the framed photographs of herself she had hung on the wall. Several of her past lovers were posed with her in front of various clubs. Why now? Why not one of the other times when the sperm was delivered by Paul, the black horn player, whom she didn't give a damn about? Her eyes moved to Willie, Abe, and finally Kirk, the only white one she had thought might please her in the way Browder had. But he was no better than all the others, and she hadn't fallen in love with any of them. She closed her eyes; she wasn't in love with Browder, either. She wasn't going to have his child, and she would get rid of it as soon as she came back from this trip. "Oh, J. P.," she whispered. "How could this have happened to you? I'm coming; it will be all right. Everything will be all right."

But her fears for her brother returned tenfold when Powers walked down the walk toward her and said, "I need to borrow or rent a car. I have a lot of research to do, and I need to get started right away." He wanted information about the DA, the sheriff, Mr. Martino's finances, the bakery, the level of integration they had achieved.

"I haven't lived here for the last ten years," Crow told him. "You talk to my mother; if she doesn't know all of the answers, she'll know someone who does."

"What about white people? Are there white people who will stand up for J. P.?"

Crow frowned. Her hands involuntarily found her stomach. "Well, the Parsons. My family has lived on their place most of their lives. They've known J. P. since he was first born." She shook her head. "But I don't know whether they'd be willing to help. You can't always tell about white people," she said, staring hard at his pale face.

Powers was unfazed. "Fair enough. Well, we can just hope for now," he said, sitting down beside her on the bench to wait for Tee Wee.

Hope. Crow turned the word over in her mind. She hadn't heard that word in a long time, and now she remembered her mother saying "There's always hope" every time a disappointment came her way. She hadn't believed in such a thing. Hoping was for fools; smart people didn't sit around hoping; they acted. Now she was the one hanging on to hope for a lot of reasons.

After Tee Wee returned, Crow was finally free to visit J. P. He was standing at the bars waiting for her. He barely resembled the boy she had waved good-bye to at the train station only weeks ago. "Hey, lil brother," she said. "Some digs you got here."

He smiled, but it wasn't his old grin that showed all his straight white teeth. "Welcome to my palace," he said.

She hugged him tightly. "Well, what did you think of Mister Powers? You feel like he's gonna help you?" Her voice was light, as cheerful as she could manage.

J. P. pressed his lips together. "Oh Crow, I feel like I let you down."

"Shush shush. You'll get out of this jail, go to school like we planned."

He looked away from her. "I did do it, Crow. I wasn't driving that car, but I have to take the blame. I let Ray drive it. I did try to stop him, but I didn't try hard enough."

"You quit thinking like that. It was an accident, pure and simple."

"Sheriff doesn't think so. Mister Larry doesn't, either. He's saying I stole that Corvette. Thinks I'm a thief, Crow." J. P.'s voice rose with anger. "Even Ray's stepdaddy is saying I'm a bad nigger."

Crow's anger matched his, but she held hers in check, knowing that cool clear heads worked better than hot ones. "Listen to me. You want to be a lawyer someday, right?" She waited until he nodded agreement. "Okay, this is your first lesson. You can't let anybody see what you're feeling or thinking. Don't let them get to you. You show emotion, you show weakness."

J. P. didn't like her words. "Easy for you to say, Crow. You're not locked up in here accused of being a thief and a killer. You never worried what folks said about you. You don't get hurt cause you don't care about people like I do." His eyes widened. "I'm sorry. I didn't mean that. I'm just so . . . so . . . I don't know what."

"It's all right. I can see where you'd think that about me. And you're right about some of it. I don't lose any sleep over whether some son-of-a-bitch is talking bad about me. And I don't care about most of the people I've run across so far. They don't deserve my time as far as I'm concerned." She reached for his hands and touched them to her cheek. "But I'm hurting for you right now." She smiled. "And you know why? You're worth all the worrying and hurting there is. I gotta go. Mama and Powers are waiting on me. I'll be back tomorrow and every day until you're home again."

"Home," J. P. said. "I never knew how beautiful that word could sound."

WHEN BROWDER DROVE past the jail, he didn't notice Crow getting into Tee Wee's truck. He had been driving aimlessly for an hour, dreading going home to tell Missy that he'd just signed away the mineral rights to his land to Dickie Webber at the Merchants Bank. Ten thousand for the mineral rights was theft. There was talk that a big oil company was buying leases in Amite County and planning on coming to Lexie County next. But he needed the loan to keep him afloat.

When he stopped for the red light on Park, Browder closed his eyes to shut out the image of Dickie's smug face as he handed him the pen to sign away those mineral rights. He flicked on his turn signal. He would go by Ruthie's house. He was worried about her. If only she hadn't married that bastard Dennis. He wished Ruthie would pack up and get the hell away from him.

Annie Ruth was at Miss Dottie's taking a ballet lesson, but Ruthie was happy to see him, and Browder was grateful for the hug she gave him that he so badly needed right now. Ruthie looked good, happy. Maybe things between her and Dennis were better than he thought. After they were settled into the wrought-iron chairs on the patio, Ruthie and Browder laughed over Annie Ruth's determination to be the sugarplum fairy for next year's Christmas recital. She had been furious when she lost the role to Katrina Markham, who had much longer legs and a lot more talent. Browder unbuttoned his cuffs and rolled his sleeves to his elbows. "Phew, it feels so good to be outside. Been cooped up in an office all morning."

"Where?"

"Merchants Bank."

Ruthie sighed. "Are you in trouble, Browder?"

"No, don't go worrying about me. I'm just a little short on cash. Missy wants a new car, says the Lincoln is too big to park. She's got her eye on a Triumph."

Ruthie pulled the potted begonia on the table to her and began removing the dead blooms. "Don't buy from Larry Martino. He's a pig."

"He is that. But people believe him and not J. P. How's Tee Wee taking it?"

Ruthie dropped the withered leaves to the concrete. "Hard. She's scared to death for him and so am I. They need a miracle. I've prayed and prayed for one, and maybe God is answering my calls for help. Crow is coming today with a hotshot lawyer who's performed a few miracles for other black people."

Browder felt a rush of adrenaline coursing through him. She was back! When he had learned of J. P.'s arrest, he had thought of the possibility that Crow might come, but no one had mentioned her. "Today?"

Ruthie laid her hand on his forearm. "Browder, stay away from her. She's here to help her brother; she didn't come because of you."

Browder moved his arm away from her. "I know that. I'm a grown man, Ruthie. I can see things for myself and I don't need you to take care of me."

Ruthie's eyes clouded. He had hurt her. She looked down at her brown sandals. "I'm sorry. I just get scared for you. I know how you feel about her, and nothing good can come of it. She's black, you're white, and you're married."

Browder rubbed his eyes. He couldn't take any more of anything today. He felt old and tired and used up. He tried to smile. "Don't worry about me. I love Missy; I'm not about to do anything that would hurt her." He wondered if this was true. So far, he hadn't done anything to hurt her because she didn't know about Crow. But if he were sure of Crow's love, what then? "Let's talk about something else. How's Dennis?"

"Dennis is fine. He's coming home for dinner on time for a change."

"I'm glad, Ruthie. I hope things work out between you."

Ruthie looked at her watch. "Oh, Browder, I've got to go pick up Annie Ruth. I wish we could talk longer. Can you promise me that you're okay?"

Browder held two fingers to his eyebrow. "I'm fine. Scout's honor."

"You were never a Boy Scout. I think you're lying to me; to yourself, too."

Browder stood up and fished for his keys in his pants pocket. "You might be right, Ruthie. I don't know how I feel about much of anything these days. I've been thinking a lot about Daddy. I wonder what he'd say if he knew that I gave away the mineral rights to the land today. Little sister, I have sold our birthright for a foreign car."

Chapter 51

ICEY WAS TRYING HARD NOT TO BE TOO HAPPY, BUT SHE KNEW that her smile crept out on her face daily like the sun from behind a cloud. With her metal tongs she fished four chocolate cupcakes from the bin and dropped them into a paper bag. "What else for you, Miz Adams?"

Sadie Adams smiled back at her. "I guess I can't resist that pineapple upside-down cake under the cover over there." She pointed to the perfectly round and level cake Icey had baked that morning. Beaming, Icey reached for a white box. She rang up the sale and helped Miz Adams out to her car, carefully setting the cake on the floorboard of the ancient Ford.

Icey hurried back inside when she heard the phone ring. It was Tee Wee asking how things were going. She wouldn't be in until later today because she had to go see J. P. and talk to that lawyer about the case. She sounded so nervous, Icey started tearing strips of paper off the register's roll. "Everthin just fine down here. I done sold two pies, a cake, and a whole mess of cupcakes and cookies. Business is good."

Tee Wee's voice came back to her like she was in a well. "I got to meet that lawyer in an hour. He says we got a lot to do before the trial. He can't get J. P. no bail, but he did get the judge to speed up the trial date."

"It'll go good, Tee. J. P. ain't done nothin wrong, and justice will win out on this here case."

"I hope you right, Icey. Pray for us."

Icey gripped the phone tighter. "Oh, I done that already, but I'll pray again. Jesus, Lamb of God, please . . ."

"Not now," Tee Wee interrupted her. "I got to go. Talk to you later."

"Okay, bye." Icey hung up the phone, then dropped to her knees, and, folding her hands, she prayed harder than ever. "Take care of Your child, J. P. Don't let him come to no harm. And help Tee Wee to take all this better than seems she is. I don't think she doin too good, Jesus. And also, Jesus, let me continue on down at this store, sellin lots, and helpin out. Be with me when I tries to make that red velvet cake. Amen."

Holding on to the counter, she pulled herself to her feet. She had gained quite a bit of weight in the two weeks she'd been helping out. Surveying the small room, she spotted a fingerprint on the glass counter, and, licking her finger, she rubbed the smear, then lifted her apron to wipe it dry. Everything looked perfect. She had surprised even herself. Deke was especially proud of her, saying he knew all along she had a head for business. Icey smiled, thinking about Deke. He was planning on leaving Parsons Place, but it was still a secret. He had a job at the Massey Harris tractor dealer in town lined up, and he would be making enough money so that they could rent a little house in East Zebulon. And she'd be close to the bakery then. Her smile vanished. What if, after the trial was over, Tee Wee didn't need her anymore? She sat down on the rocker behind the counter and picked up her tatting. Well, she'd just have to make herself necessary. She'd be the sugar in the cake, the cocoa in the fudge. She was going to get all her dolls and doilies and other craft ideas together and set them up to sell before Tee Wee got back. She'd see she couldn't do without Icey when she made so much money off them.

Around noon business slacked off to nothing. The evening crowd wouldn't begin until after four, and now Icey had time on her hands. She washed up the baking utensils, poured some Bon Ami on the stove, and scrubbed it to perfection. She mopped around the door where Mr. Wilkerson had tracked in orange dirt. Satisfied that she'd worked enough, Icey put a pillow behind her head on the rocker and dozed off.

"Icey!" She awoke to Tee Wee's voice. "I done called your name four times; a robber could've come in here, stolen all the money, and ate up the whole place without you knowin nothin."

Icey jumped out of the chair. "Tee, I wasn't sleepin. I was just restin my eyes. I knowed it was you in here."

Tee Wee crossed her arms. "You didn't hear nothin. What else goin on here I don't know bout?"

Icey waved her arm around the room. "See for yourself. Go back to the kitchen. It's cleaner than your house. Look in that register. Plenty of money I took in." She was stung by Tee Wee's words. Here she was help-ing her out when she had plenty better to do, working her fingers to the bone, and all Tee Wee got to say now is she wasn't watching for robbers. She watched Tee Wee's back as she marched around the room, in and out of the kitchen, over to the cash register, bending down to the display case. Finally, she came back to where Icey stood in front of the chair.

"Well, I got to say it, Icey. Everythin look good. You doin an all-right job down here."

Icey wanted to bask in the praise, but she couldn't help feeling some miffed still. "You seen the stove? I cleaned it good."

"Yeah, it near bout shinin. And you done a lot of business I see by the number of dollars in the register."

Icey's face glowed. "And I raised the price of cupcakes two cents and nobody cared. I figured if a loaf of bread gone up to twenty-two cents, we could get more'n a nickel for them cakes."

Tee Wee scratched her head with her index finger. "Well, I don't hold with gougin my customers, but I guess that ain't too much."

"No, and I got some more ideas to talk to you bout."

Suddenly Tee Wee's huge frame crumpled down onto the rocker. "Later. I just feel too weak now to talk about business."

Icey patted her arm. "How did it turn out this mornin?"

Tee Wee began to sob. "It ain't good. I don't understand nothin goin on really."

"What the lawyer say?"

Tee Wee's face brightened. "He's all right. He don't look like much, but he's smart. Been interviewin people all over town, and he says he may have some good news for us soon." Tee Wee stood up. "I got to go. Want to go back and visit J. P. before I go home. I came over here to get him a slice of pie, but I see the sweet potato all gone."

Icey nodded. "Yeah, but I got peach left." Icey put her hand out to touch Tee Wee's arm again. "How's J. P. holdin up?"

Tee Wee lifted her hand and squeezed it. "He gonna be fine, that boy. He tries to cheer me up every time I go down there."

Icey shook her head. "I don't know how you standin this, Tee. I just don't know."

"The Lord don't give us no burdens we can't carry. I trust in Jesus to see me through. He seen us through a lot already."

"Amen to that," Icey said. And she thought of all the sorrow she'd be leaving behind on Parsons Place. Maybe the Lord would let her lay her burdens down in town. "Amen and praise Him for walkin with us through the storms behind and ahead."

"Yea though I walk through the valley of the shadow of death, I will fear no evil," Tee Wee said. "I want to quit fearin, but oh, Icey, I is so scared."

Icey felt a ghost finger run up her back. She shivered. "Me, too," she cried.

Just as Icey was inserting the key in the door to lock up and go home, Crow came running down the street. "Hey, Icey. Wait up. I want a cake to take over to Glory's." Icey stood with the key in her hand, her eyes on Crow. Her tennis shoes didn't have a smudge on them. With her silky low-cut blouse tucked into her jeans, the big round sunglasses, and a green scarf headband, Icey thought that she looked like a real movie star now. "Thanks," Crow said. "I tried to get here sooner, but I had to meet Tyler at the Holiday Inn."

Icey opened the door. "Who's Tyler?"

Crow followed her in. "Tyler Powers, J. P.'s lawyer."

"Oh. Well, what you want? I got red velvet, cocernut, and chocolate."

Crow tapped her long pink nail to her teeth. "Mmmm. Which is Glory's favorite? It's for her and Masie. We're having a hen party tonight."

Icey reached into the case and took out the chocolate cake. "Hen party, huh? I reckon Glory and Masie would rather have a rooster or two visit them." She could understand ugly Masie not having a man, but she couldn't believe her Glory hadn't gotten married by now. She would be glad when Crow went back to Memphis. She might steal all of Glory's beaus.

When Crow leaned over to take the cake, Icey could see half of her bosom. "Yes, just us hens. We're having a picnic on the roof of their apartment building, and then I'm giving Glory and Masie makeovers."

"Well, I'm glad for Masie; that girl could use some help with her looks."

Crow stopped smiling. "She's been so sad since Lester died, and now we're all worrying about J. P. I thought we all could use some cheering up." She started for the door. "Thanks, Icey. Sorry to hold you up. Tell Deke hi for me."

Icey watched her go, balancing the cake box on her arm as she let herself out. "I ain't telling Deke nothing bout you," she said to the closed door. Crow was still capital-T trouble, but it was nice of her to fix up the girls. Glory could use some help, too, she admitted now. Her hair looked like a Brillo pad, and she was a few pounds overweight. Besides helping Glory and Masie, Crow was the one who had hired that hotshot lawyer, and although Tee Wee hadn't said so, she was sure she was paying his big legal fees. Unless she was paying with something else out at that motel. She knew for a fact that Crow wouldn't care that he was white. Her Glory might not look like no movie star, but she was a good girl.

After supper that night Icey went out to sit on her porch. Hilda was playing jacks by herself, and she thought about how different raising this last child was from the others. She didn't have any playmates, for one thing, and none of the rest of them had ever had to sit in a school desk in the middle of a bunch of white faces. The first week of school there had been a lot of white faces walking by the windows looking in at Hilda and the seven other black first-graders. They had marched back and forth with their signs that said NO INTEGRATION. NIGGERS GO HOME. WHITE SCHOOLS FOR WHITE CHILDREN ONLY. But Icey's fears that the picketing would lead to violence were unfounded. The teacher had put paper on the windows so the marchers couldn't see in, and they had eventually gone home. None of the hostilities had affected Hilda; she was smiling big when she got off the bus that first week of school. She had a brand-new workbook in her book satchel. "It ain't been erased, Mama," she said. "I'm the first one to write in it."

Now Icey looked over at her last child. "Hilda, time to go to bed. Go get your nightgown on and call me when you ready to say prayers."

As she watched her gather up her jacks and go inside, Icey noticed as she often did how much Hilda resembled Memphis. She cocked her head when she was thinking and stuck her tongue in the corner of her mouth when she was excited exactly as Memphis had. Sometimes it scared her to think like this. God had taken Memphis away; he could take Hilda, too. No. No, she wouldn't think that. Hilda was going to live a long long life and outshine all the kids. She was pretty and smart and she knew how to handle herself in the white school already. Icey rocked back in her chair. Things were changing fast around here, and when they moved into town, there would be more changing to do.

After Hilda was settled Icey went back to her chair on the porch. She was tired. Working at the bakery wasn't as hard as scrubbing floors, but the mental figuring was new to her and wore her plumb out. She looked over at Tee Wee's house. She was glad Crow was staying in town tonight. She wasn't gonna be shakin her butt in front of Deke in the morning.

"Hey, baby." Deke stood in the door. "You coming to bed? I got something in here to show you."

Icey laughed as she leapt up from her rocker. "I'll bet you has. And I think I seen it once or twice before," she said, as she followed him to their bed. She didn't need to worry about Crow; Deke still liked big women with big butts, and Icey thanked the Good Lord that she could still wiggle hers good enough to please a man.

Chapter 52

THE LEXIE COUNTY COURTHOUSE WAS DUE FOR A FACE-LIFT, and although money had been budgeted for its renovation, a dispute over the contractors' bids had yet to be settled. Most of the taxpayers in the county thought the crumbling redbrick building should be torn down and the site moved from the center of the town of Zebulon to the outskirts on the north, where a few new homes and businesses were sprouting up here and there like the volunteer pine saplings along the highway. But the small-business owners, city councilmen, judges, and the mayor argued that moving the courthouse would take away too much revenue from the shrinking town. For now the cases were presented in the same small courtroom where since the late 1800s hundreds of defendants had sat awaiting their fate, just as J. P. would on this hot July day.

In front of the courthouse two stately magnolias offered some relief from the heat by shading the lawn and sidewalk where a few people loitered, reluctant to enter the hot building. Icey brushed by them and, grabbing the black iron railing, pulled herself up the steps that led to the open double doors. She had never been inside this building, but she had no trouble finding the small courtroom located just off the marble-floored entryway. Pausing for a moment in front of one of the oscillating standing fans inside the door, she surveyed the eight rows of scarred pews separated by a narrow aisle. Both sides of the room were nearly filled, all of the Negroes sitting on the left behind the rectangular defendant's table where J. P. would be brought in soon. There were more black faces than white ones, but it was mostly white voices that rose up from the right side of the room. Icey touched her new wig, a cap of short, bright red curls, and then, spotting Tee Wee on the front-row bench, she slid into the one behind her. When she tapped her on the shoulder, Tee Wee turned and stared at her as if she didn't recognize her. Icey patted her head. "Do you like it? I think it makes me look a lot younger."

Tee Wee ignored her question. And when she didn't show any interest at all in the wig, Icey decided she wasn't going to mention her new spectator pumps and matching purse that she had bought for her debut in court. Tee Wee turned back and whispered to Luther, who sat beside her with his head down so far Icey had thought he was sleeping. Sitting up straighter, she looked around with interest at the flags behind the judge's big leather chair. One was the Stars and Stripes; the red, white, and blue one with the big X in the upper left corner was the state flag. Deke had told her that the X box on it was like the Confederate battle flag, and he said it wasn't right to have to honor a symbol that had meant fighting for slavery. Icey was determined not to look at that flag even when the lawyers were standing right in front of it. She turned her attention to the table in front of them where J. P.'s lawyer had spread out a mess of papers. She couldn't believe this was the same man she had met in front of the bakery yesterday. He had replaced his tan Bermuda shorts and flowered shirt with a suit that Icey guessed must have cost as much as a TV set. The fabric was a shiny blue shot through with tiny maroon and black lines. He wore gold cuff links attached to a pale pink shirt, and his blond hair was slicked back and held with a black band. Most wondrous of all, a huge gold cross encrusted with maroon stones lay on the middle of his chest. The man looked like a foreign movie star, and she decided that her earlier suspicions about him and Crow had to be true.

She tapped Tee Wee's shoulder. "Where's Crow?"

Tee Wee pointed to the other side of the room. "Over there. She thinks we ought to spread out so we can see and hear everything from all angles."

Icey's eyes followed Tee Wee's finger and she saw Crow, the only black person on the right side of the courtroom, sitting on the bench directly behind the Willows. In an elegant black dress with a silver circle pin over her breast, Crow sat with a straight back and an unreadable expression on her face. She reminded Icey of a white Lana Turner in that movie where she played the part of a mistress of a married man. In front of her Mr. Willow sat with his arm stretched across the bench behind his wife. They were among the few folks in the room who weren't wearing Sunday clothes. His plaid shirt, casual khakis, and her pink pantsuit made them look like country people who didn't know what to wear to the town party. Mrs. Willow held a lace-edged handkerchief that she twisted into a funnel over and over.

Icey stood up with everyone when Judge Ramsey came striding into the room with black robe billowing as the fan blasted hot air over him. She had expected an old gray-haired man with a potbelly and liver-spotted hands, but the dark hair of the judge taking the high-backed leather chair was gray only around the temples. His face and hands were the color of toast, and Icey figured he got that tan on the golf course or out on Dixie Springs Lake in a fancy boat. He sure didn't look like no farmer. His eyes swept over the crowd in front of him and landed on J. P., who had been brought in just before the judge. Icey whispered in Tee Wee's ear. "J. P. looks good, real nice in his white shirt." Icey knew that when his lawyer had told him to shave off his Afro, he had done so reluctantly, but Mr. Powers was right. J. P. looked several years younger, and that would be a good thing, wouldn't it?

"He's so thin, wouldn't make a shadow beside a fence post," Tee Wee said. Leaning forward, she squeezed J. P.'s shoulder. He turned and gave them a half smile, then slumped forward and bowed his head. An egg-shaped wet spot covered much of his back, and, becoming aware of the intense heat, Icey removed her white cotton gloves and used them to wipe the perspiration from her forehead.

When the morning sun broke through and streamed through the side windows, the heat in the room grew to roasting temperature, and most of the men removed their coats and loosened their ties. The women used handkerchiefs, checkbooks, and grocery lists for fans, and Icey made a mental note to exchange her Lycra girdle for cotton panties tomorrow. Only Tyler Powers, still wearing the jacket to his beautiful suit, seemed unfazed by the heat, and he wasn't even a southerner.

Icey suspected that the jury box was the coolest place in the room because two of the rotating fans were situated to blow over the jurors simultaneously. The hairdos of the five women on the front row chairs were destroyed by midmorning by the hot air blasting over them, but none of them seemed to care. Icey thought it was a bad sign that only one elderly colored man was on the jury, but nearly every name the clerk called was that of a white person. Icey didn't know the soft-spoken Negro man who sat on the end of the back row, but she later learned that he had been a chauffeur for the mayor's wife until he had lost his sight in one eye.

After jury selection, the judge spent a long time talking to the people who had won (or lost, depending on how they felt about serving) their seats. Icey's thoughts drifted to what would happen if J. P. were convicted. In her reverie she saw Tee Wee and herself on their way to visit him in Parchman. They were riding the bus that the state provided for families of convicts, surrounded by other women who carried food and small gifts of toiletries to their sons, husbands, and fathers. They looked out the dirty window at the cotton fields, the tasseled cornstalks, cows grazing on green pastures. Someone's transistor radio was tuned in to WTIX, and a lonely harmonica wept into the sorrowful airless bus. Tee Wee looked at her with devoted eyes. "I don't know how I could make it in this world without you, Icey." When they arrived at the prison, they were searched for weapons, and Icey shivered, imagining some white man's hands patting down her dress. No, she couldn't go with Tee Wee; J. P. could be in there for years. Tee Wee's hair would turn white, her back would bend like a willow tree limb, all her teeth would fall out, and Icey, whose gold tooth still gleamed, would help her on to the bus. They would cry and . . .

"*Mr. Powers!*" The judge had finished with the jurors. It was the lawyers' turn to talk. Icey sat up straighter; she didn't want to miss a word even if she didn't understand the meaning of some of them.

Around noon the judge mercifully called for a recess. Icey doubted half of the crowd could have lasted another hour in the heat, and nothing exciting had happened yet to take their minds off their sweating and the hunger pains of the country people, who were used to eating their noon meal before eleven.

Tee Wee had brought three sacks of food, which she spread out on the tailgate of Luther's truck. "You must of been up half the night cookin, Tee," Icey said.

"Couldn't sleep no ways, so I thought I might as well cook up some vittles," Tee Wee said as she slapped a wedge of ham onto a sliced biscuit and handed it to Luther. "How you think it's goin for J. P. so far?" she asked to no one in particular.

Luther bit into the biscuit and mumbled something unintelligible. Masie, leaning against the passenger door, said it was too early to tell, and Rufus who had come late and sat in the back of the courtroom told them that the jurors' eyes were on J. P. a lot and that was a good sign. Tee Wee nodded. "Well, you got the most experience in a court of any of us. I reckon I'll take what you say as gospel."

Luther had swallowed his food and now he repeated his words. "I said we ought to ask the lawyer what he thinks. How come him and Crow ain't eatin with us?"

Icey looked around at the faces of the people chewing and talking. She hadn't realized that Crow was missing. "Yeah, where Crow at, Tee?"

"She and Powers went off to the jail to talk to J. P." Icey looked at her friend's face and a wave of great pity washed over her. Tee Wee looked just terrible. Her eyes were bloodshot and dull as if she hadn't slept in a long time. She hadn't noticed that she was wearing one brown shoe and one black one.

Icey put her arm around Tee Wee's waist. "That's good. That lawyer sure looks sharp. I bet he can talk circles round that old Mister Gatlin." As she said this, Icey wondered if it were true. Everyone knew that Lowell Gatlin rarely lost a case for the prosecution. He was an eloquent man. All morning his powerful voice had risen above everyone else's, and as he smiled and chatted affably with the jurors, he seemed relaxed and confident. His salt-and-pepper hair was cut neatly over his ears, and his jowls flopped like a friendly puppy's as he pushed his round belly back and forth against the rail of the jurors' box. In contrast, J. P.'s lawyer was soft-spoken, seemed nearly shy, and hadn't smiled once all morning. In her heart Icey felt Crow had brought the wrong man home. But she kept her doubts to herself and complimented Tee Wee on her ham biscuit even though the dough was gooey in the middle.

It was just after one when the prosecution called the first witness, and by then the room was already a sweat box leaking horrible body odors. Icey fanned herself with her gloves as she watched Mr. Gatlin take off his coat, freeing his big belly to hang over his narrow black belt. He wiped his forehead with a blue-and-white handkerchief before he walked toward the witness chair, where the state trooper Yeager Bates sat with his legs crossed. "You were the first one on the scene, is that right?"

"Well, not exactly."

"You received a call on your radio and responded immediately?"

"Yep. I got there just before the ambulance. Two people traveling from New Orleans to Natchez got there first and stopped to help. One of them ran to the Sinclair station and called it in."

"Okay, but no one had disturbed the scene when you got there?"

Bates pulled down the cuffs of his sleeve. He must be really hot in that uniform, Icey thought. She watched his chin working back and forth as he told the court where the cars were positioned, the bodies, and J. P.

He described how the front of the Corvette crashed into the driver's side of the Mustang just at the spot where Judy Willow had sat behind the steering wheel. There were snapshots taken out and identified, and when they were passed to the jurors, two of them gasped, and all of them shuddered. Icey couldn't see them, but she knew they were the last pictures that would ever be taken of Judy Willow. Her mama sobbed out loud, and Icey knew she must be thinking about her photo album filled with pictures of her daughter opening Christmas presents, or Judy in her Easter dress, smiling at the camera, never realizing she wouldn't grow up to hide eggs for her own daughter. Icey wiped a tear from her cheek. She couldn't help thinking about Memphis; she didn't have a single picture of him.

Icey's fear for J. P. grew throughout the afternoon. His lawyer on cross-examination asked the patrolman how long he had been employed and how many wrecks he had investigated.

Yeager Bates was about Browder's age, not quite thirty. His voice was less self-assured when he answered. "Two years. I guess I've been at ten or twelve accidents."

"Ten or twelve?" Powers asked sweetly as if he were sorry about this. "Any of them fatalities?"

"One."

"So you don't know a whole lot about the ratio of velocity and trajectory as it pertains to the occupants of the vehicles?"

The trooper's face reddened, and Icey didn't think it was the heat. "Well, I know what I saw."

Mr. Powers smiled. "And that's all you can really testify to. Thank you." He walked back to his seat, his cross glistening in the sunlight that poured in through the windows. He sat down and patted J. P.'s hand as the judge told Bates he could step down.

Mr. Gatlin's next witnesses were the man and woman who were driving past just after the accident happened. They were Thomas and Delores Cain. Mr. Cain said his mama lived in Natchez and they were on their way to her seventieth birthday party when they came upon the wreck. Mrs. Cain added that they had never before seen any dead people except in caskets and she hoped she never would witness anything like this again. She still had nightmares and her heart was just broken for the poor girl's mother.

Mr. Powers didn't ask either of them a question. He waved his hand and shook his head when given the opportunity. Icey was beginning to worry about this Yankee's lack of energy. The DA's shirt was nearly soaked with perspiration, but Powers looked like he was sitting in an air-conditioned room. When the prosecutor called Sheriff Davis to the stand, he didn't look up from his pad of yellow paper. Icey had a good mind to lean over and deliver a good slap to that lawyer's head just above that horse's tail.

Before the sheriff reached the witness box, the judge said he was going to call it a day. Everybody could come back tomorrow to find out what the sheriff had to say.

Chapter 53

ON THE SECOND DAY OF THE TRIAL, J. P. SAT WITH HIS KNEES pressed together waiting for court to resume. If he separated his legs, they jiggled so fiercely he could barely keep his behind on his chair. Last night alone in his cell, he had tried to pray away his fear, and he opened the Bible Icey had sent to him, hoping to find courage in the scripture. But the words made no sense and he read the same lines over and over. J. P. closed the book and lay back on the stained mattress. He stared up at the low gray ceiling; the plaster was cracked and sagging in so many places it seemed it might fall on him in the night. He nearly wished it would. He wanted to bury his head in Tee Wee's soft bosom, he wanted Bob to lick his face, he wanted Ray to clap him on his back and tell him not to worry. Ray. Why'd he have to die? He thought of Memphis and Bob and Mr. and Mrs. Parsons. The dead rolled through his mind like a train with no destination. Over and over their faces appeared like identical boxcars that clacked over the rails in a monotonous rhythm.

"Look like nothin gonna change; everythin remain the same." Someone was singing Otis Redding's song, "The Dock of the Bay." Things got to change from this, he thought. Mr. Powers said not to worry, that he was going to prove his innocence, but J. P. thought of Judy Willow's mama and daddy sitting across the courtroom this morning. Mrs. Willow had cried nearly the entire day, and Mr. Willow's pale eyes bored into him. Every now and then, he pulled at the hairs above his lip in a gesture that told J. P. he would withstand any pain to get his hands on the nigger who had killed his daughter.

J. P. rose and began to pace across the damp floor. The singing had ended, and now he heard footsteps approaching his cell. Through the bars he saw his daddy shuffling along behind the deputy.

When Luther walked into the cell, he held his nose. "Phew, J. P. How can you stand it in here?" His daddy hadn't visited him before, and J. P. was so surprised he nearly didn't shake hands with him when he held out his gnarled fingers.

"Hey, Daddy. It's late for you to be out; you usually asleep by now."

"I wanted to see my boy. Wanted to say some things fore tomorrow." Luther sat on the cot, balanced his hat on his knees, cleared his throat. "J. P., I was some scared for you today. Everyone who got up on the stand was against you."

Daddy was right; he was going to be convicted. He tried to staunch the tears welling up inside, and when he turned his face away, Luther rose and pulled him to his chest. J. P. heard his daddy's ragged breath, a sob. He had never seen him cry, and this seemed more terrible than his own suffering. "Daddy, Daddy, I'm so scared."

"Me too. Me too. All's I been thinkin today is how I ain't never said things to you I should of said. Seem like there always somethin, a sick calf, a worm eatin the beans, weeds chokin out the garden, always somethin keepin me from tellin you what I feel."

J. P wiped his wet face on his sleeve. "It's all right. I know how it is."

"No, you don't. You my only child, and I didn't ever believe I'd have one. I love you, son." He twirled his hat between his hands. "When Memphis got killed, it could of been you, and I was some scared imaginin that. But I didn't say nothin to you, didn't tell you how proud I was when you graduated with them honors."

J. P. laid his hand on his shoulder. "It's okay."

"No, it ain't. Your mama knew it. Deke, too. He'd say to me, 'Why don't you take the boy fishin?' or 'Why not take J. P. with you when you go to town?' But I never did, and when all this happened, I was thinkin it was too late. That you'd go to prison and I wouldn't never have the chance to take you fishin or nothin."

J. P. smiled. He wanted his daddy to feel better, to go home with good thoughts. "After this is over, if I get off like Mister Powers says, then we'll have lots of time. I don't think I'll be getting my job back."

Luther grinned. "No, I spect you had enough of the car business." He placed his hat on his head, held out his hand. "Well, I gotta get on home."

J. P.'s hand went out, but when he saw the soft dark eyes beckoning him, he dropped his hand, and, leaning forward, he kissed his father's cheek for the first time.

NOW SITTING AT the defense table, J. P. looked back at Luther and his mother. Tee Wee's lips were moving in a silent prayer. When she opened her eyes, she leaned forward and whispered, "Did you eat anything?"

"Eggs and grits," he lied.

The agony of the morning seemed endless as J. P. sat mutely while a parade of men testified for the DA. Gatlin looked fresher this morning, as if the damaging witnesses he produced gave him renewed energy to bounce up and down on the balls of his feet as he led them through their testimony. Sheriff Davis repeated all the conversations he had had with J. P. in the hospital, and he read the statement J. P. made that clearly proved he was the driver of the car he had stolen. When Powers' turn came to cross-examine, he reminded Davis that J. P. had told him that he had misinterpreted his words. The sheriff laughed and said, "Yeah, the boy tried to backpedal that bike, but the race was over long before he tried."

"You said that when you arrived at the accident site, you deduced J. P. was driving because he was lying on the pavement beside the driver's side of the car."

Davis raised his eyebrows as if he were surprised this big-city lawyer didn't see that for himself. "Yep. He was lying facedown on the driver's side. The other boy was flung over in front of what was left of that poor teenage girl's car."

Powers, who was wearing an elegant tan linen suit today, tapped his teeth with his pen. "So just because that's where they ended up, that's how you determined where they began, and you never thought about the possibility that John Paul might have been thrown there or may have landed somewhere else and maybe crawled over there?"

Sheriff Davis shook his head. "Hell, no. The boy's arm was broke, head busted up, lots of deep cuts. He wasn't able to go nowhere."

Powers smiled as if this was exactly what he had wanted him to say. "Thank you," he said. "That's all."

Ray's stepdaddy, Pepper Simmons, took the stand after the sheriff. He was the only black to testify so far, and because of this, his presence on the witness stand seemed to carry more weight than his predecessors.

He sat stiffly on the small wooden chair in the jury box, keeping his eyes fixed on Gatlin's face as if he were reading the answers to the questions from the DA's sagging chin. Pepper was wearing a bright red shirt J. P. recognized as belonging to Ray. He had never liked Pepper, but his antipathy grew to hatred as he sat listening to him lie. He couldn't understand how Pepper could say that J. P. Weathersby was a wild boy addicted to hooch, whores, and knife fights. He said that it was J. P. who stole money and liquor and cigarettes from him, and it was the defendant, not Ray, who gambled on the cockfights behind Moses Jones' tenant house and then knifed Moses when he lost. When Pepper said this, Tee Wee stood up and yelled, "You shut your mouth. It was Ray who stuck Moses, and you know it."

After Judge Ramsey told Tee Wee to sit down and be quiet, Pepper looked right at J. P. and said, "No, it was him, and if Moses hadn't fell off the train and killed hisself, he would tell you him and Ray was good friends."

J. P. tried to unclench his fists and looked with wonder at his hands, which seemed not a part of him. He was nearly glad to be released from his earlier fear by this anger, and he pressed the soles of his shoes into the floor to keep himself from attacking Pepper as he swaggered down the aisle toward the back of the room. Tyler frowned at him, a warning. Then remembering Crow's advice about not showing how you feel, he took a breath and relaxed his body as best he could.

During lunch as J. P. picked at the chicken pie Tee Wee had sent to the jail, he listened to Crow's and Powers' reassurances that in the afternoon the tide would turn. But J. P. worried that no one would believe him or the witnesses who would testify on his behalf. He felt like a tree with a ribbon around it that was supposed to be saved from being cut down. Would the jury see the ribbon? Didn't it happen sometimes that a tree intended for salvation was mistakenly chopped from its roots by a logger's ax? Or was it the other way round? Maybe the ribbon he felt around his neck meant he was destined for destruction.

As Crow hugged him, saying that he would be freed very soon, her voice held no conviction. Her puffy eyes told J. P. that she was hurting almost as much as he.

"Tomorrow then. I guess I can stand one more night in this lovely hotel."

Crow smiled. "Now you're talking like you ought to be walking. Keep that thought, lil brother. Tomorrow might mean freedom."

"Freedom." He repeated the word like a mantra in his head. He remembered the first day Tyler Powers had sat on the cot in this cell. He told J. P. that he had read the published letter Bob Moses had written from the Pike County jail in '61 when he and twelve other Negroes served thirty-nine days for organizing the black voters in McComb. Powers had swept his long arms around the cell. "This is history. Those men sang freedom songs in a cell just like this. They sang 'Alleluia. Michael row the boat ashore. Alleluia.' " J. P. gripped Powers' forearm. "Alleluia. I'm going ashore," he said.

An hour later J. P.'s spirits plummeted again when Judy Willow's mother took the stand, her twisted handkerchief held to her eyes. Her testimony was irrelevant, Powers said, nothing more than a bid for sympathy. But Judge Ramsey allowed it when Gatlin said that she would testify to her daughter's excellent driving record. After fifteen minutes of sobbing and broken sentences, Judy's flawless driving record and excellent skills at the wheel were established. J. P. laid his head on the table; his freedom song had left his heart. Powers nudged him, and he lifted his head. Rising at the table, far away from Mrs. Willow, Powers told her how sorry he was for her loss. He paused and then asked, "How long had Judy been driving, Missus Willow?"

"Two months. Her fifteenth birthday was May fourth. She got her license that day," she said. "The little blue Mustang was her present."

When Larry Martino was called to the stand, J. P. turned to watch him strut past the defense table. He had forgotten how handsome Mr. Martino was. Today he was dressed in an olive leisure suit. When he lifted his hand to take the oath, he struck a pose like a male model, and with his dark wavy hair, his straight white teeth, his square jaw with the Kirk Douglas dimple in its center, J. P. thought he could have been one. As he took his seat in the witness box the females on the jury fussed with their hair and crossed their legs.

Larry Martino sat with his legs wide apart, hands dangling in front of his manhood. He looked successful, relaxed, and very sure of himself as he answered the DA's questions. When he repeated the metaphor about women's makeup and prettying up the cars, he winked at the raven-haired woman on the front row in the jury box.

Gatlin snapped his suspenders, smiling and nodding as though Mr. Larry was a stand-up comic he had hired for levity in the dour proceedings until, suddenly, he frowned. "Did you give your permission to the defendant to drive that Corvette off your property?"

Martino's face mirrored the DA's. "Absolutely not. In fact, I told him if a customer wanted to take a test drive, that they would have to come back Monday."

"So when you heard your car was wrecked, what did you think?"

Mr. Larry tilted his head and looked over at J. P. "I thought I had made a big mistake trusting that nigger."

When Judge Ramsey asked Tyler Powers if he would like to cross-examine the witness, Powers shook his head no, but he asked to reserve the right to have him recalled. The judge agreed that he could delay the cross if he so wished. He looked out into the room at the handkerchiefs and papers flapping the hot air around the perspiring faces of the crowd and banged his gavel. "Let's all go home and cool off," he said.

Disengaging the handcuffs dangling from his belt, the bailiff walked across the courtroom to the defense table. Before he held out his wrists, J. P. lifted his hands to wipe his face, pretending that the moisture on his cheeks was nothing more than sweat.

Chapter 54

STANDING ON THE COURTHOUSE STEPS DIGGING IN HER PURSE for an aspirin, Ruthie blinked her tired eyes against the bright July sun. She hadn't slept more than a couple of hours and had woken with a pounding head. She was going to be the first witness to testify on J. P.'s behalf, and she was afraid she was going to collapse before she took the stand. Although the temperature had risen to 102 degrees, Ruthie shivered. The enormity of what she was about to do had nearly stopped her blood from running through her veins.

She had made this decision three days ago after Tyler Powers came to her house and asked for her help. "A white character witness is paramount to our case. You've known J. P. all his life; you can attest to this boy's sterling qualities. We need you, Missus Wardlaw. Will you help me save J. P.?"

Ruthie told him that she wanted to help. "I know J. P. wouldn't steal a car or lie," she had said, "but I'm afraid I just can't do this. Dennis, my husband, he and Mister Willow are negotiating a real estate deal. Dennis thought you might ask me, and he said I'd have to refuse. There's too much at stake." She wiped her perspiring hands on her shorts. "You see, Dennis, he's in debt, we could lose the house, everything. If I testified, Mister Willow would back out of the deal he's made for this shopping center Dennis has invested in. We'd have to file for bankruptcy. My husband would never forgive me."

She hadn't told him that she was terrified of making Dennis angry, that her marriage was as fragile as a china vase that she must handle carefully to guard against shattering it into jagged pieces that she knew would never fit together again.

But here she was on the courthouse steps; the vase was toppling and she would let it fall when she took the stand. From across the street she saw Icey and Tee Wee getting out of Luther's truck. It was Tee Wee's love that had brought her here. On the afternoon of the day Tyler Powers had visited her, Tee Wee had knocked on her door, her face drawn with fear and worry. After she sat down on the couch beside Ruthie, she cupped her face in her hand. Looking straight into her eyes, she said, "J. P.'s lawyer called me, told me he was here today and what you said to him."

Ruthie's eyes filled with tears of shame. "Tee Wee, I wish, I wanted, it's just Dennis . . . he . . ."

Tee Wee dropped her hand onto her big black purse in her lap. Her fingers worked the latch, opening and shutting it over and over as she talked. "Shush shush, it's awright, honey. I know you scared of Mister Dennis. You ain't said nothin to me, but I seen with my eyes how it is for you." Her voice wavered. "But, my baby, J. P., Ruthie, he's in bad bad trouble. They all after him; that Mister Willow would lynch him if he could get to him."

Ruthie laid her hand on Tee Wee's. "I know. I feel terrible, letting you and J. P. down. If only things were different. If Dennis wouldn't . . ."

"Wouldn't what?"

Ruthie covered her face with her hands. "Oh Tee, I didn't want you to know. He's crazy when he gets drunk. I'm scared of what he'll do to me if I testify. He's hurt me before. Lots of times. When he's not drinking, he's a good man, a good daddy, but when he drinks, he's like Jekyll and Hyde; when he gets drunk, my nice husband turns into a monster."

Tee Wee wrapped her big arms around her. "I know, baby. I've knowed how it is for you. Every time I tried to get you to talk to me, you buttoned that lip so tight I couldn't get you to say nothin. I love you like one of my own, Ruthie, raised you up from diapers to when you married him. Why you ain't let me help you I can't understand."

Ruthie rubbed her cheek against the soft cloth of Tee Wee's dress. Here was comfort and love and the mother she had lost. "Help me now," she whispered.

Looking around, Ruthie saw that a crowd had assembled beside the walk in front of the courthouse. She didn't have any aspirin, and, snapping her purse shut, she waited for Tee Wee to make her way through the black community of well-wishers to join her on the steps.

Tee Wee had helped her. She had laid out the plan that Ruthie had followed. In secret she had packed hers and Annie Ruth's suitcases and hidden them beneath their beds, and this morning after Dennis left for the office, she had loaded them into her car and drove at breakneck speed out to Parsons Place. She would ask Browder to let her and Annie Ruth stay with them for a while, but for now Annie Ruth was safe at Icey's house. She wouldn't allow herself to think what would happen when Dennis found out they were gone. Dennis had been right about one thing. She did love Tee Wee's family more than she loved him, and she was going to do all in her power to show them her love today. God would have to forgive her. Tee Wee had promised her that He didn't want her to suffer. When Ruthie said that God expected Christians to turn the other cheek, to forgive those that persecute them, Tee Wee rolled her eyes. "The Lord might want you to forgive Mister Dennis in your heart, but He don't expect you to fry him an egg every morning," she said.

As Tee Wee broke away from the crowd and came toward her, Ruthie summoned her courage and smiled, and, arm in arm, they entered the courtroom.

The bailiff appeared and said that the trial would be delayed until after lunch because the judge was unavoidably detained elsewhere. Ruthie's anxiety grew with every hour they waited until the judge finally appeared and banged his gavel for court to resume.

Immediately Lowell Gatlin walked to the center of the room and, sweeping his arms out from his side as if he were going to bow, said that he rested his case. Returning to his chair, he hooked his thumbs in his suspenders and leaned backward as if to say he had already won and could relax now.

When Ruthie's name was called, her knees weakened as she waded through invisible water to the witness stand. She lifted her hand to her head to steady it on her neck. "Oh God," she prayed silently, "let me do this for Tee Wee. Give me the strength to do what's right." She lifted her eyes to where J. P. sat, his chin resting on his hands, his brown eyes fixed on her face. Behind him Tee Wee in her green turban nodded encouragement. "I'm okay; I'm ready," Ruthie said to Tyler.

She told the jury that she had known J. P. Weathersby since the day he was born on Parsons Place. She said that he was the finest young man she had ever known, black or white. The faces of the jurors registered their astonishment when she told them she had attended his graduation party, that he was an honor student, that he had been accepted for admission at the University of Mississippi.

Tyler looked as impressed as the jurors. He leaned against the rail in front of her. "And would you characterize John Paul as an honest young man? Do you trust him?"

"Yes, I trust him and I have never known him to lie. Ever. Not ever."

When Lowell Gatlin stood up and slowly sauntered toward her, Ruthie's heart pounded so fast and hard, she thought that surely the jurors could hear it beating. She blinked her scratchy eyes and took a deep breath.

The DA's eyes swept over her from her French twist to her black patent shoes. "Mizzz Wardlaw," he drawled. "Are you married to Dennis Wardlaw, the Realtor?"

"Yes."

"How long?"

"Ten years."

"You sell any houses for him?"

"No. I said I'm a homemaker."

Gatlin's face lit up like she had said something wonderful. "That's right. You did say you was a homemaker. And you said you are a member of the women's circle at Pisgah Church, too. But you didn't tell us that you also spend a lot of time at the hospital."

Ruthie wondered what any of this had to do with J. P., and she looked over at Tyler, but his head was bent to his legal pad. "Yes, I'm a Pink Lady, a volunteer."

"You help out with the nigras, too? Bring them water? Change their beds? That kind of thing?"

"Yes, if I'm needed."

Lowell Gatlin backed away from her as if she had suddenly begun to emit noxious fumes. "So you get chummy with the nigras down there, listen to their sad tales, how they get cheated out of their civil rights, all that, and like this Washington, DC, government lawyer sitting over there, you want to help them out, don't you?"

Ruthie opened her mouth. He had all but said the words she had heard used so many times. *Nigger lover.* She remembered that James Whitney of the *Lexie Journal* had been branded with these words after he had written an editorial entreating the citizens to integrate peacefully.

He had burned his hands trying to tear down the flaming cross in his front yard. "I . . . I'm not involved in politics. That isn't why I'm here."

Lowell Gatlin smiled. "Of course it is. But we'll let that sleeping dog lie." He turned full circle. "Speaking of lie, you said never, not ever has that boy lied. Correct?"

Ruthie found her voice again. She was angry and her head was about to explode. "No. Yes. Correct. J. P. does not lie."

"You have a little girl, don't you, Mizzzz Wardlaw? She ever tell a little fib?"

A knot formed in Ruthie's stomach. She recognized the trap she was about to step into. "Probably. Most small children do."

"Right. So you're not really telling the truth when you said the defendant has never told a lie. Never not ever. He's just as capable of fabricating a story as your own daughter, isn't he?"

Ruthie wanted to go home now. She wasn't smart enough to be here. Tee Wee should have chosen someone better to do this. She had allowed this fat bully to trick her. "I suppose so," she said in a near whisper.

"And if he's as smart as you say he is, and I *do* believe that . . . you said honor student . . . then he can probably lie even better than your little white daughter."

Powers stood up at the defendant's table. "Judge, I object."

Gatlin waved his hand. "Okay, that's all."

Ruthie barely remembered taking a seat beside Masie after she was told to step down from the witness box. She only remembered her humiliation, her heart sinking with the knowledge that she had let Tee Wee down. She had risked so much, and Dennis was right. She had lost everything and gained nothing.

The next witness Powers called was Dr. Matthews. He had aged greatly and prematurely since he had signed the death certificates for Ruthie's mother and father. He was only forty-three, but his stooped back and gray hair testified that tending to the sick and dying had taken their toll. Powers asked the doctor to detail the injuries J. P. had sustained in the accident. He confirmed the broken arm, head injury, and cuts that Sheriff Davis had referred to.

"Now, given those injuries, could a person crawl or walk twenty or thirty feet?"

"Well, it would depend on circumstance."

"Which means?"

"If a person is in shock, the brain doesn't register pain as it does normally. There are many cases of people who have performed miraculous acts when in shock or in situations where their adrenaline takes over their normal reason."

"You mean like when a hundred-fifty-pound man lifts a car off his son? Things like that, which we read about in the newspaper?"

"Yes, and in cases of head injury, extreme trauma to the brain, well, it just doesn't register information normally."

"So in your opinion, John Paul could have been thrown out of the car on the right side—from the passenger's seat—and then in shock, with his brain not recognizing his pain, crawled around the car to the spot where he lost consciousness."

"That's a definite possibility. Happens quite frequently."

Ruthie sighed with relief after Gatlin's cross-examination. He wasn't able to make a fool out of Dr. Matthews as he had her. The doctor admitted he had no way of knowing if J. P. had crawled around the car, but he was adamant that the possibility existed.

The next two witnesses, like Ruthie, were slated to testify to J. P.'s good character. The first was Zelma Whittaker, a black woman who had been his history teacher at Burglund High School. Miss Zelma had suffered a stroke and the left side of her face drooped down, giving her a lopsided appearance. Tilting her head slightly in order to see better from her disfigured eye, she told the jurors and spectators that J. P. was the best student she had ever had in her classroom. Smiling and nodding, she agreed with Ruthie's testimony that J. P. was a fine young man with a bright future. When Lowell Gatlin strolled over to the witness box, her smiles vanished. Gatlin engaged her in a long debate as to whether or not the criminal mind was smarter than most. When Miss Zelma said she didn't know, the DA asked her if it wasn't more likely that J. P. could plan a robbery down at the Merchants Bank better than most of her students with less intelligence. Tyler Powers was a jack-in-the-box, popping up and down, objecting, arguing speculation, not qualified to have an opinion, but Judge Ramsey seemed to be enjoying the repartee and shook his protests off like the flies that flitted across his face all day.

Preacher Dixon, Powers' next witness, told the court that J. P. was a member of Mount Zion, "a boy filled with the Holy Spirit." During Gatlin's cross-examination he pointed out that both Dixon and Whittaker were Negroes who would naturally feel sorry for one of their own and try to help him out. Ruthie wondered if Powers knew that Mount Zion Church had been one of the places where mass meetings of blacks and Freedom School classes were held just a few years before. Lowell Gatlin knew that fact, and he forced Dixon to admit that he had been one of the first Negroes to register to vote. After twenty minutes of cross, Dixon left the stand branded as a zealot who hated white people. Naturally, he would testify for a black boy who killed a little white girl who probably didn't even know what a Freedom School was.

Ruthie and Masie held hands as they watched the old preacher wobble down the aisle toward them with a dazed expression on his face. He had baptized nearly half of the people in the room, and all of them had witnessed his pathetic stammering denials that he was a dangerous, bigoted man. After he passed the first row of benches, people began to rise. Row by row on the left side of the courtroom, black people stood and nodded their heads in support as he walked by. When he reached Ruthie's row, she stood with Masie and saw the tears that trickled down his cheeks as he slowly made his way to the door.

After Preacher Dixon left the room, Tyler Powers metamorphosed into a completely different person. It was as if an electrical current had passed through his body energizing and transforming him into a madman. He threw off his jacket and pushed his chair back with such force that it crashed on its side. His soft voice was a memory now as he bellowed out the name of his next witness. *"Calvin Masterson!"* When the judge held up his hand, saying it was getting late, Powers beat the record for the time it took to cover the distance to the judge's bench. "One more witness, Judge. It's only three-thirty."

Judge Ramsey laughed. "You getting overtime pay?" Powers' neck reddened with anger. "No? Well, let's all get on home then. Some folks here got animals to feed, cows to milk, good dinners waiting on them." He banged his gavel. "Adjourned until tomorrow. Nine A.M."

Chapter 55

ON FRIDAY MORNING A LINE OF THUNDERSTORMS FROM THE southwest was headed toward Lexie County, and the precursor strong winds scattered the fallen magnolia blossoms across the courthouse lawn. They lay like white doilies on green carpet, but their beauty went unnoticed by Tee Wee as she walked toward the deserted courthouse. In the courtroom the overhead light globes had not yet been illuminated, but they would be needed on this dark morning. Tee Wee, her mood matching her surroundings, sat in the gloom alone. She bowed her head. "Dear Sweet Jesus, save my boy today. You made his skin black, You sent his people to this white world, and You took his brother and his friends. My soul is tired with trouble. Help us now. We ain't got nobody else to turn to." She cried into her cupped hands. "Please save my boy."

Luther's hand pressed on her shoulder, and she looked up into his sad face. He kissed her wet cheek. "You got to get hold of yourself, Tee. Don't want J. P. seein you down in the miseries."

"I ain't. I be fine. You seen any of the young'ns out on the street?"

"No, but they'll be here. All of em be comin soon."

Luther was right. Within the hour Tee Wee's family had gathered to fill three benches behind her. She looked over her shoulder and saw the beautiful faces of her sons, daughters, and grandchildren, and her eyes filled again. Tee Wee traveled back to the Martin Place where her first three children were born. She remembered stealing food from the kitchen to feed their little mouths, always open like baby birds. She saw her wild Crow crawling across the floor snatching everything within her reach. She felt again her terror when Curtis had died and left her with children to feed. Then came the miracle God had performed when he sent Luther to her. Eighteen years had passed since J. P.'s birth, and she remembered the exquisite happiness she had felt when she first saw his little round head nestled on her breast. Now she stared at his empty chair and for the first time noticed that there were letters carved into the worn seat. She leaned forward trying to make them out. She whispered the word aloud: "Mercy." This was a good omen. It had to be.

When Tyler Powers stopped beside her bench, Tee Wee's jaw dropped in surprise. Each day he had strode past her with a frown, acknowledging no one. But now he smiled and clasped her hand. "Good morning, Missus Weathersby. Mister Weathersby."

"Mornin," Tee Wee said, taking in his flowered shirt beneath his white jacket. He looked like he was about to board a cruise ship headed for a vacation island. As he leaned across to shake hands with Luther, she saw that there were, in fact, little dolphins diving all along the fabric of the blue waters on his tie. She watched as he nodded to Gatlin, to the court stenographer, to the bailiff who stood beside the door waiting for J. P. and the jailer. His smile spread wider when the jury and J. P. and, lastly, Judge Ramsey took their seats. Here her son was on trial, about to go to prison, and this Washington, DC, lawyer was acting like he was at a barbecue. When he called Calvin Masterson to the stand, he drew out the name like an emcee introducing a big celebrity.

Cal Masterson owned the Firestone store on Front Street and Masterson's Garage, which abutted the back of the store. He was Zebulon's best mechanic, and everyone knew he was fair with his prices and an expert at diagnosing engine problems. Nearly every juror had at one time or another brought their cars to him because he never tried to sell you an expensive part when all you needed was a fan belt or an oil filter.

Powers was still grinning like a Cheshire cat when he asked Cal if the sheriff's department had hired him to tow the Corvette and Mustang to his lot for impounding. Cal, whose wrinkled hands bore the embedded grease stains of twenty-eight years, held up two grimy fingers. "Yep, I hauled two cars from Highway Fifty-One to Four Eighty-Three Ninth Street."

"And since that time, have those cars been moved or tampered with in any way?"

Cal laughed. "Not likely. I got four junkyard dogs that don't like company, and everybody in town knows about the time when Dello Moak tried to steal some sheepskin seat covers out of a Chevy that my dogs was enjoying lying on. They tore a good two pounds of blubber off his rear end when he tried to climb the fence." Cal looked over at the jury. "He wasn't hurt bad, though, and if you know Dello, you know he had a fat ass and could stand to lose some of it."

Tyler Powers laughed with the jury, enjoying himself. Still smiling, he said, "So you are certain that the Corvette is in exactly the same condition now as it was immediately after the accident?"

"One hundred percent."

Powers showed Masterson a photograph of the car and verified that it was the one Ray and J. P. were riding in. Cal pointed to the chassis. "See, them Corvettes is made out of fiberglass and they kind of shred on impact. But the engine is hardly damaged."

With a pencil point Powers pointed to the driver's seat. "Is this exactly where the seat was positioned when you picked up the car?" Cal Masterson nodded. "And so this would be *exactly* where the driver was sitting before the car struck the Mustang?" When Cal agreed to that, Powers asked how he could be sure.

Cal rubbed behind his ear with his stained forefinger. "Well, there's notches on the runner beneath the seat. Locks the seat in, so's you don't go moving while you're driving. Corvette notches are curved and deep." He pointed to the photograph. "See?"

Tyler Powers nodded and passed the photograph over to Edward Starks, the jury foreman, who examined it and then handed it over to for the other jurors to inspect. "Did I ask you about the distance from the seat to the accelerator?"

The mechanic lifted his eyebrows. "Don't you remember?"

Powers smiled. "Yes, but would you tell the court about that?"

Cal explained that the seat was in the last notch, which would be used by a tall person who needed more legroom. "So a small person with short legs wouldn't be able to reach the pedals with the seat positioned way back like that, huh?"

"No way. Them sports cars sits down low and the seats slant back. I know a couple of women can't drive them even with the seat up all the way forward."

When Gatlin rose to cross-examine, Cal gave him a little wave of recognition, then quickly lowered his hands to his lap. When the DA tried to get him to admit that it was possible he could be wrong about where the seat was during the accident, that maybe it had moved on impact, Cal got angry. "If you think I don't know my business, why do you bring in that Mercury of yours every time you hear a little noise in the engine?" Before Gatlin could stop him, he went on to say that he knew more about the law than Gatlin knew about cars, and what he knew about law wouldn't fill up a fruit jar.

Judge Ramsey waited until Gatlin's back was turned and then smiled at Cal. "You can step down now and get on back to your work, Cal. Next witness, Mister Powers?"

"I recall Mister Larry Martino to the stand."

Larry Martino looked less pleased with himself than he had two days before. He was visibly nervous, jiggling the foot of his crossed leg while he waited for the first question. Tyler Powers was taking his time. His earlier jovial spirits had vanished. He flipped through pages of notes jotted on a legal pad before he lifted his head. "Mister Martino, you stated in your previous testimony that you, and I quote, had made 'a big mistake trusting that nigger.' "

Martino stared at the papers. "Something like that."

"If you have doubts, we can ask the court stenographer to read your testimony."

He shook his head. "No, I guess that's right."

"But you hired John Paul Weathersby, gave him the keys to your office, allowed him to drive expensive cars around on the lot, didn't you?" Without waiting for a reply, Powers went on. "So you must have trusted the boy. You're a successful businessman with a lot of experience, and you hired this young man over all other applicants."

Gatlin rose. "Is he gonna ask a question, Judge?"

Powers raised his pad. "Sorry. Did you have other applicants for the job?"

"Sure."

"How many?"

"Six or seven."

"All Negroes?"

"No, some white."

"Mostly white?"

"Yeah."

"But you hired this J. P., a black boy, over all the others. Why is that?"

Larry Martino shrugged. "I can't say. I guess I was feeling sorry for him; I didn't know he was going to turn out to be a thief."

Powers turned to the jury. "So J. P. didn't get the job because he was a hard worker, or because you thought you could trust him?"

"No, I didn't know him."

"And yet you gave him the keys to the office, the cars, and the outside gate?"

"Well, I needed to take my wife on that trip, and I didn't have much choice. I guess I'm just too trusting of people." He looked at the jury. "I'm too nice is all."

"How many times have you testified in this courtroom?" Powers asked.

Martino dropped his hands. He was disconcerted. "How many?" Powers stood in front of him, staring at him like he was the star of a horror movie. "Four, no five times?"

Powers shook his head. "Eight."

"Maybe." He ran his hands through his hair. "Yeah, I guess eight."

"You were the plaintiff in those cases, were you not?"

Martino covered his mouth with his right hand. His answer was muffled, but audible. "I've had some trouble with faulty loans, repos, the usual for a car business."

"And in those eight cases, how many of the defendants were Negroes?"

Larry Martino raised his eyes to the ceiling. "Let me think a minute."

"All of them, Mister Martino. Isn't that right?"

"Well, now that you say that, I guess so. Funny coincidence."

Powers smiled. "Oh I don't think it's funny or a coincidence. It's proof that you don't like blacks very much. It says to me that you're a racist, Mister Martino."

Gatlin jumped up from his chair, red-faced, sweating. "Objection!"

"Withdrawn," Powers said softly. "I apologize to the court, and I have no further questions."

As Judge Ramsey rapped his scarred gavel three times for lunch, duplicate claps of thunder shook the light globes overhead. Before Tee Wee could thread her way through the crowd to the porch, it had begun to rain. She walked to the edge of the porch and thrust her arms out into cool shower. She felt she was bathing her flesh in healing water. Jesus was listening to her prayers. "Mama, what are you doing?" Shaking the droplets from her arms, she turned to Crow. "You're getting wet. I brought an umbrella."

"I don't need one. I'm not goin off this porch."

Crow pulled on her arm. "Don't be silly. You got to eat."

She jerked her arm back. "No. I ain't. I'm stayin put. Bad luck to change anythin. Goin off this porch will put a hex on J. P. Things is goin good right now; don't make no changes." Then Tee Wee saw Crow's dull eyes, her ashy skin. "You sick?"

"A little."

"You go eat. I got sacks in the truck. Maybe y'all could find somewhere dry." As she watched Crow duck beneath her umbrella and run down the sidewalk, Tee Wee thought that something was wrong about her, but she didn't have energy left to worry about Crow right now. Every bit of her was focused on her son, and she believed that she had to continue washing in this purifying water. She thanked Jesus over and over for giving Tyler Powers a smart brain, for sending him down to them, for the man who invented the Corvette car seats, for not sending a fire to burn up the court records that proved Mr. Martino was a racist.

She was still praying when Luther took her purse and elbow and steered her back into the courtroom to her seat. When the "hear ye's" were over and Judge Ramsey was settled, Tyler Powers stood up to call his last witness. "John Paul Weathersby," he said in the sweetest voice Tee Wee had ever heard.

Twisting her handkerchief into a small rope, she watched her baby place his hand on the Bible, say his name, sit down in the chair where some had lied and some had told the truth. He was a handsome boy; everyone could surely see that, and they would all know, looking into his clear round eyes, that he was innocent.

As Powers led J. P. through his history, Tee Wee's breast swelled with pride as she listened to her son recite all of his accomplishments. Tyler asked J. P. about the conversations and statements he had given to the sheriff, and he told the court that the sheriff had misinterpreted his words. He hadn't made those things up later like Sheriff Davis had said. When Powers asked about his friendship with Ray, J. P.'s voice trembled with emotion. "Ray had a good heart; he was a good friend to me. I loved him like one of my stepbrothers," he said.

"But you and Ray were very different, weren't you?"

"Yes. Ray dropped out of school; I wanted to go to college."

"And Ray often got drunk, picked fights, took money from his father, didn't he?"

Tee Wee held her breath. She knew J. P. had protested when Mr. Powers had told him that he wanted the jury to see that Ray was a petty criminal. Was he going to save himself? J. P. didn't answer right away, but finally he nodded. "Ray was all right. He got into trouble, but he wasn't mean. He just liked to have fun, and sometimes that meant drinking too much, and then he'd go kind of crazy and do things he shouldn't."

"Did you try to stop him from driving the Corvette on the day of the accident?"

J. P. pulled his collar away from his thin neck. "Yes sir. I was on the phone with a customer and saw Ray pulling out into the street. I shouldn't have let him have the keys, but he said he was just going to listen to the horses. The engine."

"So when you saw him about to leave, what did you do?"

J. P. was talking faster now, and Tee Wee felt his panic. "I ran out there. I grabbed the door handle. I guess I was trying to stop the car. I told him to get out, but he wouldn't listen. He said he was just going around the block. I couldn't make him do what I wanted, so I thought it was best to go with him to keep him from hurting the car."

Tyler Powers held up his hand to pause the story. "So the reason you got in was to make sure he drove safely and returned the car in good condition?"

"Yes, I had just detailed it, and I hated to see him drive it off the lot to get dirty."

"But the accident occurred on Highway Fifty-One. How did that happen?"

J. P. frowned. "Ray, he said you couldn't appreciate the car unless you went fast, and he was headed out to the highway so he could feel its power." J. P. rubbed his eyes. "Well, I can't remember his exact words, but somehow we were out on Fifty-One, going fast, and I was looking out the window. I remember Ray saying we needed sunglasses to be cool, you know? And then I saw the blue. The red stoplight. The car pulling out. She didn't see us. I yelled, 'Watch out!' or something like that. I was stomping my feet on the floorboard trying to stop the car, and then next thing—" He swallowed twice. "—next thing." He shook his head. "I don't know what happened after that. I woke up in the hospital."

Tyler patted his hand, which was wrapped as tightly as a vise around the rail of the witness box. "Okay, one more thing, and then we'll be done. How tall are you, J. P.?"

"Five feet, six inches."

"Would you stand up beside me to show the jury the truth of that statement?"

Tee Wee watched as J. P. walked to where Powers stood in front of the jury box. His head didn't reach his lawyer's shoulder. "I'm six feet, two inches, tall. Was Ray about my height?" He motioned J. P. back to the witness box.

After he was seated, J. P. said, "Taller. Ray was six four. He used to tease me about being so undersized because he was shorter than me until he turned fourteen and then he just shot up like a beanpole."

"With the seat pushed back to the last notched position, could you reach the accelerator of the Corvette?"

"No sir, when I parked it on the lot, I had the seat as far up as it would go. Ray had to move it back before he could even get in."

Tee Wee was sure she heard a sigh from someone in the jury box, and she wished she knew if that was a good sign or a bad one. When Gatlin rose to cross-examine, Tee Wee ducked her head and quickly whispered, "Don't let Satan hurt my boy."

Lowell Gatlin hadn't had a good day. He had forgotten his umbrella and his suit coat was still damp from his five-minute walk to his car during lunch. He lumbered over to the witness stand. "Hmmm. You called a lot of people liars in your testimony just now. I reckon you expecting us to believe you over them. That right?"

J. P.'s eyes widened. He clutched the railing tighter. "No sir."

"Oh, you're not expecting to be believed. Is it because you're the liar?"

"No sir." Tee Wee shoved her black plastic purse into her stomach. She was fighting the urgent need to turn it into an anvil to crush that DA's head.

"Let's see. So far, you claim to know Ray better than his stepdaddy, Mister Simmons. Then you suggested that Sheriff Davis is too stupid to comprehend the meaning of your statements to him. And Larry Martino, a respected businessman in Zebulon for many years, doesn't know the difference between borrowing a car and stealing one. Is all that about accurate, college boy?"

Tee Wee grabbed Luther's arm and squeezed so hard, he winced aloud. "Don't let him blow his top, dear Sweet Lord," she prayed. She watched J. P.'s eyes looking past his tormentor. He was staring straight at Crow. "No sir. I don't think any of those things. I swore to tell the truth and nothing but, and that's what I did."

Tee Wee buried her head in her hands. "Thank you, Jesus." She jerked her eyes back to Gatlin, who was leaning on the railing of the jury box now.

"So you can't help that everyone isn't as smart as you? I reckon you got your doubts about me being smart enough to question you." He smiled at the jurors. He popped his suspenders, "Well, I'm going to go ahead and try to follow your brilliant deductions." He looked over at J. P. with an amused expression. "Say, what you planning on studying at the University of Mississippi anyhow?"

"The law."

"Ho ho." He slapped the railing. "The *law*! You want to be a lawyer like me?"

J. P.'s jaw tightened. "No, sir, I want to be a lawyer like him." He pointed to Powers, who looked like the cruise ship he was going on had sunk.

"Yeah, I reckon you would be more in-ter-res-ted"—he dragged the word out in a slow drawl—"in learning about how to strike down the rulings of our fine judges like Judge Ramsey here to get your so-called civil rights you got hurt feelings about all these years."

"I don't know any of his rulings," J. P. said. "But I do plan to fight for my rights."

"Whoo-whee," Gatlin blew air into his silver hair. "We got us a genuine firebrand here. A real crusader, a follower of the Black Panthers maybe."

Powers was on his feet. "Objection. Your Honor, Mister Gatlin is far afield from the issues he should be addressing in this trial."

Judge Ramsey seemed unable to rule, and, in the silence that followed, Gatlin struck like a copperhead. "Sidebar, Judge?"

He was awarded the conference, and while the spectators watched the three bowed heads, Tee Wee shifted her legs back and forth between Luther and Icey, who had come in late and squeezed in beside her. She hadn't done anything wrong, hadn't left the porch, hadn't eaten lunch, had prayed every chance she had. What else was God expecting from her for one favor? Icey leaned over. "It's going good, Tee. Lots better than yesterday." Suddenly, Icey's very presence was irritating her like a mosquito in the bedroom in the middle of the night. She wanted to squash her between her big hands. No, she would rather grab that silly red wig off her head and stomp on it. She would tell her that she looked like a whore in it. Oblivious to her feelings, Icey smiled. "You got to think good thoughts. You been frownin, grindin your teeths." She flashed her gold one. "You upsettin the boy. Do like me and just smile and smile at him."

Tee Wee closed her eyes. Her heart felt like it was squeezed with iron tongs, and her lungs didn't seem to be pumping any air into her organs. "Make Icey shut up, God," she begged silently.

"Objection overruled," the judge said. "And," he looked up at the wall clock over the door that led to the back hall, "if you got more questions to ask, Lowell, I think we'll just let them sit until Monday morning."

Lowell Gatlin smiled. "Fine with me, Judge."

Powers shook his head. "It's Friday. That means my client spends the weekend in jail."

Judge Ramsey ignored him. He was going deep-sea fishing in Biloxi. He rose and rapped the gavel simultaneously. "Court adjourned till Monday, nine A.M."

Chapter 56

*T*HE NOON THUNDERSTORM TOOK THE SCENIC ROUTE UP TO Jackson and was replaced hours later with an even more powerful storm that knocked out the streetlights in East Zebulon. Ruthie had slept through both storms, waking only to the prick of a needle to return to the safe cocoon of unconsciousness. She dreamed of her mother who glided to the foot of her bed. "You mustn't worry anymore. Everything will turn out all right."

Ruthie tried to speak. "Mmmmm." She couldn't open her mouth. Pain shot through her head.

"Ruthie?" The voice wasn't Mama's. She opened her eyes.

"How are you feeling?"

Ruthie focused on the face that hovered inches away from her own. "Browww?" Ruthie looked past Browder and saw that she was in a hospital bed. An IV was in her arm, the clear bag hung on the metal pole to her right. She was the patient. Now images began to flash, and Ruthie struggled to think her way out of the drug fog she was lost in. Her house. J. P. Masie. The courthouse. Annie Ruth's white bunny.

"You're awake. Can I get you something?" She stared at her brother. He looked terrible: dark stubble, red puffy eyes. She closed her eyes again. Dennis, blue shirt, curly dark hairs on his hand. Smoke. The smell of whiskey and burning hair. When she tried to raise her hand to her head, Browder held it back. "No. Don't. Lie still." His head dropped to the bed. "Oh Ruthie, you're going to be okay. I'll find him. I swear I'll kill him when I do."

"Nnnnn," the best she could manage for no. Where was her mother?

When Ruthie awoke again, she was alone in the private room in the Zebulon Infirmary. The lights were on; nighttime. She must have slept through the day. The door opened and Dr. Matthews walked to her bed. She had just seen him, where? Yes, in court; he looked even more worn out and fragile now. "So you're awake. No, don't talk yet. Your throat is raw. Smoke inhalation, and your lip is blistered."

She asked questions with her eyes. Did he understand? Yes, he sat in the chair beside her bed and nodded. "Your husband brought you in last night. Said you had fallen from a stool onto your stove. And"—his eyes looped over her head as though she were wearing a crown—"your hair caught fire. Actually your hair spray ignited and flames spread. You've got some first- and a few second-degree burns on your face, neck, and left hand." He took her wrist and placed his finger on her pulse. "Just rest now."

After Dr. Matthews left, a wave of fear swept through her. Ruthie grabbed hold of the mattress and tried to sit up, but the sharp pains and nausea forced her back to her pillow. She cried then, making inhuman sounds in her ruined mouth. She wanted someone to share this dark night with. She wanted her mother, Tee Wee. Tee Wee. The name opened the locked door of her memory. She had a headache, her name was called to testify, and everything had gone wrong.

She struggled to remember. After court was adjourned, Ruthie had waited for Tee Wee beneath one of the magnolia trees. They had kissed and hugged, and Tee Wee told her that she did fine on the stand even though they both knew she hadn't been much help. She had driven out to Parsons Place, picked up Annie Ruth at Icey's, and then hidden her car behind Browder's house. Browder and Missy hadn't asked any questions in front of Annie Ruth when Ruthie had knocked on their door holding their overnight bags, and they'd eaten dinner acting as though their presence was a normal everyday occurrence. But after Ruthie had tucked Annie Ruth into Browder's old bed and turned on the small TV set on his dresser, Browder and Missy had followed her down the hall to her old room, which Missy had made into a sewing room now. With worried expressions mirrored on their faces, they waited for her explanation. "What's happened, Ruthie?" Missy asked.

"It's complicated. It's just, Dennis. He's going to be so angry. I can't go home. Not after I testified today. I'm so tired right now. Can you wait until morning? I'll explain everything then. Thanks for taking us in tonight."

And Browder had taken Missy's arm and turned her to the door. "Tomorrow then. We'll talk tomorrow. You're safe here. Everything will be all right. Go to sleep." But she hadn't slept, had she? No, she was brushing out the French twist she'd worn to court. Her hair was tangled; she'd used too much hair spray. Annie Ruth had come into her room. Her bunny. She'd forgotten Eric, her bunny. She was crying; she couldn't sleep without Eric.

The rest of the night came rushing back to her. She knew that Browder wouldn't allow her to leave; he wouldn't understand how important that bunny was to Annie Ruth. "I'll get him, baby," she said. "Go back to bed," and she had tiptoed out the front door, was back in her car, driving into town. She wouldn't stop if Dennis was home, couldn't risk it, but she had to try. Annie Ruth was so confused and upset. She'd asked a thousand questions the day before. Where were they going? Why couldn't she tell Daddy? Would they be back at home when school started? Was Daddy coming later? And Ruthie had no answers. "We'll see. It's all a secret right now," she had said. She couldn't tell her the truth. She was too young to understand.

As she turned onto her street, she glanced at the clock on the dashboard. Seven-fifteen. Dennis usually didn't get home until eight. She prayed he would still be at the office. As she neared her block, her leg began to shake so that she could hardly keep her foot on the accelerator. "Please God. Give me strength." When she saw the taillights of Dennis' station wagon backing out of the drive, she drew a deep breath. God was with her. Dennis must have read the note she'd left on the kitchen table. "Dennis, I know you will be angry when you hear about me testifying for J. P. Annie Ruth and I are going to Jackson to a motel. Don't try to find us. I'll call you tomorrow. Ruthie." Maybe he was going to Jackson to look for them, or more likely, maybe he was headed for the nearest bar. She held her breath until he turned down the street and sped off in the opposite direction. She was safe now. She'd grab the bunny and be out before he returned.

That's what she had planned. Her hand shook so badly she could barely get the key in the lock. Dennis hadn't left any lights on, and she hurried down the dark hall to Annie Ruth's room. Where was Eric? She threw back the covers on the bed, dropped to her knees to look underneath. Her eyes swept the dresser, the nighttable, the bookshelves. Where where where? Hurry hurry. She could hear the ragged staccato gasps of her breath. She had to get out of here fast. She longed to run for the safety of her car. She flung open the louvered closet doors, where a pile of stuffed animals lay in a heap. She tossed them out: a fuzzy dog, yellow chick, Raggedy Ann, white Christmas bear with a red ribbon. She sat back on her heels sobbing now. "Where's the damn bunny?" she cried. As she slowly turned her head around the room, she saw the ballet costume lying on the floor beneath the rocking chair. Annie Ruth had dressed Eric in the pink net tutu. Ruthie crawled across the floor and grinned as she scooped him up into her arms. "There you are," she said. Before she had risen, she heard his heavy footsteps hurrying down the hall. She sat frozen on the floor clutching the bunny to her chest. He called her name. "Ruthie! Where are you?" And then Dennis was there in the doorway, his face twisted into a grotesque mask. "Well, well, if it isn't my loyal wife, Missus Dennis Wardlaw. My partner in life, my faithful whore. I thought you were in Jackson shacked up in some motel with a nigger man."

"You're drunk," she whispered.

Dennis wiped his nose with the back of his hand. "And my wife is smart, too. You're absolutely, one hundred percent co-rect. I am shit-faced."

Slowly, she rose from the floor. "I'm leaving," she said, but his body filled the doorway, and reaching out, he caught her arm.

"Wanna know why I fell off the wagon? Wanna know what did the trick?" He squeezed her forearm so hard Ruthie's knees buckled. "You, my darling loyal, faithful wife. *You.*"

Ruthie had broken away then and run for the door, but she wasn't quick enough. Dennis grabbed her shoulders, and pushed her backward into the kitchen. He shoved her back hard against the sink. "Guess who called me today? Go on. Guess. I'll bet you know already."

Ruthie shook her head. "No, Dennis, please, let's don't talk now. You're drunk."

He pushed his body into her, pinning her against the counter. "Polly parrot. You already said that. I'll tell you who called. Willow, that's who. He wanted to tell me our deal is off. *Off.* And do you know why?" He hammered his hands on her shoulders. "Because you got up on the stand and defended the murderer of his little girl."

"Stop it. You're hurting me. I'm sorry, Dennis. I had to. I couldn't let Tee Wee down."

When he dropped his hands and turned away, Ruthie closed her eyes and breathed deeply. She waited until he reached the center of the room and then began inching away from the sink. She had to get to the door, but he was blocking her exit. She halted, waiting for a chance to dart past. Dennis wheeled around. "You couldn't let that nigger down, but you could let me down. You could betray me."

Ruthie's words came out in staccato beats. "I'm so sorry sorry sorry. I wish there had been some other way, but . . ."

He pounced then, like a lion on its prey. He grabbed her hair and twisted it into a rope to jerk her over to the stove. Her back arched, the knobs on the stove bore into her flesh. Reaching around her, Dennis' hand twisted the knob. She smelled gas and her screams ricocheted across the room. The burner dug into her cheek, smoke and flames surrounded her head, she smelled the stench of burning hair. Dennis was shouting over her screams. "You took my prize; you lose yours. Your hair for a shopping center." Then she was on the floor, rolling and flailing her arms, beating her head. Excruciating pain. Someone was crying. A towel around her. The smell of whiskey in the car. Dennis was crying, and suddenly there was white light over her. She shivered, had never been so cold. "Stop. Make them stop, no water." She remembered snatches of their words. "Hair spray. Saline. Nerve endings." Then a sweet voice, Mama coming into her room.

Ruthie slept until morning when a cheerful voice awakened her. "Here. Try this." Her lips parted and closed around a plastic straw. The cool liquid trickling down her throat was soothing, and she wanted to say thank you. "Honey, you look a mess." Ruthie looked up from the hand that held the straw and saw that it belonged to a nurse she knew, Cornell Roe. Her eyes were moist, and, putting her fingers to her lips in a kiss, she touched them to Ruthie's check. "Your accident messed you up good."

Ruthie remembered Dr. Matthews saying that Dennis had told him that she had fallen on the stove. Where was Dennis? Browder had said he was going to find him, kill him. She closed her eyes formulating a prayer in her mind. Dear God, dear God, what? She didn't know what to pray for. She couldn't think.

She opened her eyes. Cornell held out a pad and pen. "Don't talk. You want something, write it here, okay?"

Ruthie nodded, took the pad and pen and wrote "mirror" on it. Cornell squeezed her eyes closed. "Oh no, hon, you don't want to do that."

"Plezzzz."

She watched Cornell pull the food tray over, flip back the center panel where the mirror was attached. Slowly, she moved it toward her.

Ruthie was waiting for the woman she knew to appear in the mirror, and at first, she thought it was positioned wrong. Bandages around the neck, someone's blistered chin and mouth, an ear bubbling out, a bandage across the right cheek. She studied the face searching for herself, then lifted her eyes to the forehead of this pitiful person and saw that she was nearly bald. A few clumps of long brown hair lay on the pillow behind her head, but mostly there were patches of pink and red flesh, smears of yellow salve. A spot the size of a quarter on the right side of her head looked like a brown Brillo pad nearly used up. The eyes were perfect, though, the skin around them undamaged, and when Ruthie looked into them, the color of bluebells, of the asters that grew in her side yard, she recognized herself. "Guhhh," she said. "My God!"

Chapter 57

ON SUNDAY MORNING CROW ATTENDED THE SERVICES AT MOUNT Zion but refused the invitation to sing with the choir. Sitting directly behind Icey's mop of red curls, she couldn't see the pulpit from where the Reverend Dixon's voice thundered out to the sparse congregation. He sounded unusually energetic for an old man. Crow supposed his fiery zeal had been sparked by his humiliation at J. P.'s trial. She wished J. P. could hear this sermon, which was an amalgam of praise Jesus and damn racist lawyers. Tee Wee's amens were reserved for the damning, and Crow noticed that Icey scrambled up to shout amen when Dixon denounced the sinners who were home sleeping in cool rooms instead of sweating with them in the hot church house. Deke was one of them most likely.

Crow's thoughts wandered around the room like the slow flies that circled overhead and executed landings on hats and songbooks. Tomorrow J. P. would take the stand again. Never before had Crow wanted more to believe that Jesus did care about them, that He would take care of the righteous and punish the wicked.

She crossed her hands over her stomach. She had begun to talk to this little being inside her. Of course, it meant nothing to her, but she had carried it to the courthouse, to the stores in Zebulon, to the field of buttercups east of town. She had begun to fantasize about keeping it. Most of the time she could push away those stupid thoughts, but occasionally, a vision of herself holding a baby to her breast crept into her mind. She had never liked squirming, smelly babies, but her fantasy child was different. This infant was beautiful and quiet and smelled like jasmine. Its skin was golden brown like maple syrup and felt like the white satin gown she had worn at the Peabody.

Crow left the church with her mother and Luther and agreed to stay for the noon meal. It would be good to get away from Masie and Glory for a while. Their squabbling was getting on her nerves, and she didn't know how much longer she could stand living in that pigsty. Besides she was really looking forward to Tee Wee's prodigious dinner. Now that her nausea had abated, she was as hungry as a stray hound most of the time.

She ate two helpings of greens, three pieces of chicken, and a huge slice of peach pie. Pushing back from the table, Crow told Tee Wee she needed to walk off some of the meal. Tee Wee laughed. "I reckon I ain't never seen you wolfin down my food as fast before now. You think worryin makes you eat more?"

"Maybe. You didn't eat much, though."

Tee Wee's eyes clouded. "No, seem like I can't care bout nothin at all; I'm just thinkin on the trial. It'll all be over tomorrow is what Mister Powers said to me when I called him at the Holiday Inn to invite him out for dinner." She began to clear the table. "He said he was workin on his summation and was gonna order a sandwich to his room." She stacked Crow's empty plate on hers and Luther's. "I admit to havin my doubts bout him, but he sure does seem like he's doin the best he can."

Luther stood up. "I wisht he had cut that horse's tail off. Mister Gatlin looks more like what I think a lawyer oughta look like." He stretched his arms over his head. "I'm gonna take a little rest. You comin, Tee?"

"No, I got ironin to do. I brought J. P.'s shirt home so's it'll be fresh tomorrow. He's got to look his best."

After her mother set up the ironing board, Crow left the house and walked down Enterprise Road toward Johnny Moore's store. When she reached the wooden rail fence that bordered the Kepper Place, Crow remembered the last day she had visited Moses there. She didn't like to think about the past: her bare feet, hand-me-down dresses, the greasy crumbled bills she stuffed into the bodice of her blouse. She thought about all the times with Browder in the pine grove, the barn, on the bank of the pond. She hadn't understood her feelings for Browder then, and she still couldn't decipher the complex thoughts that popped into her head now that she was carrying his child. What if she told him her secret?

As Crow veered off the blacktop onto the grassy shoulder of the road, she decided that there was no need to tell Browder anything. Soon she would be getting rid of this blob inside her. Shading her eyes with her forearm, she looked up at the noonday sun. Thin trails of white clouds like fingers drifted across its round face. She thought of a baby's head. "Stop it," she said aloud. "You're going back to Memphis in a few days and you can get the name of a doctor. Do it right away. Put all of this behind you. J. P. will be free, and so will you."

When she reached the vee where Enterprise Road connected to Carterdale, Crow stood beside the stop sign unable to decide where she would go now. She looked over at the lopsided sign hanging from the roof of Johnny Moore's store. The old gas pump had been removed; the front of the building was boarded up. She turned, retracing her steps. She wished she had brought a jar of water or a mint to suck on. Her mouth was dry and she tasted salt. Her eyes blurred as she looked down the road at the shimmering heat waves.

After she had walked only a few yards, a sharp pain shot through her stomach. The twisting was like menstrual cramps, and yet it wasn't. Was this the beginning of a miscarriage? She felt no blood leaking between her legs, but it might start at any moment. She walked faster; she could lose this baby right here on Enterprise Road. The mile back to Parsons Place seemed like ten, but finally the twin tenant houses framed against the background of the blue sky came into view. She had wobbled doubled over down the road, but when she turned into the drive, the pains suddenly stopped. Crow sank to the grass beside the mailbox. She wasn't going to miscarry; her baby was okay. The relief she felt was overwhelming and she folded her arms over her stomach, cradling her child. As she rocked, she cursed her weakness. "Shit. Damn. Hell. Son-of-a-bitch." She knew now that she couldn't destroy her baby. She would sing the lyrics of the song fate had composed for her. She would love this child, and now she knew that she loved Browder, too.

Crow waited until dark to call Masie and tell her that she was staying the night. "Mama needs me. I'll bring the car back early in the morning and pick y'all up for court."

If Tee Wee was surprised that Crow was staying, she showed no sign. She produced another huge meal for her daughter and said that she was going to bed early to pray for Jesus' help tomorrow. When the bedroom door was safely closed, Crow picked up her shoes and tiptoed out of the house.

As she ran across the pasture, she tried to formulate a plan to draw

Browder out of the house, and when she saw that his truck wasn't parked beside Missy's little red car, she felt great relief. He wasn't home. She could wait for him in the shadows.

In the hour that she sat beside the hydrangea bush beside the drive, Crow's thoughts whirled as fast as pinwheels in a gale wind. Her entire life had changed in one afternoon, and now she began to think about all of the problems her decision to have the baby was going to cause. She was as dumb as Ruthie had been as a child, believing in fairy tales, thinking that she was some silly princess who could kiss away the ugliness of a frog. Crow drew her knees up to her chest and wrapped her arms around her legs. Her baby rested in the dark hollow of her lap, safe and invisible for now, but soon everything would change. She would have to take a hiatus from her work; she couldn't appear on a stage ballooned out like a beach ball. She doubted any of her evening dresses would fit her even now. But other performers had children, lived normal lives, and continued their careers. She could manage that, too. She would tell Winston when she went back to Memphis; he would arrange everything. She smiled. He was such a goose with a soft heart; he might even like the idea of being a godfather to the baby. She gathered up her hair and held it in a loose bun on top of her head. The night was warm and humid, and sweat rolled down her skin between her breasts. Yes, Winston would be a wonderful godfather to her daughter. Her baby was a girl; somehow she felt sure of this.

When she saw the headlights of the truck bouncing up the drive, Crow held her breath. Maybe she was making a mistake. What was she going to say? She shouldn't be here. She would run home before he saw her. But when she stood up, the headlights of the truck swept over her, and in an instant Browder was reaching for her, lifting her to his chest. His voice was filled with joy. "I'll go inside, tell Missy that I've got to check on the horse or a cow. Meet me in the pine grove."

Browder returned in less than fifteen minutes, and when he kissed her, Crow knew that she wasn't going to tell him anything yet. She had had enough sorrow and worry for a long time now; she wanted this happiness. She sat on the pine needles, and opened her arms. "I'm back. Did you miss me?"

Facing her on his knees, he kissed every inch of her face that his lips could fill. "I missed you like I'd miss my eyes, my voice, the sound of rain. How did you know I needed you tonight? I've been wishing I could talk to you, wishing I could hold you."

Crow sat up straighter and leaned back on the trunk of a pine and Browder moved to sit beside her. He lifted her hand and kissed the center vein that ran toward her wrist. "Here we are hiding in the woods just like we did so many times back when."

"Lots has changed since then." Crow touched her palm to her stomach, then reached for Browder's neck, pulling him close. "Some things haven't changed, though."

He laid her back on the soft needles. "I love you. That's never going to change."

When he entered her, she thought of their child. There were three of them locked together now, and with this discovery, she felt a kind of happiness she had never known.

All too soon, their time together was over. "I'll be going back to Memphis after the trial. If J. P. gets convicted, I might stay longer if Mama needs me," Crow said.

"What about us?"

"What do you mean?"

Browder leaned back against the tree where she had sat earlier. "I love you. I know you love me, even if you've never said it. We belong together. Ever since we were kids, I've known that."

Crow put her fingers to his lips. "Okay, I'll say it. I love you. No man has ever made me feel like you do, and I guess that means I love you, too." She held his face in her hands. "But you're a white man; I'm a black woman. There's that fact." She dropped her hands and whispered, "And you're married."

Browder knocked his head back against the tree's rough bark. "Yeah. I'm married, but I wanted you first."

Crow didn't know what to say to him now. Her brain was a tangle of knotted rope. Her body felt limp and warm and she wanted to lie down and sleep curled in his arms. She didn't have the energy to unravel her thoughts. There would be time to talk later. "You have to go inside. We can be together after the trial is over. There's too much to think about now."

"Yeah, you're right. Crow, there's something else that's happened. Ruthie doesn't want Tee Wee to know until after the trial is over, but she's in the hospital."

"The hospital! She sick?"

"No, that bastard she married damn near killed her. Burned all her hair off her head, some of her skin. She looks terrible."

"Was it because of her testifying?"

"Yeah, that's why Ruthie didn't want Tee Wee to know. Afraid she'd blame herself for talking Ruthie into it, but it was just a matter of time anyway. I fingered him for a wife beater a long time ago, but Ruthie wouldn't talk about it, wouldn't let me help her. Protect her from that slimy son-of-a-bitch."

Crow crossed her arms over her stomach. "How did you find out?"

"Friday night after she testified, Ruthie brought Annie Ruth here to stay with us. I guess she knew Dennis would beat the hell outta her, and she was scared. Hid her car in the back in case he came looking for her." Browder rubbed his eyes and lifted them to Crow's face. "I can hardly think about anything but kissing you, holding you."

"Hold me while you talk." Crow moved closer and laid her head on his chest.

Stroking her hair, he said, "I thought Ruthie and Annie Ruth were sleeping and then Annie Ruth comes into our room and says, 'Mama's not back yet. I want Eric.' That's the stuffed rabbit she sleeps with. So after she told us this, Missy put her to bed in my old room and gave her one of her old dolls to sleep with. I ran outside and, when I saw that Ruthie's car was gone, I jumped in the Triumph and headed out to her house. When I got there her car was in the drive and the door was wide open. Soon as I walked in I smelled smoke, a terrible stink. It was her hair all singed off scattered on the stove and the floor. Big black burned places on the tile. I rushed to the hospital, and sure enough she was in the emergency room. Dennis was sitting there blubbering, trying to say she fell and had an accident." Browder's arms were tight around Crow, and she pressed closer to him. " 'An accident, my ass,' I said to him. I went crazy. Jerked him up and started punching him, kicking him with my boot when he fell on the floor." He grinned. "I think I said something like 'How does it feel to be on the other end of the fist?' Some people came and pulled me off him. Blood was dripping off him all over the floor, and a nurse was yelling at me, saying he needed stitches, and all of a sudden he took off running. Was out the door and driving off before I could get past the nurses and orderlies to get to him. I think he heard me, though. I yelled loud as I could that if he ever touched my sister again, I'd kill him. And, Crow, I would. If you saw Ruthie, you'd want to kill him yourself."

"And you don't know where he went?"

"No, probably halfway to Maine by now. He's a coward. Men who knock women around are all nothing but cowards."

"Oh, poor Ruthie. How horrible. I hope he doesn't come back. I don't want you to go to jail for killing him." She lifted her face and kissed him. "I have to tell you about something that's happened, too, but right now I'm so tired. Bone tired. I need to go home. I'll see you tomorrow. We can be together and talk after the trial is over."

Browder smiled. "Tomorrow. Oh God, I love you, Crow." He kissed her forehead, her nose, her lips, her neck, and then he bent and touched his lips to her stomach. Crow drew in her breath. If he knew, if he knew . . . but he didn't, and she could wait a while longer to tell him that he had kissed his child for the first time.

Chapter 58

IMPLE HELD THE SCISSORS IN FRONT OF RUTHIE'S FACE. "Come on now. Don't be scared. I'm not going to touch your scalp; I'm just going to snip off the frizzy pieces."

Ruthie looked into the mirror on the tray. She probably would look better without them, but her head was tender and the scissors glinted ominously above her. "Well, okay. But be careful."

Dimple waved the scissors like a sword. "Two, three swipes and it'll all be over." She closed the mirror and moved the tray to her side. "After we get your hair fixed, I'm gonna do the nails on your good hand."

Ruthie wanted to lie down. "No, I don't feel up to it, Dimple. It's good of you to want to help, but I just want to lie back down."

Dimple frowned. "You've got to stay up to get your strength back. Lying in bed just drains all the get-up-and-go outta you." She dropped the pieces of hair into the wastebasket beside the bed. "There. Take a look, much better. I'm gonna bring you a gorgeous green scarf to tie around your head till you get a wig."

Ruthie shook her head. "I'll look later." She sank back onto her pillows, and, looking up at Dimple's sad eyes, she said, "I'm sorry. You're so good to me, and I do appreciate it. I guess I'm just not good company. I can't . . . can't . . ."

Dimple sat on the bed and patted her hand. "It's okay. You've been through a horrible ordeal here. You can't be expected to feel happy, for God's sake."

Her concern made Ruthie feel worse. She should act more grateful. Browder wanted to attend the last day of J. P.'s trial, and when he'd called

Dimple for help, she had rushed over to the hospital and had agreed to take her out to Browder's as soon as Dr. Matthews released her. "What time is it?" Ruthie asked.

"Eight-thirty. Judge will be rapping his gavel in about thirty minutes. I knew you would testify."

Ruthie reached for a tissue and wiped her eyes. "I wasn't much help, though. Lowell Gatlin made me out to be a civil rights zealot. Dennis told me my testimony wouldn't make a difference, and he was right."

Dimple stood up. "That fucking phony son-of-a-bitch. I hope Browder finds him and beats the shit outta him."

Ruthie gripped Dimple's hand. "Don't tell anyone. No one, Dimple. It's too horrible. I'm so ashamed." She squeezed her tighter. "Annie Ruth must never know." She took a sip of water. "I'm having a hard time trying to forgive him."

Dimple exploded. She flew off the bed and walked around the room yelling, "Forgive him? Have you lost your everlasting mind? Forgive him? Never!"

Ruthie pointed to the nightstand. "There's a book in that drawer that tells me I must forgive him. God doesn't want me to have hatred in my heart. Forgive thine enemies; do good to them that persecute you. Remember that?"

Dimple crossed her arms. "Oh yeah, turn the other cheek, too. Take him back. Let him burn the hair off your butt next time. He might kill you next time. Then Annie Ruth might be next. Think about that." She wheeled around toward the door. "I'm gonna go see where that doctor is, so we can get the hell outta here."

Alone in the room, Dimple's words lingered in the antiseptic air. "Annie Ruth might be next." Suddenly, a knot of cold fear formed inside her chest. "Oh God, help me. Please please help me," Ruthie prayed. "I can't forgive him. I don't want him to come back. Ever."

"Here we are." Dimple walked into the room clutching the sleeve of Dr. Matthews' white lab coat. "I told this cute man that you had things to do, places to be, so he'd have to skip a few patients and get down here to Room Two Sixty-Seven." She pressed her breasts against his arm. "You didn't mind, did you?"

Dr. Matthews laughed. "Who could resist her, Ruthie? She has given me orders to pronounce you well and ready to go home. And that's just what I'm going to do."

—

AT THAT MOMENT Tee Wee was sitting in the courtroom praying that her son would be going home on this day. She was so nervous she couldn't keep hold of the lucky rabbit's foot Hilda had given her to pass to J. P. She had dropped the little furry digit tied with a pink ribbon twice before she made it down the aisle to what she now thought of as "her" bench. This morning's early sun, streaming through the window, had been a good sign. And she thanked God for sending it to her. Sitting beside Luther in his truck on their way to the jail to deliver her son's starched shirt, Tee Wee had thanked him for mending J. P.'s body, too. His cuts and broken bones had healed, the cast had been removed last week, and he had full use of his arm again. Tee Wee told Luther to wait in the truck and hurried inside the jail. There wasn't much time before this fateful day in court would begin.

J. P. exchanged the wrinkled checked shirt he was wearing for the white one Tee Wee had brought. He turned full circle. "How do I look, Mama?"

"Handsome as a prince. I like your hair short, too. Shows your pretty eyes." Tee Wee wanted to go on with this inconsequential chatter, but she felt she needed to say something important on this last morning before the verdict would be delivered. "J. P., no matter which way it go today, I'm proud of you. Any mama would want you for her son."

J. P.'s eyes sparkled, but he didn't cry. "I know, Mama. I love you. I'm gonna be okay." He held out his arms. "I'll be the best-dressed nigger in the courtroom."

"Shut your mouth," Tee Wee said. "Ain't no time for jokin." But she knew he was trying to cover the case of jitters they were both suffering from. "You stand up straight and look everyone in the eye. Even the white folks. Today you got to let them know you are a somebody." She couldn't help grabbing him and holding him to her.

J. P. pulled away. "Go on now, Mama. I'm ready. I'll see you in court."

When Tee Wee nearly fell leaving the cell, the jailer held her elbow. "Steady, there, Miz Weathersby. This is our last walk together. Your boy will be out of here by tonight."

Tee Wee wiped her eyes. "I pray to Sweet Jesus you are right about that."

When J. P. was called to resume his testimony, Tee Wee nodded approval as she watched him walk, head erect, shoulders back to take his seat. Judge Ramsey, with a sunburned face, reminded him he was still under oath. Earlier Tee Wee had overheard the judge tell Ted Withers that he had caught two snappers, a swordfish, and a lot of croakers on his weekend fishing trip.

Gatlin hadn't been fishing; he was as pasty white as ever, but the bandage on his thumb attested to some activity involving something sharp. He looked over his notes. "Let's see. We were talking about your affiliation with the Black Panthers, I believe."

Tyler Powers was on his feet. "Objection." Today he had returned to his conservative clothes, and in the dark navy suit with a plain blue shirt, he looked more like what Tee Wee thought a lawyer ought to. "No affiliation with any group has been established."

Gatlin turned and smiled at him. "Pardon me, I believe the judge ruled I am allowed this line of questioning." Before Powers could speak, the judge rapped his gavel. "You may ask the defendant *if* he belongs to that bunch."

"Okay, do you agree with the general philosophy of the Black Panther Party?"

J. P. hesitated. Tee Wee closed her eyes. "He's just a boy, Lord. Don't let him say something stupid. Put some wise words in that child's mouth."

"Some of it, but not all."

Gatlin cocked his head. "You sound like my wife when I ask her how much she spent down at the shopping center. She spent some, but not all of my money. Exactly how much of the Black Panther beliefs are you agreeing with?"

J. P. shifted his weight. He looked out at Tee Wee, and then she saw his eyes move to Crow's face. "I think Stokely Carmichael is a hero. He helped a lot of black people get registered to vote, but I know that James Meredith said . . ."

The DA interrupted him. "That's enough. So you a believer in the slogan, *Black power.* Got one of them Panther symbols on your schoolbooks?"

"No sir."

Tyler Powers was up again. "Your Honor, Mister Gatlin has not just left the path of relevant questioning, he has traveled out of the state here."

Gatlin wheeled around to face the judge. "Your Honor, I am establishing that this boy is a liar and a troublemaker. He's calling white men liars, saying his dead friend did all of his crimes. I'm trying to show him for what he really is."

Powers fists were clenched. *"Judge!"*

Judge Ramsey wrinkled his brow and winced. His sunburn was painful. "Okay." He nodded to the court stenographer. "Strike all that out. Ladies and gentlemen of the jury, ignore those statements our DA just made about the defendant." He pointed his finger at Gatlin. "And, Lowell, you get back to asking questions."

Gatlin was unruffled. "Thank you, Your Honor. Now, you told this court that you tried to stop your friend, Ray Simmons, from taking that Corvette off the car lot."

"Yes sir."

"And he just wouldn't listen to you?"

"No sir, he wouldn't."

"But you said that he wasn't smart. You're the straight-A student. So now I'm wondering why that boy wouldn't do what you told him to. Seems like he thought you had all the answers to everything. Did you really try to stop him or did you tell him to get in that car and you'd take him for a ride?"

J. P. was sweating now. His starched shirt sagged on his thin shoulders and wet circles had formed beneath his armpits. "Ray didn't listen to anybody. He was headstrong. I couldn't stop him."

"Oh, that's right. He was the wild one, not you. You didn't play poker, get into fights, steal Ray's daddy's beer and money like Mister Simmons said you did."

"No sir."

Gatlin shook his head and turned to the jury with his hands up in surrender. "I reckon I don't have any more questions to ask this witness with the faulty memory."

Powers didn't bother to stand up. "Objection," he said in a dull voice.

"Sustained. Strike that out," Judge Ramsey said, gingerly pulling his collar away from his crimson neck. "Was that your last witness, Mister Powers?"

"Yes, Your Honor."

Ramsey stood up. "Okay, we'll take a little fifteen-minute recess while you boys work on your summations, and then we'll hear them and let the jury get on with it."

Tee Wee stroked her rabbit foot. "You ain't doin your job. You got one more chance to start workin."

Icey leaned over the bench. "Tee, you goin out for some air?"

"No, I ain't leavin this seat. I'm prayin every minute till this is over."

Icey sat down. "Me, too. Oh Lord, lamb of God, save our boy from the Devil's fiery pits. Make that jackass DA mute, and let Mister Powers' words turn to gold. And, Dear Sweet Jesus . . ."

Tee Wee reached back and pinched her arm. "Pray silent, Icey. I can't think with you rattlin on like that."

Icey tucked a curl behind her ear. "Sorry. I'm just tryin to help any way I can."

Crow came to sit beside her. "How're you doing, Mama?"

"Not good. I didn't like the way Gatlin made J. P. out to be something he ain't."

Crow patted her shoulder. "I know, but Tyler will straighten things out when he does his summation. He's good, Mama. Have faith."

"I want to. The Good Lord knows I want to."

Lowell Gatlin's summation was thirty minutes long. He read direct testimony of his witnesses back to the jury in case they had forgotten any of the facts that proved John Paul Weathersby had stolen a car from Larry Martino, driven it too fast, run a red light, and killed Judy Willow. He produced the pictures of Judy's mangled body again, and Tee Wee thought he was about to cry when he reminded them that she was a good driver, that the car was a birthday present. Gatlin painted J. P. as a smart, fast-talking troublemaker, bent on having his way without paying consequences. He suggested that, if the jury found him innocent, they would possibly be seeing him on TV one day as the leader of a pack of violent blacks determined to take over the country from the whites. "He's already on his way, wants to be accepted to our fine law school at the University of Mississippi where he plans to learn how to get power over me, over all of you. Make no mistake," Gatlin said, "he's a liar, and a good one, too. He's dangerous to all of us. He's already recklessly killed one of our own, and he's not the least bit sorry."

When Tyler Powers' turn came, he seemed nearly reluctant to begin. He walked to the jury box and stood without one note in his hand, and Tee Wee's fears closed her throat so that she could barely breathe. She opened her mouth and sucked in the stale air.

Tyler centered himself in the middle of the painting that hung behind the jury box. It depicted a plantation house set far back on a long drive lined with moss-laden live oaks. There were bluebirds in the sky, tiny cotton bolls on small green plants on the left side of the house, and to the right fine chestnut horses, black manes ruffled by an invisible breeze lifted their elongated heads for the artist's eye. Powers studied the painting for a moment, then looked down from it to the faces of the jurors. "Good afternoon, ladies and gentlemen. I know you're all hot and tired and hoping to go home to a fine meal the ladies of this county are so noted for. I have been living here in the Holiday Inn in Zebulon for several weeks now and have learned a great deal about Lexie County and its good citizens. It's a lovely place to live, rich soil, elegant oaks, stately pines. The water is cool and plentiful, the voices I hear on the street are melodious like an old sweet tune my mother used to sing to me when I was a child. And the food! I mustn't forget to mention the culinary skills of the cooks in Lexie County. I've eaten okra, and greens, and crowder peas, and sweet potato pies that I shall long remember."

Powers' arms were spread out on either side of him, gripping the rail of the jury box. "Yes, Lexie County is beautiful, but besides its white cotton, its beautiful flowers, its green fields, it grows and nourishes another crop that spreads like the kudzu that proliferates everywhere in this state. I call that crop the 'dark turnip.' It grows like a regular turnip, with leaves aboveground and a bulbous root buried in the soil. The difference in these turnips is that the root isn't purple and white like a regular turnip root. It is black, and the leaves aren't green, but are the color of magnolia blossoms. The tops of these plants are pleasing to look at, fragrant and succulent. The roots are black, bitter, and smell of the earth. No one wants to unearth the roots. No one in Lexie County wants those roots to rise up and push the white blossoms over to make room for them so that they can have the benefits of the sun and rain and thereby grow into the lovely plants they were meant to be. I think you all know this is a metaphor about this young boy, the root growing in the soil that you all share. His dream is your greatest fear. This trial isn't about who was driving that car; it isn't about whether or not the car was stolen. It isn't even about the girl whose picture has been passed around in this room like it was an exhibit in a sideshow at a carnival. The best mechanic in Zebulon, Cal Masterson, whom Mister Gatlin relies on, has told you that there was no way J. P. could have been driving that Corvette when it crashed into the Mustang. Doctor Matthews, who has delivered your children, said that J. P. was in shock and that where he ended up after the accident was meaningless. So the facts bear out the truth, which is that this fine young man was as much a victim as the two who died, but Mister Gatlin asked you to ignore those facts. He wants to remind you that there are thousands of dark turnip plants growing in Mississippi. Thousands of blacks who want you to move over and let them come out of the darkness to rise up and follow their dreams. He wants you to be scared of them; he wants you to see this harmless boy as someone to fear. But he's no Black Panther; he's a follower of Doctor Martin Luther King, who showed young men like J. P. how to dream, and now the DA wants you to keep him buried in a prison cell so that his dream will die. Don't kill this boy's dream."

Tee Wee held on to the bench with both hands. She didn't know what a metaphor was and wasn't sure that the turnip crop was one, but she knew that Powers held everyone in his spell right now. Preacher Dixon didn't have nothin on him. She watched the jurors' faces. Except for the one old black man sitting on the back row studying his hands, all of their eyes were fixed on Tyler Powers as if he held them in a hypnotic trance. Powers continued citing the evidence, J. P.'s character, the lies Pepper Simmons told on the stand. Unlike Gatlin, he didn't refer to any notes as he quoted testimony from memory verbatim. Leaning into the rail of the jury box, he nearly touched the woman in front of him with his shirt front. "You are all so fortunate to live in this beautiful state, in this bountiful county. Your governor has caused you to suffer great humiliation through his public acts of racial prejudice. This is your opportunity to prove that the good citizens of Lexie County are not going to stand for any more injustice. You can get your pride back; you can nurture dreams. You can start changing your lives today. You can begin with this young, earnest black boy, who only wants to breathe the fresh air and feel the sun on his limbs. Set him free. Let him dream."

Chapter 59.

THE JURY WAS OUT FOR LESS THAN THREE HOURS. WAS THAT A good sign or a bad one? J. P. wondered. When he was brought back into the courtroom, he saw Crow and Masie holding hands sitting beside Tee Wee and Luther. Behind them Deke and Icey, his brothers, and their families, neighbors, and friends were jammed into the narrow benches. As he walked to the defendant's table, he kept his eyes away from the other side of the room where he knew the Willows were sitting hoping to hear the word *guilty.*

Not guilty, not guilty, was the chant inside his head. If he said it fifty times before the verdict was read, if someone sneezed three times in a row, if, if . . . if there was a sign, would he know it? When he sat down, Tee Wee poked her finger into his back. Turning his head, he saw the rabbit's foot in her hand. "Take it, put it in your pocket next to your heart," she said. He heard the tremor in her voice.

Tyler Powers pulled his chair close and laid his arm on the back of J.P.'s chair. Leaning over, he whispered, "Watch the eyes of the jurors when they come in. If they look at you, that's good."

J. P. nodded assent, but he knew he was going to close his eyes so that he could listen better. He couldn't take a chance on hearing the wrong words.

During the past hours it had taken the jury to reach a verdict, he had sat alone in his cell, refusing visitors. A deputy had come several times to stare in at him as if he thought he might catch J. P. digging a tunnel to escape. But there was no escaping his fear, and he didn't want anyone witnessing his panic. Lying back on his cot, he heard Tyler Powers telling the deputy that he'd be right outside if his client changed his mind about wanting to see him. Shivering with icy fear in the ninety-plus-degree cell, he planned his two lives, one as a free man, the other as a convict. Both scenarios rolled over and over in his mind like a tire bouncing down a hill. Each time he landed at the end of his reverie, he started over, going up and then down again. He remembered the myth of Sisyphus he had learned about in school. Push the rock up, let it roll down, push it up, roll it down, push, roll, push, push for all eternity. His punishment wouldn't be a choice. All of the power over his life lay in the hands of twelve people he had never met. He tried to remember the individual sound of their voices when they had answered the questions the lawyers had asked them during jury selection, but now he imagined them as one collective tongue speaking a secret language behind the closed doors upstairs. Were they saying the word *Parchman*?

J. P. remembered only one man who had gone to Parchman. He was a friend of Deke's, and J. P. had been eleven or twelve when he sat in the loft of the barn listening to their conversation as they stood beside the bush hog Deke was hooking up to the tractor. The man's name was Joshua, but he was called Carrot Top because of his orange hair. He had served five years at Parchman for stealing a bicycle for his son for Christmas from the Goodyear store where he was working. He wished now he had paid closer attention to what he said about his time there. Later, when he'd ask Deke to tell him more about the prison, Deke had laughed and said he didn't need to know more because he wasn't ever going to that place. Deke might have been wrong.

Still shivering, J. P. pressed his palm against the rabbit's foot in his shirt pocket. It was taking the judge a long time to appear, and he imagined him sitting in his big office eating a steak, drinking whiskey, but just as he thought this, Judge Ramsey strode into the room. "All rise," said the bailiff.

J. P. didn't look at the jury, but he knew the foreman must be holding the most important piece of paper he would ever not see in his life. He kept his eyes fixed on the American flag in front of him. That flag was for everyone. It stood for independence, freedom from tyranny, for liberty and justice for all. But not for him maybe. Not for him. He felt the weight of the rabbit's foot in his pocket and thought of a brown hare running from the hunter, from the copper-colored bullet that would find his heart. He knew what running for your life felt like now.

Judge Ramsey's grave voice rang out in the courtroom. "Ladies and gentlemen of the jury, have you reached a verdict?

"We have, Your Honor."

J. P. stood as instructed, but he couldn't feel the floor beneath his feet. He knew Powers was beside him because he could hear him breathing through his mouth. He closed his eyes. He heard his mother whisper, "Dear God, please."

He heard his name, the defendant. "On the charge of vehicular homicide, not guilty . . . on the charge . . . not guilty." Not guilty, not, not, not. His mama's arms were around him, lifting him up. He saw his daddy's tears, Powers' wide grin, Crow's dark eyes. He couldn't understand what anyone was saying. Over Masie's shoulder, J. P. saw the Willows talking to Lowell Gatlin. Mrs. Willow was crying. He looked away. No matter what the jury had decided, in this town he would always be the rabbit hiding from the dark barrels of accusing eyes that would haunt him forever. He turned to Tee Wee. "Mama, I'm free. Let's go home."

Chapter 60.

ROWDER SAT IN HIS TRUCK, GRINNING AT HIMSELF IN THE
rearview mirror. Today had been a banner day. J. P. was free! Crow's
brother would be going to Ole Miss after all, and that was her dream,
wasn't it? And couldn't he make his dream come true now? He thought
about Powers' turnip metaphor that had seemed so inane and yet was
obviously effective. He had become the root, too, hiding his love for
Crow, but he was going to go aboveground very soon.

Glancing at the clock on the dashboard, Browder saw that it was going on four. He'd had a couple of celebration drinks back at the McCoglin
and now he was going to be late getting home. He fumbled for his keys
and started the engine.

Browder should have turned west onto Main to head for home, but
the truck made a few turns east and then he was on Avenue L where
Masie's apartment building stood across the street from the bank.

When he saw Crow getting out of the car in front of the apartment,
he took it to be a sign, but before he pulled in next to Masie's Pinto, she
vanished into the building. He thought about following her, but Masie or
Glory might be home and he wanted Crow to himself. He couldn't say
the things he wanted unless they were alone.

Undecided, he sat in the truck watching someone's laundry dance on
a line strung out on the second-floor balcony. There was a blue work
shirt, a child's checked dress, a pair of ruffled pink panties. He was getting dizzy watching the clothes swinging back and forth as the wind
caught the line. Maybe he was a little drunk.

He dropped his head onto the steering wheel. He thought about holding Crow, telling her that he wanted to spend the rest of his life loving her. "Marry me," he whispered. "I want to marry you, Crow."

He drove away with the windows down trying to clear his head with fresh air. He hadn't been this high in the afternoon since college. Pressing on the accelerator, he sped out of town, driving past the yellow-brown broomsedge growing beside Carterdale Road, the orange and purple milkweed, late-blooming yellow lousewort. He was ebullient, dizzy now with the beauty of the world. He waved to the bobolink sitting on the fence in front of Cotton's dairy. He breathed in the scent of the sweet alfalfa and freshly mown hay. He saw a distant flock of crows and thought they were sent to guide him down Enterprise Road. He was a lucky man. He thought of the verse he'd learned in Sunday school long ago. "God's in His heaven, all's right with the world."

After passing Tee Wee's and Icey's houses, his smile vanished. There was his house, his birthright, his millstone. And inside was the woman he had lived with for the past eight years. He sighed. What would he say to Missy? Could he leave her? As he lurched past her car, he laid his hand on the hood of the Triumph and felt the heat that told him that she had just gotten home.

She was waiting for him in the living room. She sat on the couch dressed in a gray sheath with black trim that she usually wore to church.

Balancing himself on the sloping floor, Browder walked carefully and slowly toward the recliner, but Missy patted the cushion beside her. "Have you been drinking?"

"I had a celebration drink. J. P. was released today. I was there."

"You had more than one. I already heard the news about J. P. Dimple told me when she brought Ruthie out to pick up Annie Ruth. They're going to spend the night at Dimple's house. Ruthie looked just awful!" Missy's smile didn't match her words at all. Browder couldn't understand it. Maybe he was drunker than he thought, and she was actually baring her teeth like a wild animal. "I've got good news, too," she said.

Browder closed his eyes and then quickly opened them. "What's the news?" He wanted to take a shower and rest for a while. They could talk after dinner. He might be sick. She'd better hurry up and get this pow-wow over.

"I went to see Doctor Walker, the new OB-GYN, today." She took both of his hands in hers. "Look at me." He stared at her white skin, her pink cheeks, her shining eyes, and he knew. "We're pregnant," she squealed. "We're going to have a baby at last."

—

WHEN CROW WALKED into the apartment, she leaned back against the door and thought how beautiful Masie and Glory's littered home looked to her now. She wanted to call Winston right away and tell him the good news. J. P. was free! She couldn't ever remember a time when everyone had been any happier as they walked out of the courtroom to wait on the lawn for J. P.'s release from jail. Icey and Tee Wee had danced in circles, holding on to each other, laughing and jumping up and down like crazy women. Even Luther had executed a little jig on the sidewalk, and Deke handed out cigars to everyone, even the children, who giggled with pleasure and stuck them in their mouths.

Tyler Powers had rushed back to the motel to gather his belongings to make the three-thirty train to Jackson, and when he returned in the Thunderbird, Masie offered to drive it to the rental company while Crow took him to the depot in her Pinto.

As Crow and Tyler walked to the car, J. P. came running across the lawn toward them. "Mister Powers," he called out. "Wait."

"The free man cometh," Tyler said with a big smile.

"I wanted to thank you for all you did for me."

Crow hugged him and smiled. "I told you he was a good lawyer."

"I was betting on those jurors' vanity. Most of them were poor, hadn't ever had any power. I deduced that they'd jump on the chance to make people sit up and take notice of them." He grinned. "I imagine they're not feeling as good about themselves now that they're home. They won't be too popular with most of the white people in Lexie County."

J. P. dropped his head to his chest. "I know. I've already thought about that."

Crow opened the car door. "Say good-bye. Tyler has a train to catch. I think he's ready to leave our turnip green fields and go back to DC."

Tyler hesitated, but reached out and pulled J. P. to him in a loose hug. "Good luck to you, John Paul Weathersby. Study hard, make a name for yourself. It's been a true pleasure getting to know you."

At the depot Tyler took a brochure for Percy Quinn State Park from the rack beside the gumball machine. "Maybe I'll come back and camp out beneath the pines."

Crow laughed. "You're joking."

"No, I'm not. Crow, I meant what I said in my summation. This is a beautiful piece of the world. Everything I said was true. Great food, warm weather, a darkness that lies over the clover fields, too, but it won't lie there forever, Crow."

"I hope you're right, but you're not one of us. You can't understand our history."

They heard the train's whistle blasting from the south, and Tyler lifted his suitcase. "No, but I have a clearer picture of it now." He leaned forward and kissed her cheek. "Tell J. P. to have a great life. He's a fine young man."

Crow smiled. "So are you," she said.

Now in the messy apartment she searched for the phone. She tried four numbers before she finally found Winston at her own place. He was sleeping there to avoid a "persistent gentleman who pounds on my door wanting to share my bed." When Crow told him the news, he was elated and then asked when she would be coming home. A new black magazine wanted an interview. It would be good publicity for the next album.

Crow told him she didn't know just yet. She thought about telling him about her pregnancy, but she decided to wait until she returned so that she could see his true reaction. There would be plenty of time to make all the decisions that would arise. After replacing the receiver, Crow thought that the time for keeping secrets was definitely running out. She patted her midriff. "Hush little baby, don't you cry. Mama's gonna buy you a mockingbird."

As she drove back to Parsons Place her thoughts swung back and forth like a pendulum. She would tell Browder about the baby today. He would marry her. No, she and Browder could never be together. He was white; she, black. But she didn't give a damn about the rules her mama lived by. If they married, she and Browder would suffer, though; they would be hated by some people. Their child would be neither black nor white. She imagined her baby's cells on a chessboard, white and black pieces moving in patterns across the squares. Checkmate, the game is over, you lose. There's no place on the board for you.

That night lying in her mama's house waiting for everyone to fall asleep so that she could slip out and go to Browder, Crow tossed and turned in her bed. What about her career? Living in Memphis? Would Browder move away from Parsons Place? Did he love her enough? She smiled into the dark. "Yes, he loves me. He wants me," she whispered. "And I'm having his baby." Pulling back the sheet, she slid from the bed. She would tell him tonight.

Browder looked across his pregnant wife to the clock on the bedside table. It was nearly midnight. Crow was outside waiting for him. He could feel her presence. He snatched up his khaki shorts and a T-shirt and tiptoed out of the room. Crossing the yard to the pine grove, he saw her leaning against a tree. She called his name.

Crow sensed it immediately. Something was terribly wrong. As she walked toward him, her legs felt like lead pipes, her body an immovable block of steel that she had to thrust forward. When she reached him and saw the look of anguish on his face, she grabbed his arms. "Browder, what is it?"

He blurted out the words. "Missy's pregnant. That's all. She's pregnant and I can't leave her. Can't do it, Crow."

Crow tried to register his words in her brain. Pregnant. That's me. I'm having a baby. But it's Missy. Missy is pregnant. She stared at him with disbelief. When he stretched out his hand, she backed away and coiled her tongue inside her mouth.

Browder's voice was filled with sorrow. "Crow, you are all that I ever wanted. You know that. I love you, have always loved you from when we were kids. I love you but now . . ." He shook his head slowly from side to side.

This is what comes from love, Crow thought. You knew this would happen. You knew better. How could you have forgotten what you learned a long time ago? She narrowed her eyes; she hated herself; she hated him. She wanted to rake her nails down his white face, tear out his blue eyes. "Browder you are something. Did you make up that story because you found out about my lover in Memphis that I'm going back to?"

Deep lines formed on Browder's forehead. "Crow, don't lie. This may be the last time we're together. This isn't a movie script that can be rewritten to change the facts."

She exploded then. Something inside her banged and shattered into fragments. She poked him in the chest with her forefinger. Each word she shouted was a spear. "You're the one to say we aren't in a fucking movie? You. You who spent your whole life acting. Now you going to keep acting with *her*. That white bitch." Her hand shot out and struck his cheek. Backing away, she spat on the ground. "You stay up on your celluloid screen with your starlet wife." She wiped her nose with the back of her hand. "Who's lying, Browder, you or me?"

"I love you," he whispered. "That is truth."

Suddenly Crow was tired, more tired than she had ever been in her life. She needed to be alone, to lie down somewhere soft. What did any of their feelings matter now? She held his pleading eyes. Check-mate again. "Browder, go home. Leave me alone. Good luck with your baby." Turning away from him, she walked across the land toward home. As she stumbled over the tall grass, she listened for his call, but the only sound she heard was her rasping breath and the faint cry of their child.

Chapter 61

By SATURDAY AFTERNOON THE MERCURY IN THE THER-
mometer nailed to the oak tree outside Tee Wee's house had risen to
102. The iced tea glasses on the folding table in the yard were sweating,
and the congealed salad had turned to liquid. But the guests who had
come to celebrate J. P.'s courtroom victory didn't seem bothered by the
heat as they sat on folding chairs, on the steps, on the roots of the oak
tree; eating, drinking, talking, and laughing. Tee Wee brought out a pan
of chicken and dumplings, and Icey followed her with a large earthen-
ware bowl of rice. "I near bout fell down them steps, Tee Wee. They getting warped and wavy. Dangerous."

Tee Wee set the aluminum pan down on the table. "I guess the steps
at your new rent house is just perfect."

With a wide grin, Icey set the rice bowl beside the pan. "Concrete.
Last a lifetime."

"Well, now that you'll be livin in town, won't be no excuses for
showin up late at the bakery."

Icey put her hands on her hips. "I ain't never been late, but maybe
two, three times."

Tee Wee turned around. "Where's J. P., the guest of honor? I don't
think he's ate yet."

J. P. NEEDED to be alone. After being in his cell in the jail, he was unaccustomed to so many people, so much noise. Everyone had slapped his
back, hugged him in a vise grip, pumped his hand until his arm ached.

His fingers and ribs were sore, too, and he was sure he had red marks on his back. After he was released from jail, unpacking his few belongings in his room, he had caught his reflection in the cracked mirror over his dresser and hardly recognized himself. His eyes seemed larger, his lower lip had shrunk and curled inward, his wide nostrils belonged on his father's face. He felt so old now, and he couldn't keep up this smiling at all the people congregated in his yard.

J. P. slipped around the side of the house, and, taking off his shoes and socks, he dug his toes into the gray dirt. He headed out across the pasture, running full out, leaping over the cow piles, skimming over the clover on tender feet. When he stumbled and fell, he rolled over on his back and squirmed against the ground like a dog rubbing scent onto his skin. He lay still and stared up at the summer sky. He was free, and he finally understood what freedom meant to him. He couldn't leave here now. J. P. made his decision quickly, with surety. He belonged to the land, to Parsons Place, and he wasn't going to any white college and risk losing himself again. He stood up. He'd have to find Crow and tell her that she could have the college money back.

When he returned to the party, J. P. wandered among the crowd searching for Crow. She would be leaving soon and he didn't know when he'd have another chance to tell her about his decision. She'd be plenty mad, and besides her wrath, he would have to face his mama with the news.

He found Crow alone on the side of the house by the flower bed. "Crow, I got something to tell you."

She crossed her arms. Suspicious already. "What?"

He took a breath. "I'm not going to Ole Miss. You can have the money back. I've been thinking about it, and I've decided to stay here. Maybe farm with Daddy."

Crow grabbed his arm and pinched him hard. "Have you lost your mind? Did you leave it down at the jail cell?"

"Ow. Let go, Crow."

She dropped his arm, but moved closer to him. "Listen, J. P. Ever since your trial, you been acting like a nervous filly before a race. Running off here and there. Jumping at the slightest sound. You got to get hold of yourself."

Her bossy voice made him furious. "You try sitting in a filthy jail a few weeks. Try sitting in a courtroom listening to people lie about you. Try feeling like nearly every white person in the world wants you whipped like a dog. See how you'd feel then."

Crow put her arms around him. "Shush, I know. But you got to let go of all that; put it behind you. You have to be clearheaded and not let your emotions get tangled with your brains. Those white people acquitted you. Not all of them are against you."

J. P. dropped his head onto her shoulder. "I know you're right, Crow. I just don't seem to be able to forget sitting in that cell. I can't trust white people, and I can't face the thought of living with them up in Oxford."

Crow's voice was softer now. "You're right to be suspicious. But look around you. Ruthie's here; she testified. What about Tyler Powers? He cares about you."

"I know. Some whites maybe care, but there's a lot more Mister Willows out there in the world. I won't ever forget how he looked at me in that courtroom."

Crow leaned back against the house; she looked tired and upset, and J. P. felt even worse than he had. "You're right," she said. "There are a whole lot of Mister Willows and Mister Larrys, Mister Gatlins, and some of them are going to be up at Ole Miss, but you can see all this as a roadblock or as an opportunity."

J. P. kicked a rock across the yard. "How do you get that?"

"Weakness comes from never having to fight. I've fought all my life, and I'm stronger for it. You're lucky in a way, J. P. You've learned how to do battle now. You've slain one dragon; go kill some more." She reached out and held him by the shoulders. "You're smarter than most of the people you fear. Go read books, study hard, learn all you can about your enemies. Don't drop out of the war before you've had a chance to find out what all you're fighting for." She held his face between her hands. "How bout it? You going to pick up the banner for us or hide out here in the bean patch?"

J. P. thought of Lester who had fought and lost a different war for all of them. He thought of Ray sitting beside him in the Corvette. He thought of Memphis who had died before his battle had begun. He saw himself laying the silver whistle in the coffin beside Memphis, believing that he could blow it in heaven. Lester, Ray, Memphis, all the people who loved him were calling him to fight. His battle wouldn't end for a very long time, but he had won the first round. Maybe he could go the distance. He looked up at Crow, saw tears glistening in her dark eyes. He smiled. "Crow, I hate farming," he said.

She hugged him; her fingers pressed into the muscles of his back. Then, pushing him away, she shoved him backward. "Now go see to your guests. A lot of folks are still waiting to shake your hand and wish you good luck."

As Crow watched him striding across the yard, his head erect on his shoulders, she thought that he was nearly a man now and someday, who knew what he might become. The future was uncertain for all of them. She would be leaving tomorrow and this was her last chance to say good-bye to Parsons Place. She walked behind the house to the vegetable plot. There would be turnips, collards, mustard in the late fall, but most of the summer vegetables were gone. She surveyed the yellowed leaves of the remains of the squash, the brown withered plants that had held butter beans, crowder peas, and Big Boy tomatoes. Some of the rows had already been turned for new planting. Her seed had been sown, too, and she would cultivate and nourish it. No weeds, no bugs, no droughts, nothing would harm her daughter. Her child was going to have plenty of love. Winston had promised to find good jobs for Masie and Glory, and they would be coming home to Memphis with her. Together the three of them would see to this little flower. They would teach her how to grow strong and stand against the wind.

Turning to her right, Crow stared across the land to where Browder's house stood. She saw the twelve-year-old boy crawling out from beneath the house. She saw herself in a faded sundress holding out her palm for his money. She spoke his name aloud. "Browder." She would never say it again. Looking up at the brilliant blue sky, she smiled and cupped her stomach. "Tomorrow we fly away, baby girl. Fly away to Memphis to begin our new life."

AS RUTHIE WALKED toward Icey's porch where Hilda and Annie Ruth were painting on shelf paper spread out on the boards, Tee Wee caught her arm and pulled her to the steps of her house. "Sit a minute. You ain't got to leave yet." She flung her arm around Ruthie's back. "I see you wearin a new fashion look."

Ruthie had tied a blue-and-white bandanna around her head. She wore a peasant blouse and a long print skirt. A copper band encircled her wrist. She laughed. "I'm trying out the hippie look to see how it feels. I hope I don't look stupid."

"No, I like it. Sometimes a change outside make a turnaround inside." Tee Wee patted her back. "Are you okay? You healin good?"

"Yes. New skin is growing, no infection. Doctor Matthews said I'm making wonderful progress. Most of the burns were first degree. It wouldn't have been so bad if I hadn't put all that hair spray on."

"Is your heart healin, too?"

Ruthie tried to pull away, but Tee Wee tightened her grip. "It was an accident, Tee," she said.

Tee Wee slapped her lightly on the leg. "Shush your mouth. You talkin to your Tee Wee, not the law. Nobody believes that story he concocted. It's rubbish and you ain't a good liar."

Ruthie clenched her fists. Hadn't she suspected that Dennis wouldn't be believed? She surrendered her pride and laid her head in Tee Wee's lap as she had when she was a child. "Oh, Tee, I've tried so hard to forgive him, to be understanding of his problems; but I don't want him to come home. His mother calls me daily; she thinks he'll show up someday, that I'll take him back. I pray and pray, but now that Annie Ruth and I are back in our house, each day when I walk into the kitchen, it all comes back. I see him drunk, hear him yelling, and that awful awful smell returns."

"You need to get out of that house. You ain't gonna be able to forgive him until you do."

Ruthie sat up. "What do you mean I can't forgive him unless I leave?"

"Just that. I know a lot more than you. You might of taught me how to read, but there's a lot more to learn than what's in them books. You remember that doll you was always draggin round?"

"Josie."

"Uh-huh. And you remember how you hung on to her when you were too old to be playin with dolls. You finally put her on the closet shelf, but as long as she was visible, you'd go get her from time to time and be a little girl again."

Ruthie covered her face with her hands. "I remember."

"Some things you got to let go of. Things that you love even." She took Ruthie's hands and squeezed them into a tent. "You pray some more. You pray for Jesus to help you learn how to do what's right for yourself. It's hard decisions we has to make sometimes; ain't much in life comes without some worry and some hurtin. But God is good, and He don't want His children on earth to suffer. It's that husband of yours who made you suffer, not the Good Lord."

Ruthie lifted her head and smiled. "Thank you. Don't worry about me. I will heal. Skin, head, heart." She looked out over the yard filled with happy people. J. P. was pushing one of his cousins on the tire swing. God hadn't thrown him in that jail cell and maybe God hadn't set him free, either. Maybe He just watched and shook His head at the messes people made of the beautiful world He created. If J. P. was brave enough to go off to Ole Miss, couldn't she find the courage to begin a new life, too?

She kissed Tee Wee's cheek and walked across the yard toward her old home. She was beginning to see the truth of her life now. When Dennis had burned her hair, he had cremated her desire for him, and now as she sifted through the ashes of their marriage, she realized that there was nothing left to save. Staring across the span of pasture toward her birthplace, she saw herself playing with Josie beneath the chinaberry tree, her mother standing on the porch, calling for her to come inside. "Mama, I want to come home," she whispered.

Moving back to Parsons Place was an option now. When Browder had stopped by her house the day before, he had told her that she could live in the house. "It's about all that's left that I still own," he told her. "Missy and I are probably going to move out anyway. I was never cut out to be a farmer, and I don't want to live there anymore."

"But where will you go?" Ruthie had asked. "You've got the baby coming now."

Browder grinned. "Yeah, I'm getting used to the idea of becoming a papa. Feels pretty good, and Missy, she's so happy. It's like the clock turned back eight years to when we were first married. I told her about Tyler Powers' summation, how he talked about dreams. We had dreams, plans. I thought dreams were for taking, that all I had to do was go after what I wanted. I shouldn't have given up on my dreams so easily. We're talking about moving off the place, maybe to California like we planned so long ago. Who knows, maybe I'll be directing a movie someday. I'll make Annie Ruth a star."

Ruthie had laughed. "She thinks she's going to be one anyway. Thanks for the offer, Browder. I'll have to think about it some more." Then she lowered her eyes. "What about Crow, Browder?"

Browder squeezed his eyes shut. "I'll always love her, Ruthie. No matter where I go, what I end up doing on this earth, a piece of me will always belong to her." He took her hands and pulled her close so that she couldn't see his face. His voice was a whisper. "I was going to leave Missy, Ruthie. I wanted a life with Crow. But Missy told me about the baby, and in a split second everything changed."

Change. The word enveloped her. Lifting her head to the cloudless sky over Parsons Place, she spoke aloud. "Dear God, please release me from my promises. I want to come home. I belong here, not with Dennis. Give me a sign to let me know You understand." Holding her arms out to her side, Ruthie twirled around. As she spun across the grass, her scarf came untied and a puff of wind lifted it from her head. Laughing, she hiked her skirt to her knees and chased after the blue-and-white cloth waving over her head. "Thank You," she called, and as she ran, she closed her eyes and imagined that God had lifted her up and she was flying across the land.

THE PARTY WAS nearly over; as the sun was racing toward bed, its warm orange glow lit the faces of everyone lingering in the front yard. Tee Wee and Icey stood side by side on Tee Wee's porch. Their eyes traveled over their children and grandchildren scattered across the yard. Tee Wee thought of Ernestine over in Alabama and then of Lester. He should be here with them. She lifted her eyes to the leaves dancing on the oak tree. Maybe his spirit was here, and he knew that he was in his mama's heart filled nearly to bust. J. P. was going off to Ole Miss, Crow was a big star, and Masie was going up to Memphis where Crow had promised to find her a real good job. "Look at them, Icey," she said. "We got two fine families here."

Icey gazed out on the scene to find her children. Eli was still living over on the Gulf Coast, but Glory was here and Jonas had brought all five of his children, who were playing chase with little Hilda. "They make a crowd all right."

"It might be quite a spell fore we all together again. I wish Ernestine was here. And Lester."

"I reckon they all here in spirit. Memphis, too."

Tee Wee squeezed her arm. "I was thinkin the same thought."

Icey smiled. "I feel a little sentimental rememberin on my past with you. Let's walk a bit. I done ate too much."

They walked down the steps to Icey's yard and stood looking across the pasture to the Parsons' house. Icey pointed to the closed gate in front of the field. "I hate to leave the place where my baby lost his life."

Tee Wee patted her back. "Memphis lookin down on us from heaven."

"Yeah, you speakin the truth. Still I feel a little piece of him is here. You know I buried my blue nightgown that I was wearin the night I met Deke, so's there'd be something left of me here."

Tee Wee laughed. "You buried it? In the yard?"

"Yes, I did."

"Where at? I needin me a new gown."

Icey slapped her arm. "Go on, you talkin foolish." She took a breath and sighed. "Well, I guess I better get back. I got more packin to do. So many treasures to wrap up. I never realized how much stuff I got. I reckon if you and Luther ever move to town, you won't have the big job of packin I have."

Tee Wee turned and walked alongside her. "Oh, we ain't movin, Icey. We gonna stay right here. Luther done bought more'n half the place now." She tried not to grin when Icey's mouth fell open.

Icey looked around, scanning the pasture, the grove, the pond, the pigsty, the cow lots, the chicken yard, and all of the land that stretched before them. "You own half now?"

"Yep. If I keep doing good down at the bakery, one day we might just buy up the whole place."

"Whoo-whee, Tee. That'd be somethin, wouldn't it?"

"Uh-huh. I reckon folks will start callin this here land the Weathersby Place then."

Icey burst out laughing. "The Weathersby Place!" she said, bumping into Tee Wee's side, nearly losing her balance. Tee Wee grinned and grabbed her arm to steady her, and when Icey squeezed her hand, she held on to her. And the two of them, dark broad backs silhouetted in the orange glow of the evening, walked on together toward home.

Right as Rain

A READER'S GUIDE

BEV MARSHALL

Calinda Andrews, a beautiful anchorwoman for a popular television morning show in Jackson, Mississippi, has driven down to Bev Marshall's home to tape an interview with her. Bev thinks Calinda looks a lot like Crow but suspects she can't sing nearly as well. Calinda is sitting on a fake leather couch in Bev's family room, eating pound cake topped with juicy Louisiana strawberries. Bev is pretending that she made the cake, but in reality she bought it at the Piggly Wiggly just down the road from her house, five miles west of Ponchatoula, Louisiana.

Calinda Andrews: (Flashing a gorgeous smile) Delicious cake. Did you make it?

Bev Marshall: Uh, well, my mother gave me a great recipe for pound cake.

CA: This cake reminds me of all those fabulous dishes Tee Wee cooked for the Parsonses and her own family in *Right as Rain*. Why did you choose that title? I imagine a lot of city folks don't know where that expression comes from.

BM: I hadn't thought about that, but you're probably right. I grew up in an agricultural environment in Mississippi where, as you know, the summers are very hot and often dry. Rain is paramount to the farmers' livelihoods, to their very existence. A drought can mean disaster. Therefore, rain means that all will be well.

CA: So when Icy tells Tee Wee that Glory is right as rain after her recovery from her appendix operation, she's saying she's well?

BM: Yes, the phrase *Right as Rain* was coined and expanded to mean faith that all would be well. When I began writing the novel, I had faith that the lives of my characters would turn out to be right as rain and chose the title for that reason.

CA: I can't help noticing that you're not African American. (Laughs)

BM: (Laughing too) Boy, you have such sharp eyes.

CA: So why did you write in African-American voices? Four of your six characters are African American.

BM: Right again! I never intended to write in black voices. The first time this phenomenon occurred was back in 1995. I was writing a short story called "Peddling Day" about going peddling with my grandmother. She sold eggs and vegetables in McComb, Mississippi, and often she took me with her into town. I loved knocking on doors, meeting people, peeking into their lovely homes, and I wanted to set down the feelings I had as a young girl. But about halfway through the story I began to hear the voice of an African-American child named Katie. That's when I realized that this story wasn't really about me; it was about an unpleasant experience that happened to this little girl when she went peddling with her grandmother.

CA: That must have been a weird experience for you.

BM: It was, and I assumed it was a one-time aberration, but then it happened again.

CA: When you began writing *Right as Rain*?

BM: No, before that. The second time I heard a voice I was writing a story called "White Sugar and Red Clay."

CA: I think I read that story in an anthology.

BM: Yes, in *Stories from the Blue Moon Café*. It was published in *Xavier Review* first, though. And that story was supposed to be about my dad. When he was a young boy, his bulldog killed another dog, a beagle, and he had to shoot his own dog. Again, I was writing along picturing my dad in overalls, barefoot, walking down a red clay road with his dog, and then suddenly in the snapshot view in my mind, dad's skin began to darken.

CA: Are you pulling my leg? I don't believe you.

BM: No, it's true. He got darker and darker and turned into the character of J.P., who was an African-American child burdened with much more sadness in his life than my father had ever experienced.

CA: And in *Right as Rain,* J.P. is Tee Wee's son.

BM: Correct. When I began writing the novel, J.P. returned and took his place in Part Two.

CA: Okay, let me get this straight. You say you hear voices, have visions. Are you on medication for this? Because if you aren't, I know some wonderful experts in the mental health field whom I've had on my morning show.

BM: (Laughing) No, I'm not a bona fide schizophrenic, just a recreational one. Not on any medication at all.

CA: All right. I'll take your word for it. Now tell me about Tee Wee and Icey. Did you know these women or someone like them?

BM: I knew Tee Wee, but not Icey. The woman I based Tee Wee's character on was named Angilee, but her daughter's name was Tee Wee, and I chose to use her name instead. Angilee lived next door to my paternal grandmother, and I often played with many of her numerous grandchildren. My great-aunt knew Icey, and I have met her son, who lives near my dad in McComb, Mississippi. It was Icey's story that captured my imagination.

CA: Icey's story is true?

BM: Partially. Icey did have a son named Memphis who was accidentally killed when a truck ran over him after he fell from a gate on my aunt's pasture. It was actually Icey who ran over him, but I just couldn't write a story wherein a mother caused the death of her own child, so I made up the sheriff and gave him the responsibility.

CA: Okay, now let's get to the juicy stuff. What about Crow and Browder? Where did they come from? Did you know any interracial couples during this era?

BM: Oh no! In the '50s and early '60s, I thought only movie stars and famous people married interracially. This was taboo in the South. No way would an interracial couple live in the community where I grew up. Too much hostility, even rage from the racists. It would have been dangerous to stay there.

CA: How well I know! But back to my question: How or why did you put them in the novel? Where did they come from? Did some white girlfriend of yours transform into an African-American woman?

BM: Not exactly. If I had to choose a model from real life for Crow, it would be my mother because she had a lot of Crow's traits.

CA: Like what?

BM: My mother was an invalid for more than thirty years of her life. I couldn't count the number of times the doctors told us she most likely wouldn't live through an illness or operation. And yet she managed to help my father in his business, raise two children, travel . . . she even went to Tahiti after open-heart surgery. She taught my brother and me to never give up, like Crow. She believed that if you really wanted something, you could figure out a way to get it with determination and hard work.

CA: So you infused those traits into Crow as a way for her to become successful against all odds?

BM: Uh-huh. When I began writing about Crow, I didn't have a clear grasp of her character, but she fascinated me from the first time I typed her name on an old word processor. I tried to write a story about her, but I could never get it to work. I knew that she was seductive, head-strong, and independent, but I didn't know how that translated into a story. Then when I began writing *Right as Rain,* she suddenly became clear to me, and I knew how she fit into the novel.

CA: Talking about Crow leads me to sex. Your characters engage in quite a lot of it, and if they're not doing it, they're talking about it. In addition to Crow and Browder, I'm thinking of Icey and Deke and Ruthie and Dimple. Some pretty hot stuff there. You're blushing.

BM: (Laughing) I know. I'm shy about writing about sex, but the two things you can't leave out of a story are sex and God. Those two forces are the motivators for so many of our decisions and actions. When I need to write a sex scene into a story, I always imagine my dad and the ladies at Pisgah Church reading it, and I have to stop writing until I can get past that.

CA: Oh come on, don't you enjoy writing about it just a little bit?

BM: Well, truth be told I often write a lot more details in those scenes and maybe get a little carried away, but then I go back and hit the delete key, excising the parts I want my readers to imagine on their own. Sometimes what you leave out is better than what you put in.

CA: That's the truth! That's when you cut to a commercial break. How about some more cake?

BM: Back in a minute.

(Conversation resumes after Bev returns with two more slices of cake.)

CA: You should have put some recipes in your novel. The descriptions of Tee Wee's food made me hungry the whole time I was reading.

BM: Imagine how much weight I gained while writing about those meals. I have a confession to make, though.

CA: Oh good. This is the part I like best. What's the secret you haven't told?

BM: I don't know any of those recipes. I'm not much of a cook myself. I just like to eat.

CA: (Laughs) So you didn't hang out in a kitchen growing up. You must have been squirreled away somewhere writing, dreaming about becoming an author someday.

BM: No, not at all. I never dreamed I'd publish a book. All of my relatives were farmers or railroad workers. My dad was the manager of a farmers' cooperative. Sold horse and mule feed, chicken scratch, fertilizer. The only reading material we had in our home was farm journals and the Bible. Well, and a few books I found under my mother's bed and read in secret during junior high school.

CA: I imagine you learned a lot in those!

BM: (Grinning) More than I comprehended at that time. Anyway, when I went to college, my parents' dictum was to study to become a teacher. And, of course, I did later become a teacher and loved it. But like most women reared in my era, I believed that homemaking, raising children, keeping a neat house was my primary role. I was a military wife for more than twenty years, and in that capacity, I spent much of my time nurturing young wives with absent husbands. But I guess you could say that all the while I was a closet writer. I viewed writing as a hobby, like my husband's passion for golf. I saw it as a guilty indulgence.

CA: What made you come out of the closet? And how old were you when you finally confessed to being a writer?

BM: I was in my thirties. I was living in Hampton, Virginia, and I drove over to Christopher Newport College in Newport News to sign up for a parapsychology class and another class that was canceled. I saw on the schedule that a creative writing class was offered at the same time as the canceled class, so, on a lark, I signed up for it instead. At the end of the semester, when the professor told me that I had written one of the best stories he'd ever had in the class, I began to think of myself as a real writer with the potential to become a published author someday.

CA: Nearly everyone who watches my morning show knows what books I love and recommend, but what about you? Who are the authors you admire? Did any of them influence or inspire you?

BM: I love so many authors I could never name them all. I taught British and world literature at Southeastern Louisiana University and loved every author I taught to my classes. I revere the novels and plays of Southern authors like William Faulkner and Flannery O'Connor, Katherine Anne Porter, and Tennessee Williams, but I would say that the contemporary Southern writers like Clyde Edgerton, Ellen Gilchrist, Kaye Gibbons, Lee Smith, Barry Hannah, and Larry Brown have influenced my own work far more than any other authors. When I began reading their stories and novels, I thought how similar their stories were to those I had heard my relatives tell when I was a child. I realized that all of these wonderful tales would be lost with the demise of my relatives, and now I'm eager to write their stories as a kind of legacy for them.

CA: So you've got more stories to write?

BM: I won't live long enough to tell them all.

CA: So what's next? In *Right as Rain,* you've left your characters, every one, about to embark on a new life. Do you have any plans for a sequel to inform your readers as to how all of these new endeavors turn out for the characters in *Right as Rain*?

BM: So far, none of them have come back for a chat, but if they do, I'll be ready to write down their words.

CA: Well, let me know if they do and I'll drive back down for some more cake. You didn't bake it yourself, did you?

BM: Nope. But I know where to get more.

1. *Right as Rain* follows Tee Wee and Icey's friendship from their first meeting until the scene between them at the end of the novel. While they love and support each other, theirs is a relationship fraught with competition. In one scene their anger incites them to an actual physical battle. Is this friendship realistic? How does it compare to the relationships of modern women?

2. What impact does the civil rights movement have on each of the characters, especially the African-American characters? How would their lives differ today had they been born post–civil rights movement?

3. The author of *Right as Rain* is white. However, the majority of the voices in the novel are those of African Americans. How well did she depict those voices? In what passages did she fail or succeed?

4. Many of the conversations between Ruthie and Dimple center on sex and religion. How do their views differ? To what do you attribute their dissimilar views on sexuality and God?

5. Crow is one of the most complex characters in *Right as Rain*. She is determined to leave Parsons Place and, after the death of her cat, vows never to love anyone or anything. Yet, she falls in love with Browder, seemingly against her will. How and why does she recant her earlier feelings? Is this consistent with her character?

6.   Much of Part Three is devoted to J.P.'s trial. Considering the era and J.P.'s race, did you expect the verdict to be guilty or not guilty? To what or whom do you attribute the verdict? Is it a realistic one?

7.   Ruthie's relationship with Dennis is problematic throughout the novel. Trace the development of that relationship beginning in high school. Why did Ruthie marry Dennis? What factors contributed to her staying in an abusive relationship for so many years?

8.   The mother-daughter relationships in *Right as Rain* differ greatly between the African Americans and the Parsonses. Characterize and contrast the interaction between Tee Wee and Crow and Mrs. Parsons and Ruthie.

9.   Browder's obsession with films and Crow begins in puberty. Yet he marries Missy and takes over the farm after his father dies. Do you see Browder as a weak character or do you consider his actions noble? Why? Would his relationship with his father change if the novel were set in recent times and, if so, in what ways?

10.   At the end of the novel Icey and Tee Wee have become business partners. Do you think this partnership will succeed? Why? What do you foresee happening between them as they grow older?

11.   If Crow had told Browder about her pregnancy, how would he have reacted to this news?

12.   The bond between Ruthie and Tee Wee is sustained throughout the novel. Trace the development of their relationship from Ruthie's childhood to J.P.'s going-away party. How does their relationship change? How does it remain constant?

READ ON FOR A PREVIEW OF

BEV MARSHALL'S LATEST NOVEL

Hot Fudge Sundae Blues

AVAILABLE IN HARDCOVER FROM

BALLANTINE BOOKS IN SEPTEMBER 2005

Chapter 1

HE YEAR I TURNED THIRTEEN I GOT RELIGION. OH, I'D BEEN
going to church, praying like a sinner on her deathbed, but when the
Holy Spirit flew over Mississippi, it never landed on me. All through the
spring and summer of 1963, I sat beside Grandma on the sixth pew of
Pisgah Methodist Church waiting for salvation, but the Lord never spoke
one word to me. Grandma's shoulders drooped in disappointment
when, Sunday after Sunday, I didn't join the other sinners who accepted
Brother Thompson's invitation to "come on down and get wrapped in
the bosom of the Lord." She was counting on me to lead a pious life because both her husband and her daughter were bent on sinning themselves straight into hell. Every Sunday, during the hour or so we sat on
our hard wooden pew, breathing in the suffocating air of wilted gladiolas, Old Spice aftershave, and Mrs. Duncan's Midnight in Paris perfume,
Papaw would be out riding across the pasture on Jim, a dappled gray that
he claimed was the fastest in Lexie County. Mama slept late on Sundays.

So as Grandma's only grandchild and last hope for conversion, I felt a
huge responsibility to get saved, but I hadn't been able to get my feet
moving down the crimson carpeted aisle of Pisgah Methodist up until
this Sunday. Brother Thompson hadn't enticed a sinner to come up and
get saved for several weeks, and at the end of every service, he would
wearily lift his hand for the benediction. Then with his voice filled with
disappointment, he would pray for us sinners to get washed in Jesus'
blood and become whiter than snow.

So on this hot August morning, I pretended the Holy Spirit had finally lit on me because I wanted to please the preacher and Grandma,

who had had a big fight with Mama the night before and seemed more down than usual, and because Jehu Albright, the cutest boy in the ninth grade, was sitting across the aisle on the fourth pew down from us. We always sat on the right-hand pews because the morning sun bore down on the other side of the church, making it hotter than Hades, and over there you could see forty or more cardboard fans flapping faster than a wasp could fly. I had thought that Jehu was a Baptist, but his mother told Grandma that they had been attending Centenary Methodist in town and didn't like their new pastor who had posted a list of the members who hadn't sign their pledge cards on the bulletin board in the vestibule.

Today Brother Thompson's sermon was about Jesus feeding the multitudes with a few hunks of bread and a couple of little fish, and although I believed in miracles, I was having a hard time picturing the baskets filling up with loaves and fishes over and over like that. But then it occurred to me that, if what you couldn't imagine could be true, maybe Grandma wouldn't know that I was about to fake salvation. So when Miss Wilda banged out the first chords of "Just As I Am" on the old black upright piano, with my heart racing like a galloping horse, I squeezed past Grandma's knees and stepped out into the aisle. My taffeta dress, the color of a grape Popsicle, rustled applause as I slowly made my way up to the altar. When I passed Jehu's pew, I paused, tucked a curl behind my ear, and glanced over at him with what I hoped was a beatific smile. After I reached the altar rail, Brother Thompson, trembling with joy, leaned over and placed his hand on the top of my head. "Do you accept Jesus Christ as your Lord and Savior?" he whispered.

His voice was filled with such happiness I thought he might burst out laughing, and quickly I answered, "Uh-huh. Yessir."

I had been rehearsing this scene all summer on Saturdays, which was the day Grandma and I cleaned the church. Grandma had taken the job, refusing payment for her labors, avowing that menial tasks would keep us humble. She assured me that the reward of serving the Lord was compensation enough. I didn't want the Lord's rewards. I wanted cash to purchase a madras blouse and a wraparound skirt, but Grandma had refused even the paltry sum that Brother Thompson offered her from the collection of coins and bills that piled up in the silver pie plate we passed around every time the church doors opened.

After I finished my Saturday chores of dusting pews and straightening the song books, I enacted all the roles in the play I had written, titled, "Layla Jay Gets Saved and Wins a Young Boy's Heart." I pounded out hymns on the piano, switching my singing voice from soprano to alto, harmonizing with myself as perfectly as an entire choir inside my head. In the role of preacher, I gripped the lectern until sweat stung my eyes as I shouted out for the sinners to come down and be saved. I had also rehearsed the heroine's part I was playing now—that of repentant sinner tearfully asking for forgiveness. I was ready to testify, to admit to any and all sins, for what would it matter, the past? But before I could blurt out a single sin, Brother Thompson raised his hands and gave the benediction. My moment was over in less time than it took to close a hymnal. I stood beside the preacher, filled with disappointment as I accepted the first congratulatory hand that belonged to old Mr. Stokes. "Bless you, child," he said, spraying small droplets of saliva on my new taffeta bodice, which I had stuffed with a pair of socks for Jehu Albright's perusal. Then came the others; Mr. Felder, Mr. and Mrs. Frank Utley, Doris Faye Wiggins, Joan Gail Martin, Mary Lynn Sutter, Johnny Moore Jr. They shuffled past me with blessings and smiles, and suddenly there he was standing right in front of me. Blond crew cut pomaded with grease, rabbit-sized front teeth, a good strong jaw, my ideal.

"Congratulations, Layla Jay," Jehu mumbled. "You staying for dinner on the ground?"

"Thank you. Yes, I am," I whispered in the reverent tone I had practiced. And then he was gone, and Mrs. Gabe Tucker was swinging her oversized purse into my stomach as she stretched out her fat fingers to pinch my arm. "Welcome, child. You're safe in the Lord's hands now."

After pumping the remaining hands of the Lord's disciples, I escaped outside and meandered around the church grounds where I spotted Jehu lobbing pine cones at my cousin James Louis, who was firing back with cones of his own. I have hated James Louis for as long as I can remember. He is meaner than a starving bulldog, but around grown-ups, he acts like a poodle puppy, all fuzzy and soft and eager to please. Like all older women, my Grandma loves him. This is how I came to know that women can be easily fooled by men, and, since learning this fact, have resolved to never never be taken in by anyone of the opposite sex. I do not fear this happening with Jehu Albright. I will never believe that he is capable of the kind of duplicity my cousin James Louis demonstrates.

When Brother Thompson called for quiet so that he could get another prayer going, I walked over to the folding tables set up between two oak trees that served as boundaries for the little kids. Waiting for us to assemble and quiet down, he stood at the head of the table, holding up both hands like he was signaling a touchdown for the Zebulon Cougars. Jehu was standing to my left with his head bowed and his hands crossed over a pine cone behind his back.

Although delirious with happiness over my conversion, Grandma frowned when I fished around in one of the fried chicken platters for the piece that held the pulley bone. I ignored her. I needed to make a wish and I figured a pulley bone that had been blessed by a preacher would be extra good luck if I broke it right. Jehu was already going back for seconds when I took my plate over to the brick steps that led to the back of the church. My best friend, June McCormick, had saved me a spot, and when I sat down beside her, she leaned over and bumped my arm with her plate. "How come you decided to get saved today?"

I bit off a piece of crunchy chicken. "Got filled up with the spirit."

"You did not."

"Did so."

June patted her teased blond bubble hair-do that Mama said made her face look fat. "Well, I don't believe you. You just wanted to parade up to the altar to show off your new dress I'll bet."

Better to let her think vanity rather than seduction. "Well, okay. But I was planning on getting saved sometime soon anyway," I said, holding up my pinkie. "Secret pledge?"

June licked the fried chicken grease from her fingers and wrapped her little finger around mine. "Sure. I won't tell anyone. I'm your friend. You wouldn't tell on me."

Thinking that a subtle hint of blackmail was good insurance, I said, "No. I didn't tell you were the one who took a quarter out of the collection plate to buy nail polish that time." This prompted June to recite from memory all the new colors of polish sitting on her dresser, and after I offered my opinion that blue-based red polish, rather than orange-red, went with green outfits, I broached the subject I was most anxious to talk about. "Grandma said Jehu Albright's family is joining Pisgah. They switched over from Centenary."

"Yeah, I knew they were going to. My mother and his mother are in Beta Sigma Phi together. I think he's cool, looks a little like Steve McQueen, doesn't he?" I held my breath, hoping June didn't have a crush on him, too. She was far more popular than I and could get boyfriends as easily as you could catch chicken pox. She glanced over to where Jehu sat with his back against an oak tree. "But he's got big teeth and everybody knows crew cuts are passé." Breathing with a lighter heart, I tore the white meat away from the pulley bone and held it out to her. As we closed our eyes and pulled, I made my wish for Jehu Albright to love me, and got the short bone.

After everyone had eaten all their stomachs could hold, they began to gather their empty bowls and say their good-byes. As I walked to Grandma's old green Plymouth, I saw Jehu and his family driving away in their big white Chrysler Imperial and vowed that someday I'd be cuddled up beside him on the back seat of that car.

As soon as Grandma parked the Plymouth under the carport, I ran into the house to find Mama. She was sitting at the dining-room table in her green satin robe, smoking a Lucky Strike between sips of strong black coffee. I could tell by the straight lines between her brows that she had a hangover again.

When Grandma came in through the kitchen door, Mama blew two smoke circles over the table and then said, "So how was church?"

"Wonderful. Layla Jay got saved." Grandma drew the pearl hat pin from her pink pillbox and lifted it off her head. "It's a shame you weren't there, Frieda."

Mama ignored the last comment. She laid her cigarette on the ashtray and lifted her arms to hug me. "Honey, that's nice. I'm glad for you. And you look so pretty in your purple dress. Were many people there?"

"Regular crowd," I said sliding onto the chair beside her. "Brother Thompson gave me a New Testament." I drew out the small white leather-bound book from my patent purse.

Mama laughed, took up her cigarette again and blew out another ring of smoke. "I didn't know you got a prize along with salvation."

Grandma ignored the joke, but I couldn't help smiling. Next to Papaw, Mama was the wittiest person I knew. Grandma pulled at the fingers of her white gloves until they flapped off the ends of her hands and fell onto the table. She looked down the hall. "Where's Claude? Did he feed the chickens?"

Mama shrugged. "Pop was gone when I got up. Haven't seen him." She pushed back her chair. "I better get dressed. Will is picking me up in an hour."

I gripped the New Testament tightly. Although Grandma had told me that it was a sin to hate and you could wind up in hell for not opening your heart to people who didn't know God's love, she definitely hated Will Satterly. Grandma sucked in her breath, gathering air to spew out her disapproval, but before she could say a word, Mama wiggled her robe from her shoulders and naked as a newborn walked out of the room. Just before her bedroom door slammed, she yelled at Grandma. "Save your breath. I'll wait for him out front."

My mother had been dating Will for nearly a month, so I knew that he wouldn't be visiting our house much longer. None of Mama's beaus lasted for more than three or four weeks. Mama had gotten rid of Errol Newman after only one picture show, and Jake Lott held the record for keeping Mama interested for the longest time of six and a half weeks. Grandma didn't like any of the men Mama brought home, but she especially loathed Will because the weekend before this one he and my mother had come home at four in the morning to find Grandma sitting with the phone in her lap, dialing the hospital emergency-room number.

That night Mama and Grandma had argued until milking time when Papaw woke up and threatened to call the sheriff if they didn't shut up and get some biscuits in the oven. Papaw missed most of the fuss because he is a really sound sleeper, but even though I had squeezed my pillow over my ears, I heard every word they screamed at each other. Grandma called Mama a Jezebel, the devil's child, and a couple of other names I didn't know she knew. Mama retaliated by breaking two of the porcelain figurines on Grandma's whatnot shelf, and kicking the coffee table till one leg broke off, so that it looked as drunk as Mama. I was glad about the whatnots as they were a pain to move when I had to dust the shelves.

After we heard Mama's door slam, Grandma frowned at me even though I hadn't said a word. "Go change your clothes," she said. "I'm leaving in fifteen minutes."

Sunday afternoons Grandma and I visited the infirm. That's what she called anyone who belonged to Pisgah and skipped church. I was changing into a pair of shorts when Grandma came into my room and said that she had decided to go alone today because, as a newly saved Christian, I should spend the afternoon staying close to God by reading scripture and offering up prayers of thanks. I had expected just the opposite. If I wasn't a sinner anymore, it seemed to me I wouldn't need to read the Bible near as much. But I didn't argue because I welcomed the opportunity to have the house to myself. Papaw was most likely gone for the entire day, Mama wouldn't be back until late, and with Grandma out visiting, I could count on at least three hours or so of absolute freedom, during which time I planned on experimenting with Mama's makeup.

Mama's business is makeup. She sells Elizabeth Arden at Salloum's

Department Store in Zebulon. My mother got the job because she's beautiful. Her hair is the color of tobacco streaked with gold and it falls in soft waves that ripple across her shoulders when she walks across a room. Her smooth white skin, without a pimple or blemish of any kind, is as soft as a feather pillow and she keeps it that way by applying moisturizers twice daily. Since I have entered puberty and am engaged in a war with pimples, Mama has brought home jars of a variety of pimple fighting weapons that smell dreadful, but seem to be winning. I have her nose, and I'm hoping that somewhere within me lies a gene that will develop into fabulous breasts exactly like hers. Mama says I got my long slender feet from Daddy's gene pool.

My father's name is Kenneth Woodrow Andrews, and because he died before I was two, I don't remember anything about him. I'm absolutely certain he was much nicer than any of the men who treat me like a kid when they stand in the living room waiting for Mama to make her appearance. I know what Daddy's voice sounds like because he talks to me sometimes when I get the hot fudge sundae blues. That's what Mama calls them. When you're feeling as rotten and low and hopeless as you can be and you think the world's biggest sponge couldn't mop up all the tears inside you, the remedy is this: You drive to the Tasty Freeze and order the large size hot fudge sundae. And when it comes, the bright red cherry on top cheers you up a little, and then you spoon the first bite into your mouth and you taste the warm chocolate and the cool vanilla ice cream and the sweet sweet whipped cream, and you look at yourself in the rearview mirror of the car and you're wearing a white mustache, and you smile just a little, and after you've taken the last bite, satisfied and filled with that cup of joyful sweetness, suddenly you don't have the blues anymore.

But you can't always get to the Tasty Freeze, especially when you're only thirteen and you can't drive. So sometimes when I get the blues, my father comes and whispers words that sound like music and he tells me how much he misses me, how much he wishes he were here to hold me in his arms and kiss away my pain. I close my eyes and see him as he looks in the picture on Mama's nightstand. He is wearing a checked shirt with the sleeves rolled up to his elbows. His hair, black as Jim's hooves, is swept back on the sides, and one piece falls across his forehead just above his laughing eyes. He is tall, with narrow hips and long slender feet encased in shiny brown alligator boots. I can feel his strong hands on my shoulders, his lips soft on my forehead. Sometimes he makes silly faces with his eyelids turned inside out and his fingers in his mouth, stretching his lips out toward his wiggling ears. Other times his amber eyes are filled with pain, and I see his broken body lying beside the hunk of twisted metal that was his motorcycle. Mama often rode with him, but on the day of the accident, they had argued; Mama had thrown a potted plant against the wall where he stood, and she told me that he left the house brushing fine black dirt out of his hair. He hadn't stopped to pick up the helmet he usually wore. When Mama got the call from the hospital, she had finished repotting the asparagus fern and had set it on the dining table between two candles, which she planned to light when he came home.

After Grandma left, I did say a prayer, a plea for forgiveness for my latest sin. I knew that God couldn't be fooled like Grandma and Brother Thompson, so I asked Him to order the Holy Spirit to enter my heart and make things right. I also asked Him for breasts, Jehu Albright's love, and a daddy just like the one He had taken away from Mama and me.

BEV MARSHALL is the critically acclaimed

author of *Walking Through Shadows*. A native

of McComb, Mississippi, she lived as a

nomadic military wife for many years.

Marshall returned to her Southern roots

and taught English at Southeastern

Louisiana University. She now lives in

Ponchatoula, Louisiana, with her husband.

Visit her website at www.bevmarshall.com.

ABOUT THE TYPE

This book was set in Monotype Dante, a typeface designed by Giovanni Mardersteig (1892–1977). Conceived as a private type for the Officina Bodoni in Verona, Italy, its first use was in an edition of Boccaccio's *Trattatello in laude di Dante* that appeared in 1954. The Monotype Corporation's version of Dante followed in 1957.